MISCHIEF
AND
Magnolias

MARIE PATRICK
author of *A Treasure Worth Keeping*

Crimson Romance
New York   London   Toronto   Sydney   New Delhi

CRIMSON
ROMANCE

Crimson Romance
An Imprint of Simon & Schuster, Inc.
1230 Avenue of the Americas
New York, NY 10020

ISBN 978-1-4405-7572-3
ISBN 978-1-4405-7571-6 (ebook)

To my critique partners, Lexi and Ann, who are always up for a bit of mischief; to my son, who taught me what mischief truly is; and to my husband, who would never let me get away with putting molasses in his boots.

Chapter 1

Natchez, Mississippi
September 1863

Shaelyn Cavanaugh leaned against the railing of the second-floor gallery of her home and focused on the two men coming up the road, their blue uniforms unmistakable. They rode at a swift pace, a trail of dust behind them.

Since Natchez, Mississippi, surrendered to the Union forces, it wasn't unusual to see blue uniforms, especially since they'd made Rosalie, the home next door, their headquarters. But the two men didn't turn into Rosalie's drive as she expected.

Her breath caught in her throat when she glimpsed light auburn hair, much like her brother's, gleaming in the sunlight. "Ian!"

His companion had raven-black hair, though it too reflected the sun's light. Traveling with Ian, he could be only one man—the one she had promised to wait for. "James." Her hand gripped the wrought-iron railing, her knuckles white. Tears blurred her vision. Her heart beat a frantic rhythm in her chest as excitement surged through her veins.

"They're home!" she cried. "Mama!"

She lifted her skirts and ran for the outside staircase at the back of the house. "They're home!"

She jumped, missing the last few stairs, and hit the veranda at a run, her skirts held high as she ran into the house through the French doors in the small sun parlor.

"Mama!" Shaelyn darted into the central hallway, her footsteps clicking on the marble tiles as she ran to the front door, flung it open, and rushed headlong into a pair of strong arms. She rested

4

her head against a firm, hard chest, and squeezed tight. A button pressed into her cheek, but she didn't care. They were home. "Thank God," she whispered into the uniform.

"Well, that's quite a greeting," a deep, rich voice as smooth as drizzling molasses responded. Laughter rumbled in his chest. "Not expected, but certainly welcomed."

"Hmm. Where's mine?" his companion asked in the clipped tones of New England.

Shaelyn recognized neither voice nor accent and turned her head to glance at the auburn-haired man. Ian Cavanaugh did not look back at her, which meant she did not have her arms around James Brooks.

Her face hot with embarrassment, Shaelyn pulled away from the man. She drew in a shaky breath and stared. The most beautiful pair of soft blue-gray eyes she'd ever seen stared back. "Forgive me. I thought you were someone else."

"Obviously," the man replied. "Perhaps introductions are in order, although after your greeting, it may be too late." Amusement gleamed from his eyes as a wide grin showed off his white teeth in a charming smile. She wanted to touch the dimple that appeared in his cheek. "Major Remington Harte." He gestured to the man beside him. "This is my second in command, Captain Vincent Davenport."

"Miss." Captain Davenport bowed from the waist.

Shaelyn nodded in his general direction, but her focus remained on the major. She'd never seen hair so black or so thick. An insane impulse overwhelmed her—she wanted to run her fingers through that mass of thick, shiny hair and feel its silkiness. Struck by her own inappropriate thoughts, she stilled. He wasn't James. She shouldn't want to run her fingers through his hair.

"Are you Brenna Cavanaugh?"

"What?" Startled, Shaelyn shook her head. "No, I'm her daughter, Shaelyn."

Footsteps rang out down the hallway. Shaelyn dragged her gaze away from the man in uniform for just a moment as her mother joined them at the door. "I am Brenna Cavanaugh." A sweet smile accompanied the hand she offered the major. "May I help you?"

Introductions were quickly made, and Shaelyn watched the exchange of pleasantries, but her gaze was drawn back to the major. He looked dashing in his uniform. The dark blue complimented his eyes quite nicely. The material molded to his body, emphasizing his broad shoulders, lean waist, and slim hips. He stood tall, well over six feet she guessed, as her gaze swept the length of his body with admiration. She noticed a silver-tipped cane in his hand, which he leaned on. He must have been injured in battle.

She had always loved seeing a man in uniform. They stood differently: straighter, taller. Proud. They acted differently, too, as if wearing a uniform had something to do with how the world perceived them.

Her gaze met his and she felt the warmth of a blush creep up from her chest. A smile parted his full lips and her face grew hotter. She'd been staring at him and he knew it.

"Is this about Ian, my son?" Hope colored her mother's tone, a hope she had tended carefully, like one tends a garden.

"Or James Brooks?" Shaelyn added.

"May we go inside?" Major Harte gestured toward the open door.

"Where are my manners?" Brenna smiled. "Of course." She turned to Shaelyn. "Please show our guests into the sun parlor, dear. I just finished making tea."

With effort, Shaelyn dragged her gaze away from the major and the pulse throbbing in his neck, above the collar of his uniform, which had mesmerized her. "Please follow me."

Major Harte's uneven footsteps echoed in the hallway and the tip of his cane tapped on the marble tiles as Shaelyn showed them into a small, comfortable, sun-filled room at the back of the house, while Brenna pushed through the swinging door to the kitchen. "Please, make yourselves comfortable."

"Thank you." The major moved to the fireplace and rested his arm on the mantle while Captain Davenport sat on a rattan love seat.

Shaelyn sank into a chair across from the captain, her fingers settling into one of the rattan grooves, and let out a slow breath— anything to still the anxiety plucking at her spine with its icy fingers and chilling her from the inside out. After a moment, the heat of the major's gaze rested on her, negating that chill. He didn't speak as she turned to face him, nor did he smile, but the warmth in his slate-colored eyes captured and held hers.

She opened her mouth, but no words issued forth. She didn't know what to say. Or do. She'd never had to entertain Union officers, although her brother had marched off to war wearing blue. In all truth, she hadn't entertained in a very long time, and the lessons her mother had taught her about proper decorum and genteel manners simply escaped her.

Captain Davenport didn't speak either, and a heavy stillness filled the room, the only sound the rhythmic ticking of the grandfather clock in the corner. An ominous sense of foreboding stole through Shaelyn with each passing minute. Her heart pounded, not with excitement now, but with dread. A lump rose to her throat. She knew, deep down, whatever the reason for these men to be here, no good would come of it.

Brenna entered the parlor and broke the silence. "Shaelyn, would you please pour?" Her mother placed a silver tea service on the table in front of the divan and took a seat in her favorite wicker chair.

Shaelyn rose from her seat, though her entire body trembled. With shaking hands, she lifted the teapot and started to pour. A few drops of the dark brew spilled onto a linen napkin on the tray and stained it brown.

She glanced up and caught the major's wince before he addressed his second in command. "Captain, would you be so kind?"

"Of course." Captain Davenport leaned forward and took the pot from her hands.

Shaelyn gave him a tremulous smile. Every muscle and sinew in her body tensed with apprehension as she moved behind the settee, her hand resting on her mother's shoulder.

Captain Davenport handed Brenna her teacup and attempted to give one to Shaelyn as well, but she declined without a word, afraid her voice wouldn't work over the lump constricting her throat.

Major Harte straightened and limped over to the chair opposite the divan, a grimace tightening his features. Shaelyn watched his painful progress and a surge of sympathy rippled through her.

"Now, Major, please tell us why you're here. If it's bad news, don't make us wait, I beg you." Brenna's voice shook as she said the words. She grabbed Shaelyn's hand and squeezed.

He hesitated. Shaelyn wanted to drag the words from his mouth. Whatever he needed to say, she just wished he'd do it. He took a deep breath. She prepared herself, swallowing hard against the bile burning the back of her throat.

"Mrs. Cavanaugh, are you the owner of Cavanaugh Shipping and the steamboats the *Brenna Rose*, the *Lady Shae*, and the *Sweet Sassy*?"

"Since my husband passed away," Brenna replied. "Yes, I am, but Shaelyn runs the business. She's quite good at it, despite this terrible war."

"And are you the owner of record for this home, Magnolia House, and the warehouse and shipping office located in Natchez-Under-the-Hill?"

"What is this all about, Major?" Shaelyn asked. She didn't like the expression on the major's face at all. He seemed sad almost, as if he didn't relish what he needed to do, and her dread intensified, those icy fingers no longer plucking at her spine, but squeezing her heart. She stiffened against the blow that was sure to come. He removed a document from his uniform pocket, slowly unfolded it, and began to read. "By the order of the government of the United States, for the duration of this war or until they are no longer needed," he said softly, "you are hereby commanded to relinquish your home, steamboats, warehouse, and shipping office to the Union Army. Specifically, me." He glanced at Shaelyn, an apology in his eyes.

"What!" Shaelyn let go of her mother's hand and came around the sofa on legs that felt like wooden stumps instead of flesh and bone. "You can't do that. They belong to us."

She stopped in front of Major Harte and stared at him. The brief moment of sympathy she'd had for him vanished, and her face burned with anger. Indeed, her entire body felt as if fire consumed her. She grabbed the document from him, but her hands shook so badly, she couldn't read the paper in front of her.

"Indeed, I can, Miss Cavanaugh," he said, his voice no longer soft, but commanding and strong. "I have my orders." The expression in his eyes hadn't changed, though. They were still apologetic.

She knew the army, on both sides, frequently took homes and other possessions, but it didn't assuage her anger one bit. "Why my steamers? And my home?"

"The Union Army has need of your boats to transport men and supplies and your home, being in such close proximity to Rosalie, is perfect to quarter my men."

"What are we supposed to do? How will I support us if you take my steamboats? Where are we to live?" Incredulity made Shaelyn's voice sharper than normal. Although she was usually unflappable, even in the most dire of circumstances, this whole tableau had her feeling like she was someone else, someone she didn't even recognize. "What if I refuse, Major? What will you do then?"

A muscle jumped in the major's cheek as he stood to tower over her. "You have no choice in this matter, Miss Cavanaugh." His voice remained strong, but the warmth of his eyes conveyed another message. "It's nothing personal. Consider this your contribution to the war effort."

The lump constricting her throat threatened to suffocate her. She took a deep breath and swallowed hard.

"My my mother and I have already contributed far more to this blasted war than you could ever imagine." Her voice barely above a whisper, she almost choked on the words. "My father suffered a stroke when war was declared. I watched him struggle for life for two months before he succumbed." She blinked against the tears filling her eyes. "I have heard nothing from my brother or my intended in over a year. I can only hope they are still alive and were not at Gettysburg. I have lost two riverboats to shell fire. They lay at the bottom of the Mississippi, along with the people who were aboard."

She drew in her breath, tried to control her shaking body, and tried but failed to control her temper. "Now you will take my home and my business, and I am to give it to you graciously? I don't believe I can, Major."

A strong desire to do him bodily harm made her clench her fists as he stood before her, his expression impassive.

"I am sorry for your losses, Miss Cavanaugh, but we have all made sacrifices," he replied softly. His gaze held hers and he shifted his weight to his other leg, as if mentioning the word *sacrifices* made him remember his own. "Some more than others. It is the way of war."

"Your war, not mine!" The words exploded from her, despite the constriction in her throat. How much more would this blasted war take? How much more could she give? Had she brought this on herself by applying for a government contract? She'd been denied, of course, and immediately tried again and again. Had she drawn attention to Cavanaugh Shipping by her sheer persistence? Instead of getting the contract she so hoped for, she had her possessions taken.

A small sound drew her attention. Shaelyn tore her gaze away from the major and glanced at her mother. Brenna had not moved, had not uttered a sound except for a small whimper, but her face had lost all color. Her chin trembled and tears shimmered on her lashes. Pain and confusion flashed in her eyes. Shaelyn's heart came close to shattering.

She had promised her father she would always take care of her mother, a privilege she gladly accepted. She wouldn't break her promise now. She took a deep breath and managed to smile at her mother to let her know it would be all right.

"I'm certain you are a reasonable man, Major." She forced her gaze away from Brenna and faced the man who stood to take everything from her. "We have nowhere to go, sir. No family left, no friends able to take us in. The war has seen to that." She took a deep breath and tried to keep her anger under control. "Perhaps we can strike a bargain?"

• • •

Intrigued, Remy cocked a dark eyebrow. He hadn't missed the look she'd given her mother, nor could he mistake the devastation on the older woman's face and his part in putting the desolation there. He hadn't had this issue with the other homes where some of his men were now staying. "A bargain, Miss Cavanaugh? What did you have in mind?"

"Perhaps we can discuss this privately," Shaelyn suggested, and nodded toward Brenna.

"Of course," he conceded, and followed her from the parlor. They stepped across the hall, toward the front of the house, and into a well-appointed study. Remy limped to the desk and leaned against it, taking the pressure off his leg in an effort to alleviate the pain, which never seemed to abate.

Shaelyn shut the pocket doors then moved to the center of the room. A ray of sunlight fell on her, and Remy sucked in his breath. *Heaven help me, she is a beauty. Damn Jock MacPhee!* Her light auburn hair, twisted haphazardly into a loose knot atop her head, left wispy tendrils to frame a lovely, heart-shaped, and at the moment, angry face. Bright patches of color stained her cheeks. Dark brows arched over smoldering eyes the color of cobalt. Her pert nose turned up slightly at the tip. He had no doubt her mouth, now compressed in annoyance, broke hearts when she smiled.

She had spirit. He'd give her that. Her rage was tangible; he felt the heat radiate from her from across the room. Her eyes never left him. They sparkled with dangerous intent.

"You have my undivided attention." He hid a smile as she stomped toward the desk, the lace at the hem of her dark plum skirt swishing like ocean foam. He wondered briefly if the skirt had had lace originally or if she had used it to hide a badly frayed hem like so many other young ladies did during these difficult times. She wore no hoops or crinolines beneath her skirt, but he did glimpse pristine white petticoats and the tips of her worn, scuffed shoes.

Shaelyn said nothing. The expression on her face spoke for her. Remy kept his gaze steady on hers, frankly admiring her blushing cheeks and flashing eyes.

"You're staring daggers at me, Miss Cavanaugh. Does the color of my uniform offend you?" he asked, unable to resist.

"The color of your uniform makes no difference to me, sir." Her eyes narrowed as she spoke, yet still glittered like rare dark sapphires. "What offends me is the color of the blood that runs so freely because of this war. What offends me is the way you all do whatever you all damn well please, without thought for the consequences of your actions. What offends me, at the moment, is you!"

"I'm sorry you feel that way, Miss Cavanaugh." He'd always admired a woman with strength and courage, with character, with what his mother called fortitude. Shaelyn Cavanaugh seemed to have all that and more, and he rather enjoyed this confrontation, despite the circumstances, despite how her attitude had changed. It made him feel alive in a way he hadn't felt in quite some time. "Regardless of your feelings, this is the way it is. You must accept it as fact."

He straightened and took a step toward her. Before they'd left the parlor, she'd been willing to swallow her anger and strike a bargain. Now, however, she didn't seem so willing. "I find it remarkable how much your manner has changed since we left the parlor."

She glared at him, her head tilting back on her slim neck, but she didn't move, didn't back down.

His attitude softened as she stood in front of him, defiant and bold. He expected her wrath, even her resentment. Almost welcomed it. He would have been in full fury if his home and business were taken away. "You wished to strike an agreement?" he reminded her.

"My mother is an excellent cook. She will prepare meals for you and your men and I will clean, do your laundry—" she paused and licked her lips "—and anything else you need to have done if you will allow us to stay in our home."

Her words finally penetrated his brain. No wonder she looked at him as if she would happily stab him through the heart. His blood ran cold as he realized she assumed by confiscating her home, he'd be asking—no, telling—them to leave, throwing them into the street. He'd seen it happen before. No doubt they had, too. Truthfully, he *had* planned to ask them to leave, though Jock had asked him to allow Shaelyn and her mother to stay. He hadn't quite made up his mind….not until he met her and then everything changed in a split second.

He should disabuse her of her misinterpretation at once but just…didn't want to. No one had dared to stand up to him such as she had in a very long time, and the longer they stood staring at each other, the more fascinated he became. She drew in her breath, the flesh above the décolletage of her white blouse turning red. A vein throbbed along the side of her neck, drawing his attention to the soft column of her throat. His gaze rose higher and he watched the subtle shading of her eyes darken to almost violet.

He hid the smile that threatened to turn up the corners of his mouth. "You and your mother may stay with conditions."

"And what would those conditions be?"

"You will treat my men with respect, regardless of the color of their uniform or the reasons they are here."

"I would have it no other way," she told him, her mouth set. "By the same token, I will have the same from you. My mother is a kind, gentle woman, Major, and naive in many ways. I will not have her abused or mistreated, by either you or your men. If we must treat you and yours with respect, then I demand you treat my mother that way as well."

"You aren't in any position to make demands, Miss Cavanaugh."

"I understand. I still ask you to honor my request."

Remy's heart skipped a beat as he gazed into her flashing eyes. They didn't merely sparkle; they danced in her lovely face. He detected no fear in those glimmering orbs of blue, just fury. What would she look like with her temper—or her passion—unleashed?

"It will be as you wish, Miss Cavanaugh," Remy conceded. "My men will show your mother the respect she deserves." He took another step forward and smelled the warm, inviting fragrance of her perfume. The alluring scent conjured images in his mind, images better left alone. He wanted to touch her, to kiss the spot on her neck where her pulse throbbed, to rub his thumb against her lips and feel them soften. "And what of you? Do you not deserve the respect of my men as well?"

"I expect nothing less."

Intoxicated. That's what he felt. As if he'd drunk all the whiskey his father distilled. Her scent wafted gently to his nose and a vivid vision filled his mind. He saw her in his arms, saw them making love until they were both breathless, moonlight glowing on her bare skin, passion flushing her lovely face—

She's taken, promised to another.

The reminder did little to stop the kaleidoscope of visions cascading through his mind. With a bit of disappointment, Remy mentally shook himself and moved away from her, more to save himself from her sensual, alluring fragrance and the images in his mind than anything else.

"I realize this is an inconvenience for you, Miss Cavanaugh, but I will try to make it as pleasant as possible." He gazed into her eyes. The most peculiar sensation settled in his chest, one he could not define, but which made his heart a little lighter. "I suggest we both make the best of a bad situation. I am willing to allow you and your mother to stay. Do we have an agreement?"

Slowly, she let out her pent-up breath and stuck out her hand. He grasped it firmly and a jolt of desire slammed into him. He wanted to pull her into his arms and kiss her tempting lips. Now. If she felt it too, she gave no sign.

He pulled his hand away quickly and cleared his throat. "Please show me the rest of the house."

"As you wish." She led him out of the study, her hands balled into fists at her side, and into the central hallway. Remy followed, admiring the subtle sway of her hips beneath the plum skirt, the long line of her back, the wispy tendrils curling at the back of her neck, begging for his touch.

From the study, they took the marble-tiled corridor toward the rear of the house. She poked her head into the sun parlor, where

Brenna held Captain Davenport in subdued conversation. Her mother looked up. Shaelyn said not a word, but the expression of relief on the older woman's face could not be denied.

Shaelyn opened the swinging door to the kitchen a moment later and stood aside. She said nothing as he inspected the room, but her anger smoldered. The heat he'd felt earlier shimmered around her. He couldn't concentrate on the room's appointments. Instead, he felt the intensity of her stare and turned to face her.

A blush spread across her face, but her eyes never left his.

Is that a challenge I see?

He tore his gaze away from her and walked around the kitchen, opening all the cabinets and drawers, inspecting their contents, satisfied his stay at Magnolia House would be a comfortable one.

He finished looking into the cabinets and moved to a door to his left. His hand rested on the knob. "Where does this lead?"

"The cellar, backyard, and a small room where one can remove muddy boots." Her answer was clipped, bordering on rude. "Also the servants' stairway."

Remy ignored her tone as he nodded and limped to another set of doors. "And these?"

"Servants' quarters."

He opened the door to the first room, noticed it was clean, the small bed made, but vacant, as if no one had resided there in a long time. "Where are they now? Your servants, I mean."

"Gone. I couldn't afford to pay them anymore."

He closed the door and walked around the butcher-block counter in the middle of the room. A set of carving knives sat on the surface, and he wondered if he should remove them before they became an enticement for her.

Another swinging door led to the dining room. Shaelyn pushed through it a few steps before him and let it swing back. He drew in a deep breath and stopped the door from hitting him in the face with his hand.

This is going to be more difficult—and more entertaining—than I thought.

He didn't take more than a moment to glance around, but in that time he saw all he needed to see. The dining room table, covered in a lace cloth, seated twelve comfortably. Extra chairs lined one wall and a long sideboard sat across from it against another. The hutch stood empty—perhaps the fine china had been sold to put food on the table.

Shaelyn left and waited in the hall. Impatient, her foot tapped a beat on the marble floor. Remy grinned and slowed his pace to annoy her a bit more.

The ground floor of Magnolia House held a myriad of surprises, not the least of which was a billiard table in the game room and a fine piano in the music room. No artwork adorned the walls, but he noticed bright squares on the wallpaper where pictures had once hung. No carpets covered the floor, either, and the rhythmic tap of his cane seemed very loud, especially in the room he suspected was the formal parlor, which contained not a stick of furniture, not even a plant. Perhaps the furniture and paintings had been sold as well. Or bartered.

"This is a lovely home, Miss Cavanaugh."

"Yes, and I'd like to keep it that way, Major. I would appreciate it if you and your men leave it exactly as you find it." She led the way upstairs to the bedrooms at a quick step. Remy followed slowly, using his cane and the carved banister for support. After so many hours on horseback, his leg felt like a foreign appendage made of lead as he placed one foot in front of the other on the treads. Each time he put pressure on his leg, a fresh wave of pain shot through him. Sweat beaded on his forehead. Still, he endured, welcoming the burning rush. His circumstances, like so many others, could have been much worse and he could have died, several times, since the day he'd been shot.

Shaelyn waited at the top of the stairs, her fingers gripping the banister, knuckles white. He looked at her for a moment, saw how stiffly she stood, and forced himself to move faster. He had too much pride to show her his weakness.

When he reached the landing, he took a deep breath. He didn't apologize, nor did he acknowledge her as his gaze swept the upstairs hallway.

There were six bedrooms in all on the second floor, some with adjoining sitting rooms, some without. All led out to the gallery, which encircled Magnolia House. He inspected each bedroom, mentally naming who would occupy which.

The manse more than met his expectations. His officers, those who had elected to stay with him and not somewhere else in Natchez, including the apartments over the Cavanaugh warehouse, would be quite comfortable here for the duration of their stay. The proximity to Union headquarters at Rosalie was perfect.

Between the last two bedrooms stood a closed door. Thinking it held linens and such, Remy opened it. A smile curved his lips.

"The bathroom," Shaelyn said from behind him.

The small room contained a commode, a sink with brass spigots, and a large clawfoot bathtub. "Indoor plumbing," he remarked with pleasure. He entered the room and faced the sink, then turned the tap and waved his finger beneath the flowing water. Steam rose to coat the mirror and he wondered if there was, perhaps, a copper tank somewhere in the house that kept water heated. It didn't surprise him. Sean Cavanaugh owned steamboats. Surely he could devise something…or pay someone to devise something. Remy didn't ask though. Instead, he wiped the steam away and caught his grinning reflection. And something else—a tile-floored structure in the corner of the room. "What is this?"

"We call it a rain bath." Shaelyn moved into the room, opened the wooden door, and pulled the lever connected to the pipe leading up to a wide, round brass…thing. Water flowed onto the tile floor, like it sprinkled from the sky during a rainstorm, before she turned it off. "Instead of taking a bath, you can stand in here and let the water flow over you to get clean."

He'd heard about them, but had never seen one. And couldn't wait to try it. The structure gave a completely new way to keep clean, and after what he'd been through, cleanliness was something he valued. He said nothing more as she moved past him and stood by the door to the last room, her arms folded against her chest as she waited for him.

Remy poked his head through the doorway. He liked the stark simplicity of this room. The walls were papered in a soft white with sprigs of purple violets and green leaves. The draperies repeated the pattern. An intricately carved four-poster bed took up space between the French doors leading to the gallery. The bed looked inviting with its plump pillows slanting against the headboard.

"This will be my room."

"But…but this is mine," Shaelyn sputtered.

"No longer," he said as he made his way down the hallway. "Have your possessions removed before dinner. Your mother's also."

"And where am I supposed to sleep?"

He turned and grinned at her, couldn't help it. "You could stay with me."

Her eyes widened and color stained her cheeks. She drew in her breath sharply. "How dare you even…suggest…such a thing!"

Remy shrugged. "It's your choice." The idea of her warming his bed brought a vivid image to his mind.

"I am not that sort of woman!" Her eyes flashed with pride.

He took pity on her and relented. She didn't know him, didn't know his sense of humor. She couldn't have known he wasn't like most men, who would have taken advantage of this kind of situation. "You may move into the servants' quarters for the duration," he said over his shoulder as he continued down the hall.

"I thought we had an agreement, Major. You said you'd try to make your stay as pleasant as possible." She caught up with him and grabbed his arm, stopping his progress. Her eyes narrowed. "You said—"

"I know what I said, Miss Cavanaugh." He looked at her small white hand on his arm and felt an infusion of warmth seep through his sleeve. Her touch ignited a fierce yearning in him. In another time and place—he didn't allow himself to finish the thought. "I am allowing you and your mother to remain here, but make no mistake. I am in command. My orders will not be questioned. I don't accept it from my men and I won't accept it from you. Do I make myself clear?"

Shaelyn nodded and stepped back, releasing her grip on his arm.

"I'm glad we understand each other. We are in the middle of a war. We all must make sacrifices."

"Yes, Major, we are in the middle of a war," Shaelyn said, her voice strong with defiance, her body stiff and unyielding. "But your battle has just begun."

She spun on her heel and sashayed down the stairs. Remy watched her, fascinated. "If it's a battle you want, Miss Cavanaugh, it's a battle you shall have."

Chapter 2

Shaelyn heard his words and cringed as the front door slammed shut behind her. She needed more than a moment to gather her thoughts and bring her temper under control. When she told her mother of the agreement she'd made with Major Harte, she wanted to be perfectly calm. Right now, calmness seemed beyond her capability.

She walked the garden path to the edge of the bluffs. A stone bench shaded by magnificent magnolia trees awaited her, and her gaze swept the horizon as she sat.

"Oh, Papa." She stared at the Mississippi flowing so peacefully below her. "I'm so sorry. I couldn't stop them from taking everything—the house, your business, your beloved riverboats. I couldn't save what you loved so much."

She allowed herself the luxury of a few tears then took a deep breath and forced herself to stop. Crying never solved anything. Although her heart remained close to breaking, she would carry on, as she had done every day since the Civil War broke out, since burying her father and watching her brother march off to join the battle.

Sean and Brenna Cavanaugh had not raised a spoiled child. Shaelyn had not been coddled overmuch, although she knew she had been loved deeply. Her parents always encouraged her to be confident and independent, spirited and outspoken— within reason—and she'd done her best to make them proud. She wouldn't let the Union occupation of her home change her.

A soft breeze rustled through the trees and several leaves fluttered to the stone path, the scent of autumn heavy in the air. For the moment, a sense of peace flowed through her, as if Sean Cavanaugh understood. "Thank you, Papa."

Her resolve once more restored, she rose and took two steps toward the kitchen door before a rumbling noise caught her attention. She looked up. Not a single cloud marred the darkening violet sky stretching into the distance. The sound grew in volume until it seemed to thunder all around her and the earth shook beneath her feet.

Shaelyn followed the flagstone path around to the front of the house, her feet lightly skipping over the stones in her haste. She stopped and stared at the sight before her, unable to move a muscle.

The entire Union Army filled her driveway. Or what seemed like the entire army. Wagon after wagon pulled to a stop on the circular path. Men in uniforms jumped over the sides and quickly set to work.

The front door of the house swung open. Captain Davenport came out and stood on the steps, his hands on the wrought-iron balustrade. A wide smile parted his lips.

"I see you found us without problem." Shaelyn heard him say as several officers climbed down from the carriages. They joined him at the top of the stairs.

One of the officers, a man with gray in his sideburns, shouted, "Start unloading. Bring the provisions into the house."

The men formed a line up the steps, past the officers, and into Magnolia House's central hallway. Item by item, they unloaded the wagons. Sacks of flour, sugar, and coffee were tossed man to man down the line. Barrels were rolled up the steps and down the hall.

Shaelyn raced up the curved staircase and pushed her way through the circle of officers on the veranda, her focus on Captain Davenport.

"Are you in charge of this this chaos?" The temper she had tried so hard to control simply broke loose. She couldn't help it, nor could she stop it. "You couldn't have them pull around to the back of the house to unload the wagons? There is an entrance to the cellar, right off the kitchen, Captain. Look what they're doing to my floor!"

Captain Davenport turned and glanced at the dirt being tracked into the house. Scratches from the barrels marred the beautiful marble. "I beg your pardon. I didn't realize—"

"No, of course not," Shaelyn exclaimed. "Why should you realize what you're doing to my house? You're only here for a short while. Why should you care if you leave my home in shambles? You won't be here to make it right!" She threw her hands up in disgust and pushed past him, slamming the front door in the face of a young private tossing a sack of flour to the next man in line. The sack hit the door with a thump.

"My word!" one of the officers exclaimed. The statement traveled through the closed door and open windows into the hallway, where Shaelyn stood trying to calm herself before she approached the major. She drew in her breath and watched the line of men standing in the corridor, waiting for the next item to be passed their way.

Another voice, one she did not recognize, floated through the open window. "Who is that lovely young woman?"

"That," she recognized the clipped speech pattern of Captain Davenport, "is Miss Shaelyn Cavanaugh. She is the daughter of the woman who owns this home. Beware. She has a temper."

"So I see," the second man said with a chuckle. "When will she be leaving?"

"She's not." Again, Captain Davenport answered, his accent placing him from Boston, an accent Shaelyn had become familiar with when she attended school there. "She came to an agreement with Major Harte. She and her mother will be staying."

"Is the major out of his ever-loving mind?" A third voice joined the conversation, and Shaelyn wondered if the tall man with the gray in his sideburns had uttered the question. It didn't matter. She had no intention of learning their names. "What is he thinking?"

"I wasn't privy to the conversation. All I know is they are staying. Mrs. Cavanaugh will cook and that young lady will be cleaning up after us." He paused then ordered, "Please put my trunk upstairs in the hallway."

Shaelyn moved away from the door and stormed into the library with one purpose—to give Major Harte a piece of her mind.

He didn't look up from the paperwork spread out on the desk—her father's desk. "What can I do for you, Miss Cavanaugh?"

"I see your word means nothing," she stated, her voice cracking in her ears.

Remy finally glanced at her. One dark eyebrow rose in question. "Excuse me?"

She pointed toward the hallway and the line of men standing idly, waiting to pass more foodstuffs. Mud from their boots splattered on the marble tile. "Your men are ruining my home! Why drag everything through the main house when there's a perfectly good entrance to the cellar in the back?"

Remy looked past her, his mouth settling in a thin line. "I'll take care of it." He rose from his chair with a wince of pain, grabbed his cane, and left the room. Shaelyn followed. Their footsteps tapped on the marble floor; her two to every one of his, despite his limp.

"Vince," Remy said when he walked out the front door and stepped into the pile of flour. White puffs shot into the air. "Have the men bring the wagons around back to unload." He glanced down at his boots and the flour coating the high gloss shine. "And have someone clean this up." He turned to Shaelyn. "Satisfied?"

"No, Major," she said, her voice sounding strange to her own ears. "What would satisfy me is having you leave."

"I'm afraid that's not going to happen." He turned on his heel and went down the hall in his uneven gait, his back ramrod straight as he returned to the study.

Shaelyn watched his progress and exhaled slowly. *This is not going to work at all. I don't want these men here.*

She knew she had no choice though. Neither did anyone else whose home had been invaded by these men in blue, but at least Shaelyn and her mother were being allowed to stay. So many others found themselves homeless. Shaelyn squared her shoulders and took a deep breath. She turned to face Captain Davenport and the other officers. Her cheeks burned as she eyed each man and waited for one of them to give the order.

They stared back at her, almost mesmerized.

"Well?" She cocked an eyebrow and put her hands on her hips. "Will one of you give the order or shall I?"

The man with the gray in his sideburns gave an exaggerated bow. "My pleasure." He turned toward the men and gave the command. In moments, the men rushed to obey.

Shaelyn turned on her heel and marched toward the kitchen. One battle won. How many more to go?

Her mother was standing on a step stool when Shaelyn entered the kitchen, pulling glasses from a cabinet high above the sink, then bending low to place them on a rolling cart. Fading sunlight coming in through the window created a warm glow around her. "You shouldn't be doing this, Mama." She took the glasses from her mother's hands, placed them on the cart, then helped her from the stool. "Why are you bringing all the glasses down?"

"I thought I'd make some cold tea for those poor soldiers. They must be very thirsty. Did you see all the food they brought in?"

"You mean dragged through the house?" she asked, her tone tart. "Yes, I saw. I also saw the scratches on the floor, which I will try to remove later. Leave it to a man to make things harder than they should be. I suggested to Major Harte he bring everything into the cellar."

Brenna frowned, the delicate lines around her eyes becoming more pronounced. "Suggested? Or did you use *that* tone with him?"

Shaelyn said nothing, but stared into her mother's eyes. She clearly saw the reprimand in their azure depths.

"I thought as much. Shaelyn, you can't—Never mind. I can only hope someone is looking after your brother like this." She sighed then started to rinse the glasses. "I could feed an army for a month with all the food they brought."

"You'll probably have to." Shaelyn struggled with a sack of flour some young man left in the middle of the floor. She dragged the sack into the pantry.

"What, dear?" Brenna went back to rinsing glasses, but spoke over her shoulder. "I knew everything would be all right when you poked your head into the parlor and gave me that look. Oh, Shae, I was so relieved. I didn't think I could bear having to leave—"

"Mama, this isn't all good, as you might think. In order for us to stay, I made an agreement with the major."

"An agreement?" Brenna grabbed a dishtowel and a glass. She turned slowly, her eyes wide with confusion. "What kind of agreement?" Her voice trembled.

"You're going to cook for Major Harte and his men. And I'm going to clean up after them."

Visibly relieved, Brenna smiled. "That's not so awful, dear."

Shaelyn shook her head. "There's more. We're to move our belongings into the servants' quarters."

Brenna tilted her head as she commented, "Still, it could be so much worse, Shae. We could be homeless like so many others. Why, I just heard Mrs. Merr—"

"I don't want them here." Bitterness colored her voice, but she couldn't help the caustic bite of her words. The sound of men stomping up and down the cellar steps echoed in the kitchen before sweet, blessed silence met her ears.

Brenna took a breath and opened her mouth to speak, but never had the chance. Her gaze drifted past Shaelyn. "Yes, Major?"

Shaelyn jumped and whirled around to come face-to-face with Major Harte. She knew he'd heard her comment and her face grew warm with embarrassment.

"Might I have a moment of your time?" he asked, his voice congenial, as if he'd heard the acid tone in her words but chose to ignore it. "I'd like you to meet the rest of my officers. At least, those who will be staying here."

"Of course, Major," Brenna replied, and to Shaelyn's mortification, patted a stray auburn lock back into place then actually smiled at the man.

Shaelyn stood rooted to the spot and gazed into the major's eyes. He offered his hand to her and grinned. She noticed how one corner of his mouth quirked a bit higher than the other, making his smile a little crooked…and definitely sweet, in a little boy way. "Miss Cavanaugh."

She drew herself up straighter, appalled she could even think his smile sweet. "I have no desire to meet your men."

"But meet them you will and you will be pleasant." His tone demanded obedience.

She chewed her bottom lip in indecision, caught between her desire to defy him and the command in his voice. The understanding and sympathy she saw in the warmth of his eyes confused her. She glanced at his hand then back at his face. His stern countenance convinced her. Disobedience would not be tolerated. She rushed past him into the hallway, her face aflame as if it were on fire. She leaned against the wall and drew in a deep breath to still the swift beat of her heart.

"Time, Major," she heard her mother say, then watched them leave the kitchen, Brenna's hand tucked into the crook of his arm. Shaelyn moved away from the wall and followed.

Remy's officers rose from their seats as he and Brenna entered the parlor. He brought her mother to stand directly in front of them. Shaelyn watched from the doorway where she stood.

Remy turned and faced her. "Miss Cavanaugh, would you please join us?"

She had no choice, she knew. Resentment reared its ugly head, but she tamped it down. With a great deal of reluctance, she joined her mother in front of the men.

"Mrs. Cavanaugh, Miss Cavanaugh, please meet Captain Bonaventure."

"Daniel, please," Captain Bonaventure, the man with the gray in his sideburns, said as he took Brenna's hand and brought it to his lips. His thick, woolly mustache tickled her hand and she giggled with delight.

"You must call me Brenna."

Shaelyn gawked at her mother, surprised by her warm, inviting manner. She shouldn't have been surprised, though, as Brenna had always been a gracious hostess, no matter the circumstances. Brenna's face beamed and a momentary flash of guilt rushed through Shaelyn. She should take the example and be kind to these men, but she just couldn't bring herself to do it. As it was, she had to grit her teeth when Brenna uttered "A pleasure, Daniel" with much warmth.

Daniel blushed then looked at Shaelyn. "Miss."

"Captain," Shaelyn replied coolly. Every muscle in her face strained with the effort to keep her smile firmly in place.

"Captain Peter Williams." The next man in line bowed before Brenna. He couldn't have been more than twenty-five, his light brown eyes bright with all the promise of a life ahead.

"Lovely to meet you, sir." Once more, Brenna flashed a beautiful smile, welcoming these intruders into their home as if they were about to share afternoon tea, or were being introduced at a grand ball, instead of having their home overrun by blue uniformed men.

"Aaron Falstead." A young man, no older than her brother, came forward, exuberance in his step and in his manner. How he reminded Shaelyn of Ian with his charming grin. He bowed from the waist before he took Brenna's hand. "A pleasure to make your acquaintance."

Brenna nodded in that regal style she had. "And what is your rank, sir?"

"Captain, ma'am." The man blushed to the tips of his dark blond hair, turning the few blond whiskers on his face almost pink as he stepped back into line.

"Randal Beckett, ma'am. Captain."

"Lovely to meet you, Captain." Again, Brenna's manner conveyed a warm welcome. Shaelyn clenched her jaw then narrowed her eyes when Captain Beckett winked at her.

The last man in the group stepped forward and again, Brenna's hand was kissed. "Captain Courtland Ames, ma'am. Please call me Cory." He glanced at Shaelyn and nodded in her direction.

"There is one more officer," Remy said quietly, "but he hasn't arrived yet. Perhaps—"

"Please excuse my lateness, Major Harte."

Shaelyn heard the familiar voice from behind her and whirled around. Angus "Jock" MacPhee, old family friend and honorary uncle, stood in the doorway, a huge grin stretching the ginger mustache across his upper lip. His light green eyes twinkled merrily as he opened his arms wide.

"Uncle Jock!" Shaelyn rushed across the room and flew into his arms.

"Sassy, lass," Jock murmured in her ear. "I thought ye might like to see a friendly face."

"Oh, Uncle Jock, I'm so glad you're here." She squeezed him tighter. Tears burned her eyes and her heart beat a frantic rhythm in her chest.

"'Twill be a'right, Sassy lass."

Shaelyn pulled away when she felt her mother behind her.

Brenna fell into the circle of Jock's arms. "Angus MacPhee, you are the most surprising man," she whispered as she rested her head against his broad chest then burst into tears.

Shaelyn stood back and watched while Jock rubbed Brenna's back in a reassuring manner, offering comfort.

"Don't cry, my fine Irish rose. Everything will be all right," Jock murmured, his thick Scottish brogue more pronounced than usual.

Whatever brave face Brenna had shown to the world, her inner turmoil and pain were now more than evident. Shaelyn knew her attitude hadn't helped, and a strong sense of guilt overwhelmed her as she watched the man she'd known all her life lead her mother to a chair by the window.

The other officers gathered around Brenna, their voices a low hum as they, too, offered comfort.

Shaelyn felt someone watching her and glanced at Major Harte. Sympathy radiated from his eyes. The simple expression was her undoing. The tears she'd fought so hard to contain clouded her vision as she ran from the room.

Chapter 3

Remy watched Shaelyn run into the hallway, but not before he saw tears fill her magnificent eyes. The rush of sympathy he'd felt earlier doubled, then tripled, and the inclination to comfort her surged through him. And yet, he wouldn't allow himself to move forward.

As long as they were here, he would be in command, and the sooner she learned that, the better off she'd be. That didn't mean he couldn't be pleasant, show her he was a man of his word, a man of honor.

He glanced at Brenna. As gracious and sweet as Jock said she was. There would be no fireworks, no battles, no questioning of his orders from her. Her tears had dried, leaving tracks on her cheeks, but the smile now spreading her lips remained as warm as when they'd first met. She sat on the rattan sofa, surrounded by his men, the last rays of the sun coming in through the window to highlight her dark auburn hair, the color of rich mahogany.

A smile twitched the corners of his mouth. No wonder Jock MacPhee had suggested this home and the Cavanaugh steamers. The Scotsman loved this woman, and had for quite some time, if the warmth glowing in his light green eyes was any indication.

A long sigh escaped him and the pain in his leg throbbed with each beat of his heart. He shifted his weight and leaned on the cane, his constant companion for the past three months. There was much to do and he had no time for the relentless reminder of his injury, nor for the love for Brenna he saw reflected in Jock's eyes.

"Gentlemen," he said as he turned and limped over to his officers. "I have assigned your rooms. If you'll join me in the study, we can begin getting settled." As one, his men rose and departed the room, their boot heels heavy on the marble tile in the corridor, leaving him alone with Mrs. Cavanaugh.

He studied her for a moment. A handsome woman by anyone's standards. An ageless beauty, enhanced by her sweet nature, with not one hint of her daughter's fiery temper. No raised chin, no daggers shooting from her clear blue eyes, which regarded him now with curiosity.

Remy cleared his throat. "Mrs. Cavanaugh, would you be so kind as to prepare supper? I am certain everyone is hungry. I know I am." And as if to prove his statement, his stomach rumbled. He covered the sound by clearing his throat once more. "You may use whatever provisions you like and if you should need anything else, please let me know."

"Of course, Major." She stood and smoothed the wrinkles from her long skirt. "And you must call me Brenna. Please." Her smile radiated her good nature as she touched his arm, her fingers light on his uniform sleeve. "I have a feeling you and I are going to be friends." She held his gaze with her own and sighed. "The same may not be true for Shae and yourself, and I apologize for her behavior. She is not normally rude. Truly, she is a sweet girl."

"No apologies necessary, ma'am. I quite understand. She's had quite a shock, as I'm certain you have had." He escorted her to the kitchen, now fully stocked with the foodstuffs he had purchased with his own money.

"Thank you for your understanding. And thank you for letting us stay. You could have thrown us into the street."

He nodded once then left the kitchen, uncomfortable with her gratitude, and limped down the hall to the study.

His men waited patiently, Daniel and Jock sitting in the oversize chairs in front of the desk, Peter and Cory lounging on a comfortable leather couch with Aaron behind them at the window. They were good men, chosen not only for their expertise, but for their integrity and honor.

Vince studied the collection of books on one of the shelves and glanced at him as he closed the pocket doors. "How's your leg?"

Remy grinned despite the pain as he moved across the floor and took the chair behind the desk. "Still with me." He made himself comfortable then propped his cane against the side of the desk and focused on the short list he'd written earlier. After each man knew which bedroom would be theirs for the duration of their stay, he said, "By the time we unpack our belongings, Mrs. Cavanaugh should have supper ready."

"Do you think it's wise to allow Mrs. Cavanaugh and her daughter to stay?" He caught the curious gleam in Daniel's eyes as the man asked the question. "Miss Cavanaugh has quite a temper."

"That she does." He couldn't help the small chuckle that escaped him. "As we've all seen. Whether it's a wise decision or not—" he shrugged his shoulders "—I don't know. It isn't the color of our uniforms that upsets Miss Cavanaugh. It's the fact that we all do what we damn well please, as she so clearly informed me, but from what I can see, she's more interested in keeping her house in good condition and keeping both her mother and herself safe. I understand that. I can respect that." He stood and moved to the window, aware that his leg had already begun to stiffen. "Besides, they have nowhere else to go."

Vince shot him a glance, one brow raised. "When did you become so sympathetic?"

He ignored the question. How could he answer? How could he explain that something in Shaelyn's flashing eyes had touched him and brought out every one of his protective tendencies? He thought of his mother and sister, sweet and gentle women both, and what would have become of them had they found themselves in the same circumstances. How would his officers feel if the situation were reversed and it was their mothers, daughters, sisters, or wives whose homes were confiscated? Could they have cruelly tossed those women out with nothing more than the clothes on their backs and a few coins, if they had any, in their reticules? And there was Jock MacPhee to consider as well.

He turned and faced them all. "Don't mistake my kindness for weakness. I have my reasons for allowing them to stay." He grinned. "I am sure none of you want to enjoy my cooking."

"Nay, ye don't. Trust me. I've tasted his cookin'," Jock teased with a laugh and tapped his chest with his closed fist. "I'm still tastin' his cookin'."

"We have an opportunity to do some good here, gentlemen, an opportunity to prove to these genteel Southern women that we are not cruel, heartless bastards. Now, go find your rooms and unpack."

As the men started to leave the room, he stopped them. "One more thing. You will treat these women with respect. Think of them as your mothers or your sisters. Be kind. Be courteous." His eyes narrowed as he pinned each one of them with a steely stare. "I will tolerate nothing less."

The Scotsman remained behind as the other men left the study. He approached Remy and laid a gentle hand on his shoulder, slipping easily into the role of favored uncle, though they shared no blood ties. "Thank you, laddie. I'm glad ye decided to let Brenna and Sassy stay. I was hopin' ye would."

"I only hope I don't regret my decision."

A gleam lit the older man's eyes and a smile spread the ginger mustache across his lip. "Ach, ye won't, laddie. Ye have my word."

Remy watched the man leave the room and wondered why the Scotsman grinned as he did. He'd known Jock MacPhee for many, many years—from the moment he'd taken his first steps. A friend of his mother and father, Jock had spent a great deal of time at the Harte family home and distillery when he wasn't captaining the riverboats that plied the Mississippi River.

Was there something the man hadn't told him?

• • •

Shaelyn took a deep breath and swiped at the perspiration dotting her forehead, despite the cooling breeze coming in through the open French doors. Candlelight flickered on the walls as she took another frayed and tattered skirt from the armoire and tossed it on the bed, adding to the pile growing on top of the comforter. She had already moved her mother's belongings downstairs and now worked on her own.

With each piece of clothing making the mound higher, her anger grew. "Damned bluebellies," she murmured under her breath. Her fingers grasped the silk fabric of a ball gown in the back of the armoire. A sigh escaped her as she pulled it out and held it against her body. Such happy memories were associated with the white gown splashed with hunter green leaves. She'd worn it when James had asked her to wait for him, when she'd kissed him and sealed the promise.

Tears sprang to her eyes as those memories faded, replaced with the reality of what her life had become. Balls and soirees and barbecues were pleasures of the past, as each day became a struggle simply to survive the ravages of war. There had been no extra money for anything frivolous.

In truth, she hadn't had a paying customer on any one of her steamboats in quite some time and even if she'd had, she didn't have a captain or navigator. She could have piloted the steamers herself, but without a crew, the task would have been impossible, and no one wanted an unlicensed pilot, no matter her skill and experience.

The warehouse in Natchez-Under-the-Hill had been empty for some time as well. The account at the bank had no funds. Simply keeping food on the table had necessitated selling off her mother's fine china and several of the paintings her parents had collected for much less than half their worth. She would have sold the piano in the music room if she could have found a buyer. Her mother no longer played.

She couldn't remember the last time she'd had a cup of coffee that wasn't full of chicory, and now she had a house full of Union officers to contend with. At least they'd brought provisions with them.

She tossed the gown on the bed and swiped at the tears blurring her vision. Forcing herself to take a deep breath to calm her shattered nerves, she continued to remove her clothes from the armoire. The drawers in the bureau were open and already empty.

Noises in the hallway drew her attention. Male voices, which hadn't been heard in this house for the past two years, raised in camaraderie, followed by the sound of heavy objects sliding across the floor.

Shaelyn glanced through the open door and clenched her teeth so hard pain radiated from her jaw. Instead of two people lifting the heavy chests, each one grabbing a handle, the officers pushed and tugged them to their assigned rooms. A reprimand built on her tongue. Who had raised these men that they couldn't come up with the idea to work together to avoid scratching the marble tiles she spent so much time cleaning and polishing?

She gathered the pile of clothing in her arms and left her bedroom, intending to give them a piece of her mind. Or at the very least, suggest how they could move their trunks without ruining her home, but the words died on her lips as she collided with Major Harte's hard body.

She swallowed hard as her gaze rose to his. Her mouth dried and her heartbeat picked up its pace to match the vein pulsing in his neck.

"Excuse me," she managed, although how she could speak was beyond her, especially when he put his arms around her to steady her. His warmth seeped through his uniform and she smelled his clean scent of citrus and soap.

Her pulse pounded in her ears. In the brief moment his hand touched her arm, she saw a vivid image in her mind. Of them. Together. His hand possessively caressing her flesh, his lips touching hers.

"Of course." He released her and she almost staggered on legs that had turned to butter on a warm day. "Be careful, Miss Cavanaugh." He grinned and her world turned upside down. Indeed, her world had been upside down from the moment she wrapped her arms around him on the front porch, and nothing had changed in the hours that followed. She felt…unbalanced, unsure, unable to hold a coherent thought in her head, as if some awful spell had been cast on her. The lights dancing in his eyes didn't help, nor did the charmingly crooked smile spreading his lips.

Shaelyn blinked and inhaled deeply, to still the frantic pounding of her heart, before she turned on her heel and fled down the hallway to the dumbwaiter built into the wall.

She stuffed her clothing into the dumbwaiter, aware of the warmth of his gaze on her. A shiver raced up her spine and heat rose up to settle on her face. Her whole body felt flushed before the feeling disappeared as if it never happened. Shaelyn glanced behind her and noticed she was alone.

She pulled air into her lungs and let it out slowly, then yanked on the cord that would lower the dumbwaiter to the small room behind the kitchen.

What was that? What happened to me?

She'd never, ever felt that way and even now, as she went downstairs, her pulse still beat an erratic tattoo in her ears. She closed her eyes for a moment, her hand resting on the wrought-iron banister, and tried to erase the vision she'd seen from her mind, but no matter how she tried, the image remained strong. So did the scent of citrus and soap.

As soon as she stepped into the small room behind the kitchen, the smell of freshly brewed coffee overpowered the fresh, clean scent of Remington Harte, for which Shaelyn was extremely grateful. She removed her clothing from the dumbwaiter and sniffed, her mouth already watering with anticipation. She entered the kitchen, her arms full of skirts and blouses and her favorite ball gown. "Is that real coffee I smell?"

Her mother turned from the stove, her eyes as bright as her smile. "Yes, it is. No chicory." Her grin brightened and for the first time in a long time, Brenna seemed like her old self. "You should see all the food Major Harte brought. I have a lovely ham in the oven, but there's beef, sausages, and bacon."

"Bacon?" Shaelyn stopped listening and repeated the word as if she were dreaming. How long had it been since she'd had bacon? Or beef, for that matter? How long had it been since they'd had any kind of meat? Granted, there were three pigs in a small enclosure behind the carriage house, but none of them were fat enough to make a trip to the butcher. Eggs and vegetables were plentiful because of the henhouse and garden, but even her connections in the black market couldn't provide her with meat, even if she'd had the coin to pay the exorbitant prices.

Perhaps having *them* here wouldn't be so awful.

After she put her clothes away in her new room, she came into the kitchen, grabbed an apron from one of the drawers, and tied it around her waist. "What would you like me to do?"

"Set the table, please."

Shaelyn did as she was told then returned to the kitchen. "What now, Mama?"

"I'm not sure. Do we still have the asparagus that we put up last year? Maybe green beans? Or beets? Just pick something." Shaelyn watched her mother as she basted the ham with a mixture of brown sugar, ground mustard seed, and vinegar. The aroma scented the air and made her mouth water almost as much as the coffee. "Oh, and see if we have any peaches left. I didn't have time to make dessert."

"Yes, Mama." She grabbed a lantern, lit it, and went downstairs to the cellar. She stifled an oath—indeed, she stifled a scream of frustration—when she saw the mess the soldiers had left.

She wended her way through the small path between sacks of flour and potatoes and other foods she couldn't identify at the moment, found a spot on the table where she could put the lantern, and began setting the room to rights.

A short time later, the cellar had some semblance of order. Smoked meats hung from hooks in the sturdy beams above her, and everything else had been stacked neatly, clearing a wide path to the shelves in the back where Brenna stored the vegetables and fruits they had preserved. Shaelyn loaded two jars of green beans and three of sliced peaches in heavy syrup into the well she'd made with her apron and brought them upstairs.

Warmth from the oven heated the kitchen. Fine tendrils of her mother's dark hair clung to her forehead and cheeks, and yet she didn't seem to mind. Indeed, she seemed quite happy, if the tune she hummed was any indication. Her mother had always enjoyed cooking and toyed with the idea of writing a cookbook one day.

"Look at you!" Brenna exclaimed when she turned around and spotted her daughter placing the jars on the table. "What took you so long? Did you decide to roll in the dirt?"

"No, Mama, I straightened the cellar."

"They did leave it in quite a mess, didn't they?" A warm chuckle rose from Brenna's chest as she swiped at the perspiration gleaming on her forehead. "Go get yourself cleaned up. By the time you finish, they should be finished putting their things away and ready for supper."

Again, as she never wanted to see her mother as upset as she'd been earlier, Shaelyn did as she was told.

Deep, rich voices in a multitude of accents alerted her that the officers had arrived in the dining room. Presentable in a clean skirt and blouse once more, she stepped out of her room just in time to grab the coffeepot and a pitcher of cold tea.

Major Harte sat at the head of the table, in her father's customary spot, although she hadn't set a place setting there. The sight of him in that chair brought a flash of anger, yet at the same time, a comfort she couldn't explain. His officers had taken places on either side of him and seemed relaxed in each other's company, as if they'd known each other for a long time, which she supposed they had. The major watched her, his warm gaze bringing an uncomfortable flush to her cheeks and a slight tremor to her hands.

Back and forth through the swinging door, Shaelyn brought the mashed potatoes, the green beans, bread and butter, and a gravy boat filled to brimming with the leftover brown sugar glaze. With each trip, she felt more and more self-conscious, especially with the major's eyes watching her every move. She didn't look at any of them until she heard Jock clear his throat. She glanced at him and caught his wink, his light green eyes, the color of new leaves, glowing with merriment and not a little bit of mischief, before she scurried back to the kitchen and the last item to be brought to the table.

"I must admit, I am anxious to see these riverboats you've boasted about, Jock." The comment came from Aaron Falstead, who grinned, showing off a complement of pearly white teeth.

"Ach, ye're in for a treat, laddie," the Scotsman replied, smiling. His eyes sparkled as he winked at her once more. "Finest riverboats on the Mississippi."

"Tomorrow will be soon enough," Remy said as he draped a linen napkin over his lap and took the platter of ham from Shaelyn's suddenly shaking hands. He flashed that charming smile that sent liquid honey gathering in the pit of her belly and, without a word, passed the heavy plate around, making sure everyone had theirs before taking several slices for himself. He placed the platter in the middle of the table. "Thank you, Miss…Shae."

The way he said her name sent a jolt of pleasure to her heart, and the warm honey that settled in her stomach spread outward, speeding through her veins one pulse beat at a time. Excused, she pushed through the swinging door and let out the breath she'd been unaware she'd been holding.

Brenna, bless her heart, sat at the small table where the servants—when they had had servants—had taken their meals, two plates heaped with food in front of her. Her hands were folded in her lap as she waited, but her eyes were bright, and the smile Shaelyn loved so much softened her features.

As soon as Shaelyn slipped into a chair, Brenna reached across the table and grabbed her hand.

She prayed, thanking God for the food on the table, asking Him to watch over them and to bring Ian home safe. To Shaelyn's surprise, her mother included the soldiers in the dining room in her prayer.

While she picked at her meal, she listened to the conversation in the other room. She learned that Daniel Bonaventure had a wife and three strapping boys in Pittsburgh. He hadn't seen them in quite some time and sadness reflected in his voice.

Aaron Falstead had a fiancée in Keyport, New Jersey, where he grew up and where his father owned a steamboat company that plied the shoreline from New York to Red Bank. They planned to be married once the war ended.

Cory Ames had a new daughter he hadn't yet met.

Peter Williams had no wife or fiancée waiting for him, but said he planned to remedy that as quickly as possible. Life was too short, he said.

Captain Becket didn't contribute much to the conversation. Out of all the men in her home, he was the quietest. If he had an opinion, he didn't share it.

Captain Davenport had neither wife nor sweetheart and didn't seem interested in obtaining either one. Or so he claimed in his clipped New England tones.

Major Harte said very little, although he did laugh, which for reasons she couldn't fathom, warmed her. A long sigh escaped her as she pushed the mound of mashed potatoes around her plate. Her appetite fled as a startling realization came to her. The men who had invaded her home were not monsters. They were just men who happened to wear blue uniforms. They felt sadness and happiness, loneliness and companionship, just as she did.

"You're not eating."

Shaelyn glanced up from her plate to find her mother's gaze on her. "I'm not hungry."

"Of course," she said, then pushed away her own plate. "I know it doesn't seem like it now, but having them here may well turn out to be a good thing, Shae." She stood and moved to the butcher-block table, where she opened the jars of peaches and poured them into one of her beautiful serving bowls. She added a serving spoon then took several smaller bowls from the cabinet and put them all on a tray. "Try to finish a little more, dear, then bring that other pot of coffee."

Brenna pushed open the swinging door separating the kitchen from the dining room, the tray in her hands. Before the door swung closed, she heard her mother say, "My apologies, gentlemen, I have no dessert for you this evening, but I thought some peaches Shae and I put up last year might be the perfect thing to end your dinner."

Shaelyn dragged herself from her chair, grabbed the coffeepot from the stove, and followed. As she refilled their cups, every one of the men around the table said "thank you," which didn't surprise her. All of them were courteous and kind and polite to a fault.

A short time later, the officers left the dining room, and a hush fell over the house as they closeted themselves in the study.

Shaelyn glanced at her mother and noticed the fine lines around her eyes seemed deeper and more pronounced. "Why don't you go to bed, Mama? I'll clean up."

"Thank you, dear. Having all these men here just reminds me of how much I miss Ian and your father." She sighed. "It's been such an eventful day. I must be tired."

As Brenna slipped inside her room, Shaelyn filled the sink with hot soapy water then rolled up the sleeves of her blouse and began to clear the table, saving the scraps for the pigs, who would eat heartily tonight.

By the time the pigs were fed, the dishes done and put away, and the kitchen gleamed in the lamplight, exhaustion overwhelmed her. Not only exhaustion, but a queer, curious tingling in her belly as she placed the roasting pan in the cabinet beside the stove. She turned quickly to find Major Harte standing in the doorway, watching her every move. He limped closer and stood on the other side of the butcher-block table.

"Might I have a moment of your time?" His voice, when he finally spoke, seemed weary and yet still commanding.

Lamplight reflected on his thick black hair and again the insane impulse to run her fingers through the silky strands overwhelmed her. Her voice stuck in her throat, she simply nodded.

"Please thank your mother for a lovely supper. I've not had such fine cooking in a very long time."

Shaelyn swallowed hard. "I'll tell her."

"There is one more thing." He withdrew a folded paper from his pocket. For a moment, she thought he might have changed his mind about letting them stay. Her heart began to pound in her chest, and she twisted her hands in front of her to keep them from shaking.

"This is a list of instructions I expect to be followed for as long as we are here," he said, his voice lowering, sending chills up her spine. He unfolded the paper and handed it to her. Their fingers touched. Shaelyn sucked in her breath as a heat rushed up her arm and the vision she'd had earlier returned, clearer and more vivid.

"Good night, Shae." As before, when he spoke her name, liquid honey pooled in the pit of her stomach. She willed the feeling away, but it remained even after he left the room, and she reminded herself that she hated his intrusion into her home.

Chapter 4

A sharp knock on the door woke Shaelyn with a start. Her eyes flew open. With a groan borne of a lack of sleep, she rolled from the narrow bed in the servants' quarters.

Though she'd been exhausted, her rest had been fitful at best. She'd spent most of the night listening to the clock on the bedside table tick away the hours, her mind filled with thoughts of mere survival in a house full of strangers—strangers she now labored for. Even though keeping house for the officers had been her suggestion, it did not sit well with her.

She lit the candle on the bedside table with trembling fingers. The fury of yesterday had not lessened with the dawn of a new day. Her heart pulsed with anger and revenge—and something else she couldn't define. The vivid images she saw in her head each time Major Harte touched her haunted her dreams when she did sleep, leaving her confused and mystified.

The war wouldn't last forever. Major Harte would someday leave Magnolia House. She'd have her life back, with her home and her business intact because of the sacrifices she and her mother made. In the meantime, Major Harte would come to regret his decision to confiscate her home and her riverboats.

Her gaze found the list the major had given her last night after supper. Bold yet neat handwriting filled the page, his instructions explicit. He expected breakfast promptly at seven, a small repast at one, and supper at six thirty. Prior to breakfast, he required a cup of coffee, black. Per his instructions, the coffee should be brought to him at six.

In addition, she would prepare his bath, sharpen his razor, and mix his shaving soap into a rich lather.

He wanted his uniform neatly pressed and his boots shined to a high gloss. The bed sheets were to be changed, dirty laundry would be gathered, washed, dried, ironed, and put away before the end of the day, and the room he occupied—her room—would be cleaned. She would do the same for the other officers, except for the personal attention he required.

Shaelyn grit her teeth as she read over the list once more. In truth, she had asked for this, made this bargain that would allow her and her mother to stay, but she didn't have to like it.

In the few hours he'd been at Magnolia House, Shaelyn saw Remington Harte, like his list, to be a highly regimented man, rigid not only in his posture, but in his command as well. His men followed his orders to the letter and without the slightest hesitation. Even Jock MacPhee deferred to his wishes, and that particular Scotsman didn't take orders lightly.

In Major Harte's world, his word was law. No one dared to contradict or question him, and yet he tempered his orders with kindness. Always, he said "please" and "thank you" and treated everyone with the utmost consideration. Even her.

His officers respected him; that much Shaelyn saw for herself. The respect seemed to be mutual, and that was a good sign. It meant he would keep his word as best he was able.

Another sharp rap on the door startled her. "Yes, Mama," she called out, her voice still groggy. "I'm coming."

A sudden smile curved her lips. If Major Harte expected complete compliance from her, he'd be woefully disappointed. *She* was not military. *She* did not belong to his contingent of men. *She* did not have to follow his orders.

But she did. If she wanted to stay in her home…

The clock in the hallway chimed five times. Shaelyn shook herself out of her musings, washed her face, brushed her teeth, and dressed quickly in a simple skirt and blouse, though both were a bit frayed and well-worn. She twisted her hair into a loose knot atop her head and left the room to find her mother in the kitchen, tying an apron around her waist.

"Good morning," Brenna greeted her, her lovely face a beacon of sanity in an otherwise insane situation. "I trust you slept well."

"No, Mama. I did not sleep well at all."

Brenna reached out and caressed Shaelyn's cheek. "Try not to be too angry, dear."

"Anger doesn't even begin to touch the surface of what I feel." The words were out of her mouth before she could stop them.

Her mother sighed, her eyes conveying her understanding. "Sometimes, we must accept what we cannot change."

Brenna might have been naive in many ways, but in this she couldn't have been more right. Shaelyn heard the wisdom in her mother's words, yet still railed against acceptance. But after yesterday's tears, she didn't want to upset Brenna again. Her voice softened. "I may have no choice, but I don't have to like it."

"No," Brenna conceded. "You don't have to like it. Just try to make the best of it."

"Yes, Mama." She met her mother's direct gaze, but said nothing more.

After a moment, Brenna sighed and turned away to make coffee. Over her shoulder, she said, "Please set the table."

"Yes, ma'am."

It didn't take long for her to prepare the dining room and rejoin her mother in the kitchen.

Brenna cracked eggs into a large bowl, added milk, and beat the concoction until it frothed. Slices of ham, left over from last night's impromptu dinner, were crammed into a skillet on the stove. They began to sizzle in the pan. The aroma of real coffee scented the air.

"What can I do, Mama?"

"Peel some potatoes," Brenna replied as she added butter, a staple neither one had seen for a long time, to the skillet for the eggs.

Dutifully, Shaelyn peeled and shredded potatoes without saying a word, leaving a pile in a bowl, waiting to be fried.

At five fifty-five exactly, Shaelyn made her way upstairs to the room Remy now occupied, carrying his cup of coffee on a tray. She hoped he'd enjoy the generous dollop of vinegar she'd added to the hot brew behind her mother's back.

She didn't knock, just opened the door and walked in, fully expecting him to be lazing about in bed, waiting for his coffee. She stopped, the door wide open, her hand still on the knob, and sucked in her breath. Her hands shook so badly she almost dropped the tray.

Sweet merciful heaven! She'd never, ever seen anything quite like Major Harte. He stood beside the bed with his back toward her, completely and unabashedly naked. His broad shoulders tapered to a slim waist and firm, rounded behind, his legs were long and tightly muscled. Sinews rippled in his back as he reached for his robe. He didn't seem concerned with her presence as he slid his arms into the sleeves.

"Excuse me," she muttered, quickly averting her gaze to stare at the floor.

"Good morning, Shae." He turned as he tied the sash around his middle. "Perhaps, in the future, you should knock before you enter a gentleman's room." He grabbed his cane and came forward to meet her. His robe flared open and she caught another glimpse of his muscular legs before her eyes were drawn to the long, jagged scar on his thigh. The wound did not look good at all. It was red and swollen; no wonder he limped. She could almost feel his pain.

She said nothing as she raised her gaze to his face. Yesterday, when she'd first met him, she'd been struck by his handsome visage. This morning, with his dark hair sleep tousled and his face scruffy with whiskers, he was even more so.

The warmth of his gaze touched her in ways she didn't comprehend. Her heart fluttered painfully in her chest and a queer quiver settled in her stomach as he advanced on her. She took a hesitant step back then stopped and drew in a deep breath. Silently, she handed him the coffee. Her hand trembled and she quickly hid it behind her back after he took the cup.

"Thank you."

Anticipation and a touch of fear coursed through her as he raised the cup to his lips and swallowed. His eyes widened in surprise. His throat moved convulsively as his mouth pursed and an eyebrow rose in question, but he said nothing. He didn't need to. The look in his eyes said it all, and yet he didn't seem angry. Not one bit.

He might not show anger, but that might not mean he wasn't angry. Wishing she hadn't doctored his coffee with vinegar, Shaelyn took another step back, placed the tray on the bureau, and fled the room without saying a word.

She stood in the hall, trying to catch her breath and still the painful pounding of her heart. Once she calmed herself, she rushed to the bathroom to start his bath and mix his shaving soap. How far could she push him before he retaliated? How much would he take before he said "no more"?

Her stomach clenched. Had she already gone too far? He didn't seem angry, yet she couldn't be sure. She didn't know him well, didn't know what kind of man he was beneath the veneer of civility she'd seen so far, but if it would help to make him leave Magnolia House, she'd do whatever it took.

She mixed his shaving soap into thick, rich foam then started the bath water, running her hand beneath the spigot to test for temperature. Despite her fear of retaliation, the water splashing from the spigot remained cold.

That'll teach him to invade my home!

"In medieval times, it was customary for the women of the house to help a guest bathe." He stood behind her. She hadn't heard him enter the room over the sound of the rushing water. "They considered it an honor." Humor tinged his voice.

Shaelyn straightened and whirled to face him. His smile could have charmed the drawers from an old woman, much less what it did to this young woman. Her palms grew damp. She couldn't breathe, couldn't take her eyes off the crooked grin on his face. "You are not a guest," she managed, although her mouth had gone dry.

"Be that as it may, the offer still stands." He untied the sash holding his robe closed.

Shaelyn heard his laughter as she fled the room. Her face burned even hotter.

Off balance. Confused. Not in control of herself. Angry. The variable mix of emotions frightened her. She'd never felt this way before, which made her angrier and more befuddled. From the moment he'd walked through her door, the world she knew ceased to exist. She drew a deep breath and let it out slowly, then entered her old room.

Well, he's certainly made himself at home. His brush and comb were neatly aligned on the bureau alongside a bottle of cologne, a small knife, a pocket watch, and a gold coin. Shaelyn picked up the bottle and smelled the cap. A fresh, clean scent with a hint of citrus assailed her nose. The memory of pressing her face into his chest when they first met flitted through her mind. She put the bottle down then turned toward the bed. A book lay on the bedside table, a red ribbon marking his place. She glanced at the title and tried not to smile as she recognized one of her father's favorites, *The Last of the Mohicans.*

The bedclothes were half on the bed, half dragging on the floor—as if he hadn't been able to find a comfortable position and instead tossed and turned all night, as she had done—but the pillow retained the indentation of his head. She smoothed the pillowcase and the scent she now identified as his rose to her nose.

"Nice," she murmured and pulled the sheets from the bed, tossing them in a pile on the floor.

His uniform jacket hung on the doorknob of the armoire. She smoothed the collar, releasing the smell of sun-warmed citrus and soap, then retrieved the pile of dirty laundry from a chair. A pair of soft woolen undergarments fell from her hand and she picked them up. Not the typical drawers that went down to mid-calf like most men wore, these, she assumed, had been specially made for Major Harte. Made of the finest wool, they stopped at the thigh, allowing the rest of his legs to be uncovered beneath his trousers. She wondered if he'd had them made to accommodate the ugly scar on his thigh.

An idea popped into her head and made her chuckle before she dropped the pile of dirty laundry in the hallway and grabbed clean sheets from the linen closet. She could hear him humming in the bathroom amid the sound of splashing water as he shaved. He wouldn't be humming for long. She finished making the bed and made a hasty exit before he stepped into his cold bath.

• • •

Remy watched Shaelyn come through the swinging door for the fourth time. Using a dishtowel to protect her hands from the oven-hot plate, she carried a platter heaped with johnnycakes and started making her way around the table. She had already dished out eggs, ham, and fried potatoes on her previous trips before placing the leftover food in chafing dishes on the sideboard.

Remy rose from his seat. "I'd like it if you and your mother would join us for breakfast."

She stopped and looked at him, the hot plate in her hands coming perilously close to Captain Ames's head. "I'd rather not."

He tilted his head slightly. "That was not a request. It was an order." He took the platter as well as the dishtowel from her hands, setting it on the sideboard with the other food, then grasped her elbow and guided her to the table, where he pulled out the chair next to his. "Please."

Shaelyn sat. Remy pushed in her chair. He recognized the defiance in her eyes as she stared at him, and he hid the smile that lifted the corners of his mouth.

He felt her gaze as he limped over to the swinging door and pushed it open. "Brenna, would you please join us?"

"Of course, Major. Thank you." Brenna smiled as she untied her apron and tossed it over a chair back. She entered the dining room and went directly to the sideboard where she helped herself to breakfast then took the seat opposite Shaelyn, next to Jock.

"You must be hungry," Remy commented to Shaelyn as he moved to the sideboard. He spooned scrambled eggs onto her plate and added a slice of ham and a spoonful of potatoes. He placed the dish on the table in front of her then went back to the sideboard and poured coffee. He held out the cup, forcing her to take it from him. With a flourish, he grabbed the napkin from her place setting, snapped it open, and draped it across her lap.

He took his seat next to her, picked up his napkin and placed it on his lap, then folded his hands and watched her. And waited. He could be patient when the moment demanded it and as he gazed into her lovely face, he felt like he had all the time in the world.

"You're not eating," he said after a while.

"I'm not hungry."

"You must eat, if for no other reason than to keep up your strength. You have a lot of work to do."

The hatred in her eyes almost singed him. He watched her gaze sweep the table. All eyes were focused on them, including Brenna's. Amusement made the corners of his mouth twitch as her gaze slid back to him. She raised an eyebrow. "Afraid the food is poisoned, Major?"

All motion ceased. Cups stopped halfway to lips. Forks, full of food, hovered in mid-air.

"The thought had crossed my mind." His lips parted in a generous grin. "Have some coffee."

Her eyes still filled with defiance, Shaelyn did as she was told and brought the cup to her lips. She took a sip.

"More."

He touched the bottom of her cup with his index finger, easing it to her lips. Obediently, Shaelyn swallowed, but her gaze remained on him over the rim. She put the cup down.

"Happy?"

"Not quite." He lowered his voice and leaned forward. His smile widened. "Eat."

"As you wish." She picked up her fork, speared a mound of fluffy eggs, and took a bite.

"Swallow."

Obediently, Shaelyn swallowed.

Remy nodded, glanced at Brenna briefly, then brought his attention back to Shaelyn. "You and your mother will continue to eat all meals with me and my men." Feeling mischievous, he added for her ears only, "Coffee tastes much better without the vinegar. And I don't appreciate cold baths, either. Don't do it again, Shae. I can guarantee you won't like the consequences."

Shaelyn's eyes widened. She almost choked on her eggs. Remy watched in fascination as she blushed becomingly and ate the rest of her meal in silence.

Perhaps I am up to the challenge, Remy mused as he watched a vein pulse in her neck. His gaze drifted to her eyes and he bit the inside of his cheek to keep from grinning. He'd angered her. He could tell because the color of her eyes had changed from vibrant cobalt blue to nearly violet.

Amused, he dug into his meal.

Between bites of scrambled eggs and ham, he addressed his officers. "Today, gentlemen, we'll inspect the Cavanaugh steamboats. I don't know when our first shipment of supplies will be here, but I'd like to be prepared. I expect everyone to be ready by eight thirty."

"I'd like to go with you." She spoke so quietly, he wasn't certain he'd heard her. He turned slightly and gave her his full attention. Again, her face colored, the flush rising up from her neck to stain her lovely features. Her beautiful eyes were wide, glowing with…what? Warmth? Determination? Her small pink tongue darted out to lick her lips.

Remy's inclination was to deny her request outright, but what better way to keep an eye on her? What better way to make sure she didn't put nettles in his bed? Or do something else to him?

Aware his officers watched him, he nodded slightly. "You may join us, but I will not wait for you. We leave at eight thirty sharp, whether you're with us or not."

Shaelyn gave a slight nod then pushed her empty plate away. She rose from the table and started collecting the dirty dishes. He saw her glance at the clock against the wall, perhaps judging her time, and move a little faster.

• • •

He didn't have to wait for her. Shae was already standing on the porch, her hands resting lightly on the wrought-iron railing, when he stepped through the front door and closed it behind him. A slight smile crossed his lips. She had changed from the serviceable skirt and blouse to a day gown in vibrant colors of gold, green, and red stripes. Still, she wore no hoops, but he could see the frothy lace of her petticoats beneath the hem of her skirts.

Captain Falstead brought an open carriage around to the front of the house and remained in the driver's seat, the reins to the matched pair of bays held loosely in his hands.

She didn't speak as she walked down the steps, but did allow him to hand her into the conveyance, her small hand resting in his much larger one. The warmth of her touch sent a thrill coursing through him, one he couldn't deny...but should.

"Thank you," she whispered as she adjusted her skirts and took a seat, her intent stare never leaving his face until she lowered her eyes to study her shoes.

Remy sucked in his breath as he climbed into the carriage and sat across from her. Jock had been so right when he'd claimed that her steady gaze could see into a man's soul. Despite his cold bath earlier, desire surged through his veins, heating his blood. Her tempting lips curved into a smile and all he wanted at that moment was to taste them. Would her kiss be sweet? Or bitter like the vinegar in his coffee?

He had no time to learn the answer, as the rest of his officers came down the curving staircase and joined them, the carriage moving as they climbed in.

"Where's Davenport?"

"Right here." Captain Davenport rode up to the carriage astride a beautiful black stallion then tugged on the reins, bringing the horse to a stop. "I'm going to stop at Rosalie. I'll meet you on board the riverboats." He said nothing more as he nudged the horse, setting him in motion, and disappeared down the long drive in a cloud of dust.

The drive from Magnolia House to Natchez-Under-the-Hill took no time at all, and yet, time seemed to stop for Remy. Shaelyn sat across from him and he couldn't tear his gaze away from her. Excitement reflected in her softly glowing eyes. Obviously, her riverboats were not simply a means to an end for her. They didn't just provide for her livelihood.

They were something more.

She loved them, if the expression on her face was any indication. They were a part of her. Pride flickered in her eyes and despite being in a carriage filled with Union soldiers, she couldn't hide the smile on her face.

She glanced in his direction and flushed to the tips of her ears, then focused her gaze on the steamers lining the quay.

He could see why she loved them. The Cavanaugh riverboats were a sight to behold. Tethered to huge stone moorings, they bobbed in the water as the carriage came to a halt. Both the *Lady Shae* and the *Brenna Rose* were side-wheelers, their huge paddles on the sides. The *Sweet Sassy* was a stern-wheeler, the big paddle, painted scarlet, in the back.

His men climbed down and stood on the wharf, talking among themselves. Remy climbed down as well, then reached up and offered his hand to help her. She laid warm, slim fingers against his, and again a tingle raced up his arm and settled in his chest. Her lips parted in surprise, as if she too felt that tingle.

Something flickered in her eyes as she pulled her hand from his grasp and walked toward the *Lady Shae*, lifting her skirts just enough to show the lacy white petticoats beneath the hem. Remy sucked in his breath, his gaze focused on her slim ankles.

He blinked, forcing his gaze away from her ankles, then grinned in spite of himself as his eyes found and settled on her backside, swaying beneath the yards of shimmering fabric. As if in a trance, he followed her up the landing stage, the cane in his hand tapping on the wooden planks beneath his feet.

He felt an intense stare and turned slightly to see Jock's eyes on him, a huge grin stretching the ginger mustache across his upper lip. The older man said nothing, but he winked and picked up his pace, making his way toward the pilothouse aboard the *Lady Shae*.

One by one, they inspected the riverboats. All were in excellent shape, the paint new, the brass gleaming in the morning sun, the engines well oiled, and he wondered how Shae had managed it all. He'd seen the brighter squares on the wallpaper in her home where paintings had once hung and had assumed she'd sold them to keep food on the table, but it may well have been to keep her riverboats in tip-top shape, despite the fact there hadn't been passengers in quite some time.

"These will do quite nicely," he murmured as he approached her. She stood at the bow of the *Sweet Sassy*, her face turned toward the deceptively gentle waters of the Mississippi. Several strands of her hair escaped the loose knot at the back of her head and fluttered in the breeze. "Who maintenances them? I'd like to hire him."

Startled, she jumped, then whirled to face him. "I do."

Remy cocked an eyebrow as he studied her face, noting how sad she seemed, noticing, not for the first time, how her throat moved when she spoke or swallowed, the white column soft and supple…and begging for the touch of his lips. "You?"

"Surprised, Major? Did you think me incapable of getting my hands dirty?"

He said nothing, mesmerized by the sudden flash of anger in her eyes as she looked up at him. Jock had said she was like no other woman he'd ever known, and now Remy could see why. Wisps of titian hair framed her face. He wanted to tuck them behind her ears and feel the softness of her skin beneath his fingertips.

"My father always said it wasn't enough to own these beautiful steamboats. One should know how they work and should be able to do every job on board." Pride replaced her anger. "My brother and I learned everything we could from Papa. I can pilot and navigate as well as or better than any man. I can read the maps, stoke the firebox, paint and polish, and I can fix the engine."

Such dignity radiated from her, he stopped listening as she spoke of all she could do. Admiration for her fortitude and ingenuity made him smile. He could picture her, grease on her hands and in her hair, perhaps a smudge on her smooth cheek, as she wielded a wrench. He saw her at the wheel, her hands gripping the solid wood, or studying the maps spread out on the table in the pilothouse.

Could he trust her to not tamper with the engines and leave them at the mercy of the Mississippi's strong current?

He studied her, saw the pride and passion on her face. Without a doubt, she'd never do anything to damage her riverboats. Oh, she might put vinegar in his coffee, but her steamboats? Never. And so he asked, "Would you consider continuing to maintenance your steamers? For me?"

The question caught her by surprise. Her lips parted and her eyes widened for a moment before they narrowed. "Why should I?"

Remy grinned at her, mesmerized by the way her chest seemed to puff out, exposing the silken tops of her breasts above the décolletage of her gown. "Why wouldn't you? Knowing how you feel about your riverboats, why would you trust anyone else? Especially if he happens to wear blue?"

She seemed to consider his offer, drawing her lower lip between her teeth as she thought, the sight erotic and spellbinding. After a moment, she inclined her head. "Yes, I will."

Those three words, spoken so softly, touched him in a way he hadn't thought possible, and he couldn't help smiling at her.

• • •

Shaelyn let the breath ease from her lungs. There was undisguised pleasure in the softness of his blue-gray eyes, although why that should matter, she didn't know. The last thing she wanted to do was please him. She didn't want to see him smile because of what that smile did to her. She didn't want to see the lights dancing in his eyes either. She still hated his intrusion into her home…into her life…and wanted him gone from both.

She turned away and left him standing at the bow, aware that his gaze followed her, causing her heart to beat a little faster in her chest and her blood to pound in her ears. Confusion and bewilderment swirled through her mind to cloud her judgment.

This is ridiculous! He's just a man. A man I don't want in my house. And I've only known him two days!

Shaelyn scowled as she climbed into the carriage and took her seat to wait for the officers, anxious to be home and away from *him*. She closed her eyes and concentrated on breathing deeply in an effort to tamp down the alien feelings arising within her.

After a moment, her breathing returned to normal, her heart rate slowed, and she thought she'd succeeded…until the major climbed into the carriage and sat beside her.

Shaelyn didn't know which was worse…seeing his handsome face and charming smile across from her, or feeling the heat from his body from shoulder to thigh pressed against her as he made room for the other men.

And there was heat. Seeping through his uniform, burning her, making her so *aware* of him as a man and not just someone who'd upset the plans she'd made for her life. Now, more than ever, she wanted him gone.

She turned her head and stared at her riverboats as the carriage moved toward home, ignoring the major as well as the other men. The officers talked among themselves, a conversation she was glad she didn't need to take part in.

By the time Magnolia House came into view, perspiration had trickled between her breasts and dampened her back, and his scent had invaded her brain in the same way that *he* had invaded her home. Shaelyn couldn't wait to get out of the carriage and away from him, but such was not to be.

As the carriage halted, Remy climbed from his seat and stepped down. He turned and raised his hand to her. Shaelyn glanced at his face. A charming smile curved his lips and his eyes, the color of a storm-filled sky, glittered with amusement and something else she didn't want to define. Her gaze lowered and focused on his big hand and long, strong fingers. She had no choice but to accept his offer of help, but as soon as their fingers touched, as soon as his warm hand clasped hers, the tingling in her belly began all over again. Worse, the vision she'd seen of them—together in her bed, his mouth laying claim to hers—flared to life as well.

Shaelyn sucked in her breath, certain he saw that vision too, but how could that be?

"Thank you, Shae, for a lovely morning and for showing us your riverboats."

Oh, his voice was too deep, his touch too warm for comfort. Shaelyn slipped her hand free from his and raced into the house, hoping to find blessed escape from the feelings that threatened to overwhelm her senses.

Chapter 5

Shaelyn groaned as Beelzebub crowed right beneath her window. Mean and ornery, his name fit him well. Stars still shined in the night sky as she cracked open one eye and glanced in that direction.

"Blasted rooster can't tell time," she mumbled as she glanced at the clock on the bedside table ticking away the hours. Three forty-five. Another groan escaped her, but despite being exhausted from cleaning up after a houseful of men for the past several days, she knew she'd never be able to go back to sleep. If she closed her eyes, she might dream of *him* again, as she had done every night since they'd met. "Might as well begin the day," she mumbled with a sigh as she tossed back the light sheet she slept beneath and climbed from bed.

She washed, brushed her teeth, and dressed, then wandered to the kitchen. Behind the closed door of Brenna's temporary room, she heard the soft sounds of her mother's ladylike snore. She prepared coffee and set it on the stove to boil, then gathered the officers' boots and brought them to the table, which she covered with old newspaper.

One by one, she brushed off the caked-on mud and brought each boot to a high-gloss shine. In truth, she didn't mind this task so much. It allowed her mind to wander while her hands were busy, but perhaps that was a mistake too.

More so than ever, she wanted these men out of her house, out of her life. Especially the major. Not because of the color of his uniform, but because of what he made her feel—sensations that were strange and frightening and thrilling all at the same time. She reminded herself she was spoken for.

In truth, the major seemed to be kindness itself—and his kindness was killing her. Slowly. Little by little. Day by day. The longer he stayed, the more confused she became. The tingling in her belly remained constant, a low buzz that warmed her blood and spread to her limbs. Her heart thundered in her chest every time he looked at her, and she found his gaze on her more often than not.

And the things she saw in her head! She couldn't close her eyes without seeing him—*them!*—arms and legs tangled within the sheets. She'd never, not once, thought of herself and James like this. Truthfully, she hardly thought about James at all, not since a tall, handsome major had come into her life and filled her mind with images and ideas she shouldn't have.

Even now, as she polished his boots, the visions were clear—his dark head bent toward her, his lips and mouth taking possession of hers, touching her, tasting her, his big hands caressing her body.

Shaelyn groaned in frustration and put all her concentration, all her efforts, into polishing his boots and trying to remember how much she wanted him gone from her home.

Finished, her fingers now stained with the blacking she used, the rag in her hand equally black, the surface of his boots shined in the lamplight and reflected her face, as did all the others. A devilish thought came to her and she couldn't help smiling. She rose from her seat and went into the pantry. Spying the object of her desire, she pulled the jug from the shelf and returned to the table, where Major Harte's boots waited. Removing the cork stopper, she poured molasses into his boots and tried not to giggle as she imagined his face when he felt the sticky, gooey mess.

• • •

After enduring only one of the cold baths Shaelyn had prepared for him, Remy struck that particular chore from her list and used the rain bath instead. He loved it. Loved how the water sluiced down his body, loved the feeling of being clean.

He flipped the lever, turning the water off, and opened the door so he could grab a towel hanging from a rack between the rain bath and the clawfoot bathtub. None of his officers utilized the contraption except Jock, who loved it as well—in the evenings, one could hear the Scotsman's voice raised in song as he bathed beneath the flowing water. The rest of his men preferred an old-fashioned soak in the clawfoot bathtub.

He dried off then wrapped the towel around his waist and moved to the sink. Steam coated the mirror and he wiped it away, then smoothed shaving soap on his face with a horsehair brush. Several strokes with a straight-edge razor later, he removed the excess soap and dried his face.

Haunted blue-gray eyes in the mirror studied him closely as a long sigh escaped him. Being clean did not stop the memories from assaulting him. How could it when the constant throbbing in his thigh reminded him every day of the carnage he'd seen, the friends he'd lost? Or the smell of death and the moans of pain as he lay in the hospital bed, struggling to save his leg, struggling to live, as the men around him died from their wounds?

He sucked in his breath and closed his eyes for a moment, trying in vain to erase the vivid images rushing through his mind. Shutting out his reflection did nothing to relieve the ache in his heart. Despite his efforts, the pain increased as the memories flashing before his eyelids grew in intensity. Not only could he see the past, but he could hear it and smell it as well. The sharp report of gunfire, the sound of bullets whizzing past his ears, the nervous whinnies of the horses, the screams of his men as metal hit flesh and bone. He could still see their faces, hear their voices. And the maniacal laughter that had rung out before a bullet screamed past his head.

Only two had survived the ambush—himself and General Sumner. The rest of his small contingent had perished in the blood-soaked mud, the smell of copper invading his nose as he too lay in the mud, his leg twisted beneath the weight of Soldier Boy's heavy body.

He opened his eyes, took another breath and let it out slowly, then did it again. After a few moments of deep breathing, he managed to still the images flashing before his eyes.

Towel wrapped around his waist, he limped into the bedroom and finished drying himself, mindful of the scar throbbing in his thigh.

He inspected the puckered skin and sighed. Ugly and swollen, the jagged line pulsed as if it had a life of its own, and yet he remained grateful to still have his leg. He could walk, despite the pain, and still breathed when so many others did not.

It had been close though. The surgeons at the makeshift field hospital had wanted to take his leg, declaring the bone protruding from his thigh too damaged to ever support his weight again. He remembered begging the doctor holding the saw in his hand, bargaining with him, promising him the moon and the stars and every cent of his worth if he would put the saw down. He'd made promises to God, too, and whoever else would listen. When infection set into the wound, it had nearly killed him. If it wasn't for the timely intervention of General Sumner, Jock, and his father, he wouldn't be here now. They had kept a vigil, the three of them taking turns feeding him broth, keeping him clean and cool, and urging him to fight to survive.

Coming so close to losing his life had changed him in so many ways. Accused of being arrogant and self-centered in the past, he now chose the other road, and though sometimes it was hard, he tried to remain kind, tried to see humor where little existed, tried to take the feelings of others into consideration when he made decisions.

With effort, Remy pushed the memories from his mind, except for his promise to learn the identity of the traitorous bastard who'd betrayed them to the enemy.

He dressed in his uniform then brushed his hair back from his forehead. He didn't inspect his reflection in the mirror, afraid the visions might assault him once more.

Instead, he sat on the edge of the bed and pulled his boots closer. A slight smile crossed his face as he inspected the shine. Shaelyn Cavanaugh may resent him for being here, her attitude described as prickly at best, but he certainly couldn't find fault in the high gloss on his boots.

He slipped his left foot into the boot. His smile disappeared as the oddest feeling came over him. Something wasn't right. His foot, encased in a heavy wool sock, had become wet, his toes sliding against each other as he wiggled them.

He removed his boot and inspected the sock. Thick, dark-brown syrup coated his sock and plopped to the floor one sticky drop at a time.

Molasses!

He should have been angry, should have raised the roof with the sounds of his displeasure, but none of that happened. As he studied the sock dripping molasses, a rumble of laughter rose from his chest. He couldn't help it. Vinegar in his coffee, cold baths, now molasses in his boots. What would the feisty, spirited woman think of next?

He almost couldn't wait to find out.

Exchanging his molasses-covered sock for a fresh pair from the drawer, he finished the last of the coffee Shaelyn had brought him earlier—stone cold but vinegar free—then padded down the stairs in his stocking feet, boots in hand, and sought out the vixen who dared so much.

Remy strolled through the dining room and noticed the table had been set. Warming trays were on the sideboard, one already filled with grits, another with cornbread, a third with small link sausages perfectly browned.

Daniel was the only officer already at the table, uniform clean and pressed, pen in hand, paper spread out before him. He looked up from his correspondence and took a sip of coffee. An eyebrow rose and a grin created dimples in his cheeks as his gaze landed on Remy's sock-clad feet and the boots in his hand, but he said nothing, simply nodded briefly then went back to his letter, his pen scratching out the words Remy suspected were to his wife.

He pushed open the swinging door between dining room and kitchen quietly and found the object of his search. She stood in profile, wispy tendrils of glossy mahogany hair brushing her flushed cheek. He caught a glimpse of the long, slender column of her throat exposed by the open collar of her blouse and the thrust of her breasts beneath the cotton, which expanded as she breathed. He said nothing, mesmerized by her beauty, and simply watched Shaelyn pour cake batter into round pans then lick the creamy concoction from the spoon.

In an instant, his body responded. Seeing her small, pink tongue against the bowl of the spoon had his belly tightening, his heart rate picking up its pace. Blood surged through his veins, resulting in an almost painful arousal that pushed against the fabric of his trousers.

He shook himself, tamped down the rampant desire shuttling through him, and said, "Good morning."

Shaelyn jumped, startled, and whirled around, the spoon still in her mouth. A lovely blush stained her face, making her incredible eyes glow as she glanced down at his feet then back up to his face. The blush deepened, rising up from her chest to encompass the soft flesh of her throat.

"Planning to put broken glass in that?"

She swallowed, the muscles in her neck moving. "I wouldn't waste chocolate like that, Major."

He took a step closer. Despite the lingering aromas of coffee, grits, and sausage, Shaelyn's alluring, seductive perfume reached his nose. Remy inhaled and let the scent fill him as he took another step toward her.

She watched him come closer. No fear sparkled in those hypnotizing eyes. Humor? Most certainly, but no anxiety, no panic or fright. The corner of her mouth twitched, as if she tried not to smile, and his heart pounded a little faster in his chest.

My God, she is beautiful!

She didn't move, although her chest rose and fell with each breath she took. Her mouth parted, her small, pink tongue darting out to lick her lips. If he took one more step, he could sweep her into his arms, press her body close to his, and touch the lips that spread so generously into an innocent smile.

Remy took that step…

Just as Brenna swept into the kitchen, fresh herbs clutched in her hand. Shaelyn's eyes widened as he gave a guilty start. His face heated beneath her direct stare and he moved away from Shaelyn, who hadn't moved at all. She still held the spoon in her hand, although now the metal seemed to be misshapen. Had she clutched it so hard she'd bent it?

"May I help you, Major?" Brenna asked. "Did you wish for something special for breakfast this morning?"

"No, ma'am. I was just…I mean…I…" *Good God, I'm stammering like a schoolboy!*

Brenna raised an eyebrow in question as her gaze drifted to the boots in his hand. "Major, shouldn't your boots be on your feet?"

"They should, ma'am, however, I seem to have a problem."

The corners of Brenna's mouth lifted as her gaze went from the boots to his face, then finally settled on her daughter. "And what is the problem?"

"You might want to ask Shae."

Brenna slowly shook her head. "I'm almost afraid to, Major." Humor tinged her voice as if she already knew what mischief her daughter had participated in, but to her credit, she did not smile.

Her eyes, however, snapped with laughter. "In fact, I don't think I will. You and Shaelyn will have to work this out yourselves. However you see fit."

"But Mama—" Shaelyn glared at her mother, but Brenna held up her hand, stopping whatever argument the girl could send her way. "Yes, ma'am," she muttered, but she didn't hang her head in contrition or apology. Oh no, not Shaelyn Cavanaugh. She stood tall, her head held high, her eyes glittering.

Remy thought for a moment as he studied her and tried to devise the most devious penalty he could think of. He couldn't help the thrill that coursed through him when the idea popped into his head. "As punishment," he said slowly, addressing the young woman whose stare saw directly into his soul, who dared to pour molasses in his boots, who stood so defiantly before him, "you will accompany me while I buy new boots. In fact, you and I will spend the day together, after, of course, you finish your chores."

Shaelyn gasped and her eyes widened. The blush that seemed to be a permanent fixture on her face darkened as her mouth gaped open. She closed her mouth with an audible click and swallowed hard. She turned toward her mother. "But Mama—"

Brenna held up her hand. "No 'buts,' my dear. You brought this on yourself. In truth, I don't believe the major's punishment is all that terrible. Certainly no worse than you deserve." A long sigh escaped her as she turned her attention to Remy. "In the meantime, there might be a pair of shoes in the attic that might fit you, Major." There was no mistaking the attitude or the expression on her face when she directed her gaze on Shaelyn. "After breakfast, you will accompany the major to the attic and find a pair of shoes that fit him."

Remy inclined his head toward Brenna then pushed through the swinging door. He stood on the other side as the portal closed and heard Brenna's reprimand and Shaelyn's hotly whispered outrage. For some reason, both made him smile, and he looked forward to—at the very least—an interesting day.

Chapter 6

Remorse. Regret.

Both emotions filled Shaelyn. Oh, not for putting molasses in the major's boots—which she'd truly enjoyed—but because her punishment was to spend the day with him...and it wasn't as awful as she thought it would be. Or should be.

In fact, to her utter surprise, being in his company like this was quite enjoyable. He seemed a little more relaxed, a little less rigid.

From the cobbler, where measurements for a new pair of boots were taken, to the butcher, where Remy paid an exorbitant price for a roast and a leg of lamb to be delivered to Magnolia House, to the baker, where they bought sugar cinnamon buns, they walked around town. And talked. And laughed. Despite herself.

Oh, and it felt so good to laugh, even if it was with *him*.

Who would believe the man walking beside her was the same one who'd invaded her home not too long ago? The one who'd nearly thrown her and her mother out on the streets?

Charm seemed to ooze from every pore as he regaled her with stories of his childhood and the mischief he'd often engage in, though he'd never poured molasses into someone's boots.

And his smile! Good Lord, even the old ladies he bestowed that crooked grin upon giggled like young girls.

"So what happened to that little girl who stole kisses from you?"

Remy shrugged his shoulders. "She grew into a very lovely young woman and married a good friend of mine."

"Did that break—"

"Shae, is that you?"

Shaelyn jumped as the familiar, honey-sweet voice met her ears. Even before she turned around, she knew who stood behind her and could just imagine the curiosity burning in Millie Hunnicut's cat green eyes. She stifled the groan building in her throat. Of all the people in Natchez, why did she have to run into Millie? Why now, when her hand rested lightly on the major's arm? When she'd been having such a good time in his company, laughing at his stories?

Another groan built in her throat as she turned and faced the woman. Her stomach tightened. She knew, before night fell this evening, everyone would know that she had been seen in the company of a man not her father, not her brother, and certainly not James Brooks, the man she had intended to marry. Worse, the man in question was a Union officer.

"Oh, it is you! I haven't seen you since...since your father's funeral." The young woman rushed forward and kissed the air in the general vicinity of her cheek. "Where have you been keeping yourself?"

"Hello, Millie," Shae managed, though she wished she was anywhere else—purgatory came to mind—instead of standing on a sidewalk with her fingers still resting on the major's arm.

"Aren't you going to introduce me to your...ah...friend?" Honey dripped from her voice, a voice Shaelyn knew Millie practiced in front of a mirror from the time she'd given up short dresses. Never close friends, she and Millie had been thrown together at various barbecues and socials from the time both had been old enough to attend such events. She'd seen, firsthand, the hope growing in a young man's eyes when Millie played the coquette. Shaelyn's brother, Ian, had fallen under her spell, only to be thrown over for the next handsome man. At one time, James too had succumbed to those lush lashes batting over beautiful green eyes.

Shaelyn's teeth clenched together, yet her smile remained in place. Perhaps, if she performed introductions quickly, she could make a fast escape. "Millie Hunnicut, please meet Major Remington Harte."

"Major, is it? Oh my. And for so young a man."

Shaelyn rolled her eyes as Millie poured on the charm. She couldn't help it. And the major made matters worse by taking Millie's hand in his own and bringing her gloved fingers to his lips to brush a kiss against her knuckles. Millie, eyes almost as wide as her smile, blushed a pretty pink, which Shaelyn thought might be as practiced as her honey-toned voice.

"A pleasure, Miss Hunnicut."

If she didn't know better, Millie looked ready to swoon, another maneuver practiced many, many times over the years. A quick pinch to the woman's arm might stop the fake faint, but she never had the chance. Millie forced her way between her and the major, insinuating her body in such a way that Shaelyn was pushed out of the way.

"I've never seen you before, and I know everyone in Natchez. Are you a relative of Shae's?"

Shaelyn's jaw clenched a little tighter and her stomach turned. Heat rose to her face, burning her cheeks. She didn't want Millie to know Magnolia House no longer belonged to the Cavanaughs and she only had a roof over her head because the major had been kind. That would be just the sort of tidbit Millie would need to start spreading the word throughout town, and she needed to stop Remy from saying anything. "It's been lovely to see you, but the major—"

At the same time, Remy said, "My men and I have been staying at Magnolia House, Miss Hunnicut."

Too late. Millie knew. The woman turned, a knowing look in her eyes. No sympathy radiated within the depths of green. No kindness either, just a sort of smug satisfaction the Cavanaughs were not immune to hardship.

"I see." The woman inclined her head to the side, and a smiled played over her lips, as if she couldn't wait to start gossiping. Which she probably couldn't.

Shaelyn wanted to hide. Better yet, she wished the earth would simply open up and swallow her whole. She opened her mouth, ready to voice an excuse to be running along, for the longer she stood there, looking at the expression on Millie's face, the more embarrassed she became. Not only embarrassed, but ashamed, which made her angry, because she shouldn't be feeling any of those emotions. Many people in Natchez had had their homes taken over by Union forces.

Yes, but not all of them are laughing with the enemy. Laughing! And hanging on every word!

She was saved from making excuses.

"Oh, look at the time!" Millie exclaimed as she glanced at the timepiece pinned to her bodice. She dipped a slight curtsey. "Major, it's been a pleasure to meet you, but I must be on my way."

"The pleasure has been all mine, Miss Hunnicut." He kissed her gloved knuckles one more time then released her hand. "Perhaps we'll see each other again."

The words brought more color into Millie's face, but only succeeded in making Shaelyn mumble beneath her breath. She didn't miss the warm twinkle in Remy's eyes as he watched Millie walk away.

Shaelyn watched Millie leave as well and released her breath in a long sigh. Whatever pleasure she'd found in the afternoon dissipated like smoke from a chimney winding its way upward. "We should be getting home as well."

He said nothing. Did not agree or disagree, but he didn't move either. Almost as if he couldn't.

Shaelyn studied him and realized the sparkle in his eye wasn't from flirting with a beautiful young woman or from watching the gentle sway of her hips as she hurried up the sidewalk, but from extreme and utter agony. His leg, or rather the ugly scar, must be smarting something fierce.

The charming grin when he'd spoken to Millie was replaced by a grimace. His lips pressed together, a white ring forming around his mouth. His hand gripped the silver head of the cane. She glanced at his feet, and the shoes she'd found for him in the attic. He'd said they were a good fit, but now she wondered.

She realized, before Millie had stopped them, their pace had slowed without her noticing, so caught up had she been in his recitation, in the pure delight of laughing aloud. His limp had become more pronounced than when they'd started out earlier and she'd unconsciously matched her stride to his.

He moved, finally. Stumbled, just a bit, not so much anyone would truly notice unless...unless they'd been paying attention, as she did now. She didn't want to notice these things about him, didn't want to feel the rush of sympathy coursing through her, making her heart hurt. Or the guilt cascading through her. She'd done this to him by ruining his boots, which, now that she thought on it, must have been specially made for him. She didn't want to feel these things and yet, she did. She wasn't so cold and unfeeling she wished him pain. "Would you like to rest? There's a park not far from here. Or I could go back and get the buggy."

"It isn't necessary," he murmured, but even that short sentence told her he suffered more than he let on.

"Yes, it is. You're hurting."

A long sigh escaped him as he slowed his pace even more. Through gritted teeth, he murmured, "Pain is good."

Though she didn't want to feel it, she did. Empathy. Compassion. And the realization that she felt these emotions hurt her just as much as his leg hurt him. "You're a fool, Major. Anyone in their right mind would have rested long before now, would have said something."

"Shae."

There was a warning in the way he said her name, but she chose to ignore it. "You wait here. I'm going back for the buggy."

"We'll both walk back."

"Stubborn Yankee mule." The words exploded from her without thought, without effort. Anger exploded from her, too. With him and with herself. Why should she care? "You really are—"

Dark brows slanted over his eyes, creating a furrow between them, the warm gray-blue darkening to polished pewter. "What did you say?"

"I called you a stubborn Yankee mule, but maybe I should have said 'ass'!"

"Madam, you go too far." His voice harsh, yet strained at the same time, he warned, "I would consider my next words very carefully."

They were there, right on the tip of her tongue, everything she felt about him and his invasion into her home, the good and the bad, but the expression on his face stopped her from uttering a single one.

With an exasperated sigh, she turned away and started walking up the street. After a few moments, she stopped and waited for him to catch up, though she didn't look at him, not even when he took her hand, placing her slim fingers once more in the crook of his elbow. Beneath the fabric of his sleeve, she could feel the tension in his hard muscles and wondered what toll walking beside her right now took on him.

The buggy waited exactly where they'd left it, Jezebel's reins tethered to a metal post in front of the cobbler's shop, though each step he'd taken seemed to be a struggle. His breathing became more labored, and redness stained his features. From pain? Embarrassment? Exertion? Shaelyn couldn't tell. And she didn't ask. Nor did she apologize. She couldn't. The words were lodged in her chest like a boulder, weighing her down, but even if she uttered them right now, she doubted he would accept.

He didn't say a word as he helped her into the buggy and limped over to the other side. Perspiration made his face shiny as he climbed in beside her and settled himself with another grimace.

Shaelyn didn't speak either as he handled the reins, leading Jezebel and the buggy to Magnolia House. "Stubborn Yankee mule," she murmured more than once, but beneath her breath so he wouldn't hear. The expression on his face did not invite conversation, nor did it invite insults. By the time they arrived home, sweat soaked through the major's uniform jacket and his eyes glowed, but not with humor. Indeed, he seemed feverish. And angry. Perhaps frustrated as well.

He brought the buggy around to the back of the house and pulled on the reins, drawing the vehicle to a stop. Shaelyn glanced in his direction, saw him close his eyes and draw a deep breath. He winced as he started to climb out of the buggy. Shaelyn slipped out of her seat and came around to his side of the vehicle. She reached up to grab his hand. "Let me help you."

"I don't need your help," he all but roared, pain not only showing on his face, but clear in his voice as well. "Stop fussing over me. I'm not an invalid."

Shaelyn jumped back. Without warning, unwanted tears filled her eyes and she sucked in her breath. "Damn stubborn Yankee."

He glared at her. The skin around his eyes had a yellowish green tinge. She'd seen that particular color before—on Papa's face just before he had an infected tooth pulled.

"Just full of pride, aren't you? Can't accept help from anyone, can you?" She returned his unflinching glare with one of her own. "Have it your way, Major. You always do."

He turned away from her then, but not before she saw something flash in his eyes. An apology perhaps? She had no time to discern the look as he limped up the back steps and disappeared into the house, his body stiff, shoulders tight. She couldn't see his face, but knew pain radiated from every fine line around his eyes and mouth.

"He'll be all right, lass. Just give him some time."

She glanced to her left and saw Jock rise from a rocking chair, a meerschaum pipe clenched between his teeth. He leaned against the veranda railing for a moment, then sauntered down the back steps. "Here, let me take Jezebel."

"No, I'll do it. Why don't you check on him?"

Jock simply smiled, took the pipe from between his lips, and shook his head. "I'm not that much of a fool," he said, his Scots brogue heavier than usual. "I've known him long enough to know he don't want no one with him now. And lass, he's embarrassed you saw him this way."

Shaelyn said nothing. She couldn't. The lump in her throat didn't allow her to speak. Instead, she shrugged and strode away, leading Jezebel and the buggy to the carriage house, berating herself for a fool with each step she took.

She'd forgotten. Between the beauty of the day and the warmth of his smile, she'd forgotten she didn't want him here. Forgotten that she hated his intrusion into her life.

Didn't she? So why did she care that his beautiful eyes revealed his pain? Why did she feel hurt they had argued? That she'd called him a stubborn Yankee ass? Indeed, it would be best if he left Magnolia House and she never saw him again. Anything would be better than the utter desolation she felt now.

• • •

How stupid!

Remy pressed his lips together in annoyance and continued to massage the cramped, bunched muscle in his thigh, though his efforts had little effect. His leg throbbed, the pain more intense than it had been in a long time.

He leaned against the desk, where he poured himself another glass of whiskey and took a long swallow, hoping the heat from the liquor would help to relieve some of his stiffness, his soreness.

What made him think he could traipse about town? What made him think he was the same strong, powerful man he'd been several months ago? And could do the same things that man had done?

Ah, but he knew the answer. With Shaelyn beside him, her fingers pressed into the crook of his elbow, her face animated with laughter, he'd thought he could do anything.

Oh, how wrong he'd been.

What if General Sumner saw him like this? Would he be deemed unfit to command? Would someone else be put in charge? Here? At Magnolia House? Would Shaelyn and her mother be allowed to stay?

The questions crashing against each other in his head were almost as painful as his leg, which still wouldn't hold the weight of his body and gave out one more time. He almost fell to the richly patterned carpet, but managed, by sheer force of will, to maintain his balance. Leaning on his cane, he made it to a high-backed leather chair and collapsed within the buttery softness of the cushions.

He counted himself fortunate he'd been able to make it back to Magnolia House and inside before he tumbled to the floor, but not before Shaelyn had seen his pain, his weakness. What's worse, she'd shown sympathy, her eyes shining with unshed tears, her actions solicitous and caring…much more than he could take.

A long sigh escaped him before he tilted the glass and swallowed more of the dark amber brew. Warmth trickled to his stomach and spread outward as he leaned forward and removed the shoes from his feet. Another burst of searing pain shot through him, the rising tide of biting agony stealing his breath. He took another sip of whiskey, wiped the sweat from his brow, and prayed the keen throbbing would stop. He closed his eyes as the pain slowly receded.

• • •

Shaelyn rubbed her eyes in an effort to get them to focus once more. The candle on the bedside table didn't provide enough light for the task at hand. Despite the lateness of the hour and the strain on her eyes, she continued using small, delicate stitches to sew up the legs in Major Harte's undergarments.

As she plied the needle, she wondered what punishment he would think of for this prank and couldn't help the delicious shiver that snaked down her spine. Despite running into Millie, despite the pain in his leg, and the way the day had ended, she had enjoyed spending time with him.

In another time, in another place, she might have harbored the thought they might court. Handsome—and charming when he chose to be—Remington Harte was the kind of man her father would have chosen for her. Even more, Sean Cavanaugh would have liked him tremendously, as her mother did.

Ah, but this was war. His charm didn't matter. His good looks didn't matter. Neither did his kindness. After all this time, he was still an invader in her home, an unwelcome guest.

But was he really? If she admitted the truth...

Shaelyn drew in a deep breath and laid her sewing aside as the realization stung her. After laughing with him and listening to him speak with such love about his family, she had to admit he certainly wasn't the enemy she'd thought him to be when he first came to Magnolia House. He didn't have to show her the kindness he had. Indeed, he didn't have to let them stay. For that alone, she should be grateful. And she was.

And though he remained an unwelcomed guest, she couldn't say with any accuracy that his being here had made her life worse. In truth, things had become easier. Just a little. At the very least, she did not have to worry about putting food on the table. Major Harte had taken care of that burden by filling the pantry with a variety of goods, some of which she hadn't seen in a very long time.

The candle flickered on the nightstand beside her, the flames making shadows dance on the walls. She caught her own reflection in the mirror and studied the face staring back at her.

Never before had she felt this way. She'd always known exactly what she wanted, but…he confused her, muddied her thinking until she couldn't hold a coherent thought in her head if she so wanted. Her thoughts and emotions were jumbled now, colliding with each other, clicking off one another like billiard balls on a smooth felt table, and she didn't like it. Not one bit. One moment, she hated him. The next, she didn't, and if butterflies would stop fluttering inside her belly every time he looked at her, if she didn't feel a tingle and a surge of heat every time he touched her, maybe she could stop the whirlwind of conflict inside her head. Maybe she could stop caring about him.

He'd shut himself in the study as soon as they'd come home. Because he couldn't climb the stairs? Shaelyn had no way of knowing. He had refused dinner, refused to let anyone come into the study, friend or foe, simply requesting to be left alone. He hadn't come out by the time she'd finished cleaning the kitchen and retired for the night—to sew up the legs in his undergarments—which she now thought was juvenile and mean-spirited, but had been part of her plan, one that she had been determined to follow through to the end. At least, until he packed his bags and left Magnolia House. But that didn't mean she couldn't check on him, see if he needed anything. That didn't mean she was pleased to have him in her home. She wasn't, and would do anything to help his decision to leave.

She chewed at her bottom lip, unsure and uncertain, torn between what her heart wanted and what her head wanted.

An hour later, her vision so blurry she could barely see, her fingers cramped with the effort of removing all those tiny stitches, Shaelyn put her sewing kit away, neatly folded the major's undergarments, and rose from the bed. She stuffed her feet into worn slippers and her arms into a thin wrapper, tied it securely around her waist, grabbed the pile of undergarments, and took the servants' stairs to his bedroom.

Once in his room, she went quickly about her business. Opening the bureau drawer, the scent of fresh air and citrus assailed her nose. *His* scent, the one she could smell even when he wasn't near. A small smile lifted the corners of her mouth. The other officers smelled of bayberry, except for Jock, whose fragrant tobacco drifting from his ever-present pipe scented everything he wore.

Shaelyn tucked the major's undergarments into the drawer and left the room through the gallery doors. Beams of moonlight danced on the mighty Mississippi in the near distance. A slight chill in the air made her shiver and draw her wrapper closer.

With a sigh, she took the gallery steps down to the veranda and peeked into the study through the open French doors. Several candles were lit against the darkness, but she didn't see him. She entered the room on tiptoe and spotted him reclined in a big, overstuffed leather chair, one sock-clad foot on the tufted ottoman in front of him, the other on the floor. His right hand clutched the head of his cane, as if fused to his palm, his left lay across his chest, rising and falling with each breath he took.

A bottle of whiskey sat on the small, round table beside him. Even in the candlelight, she could see the bottle was empty, the glass beside it empty as well.

She came further into the room, intending...she didn't quite know what she intended...and tripped over the shoes he'd been wearing earlier. She grabbed the back of a chair to keep from falling with a muffled "Heaven help me," and continued to his side.

Without thought, she leaned over him and laid her palm against his forehead, as her mother had done when she was younger and not feeling well. No fiery heat seared her hand. His breathing seemed normal. The pain must have receded, just enough to allow him to rest. She ran her fingers down the side of his face, feeling the roughness of his whiskers and the softness of his skin beneath.

She straightened, moved quietly to the window seat, and moved one of the cushions aside. She pulled up on the panel beneath, grabbed a thin throw from the compartment, and put the cushion back in place.

Approaching him once more, she spread the blanket over him. "I wish you would just leave," she whispered, even as she tucked the flannel around him. "I want my life, such as it was, back."

His eyes flew open as his hand snatched her wrist, the grip like an iron band around her bones, yet gentle and caressing at the same time. Shaelyn jumped, a startled squeak stuck in her throat.

"That's not going to happen, Shae." His gruff, pain-filled voice struck her heart. A low heat flooded her belly, and her breath stuck in her throat. "Until either I get reassigned, which might happen because of this—" He gestured to his leg propped up on the ottoman. "Or until this war is over, I'm staying. You'll just have to come to terms with that." He lowered his voice, but his gaze never left her face. His eyes glowed in the candlelight. "Now leave me alone."

Shaelyn swallowed, took one look at his pain-ravaged face, and ran from the room, hurt beyond reason and a little angry she had removed all those tiny stitches from the legs of his undergarments.

Chapter 7

Major Harte had made himself comfortable in her home and refused to budge. Nothing she did to drive him out—vinegar in his coffee, cold baths, molasses in his boots—none of it had the desired effect. He remained at Magnolia House, charming and pleasant as always, finding her pranks amusing, laughter smoldering in the blue-gray of his eyes. He never, not once, mentioned the incident when the pain in his leg had become too much for him. He never apologized for it either.

Frustration ate at Shaelyn. What else could she do to him? What would make the man finally realize he'd come to the wrong place and simply depart? She'd run out of ideas.

On the bright side, she no longer had to prepare his bath—he'd fallen in love with the rain bath and preferred that to soaking in the bathtub. She no longer had to mix his shaving soap into a frothy foam, nor shine his new boots either. She still had to do his laundry and clean his room, but those were tolerable tasks.

Shaelyn watched the time pass, cleaning up after men who for the most part seemed to take care of themselves, and maintaining her beloved riverboats. One day flowed into the next and the next until, before she knew it, September turned to October. Leaves changed their colors to brilliant scarlet and stunning gold, and a briskness filled the air as they floated to the ground.

She entered the kitchen on a bright fall afternoon, a basket of folded laundry in her hands. The bed linens were still warm from hanging in the sun and smelled of sweet, fresh air. She stopped short.

Her mother and Jock MacPhee stood side by side in front of a big pot on the stove, aprons tied around their waists, sleeves rolled up to their elbows. They spoke softly to each other, their conversation intimate.

A private moment Shaelyn shouldn't have seen.

She watched her mother. Brenna's eyes were bright when she faced Jock, a soft smile on her lips. She laughed, a sweet sound Shaelyn had not heard in a long time, not since her father had passed away.

Jock lifted a spoon to Brenna's lips. She sipped delicately and a dreamy expression stole across her face. "Oh, Jock, that's wonderful."

Shaelyn's face flushed. She *had* intruded. She struggled to breathe over the sudden lump in her throat, her eyes stinging with unshed tears.

She must have made a sound, for they both turned. Jock blushed to the roots of his ginger hair and the mustache across his upper lip twitched. "Excuse me," he stammered, removed the apron from around his waist, tossed it on the table, and made a quick, embarrassed exit.

Shaelyn did not miss the look of longing the man sent her mother before the door closed behind him.

"What were you doing, Mama?" she asked as she put the basket down.

"Jock was just showing me a new recipe for seafood gumbo," Brenna said softly as their gazes met and held, her mother's eyes still dancing with bright lights. She tilted her head, her direct stare never leaving Shaelyn's. Her chest rose and fell as she took a deep breath and let it out slowly. "He's still the same Uncle Jock you've known all your life, Shae. He hasn't changed because of the war. He isn't your enemy. None of these men are."

Shaelyn said nothing as she studied her mother and noticed the blush coloring the apples of her cheeks, the warm glow that seemed to infuse her. How could she explain the feeling of betrayal that settled in the pit of her stomach at seeing her mother flirt—yes, flirt—with another man, even if he was a man she'd known all her life? Jock MacPhee had been her father's best friend, had piloted the Cavanaugh steamers for as long as she could remember.

"He's always loved me, Shae." Brenna's voice reflected her happiness. "And I…I always loved him. I just loved your father more. You know that. I'll love Sean until I take my last breath, but things have changed. Your father is no longer here and I think—no, I know—I deserve a little happiness. If I can find that with Jock, I'm going to."

Shaelyn still couldn't find her voice, despite the pleading tone in her mother's words. What could she say? She was happy? She approved?

In truth, she didn't know what she felt, couldn't define the emotion if her life depended upon it. So many things had changed, so much had happened to throw her well-ordered routine into a spinning, muddled mess.

She swallowed against the lump taking permanent residence in her throat.

"It's all right, dear. You don't have to say anything. The expression on your face is enough." Sadness crept into Brenna's voice and a sigh escaped her before a hint of defiance glimmered in her eyes. Her voice grew stronger, her tone no longer meek. "You don't approve. Well, that's fine. You don't have to. I'm not looking for your permission or your blessing. I'm a grown woman, able to make my own mistakes, if that's what this is. I'm willing to take that chance. What about you?"

Brenna's attitude changed as she asked the question. She stepped forward, hands on her hips, the sadness in her eyes gone as quickly as it came, the expression on her face one Shaelyn remembered from before they'd both been thrown into this…this turmoil of war. "Admit it, Sassy," Brenna demanded, using the nickname she hadn't used in years. "You find the major attractive. If circumstances were different—"

"I find no such thing!" Shaelyn declared hotly, finally finding her voice. "Have you forgotten I am in love with James? He will come home, I'm sure of it. And he'll bring Ian home with him."

Brenna gently caressed her hand, still grasping the handles of the wicker laundry basket, and whispered the truth neither one of them was willing to admit. "I don't think either of them will come home, Shae. I think they're both gone or we would have heard something by now. A letter from one of them at least, telling us they are all right."

"I refuse to believe that, Mama."

Brenna shrugged. "Believe what you will, my dear, you always do." She turned and walked away, back to the pot on the stove. As she picked up the spoon and began to stir the simmering contents, she commented over her shoulder, "I've seen the way Major Harte looks at you."

Shaelyn stiffened beneath the casually uttered words and did the first thing that came to her mind. She lied. "I don't know what you mean."

But she did know. She had seen him watching her as she did her chores, his eyes glowing softly, the warmth of his gaze making her feel clumsy and awkward. The niggling fluttering in her belly hadn't lessened with time nor dimmed with familiarity. Indeed, the feeling had grown over the past few weeks. The afternoon they'd spent together, though it ended badly, still lingered in her mind as one of the most pleasant outings she'd had in a very long time. He'd been a gentleman—caring, thoughtful, and so very charming. He was still a gentleman, his kindness at times overwhelming. So many possibilities had run through her head during their lovely afternoon, but in truth, he was still an intruder in her home. One she wanted to leave. Or did she?

• • •

Shaelyn followed her mother through the swinging door to the dining room, a tureen of seafood gumbo on the serving cart she pushed.

As one, the officers rose then took their seats once more, as Jock pulled out the chair beside him for Brenna.

"We won't go all the way to New Orleans," Remy said to the group of men around the table as he charted the journey on a map of Louisiana. "We'll stop just north of there, right here." He marked the spot with a pencil and passed the map around. "I'll arrange to be met by another unit and we'll unload the men and the equipment. The journey will be finished over land."

As she ladled the steaming stew into their bowls, Shaelyn listened intently. The Union Army occupied New Orleans, but getting there remained a challenge.

Trains would be the best mode of transportation, but dangerous, as the rails were destroyed time after time.

Those around the table were aware of a rebel band of Confederate soldiers who had taken it upon themselves to fight the war their own way. Led by a man known simply as the Gray Ghost, they were the ones responsible for sabotaging the rail lines.

Trains weren't their only target, though. Along with the smugglers plying the Mississippi River looking for any unsuspecting target, this rebel band also attacked Union vessels, stealing cargo, food supplies, and ammunition. The steamboats were gutted and sunk. No one seemed to know what happened to the troops aboard those riverboats. The assumption was either they lay in a watery grave or had been marched to one of the prison camps.

Trepidation filled her, and her mind raced. It would be the first time since her riverboats were confiscated that they would be put to use. "Which will you use?"

"The *Brenna Rose*."

Brenna gasped and Shaelyn sent her a sympathetic glance. The *Brenna Rose* held fond memories for them both. The first steamer in the Cavanaugh fleet, it was where Brenna and Sean Cavanaugh had been married, in the pilothouse. They had lived on board for the first four years of their marriage, until Sean had enough money to build Magnolia House and begin his empire.

"Do you have a pilot and a navigator?" Shaelyn asked as she continued around the table and stopped before Remy. She held the ladle in her hand, hesitating, waiting for the answer. Though these men had been in her home for the past month or so, she didn't have the vaguest clue what they did.

"We all have experience, Miss," Daniel said as he unfolded his napkin and laid it across his lap. "Except the major and Captain Davenport. Before the war, I was the pilot on the *Moonlight Lady* out of St. Louis and Captain Williams was my navigator. Falstead captained the *Holly Lauren* out of Monmouth, and Captain Carroll was navigator aboard the *Memphis Belle*." He gestured to the men as he spoke. "Captain Becket piloted the *Delta Queen* out of New Orleans. Captain MacPhee, of course, you know. He's piloted your own steamboats. That's why we were chosen. Your steamers will be safe with us." The captain, aware of Remy's withering stare, mumbled an apology, and quickly became engrossed in the bowl of gumbo before him.

Though she acknowledged his statement, Shaelyn remained unconvinced. The men around the table had experience, but that didn't matter—the steamers they'd all spent time aboard weren't *hers*.

"We'll manage," Remy said as he turned his gaze to her once again.

Her mouth set in a grim line, Shaelyn came to a decision. She didn't want anyone at the wheel of the *Brenna Rose* except herself. She could trust no other to make sure her beloved steamboat survived the journey. "I want to go," she offered boldly. "I'll pilot or navigate or anything you wish, but I want to go."

Remy's brows raised in question and a smile quirked the corner of his mouth. "Why would you do that? It's more than evident you have no love for us Yankees, so why would you help us?"

She glared at him. "Please don't mistake my intentions, Major. This has nothing to do with you."

"Then why?" The intensity of his gaze warmed her. Heat rose to her face. Indeed, heat seemed to warm her entire body. Her heart beat faster in her chest.

"My concern is for my riverboats," she said, although how she could speak was a mystery. "This war will be over someday. I'll need those steamboats in good condition so I may provide for my mother and myself."

He nodded, his eyes never leaving her face. The warm tingle taking up permanent residence in her belly spread outward. If she listened, she could hear the pounding of her pulse in her ears.

"What qualifies you as opposed to them?" He gestured to the officers around the table then folded the map and laid it beside his plate.

All too aware of his eyes on her and the warmth rushing through her body, she said, "I cut my teeth on the wheel of the *Brenna Rose*, Major. I stood in front of my father while he guided our steamers, his hands over mine until I was tall enough to take the wheel myself. I've learned the feel of the water beneath the bow, and how the steamboats respond to touch." Pride and passion made her voice stronger. "The Mississippi is a treacherous river, full of snags and sandbars, constantly changing, but I've studied the maps. I could get your troops and supplies safely to wherever you wish to go."

"So can my men." Remy reached out and grasped her wrist gently, his fingers hot on her delicate skin. "Why should I trust you?"

She felt as if they were the only two people in the room, even though she was aware of the many eyes turned toward them. His thumb lightly caressed the soft skin of her wrist while his eyes bored into hers. Finding words became difficult. Holding onto a coherent thought seemed impossible, and yet, she tried.

"Trusting me is your issue, but you didn't seem to have this problem when you asked me to continue maintaining my boats." She heard the trembling in her own voice and her frustration grew, with him, and with herself. "Let me make it perfectly clear to you, Major. I will never let harm come to my boats. Or anyone who happens to be aboard them. To you, they are a means to an end, simple transportation, but to me, they are a way of life. This house was built with the money those steamboats provided, this dress was bought, these dishes, the very chairs you sit upon were purchased through the benefits of my steamers."

She took a breath, her heart beating a rapid tattoo against her ribcage.

"Both my brother and I were born on the *Brenna Rose*," she told him proudly. "My father named the *Lady Shae* and the *Sweet Sassy* after me."

"Sassy," he interrupted, the nickname falling from his mouth in a slow, seductive tone. "I thank you for your offer, but this is a military operation. My men will handle it."

Shaelyn's eyes narrowed and the inclination to pour the contents of the tureen into his lap flared in her brain. The urge became almost overwhelming, but as if he could read her thoughts, a certain expression came into his eyes and the message was clear. He had looked upon her previous pranks with amusement, but this… there would be no way on earth he'd forgive her for dumping hot gumbo in his lap. The consequences of such an action would be nowhere near as pleasant as being forced to spend the day with him.

Carefully, making sure she didn't spill a drop, she ladled the thick stew into his bowl. "I'll never forgive you if something happens to my steamer, Major. Never." She dropped the ladle into the tureen, spun on her heel, and left the room at a near run, hoping no one would see the tears of frustration, anger, and hurt fill her eyes.

Chapter 8

The hour grew late as Remy sat at the desk in the Cavanaugh study, maps of the Mississippi River spread out before him. Captain Davenport's ledger, containing all the supplies and artillery stored in the warehouse, lay open as well. Beside the ledger was a thick sheaf of papers—a registry of soldiers who had experience with steamers, from cabin boys to those who had stoked the fires, an inventory of the artillery and armaments to be boarded, a list of food supplies for the troops. All was in readiness. Or as ready as he could make it.

He heard the men say goodnight to each other and climb the stairs to their rooms, heard a few rustlings, doors closing, soft footsteps on the floor above him, then silence. He leaned back with a sigh and rubbed his leg.

His thigh ached and throbbed. He'd been sitting too long, staring at the maps as he tried to decipher all the little markings. He needed to move. He needed to sleep, too, but sleep, he knew, would be a long time in coming. He didn't relish the nightmare that awaited him when he closed his eyes, but then, his eyes did not need to be closed in order to remember the devastation of being ambushed.

Wearily, he ran his fingers through his hair, took a deep breath, and slowly stood, gingerly testing his leg for strength. A sharp, grinding pain shot through him and he sat quickly, before his leg collapsed, unable to bear his weight. He cursed.

Remy hated weakness and loss of control, more so in himself than in anyone else. Frustration filled him. After five months, he should be able to move about freely, without fear his leg would give out on him. He did have to admit, though, he was getting better, the bouts of infirmity getting farther and farther apart. Still, at times like this, that knowledge wasn't helpful.

He took another deep breath, mentally preparing himself for the inevitable rush of pain, and stood again. This time, his leg held. He grabbed the cane leaning against the desk and limped toward the window.

He spread the heavy drapes and gazed into the moonlit night. His gaze found and settled on a lone figure sitting on a bench beneath the huge magnolia trees for which the house had been named.

He smiled and whispered, "Sassy." The name truly did fit her. She was spunky, feisty. Another woman would have crumbled when faced with the circumstances she had been faced with. To lose one's home and one's business in one fell swoop to a man she considered an enemy would have broken a weaker person, but not her.

She had surprised him tonight with her offer to pilot the *Brenna Rose* down the Mississippi, but then everything she did surprised him. Indeed, amused him and made him want to laugh, made his heart pound harder in his chest.

His smile faded as he stared at her through the window and wondered what thoughts roamed through her mind. Was she still upset about the *Brenna Rose*? Or thinking of new ways to torment and tease him? Was she confused? He knew he was. Would she ever look at him with the same passion that had darkened her eyes when she spoke of her beloved steamers? Did he want that from her?

Yes, he did. From the moment she'd flown into his surprised embrace, he'd wanted to take her in his arms and kiss her sweet, tempting lips. Nothing had changed in the time he'd been here. His feelings for her had grown stronger as she tempted him with every saucy turn of her head.

But did she want him as much? Her heart had beat faster when he held her wrist. He had felt her pulse against his fingers as he caressed her velvety skin. He had seen her watching him, her gaze drawn to his face more often than not.

Moonlight filtered through the trees now, illuminating her light auburn hair and delicate features. She looked like a statue he'd once seen of the goddess Diana.

Despite the pain in his leg, a decision came to him. He should stay closeted in the study, going over all his paperwork to make sure every piece of equipment made it onto the *Brenna Rose*, but she drew him as surely as the moon drew the tide. And he just couldn't resist. Didn't want to resist spending a moment or two in her company, as prickly as she might be.

He gathered a silver tray, two cut crystal glasses, and a bottle of Harte's Private Reserve whiskey and exited the study through the French doors. He moved slowly, balancing the tray on one hand and leaning on this cane with the other, praying with every step his leg would not give out on him. Pain jarred him, but at least, it was bearable. Even so, he could feel the dampness of perspiration on his back.

"It's rather late, Shae," he said as he approached her. "May I?" He nodded toward the empty half of the stone bench.

Shaelyn turned to face him. "Why ask? You'll do as you please anyway."

Taking her tart statement as an invitation, he placed the tray on the bench then eased down with an audible sigh and placed his cane within easy reach. "Would you like a drink?" He didn't wait for her to respond. He poured a small amount into a glass and handed it to her.

"I see you found my father's private stash," she commented when she saw the familiar bottle. "This was his favorite. He only brought it out on special occasions."

Remy smiled. "That pleases me." She raised a questioning eyebrow. He pointed to the label. "Harte's Private Reserve. That's my family. My father and grandfather have been making this fine sipping whiskey for more years than you and I have been alive." He took a long swallow and savored the warmth of the liquor as it eased down his throat. "My grandfather says a glass a day is the key to a long and healthy life. He'll be eighty-two on his next birthday and still taste-tests every batch of whiskey we produce."

She took a sip and shivered but said nothing as she clutched her glass. Indeed, she didn't even look at him, but kept her gaze on the amber liquid shimmering in the cut crystal.

"Why are you up so late? Thinking of what else to do to me? It wasn't enough to put vinegar in my coffee or molasses in my boots?" She didn't say a word as she glanced at him, but her lovely face flushed in the moonlight. He lowered his voice. "I will say I admire your creativity."

"I apologize for behaving like such a spoiled brat." Humor touched her voice and floated over him like a silken web. She took another sip of the whiskey. "I shouldn't have done those things to you. Call it impetuousness on my part. I was trying to make you leave. I realize now that you're more stubborn than a Yan—well, more stubborn than I could have anticipated." She turned to face him.

Sweet heaven! She is beautiful. Remy struggled to breathe. All he could do was stare at her as the words he wanted to say became stuck in his throat.

Moonlight glinted off the loose knot of hair at the top of her head, turning the light auburn locks to liquid fire. Wispy tendrils framed her face. He had a strong desire to pull the pins and let the mahogany tresses cascade down her back. He'd never seen her hair loose, but he had imagined what it would look like, imagined running his fingers through the fine silken strands too many times to count.

"We made a bargain, you and I," he said when he found his voice. "Perhaps, what we really needed, Shae, was a truce."

"A truce?"

She looked at him, and he all but melted within the warmth of her gaze.

"Yes. For the good of us all." He reached for her hand then thought better of it. She would only pull away. "You and I need to declare peace. I'm finding it increasingly difficult to concentrate on my work when I'm wondering what you'll come up with next. Frankly, I can do without the distraction."

He didn't tell her that just looking at her distracted him. He didn't tell her that the alluring scent of her perfume conjured visions in his head or that the mere touch of her hand sent his heart racing. The simple truth was, since the moment they'd met, she disturbed his every thought, waking and sleeping. When he should have been concentrating on gathering the appropriate supplies and armaments needed for his Union brothers, he was thinking of her.

"All right, Major." Her soft voice sent a shiver up his spine. "We'll call a truce." She put her empty glass on the bench beside her then stuck out her hand.

Remy laughed. "I don't think so. The last time we shook on an agreement, you short-sheeted my bed. No, I think this time, we'll seal our bargain with a kiss."

Her eyes widened and she sucked in her breath. "A kiss, Major?"

He grinned at her startled expression. "Why not? Or do you still consider me your enemy?"

"No, you're not my enemy." Her sweet, tempting lips curved generously into a smile that nearly took his breath. "You're more of a thorn in my side."

She touched him then, just patted his hand, and Remy felt his whole world turn upside down, more so than when he held her fragile wrist and felt her pulse beat beneath his fingers.

She puckered her lips and leaned forward, eyes closed. Remy grinned. That kind of polite, chaste kiss was not what he had in mind. He wanted to feel her lips soften and open beneath his, wanted to feel her response as his mouth moved over hers. Very slowly, he placed his hands on either side of her face, his thumbs caressing her cheekbones. He lowered his lips to hers and tasted her tempting mouth.

The first touch of his mouth on hers held a spark of surprise. He'd imagined her lips would be soft, but not so incredibly warm and pliable as they molded to his. He didn't expect the sudden rush of heat coursing through him, either, nor did he expect the response of his own body.

He didn't expect to feel the compelling desire to keep kissing her until neither one of them could breathe.

Her breath quickened as he deepened the pressure of his mouth on hers. His tongue slid along her lips before slipping inside to taste the warm confines of her mouth and the whiskey she had drunk.

A small sound escaped her. A sigh? A moan of desire? Or revulsion?

She placed her hand on his chest and his heart responded, beating harder.

Does she feel it? Can she hear it? Does she know what she's doing to me?

He'd kissed women before, but never had he felt like this—as if he were a drowning man finally coming up for air, all with the softest touch of her lips.

He smoothed her hair away from her face, something he'd been longing to do since he first saw her, and pulled the pins from the topknot, dropping them to the ground. Silken curls tumbled down her back, releasing a fragrance uniquely hers. He entwined his fingers into the burnished copper tresses as his mouth moved over hers.

The whiskey bottle tumbled off the bench onto the grass, unheeded, as she broke the kiss and moved her head to the side. Her breath brushed against his cheek, fast and warm. "Is this how the military signs a truce?"

"No, Sassy." He murmured the words against her throat as his lips moved lower. "This is very unmilitary. This is something else. Something wild and bright and remarkable."

"Oh," she breathed as she offered more of her neck to him.

Remy felt her shiver, her body trembling against his as he rose from the bench, bringing her with him. They stood in the moonlight, their bodies pressed together, his mouth and hands making promises he fully intended to keep.

"We shouldn't," she murmured against his lips, even as she wound her arms around his neck and pulled him closer.

Her soft breasts were crushed against his uniformed chest. He felt her heat through their clothing. "Yes, we should."

Heat curled in his stomach and moved lower as he tightened his embrace. He smoothed his hands down her back and cupped her behind through the material of her skirt and petticoat, drawing her closer against the undeniable urgency surging through him. His trousers became tight and uncomfortable and he shifted, moving his leg between her thighs.

Shaelyn gasped at the sudden intrusion. "Major! We must stop." She turned her face away, although she remained in his arms, the slender white column of her throat exposed to his lips, her breathing heavy and labored.

He respected her wishes and released her, although letting her go was the last thing he wanted. He hadn't intended for their kiss to become so heated, but he hadn't been able to stop himself. The feel of her soft lips and her passionate response had encouraged him to take more. He wanted more still, wanted to lie with her and touch every inch of her velvety skin, wanted...everything.

"It's getting late. We should go inside." Shaelyn's hands shook as she smoothed the wrinkles from her gown. Her voice shook as well, but she hadn't run from him or slapped him across the face, which surprised yet pleased him.

"Of course." Remy loaded the tray with the bottle of whiskey and the glasses, then picked up his cane. He didn't apologize for his behavior. In truth, he wasn't sorry he had kissed her. "Will you walk with me? I promise—hands off."

He watched her as he waited for her answer. Her mouth seemed swollen from his kisses and her face still bore the flush of passion. In the glow of moonlight, he saw the blush staining her cheeks, and her eyes! How they twinkled, like the stars gracing the heavens above.

She returned his gaze, nodded, and fell into step beside him. "What happened to your leg?" Curiosity and boldness colored her sweet voice before she sucked in her breath and her tone changed to one of embarrassment. "Forgive me. That was awfully rude of me. I shouldn't have asked and you don't need to tell me if you don't want."

"It's all right. I don't mind telling you. I was leading a small contingent of men on a scouting mission when we were attacked by sharpshooters. Or at least I think they were sharpshooters." He frowned. He didn't mention that he took the bullet meant for his commanding officer or that he lay in the blood-soaked mud, his leg nearly crushed beneath Soldier Boy's heavy weight, his body a mass of pain for hours. The memory still had the power to make him shudder.

"I spent four months in a hospital, recuperating." Sympathy glowed in her eyes and he knew he had her rapt attention. "I almost lost my leg. What am I saying?" he asked with a chuckle. "I almost lost my life. Too many wounded. Not enough doctors and nurses. The smell of—Forgive me. You don't need to hear that." He nodded toward the bottle on the tray. "General Sumner, my superior officer, my father, and grandfather along with a bit of Harte's Private Reserve saved my miserable hide."

"You were fortunate to have them." Her soft voice floated over him like fine mist and eased some of his horror. "If you were a scout, how did you come to be here? In control of my steamers and everything else my family owned?"

He held up his cane. "As you can see, I never completely healed from my injury. Sitting on horseback for days at a time would probably cripple me for life. I knew I couldn't do it." A long sigh escaped him. He still missed the feel of good horseflesh beneath him. Short trips on horseback he could handle, but anything longer than thirty minutes or so left him nearly crippled. Despite that, he never again wanted morphine, which the doctors had given him to ease his pain. The drug had the desired effect; however, he didn't feel in control of himself or his actions when he took it, and loss of control was tantamount to a death sentence.

"On one of his last visits at the hospital, the general asked what I wanted to do. I could have gone home, but I've been a military man since I was sixteen. I wouldn't have known what to do with myself." He tucked his cane under his arm and walked rather slowly beside her. In truth, he slowed their pace because he didn't want to lose her company, and he would as soon as they entered the house.

"I'm not quite ready to take over the family business and truthfully," he continued, "the business isn't for me. Oh, I can take care of the books and distribution and the day-to-day operation, but my brother, Win, is much better suited. He has a talent, much like my grandfather, for distillation." He glanced at her. She hadn't taken her gaze from him since they started walking. "It doesn't matter anyway. My father isn't quite ready to give it up. Neither is my grandfather."

He grinned. "The last time I tried to brew a batch of Private Reserve, I singed my eyebrows and eyelashes, and burned my hand." He held up his hand and nodded toward the scar, almost invisible now after so many years. "I almost blew up one of the stills. My father, the very patient, very loving Jackson Harte, immediately banned me from the distillery, but honestly, it was a pleasure to go back to West Point."

"You haven't answered my question. How did you come to be here?"

"The general again," Remy replied. "He found the post, but not the place. Jock MacPhee provided the location. He claimed your steamers were the best on the river." He glanced at her and smiled. "You have your Uncle Jock to thank for the intrusion into your home."

Shaelyn said nothing as she passed through the door he held open for her. A single candle burned in the middle of the kitchen table, where he placed the tray, the light shimmering on the walls... and on her hair, which tumbled down her back in wild, burnished curls. Tomorrow, he'd have to find all the pins he'd pulled from those shimmering tresses and return them to her, but for now, he wanted once more to run his fingers through the heavy, silken weight. He took a step toward her and raised his hand, intending just that...one more touch of her hair, and perhaps an opportunity to pull her close and feel the heat of her body next to his again.

As if his intentions were clear to her, Shaelyn's eyes widened, the candlelight reflecting in the deep blue. She neatly stepped away from him and slipped into her room before he could act on his thoughts. "Good night, Major."

"Good night, Sassy." Remy lowered his hand as she slowly closed her bedroom door.

• • •

It was just a kiss.

Shaelyn knew she lied to herself as she leaned against the closed bedroom door and listened for his footsteps to recede. It wasn't just a kiss. Not if she could still feel the touch of his lips on hers even now. The usual tingle in her belly had turned into a raging fire within her, the flames licking at her insides, heating her blood, making her heart pound, all because he'd held her in his arms, and his lips had tasted hers.

She'd never felt like this before.

Not even when James had kissed her.

James.

She realized she hadn't thought of him in some time.

James's kisses had been chaste, to say the least. She had never opened her mouth to him and he had never asked it of her—their tongues had never touched, never tangled, never slid against each other. James had never pulled her into his arms and held her as if he were drowning and she his salvation, his only hope. Nor had he ever had the audacity to hold her closer so she could feel the solid hardness of him through her skirts as he insinuated his thigh between hers.

She let out her breath as she heard the major's footsteps lead away from her door, unaware she'd been holding it, but instead of relaxing, she held herself rigid against the exciting—and frightening—sensations rippling through her.

She undressed in the silvery light of the moon and slipped into a nightgown. The soft cotton brushing against her body simply added to the sense of urgency and need already sweeping through her. With trembling fingers and a heartfelt sigh, she fastened the buttons on the bodice and tried to ignore her growing fascination with both the major and the things he made her feel. She crawled into bed, pulling the light blanket over her.

She should get some sleep. Tomorrow, she planned on being aboard the *Brenna Rose* while Remy's men loaded the supplies and armaments for New Orleans. But how was she to sleep when he still filled her senses?

Her eyes wouldn't stay closed. Well, that wasn't the truth. The truth was, when she did close her eyes, she saw *him*—his blue-gray eyes mesmerizing, hinting at a passion he kept at bay, his crooked grin that tugged at her heart as much as she wanted to deny it.

It was just a kiss.

But it wasn't, and she was fooling herself to think otherwise.

Frustrated, not only by the circuitous route her thoughts were taking, but also by the physical ache building within her, she flipped her pillow to the cool side, punched it down a bit, and laid her head in the indentation. It didn't help. The moment she closed her eyes again, she felt his lips on hers, tasted whiskey, and smelled fresh air and citrus.

Oh, this will never do!

She slipped from the bed and moved to the small desk in the corner, where she lit a candle. Pulling several sheets of paper from the drawer, Shaelyn settled herself in the chair and began to make a list of the reasons why she should never allow Major Remington Harte to kiss her again.

Chapter 9

Shaelyn grabbed the last breakfast dish from her mother's soapy hand and almost dropped it in her hurry to be done and on her way.

Exasperated, Brenna let out a long sigh, grabbed the dishtowel draped over her shoulder, and dried her hands. "Shae! What is wrong with you this morning?"

Shaelyn stood on tiptoe and carefully placed the plate on the stack in the cabinet. "I can't let them leave without me."

"What are you talking about?"

"They're loading up the *Brenna Rose* today. I want to be there."

"I doubt they'll enjoy having you there, pointing out their every mistake."

"Whether they enjoy my presence or not, I need to be there. You didn't see them moving their trunks into their rooms when they first came here, Mama. There are still scratches on the floor." She glanced at the timepiece pinned to her blouse and swallowed hard. Five minutes to eight. "I'm sorry, Mama, but I need to go." She dropped the dishtowel on the table. "I don't want him to leave without me, but I'll finish my chores when I get home."

Brenna cocked an eyebrow but said nothing, although Shaelyn saw the smile tilting the corners of her mouth, as if she knew something but would keep the information close to her heart.

Ignoring her mother's mischievous grin, Shaelyn ran down the hall toward the front door, checked her appearance in the mirror above one of the few remaining ornate tables there, then grabbed a straw hat from the hook where it resided and plopped it on her head. The plain black skirt and white blouse she wore would suffice—she didn't have time to change anyway—but she smoothed the wrinkles before slipping into a fitted red, black, and gray plaid jacket with big black buttons.

The briskness in the very air lifted her spirits as she stepped through the front door and closed it behind her just in time to see Captain Davenport race by on his horse. She checked her watch once more and grinned. She had two minutes to spare—two minutes in which to relive, as she'd done several times already this morning, the kiss she'd shared with Remy. And how could she not? The taste of him lingered on her lips, as sweet as it had last night.

The sound of hooves and hard wheels on the crushed shell of her drive drew her attention away from the memory and she started down the stairs long before Captain Ames brought the landau to a halt in front of the house. He climbed from his perch and checked the horse's rig one more time, making sure everything was as it should be. He grinned as she approached. "Will you be joining us today, Miss Shae?"

"I thought I would, yes."

He gave a slight nod, bowed, then offered his hand, helping her into the carriage. She didn't have very long to wait before Remy and the remaining captains appeared. If nothing else, the major was punctual. When he said eight o'clock, he meant it.

A frown darkened his features as he made his way slowly down the steps, cane in hand, his eyes darkening to polished pewter… and trained on her.

He stood beside the landau, one hand resting on the side and stared at her. The crooked smile she'd come to adore was nowhere to be seen. Instead, his sensuous lips pressed together in annoyance. "What are you doing here?"

She took a deep breath and returned his unrelenting stare with one of her own. "You're loading the *Brenna Rose*. I want to be there."

An eyebrow rose, then the corner of his mouth rose as the other officers climbed into the carriage and pretended they didn't see what was before their eyes. "I can order you to stay here." His voice caressed her, much as his fingertips had last night.

"But you won't," she said, confident by this time that she knew him, just a little. If nothing else, Major Remington Harte was a fair man, though praying he'd understand didn't hurt. "You know how much the *Brenna Rose* means to me. Please."

"Ach, let her come, laddie. What's the harm?" Jock climbed into the carriage and adjusted the crease in his trouser leg as he sat across from her. She graced him with her widest smile, glad at least one person sided with her.

"Then she'll be your responsibility." Remy pinned the Scotsman with a steely stare, then stepped into the vehicle and sat in the only place open, beside her.

"I don't need anyone to be responsible for me." She turned to look at him. The sharp spark of anger along with the undeniable physical awareness of *him* jolted her senses. "I'm perfectly capable of taking care of myself."

Remy said nothing as he crossed his arms over his chest and looked straight ahead.

"Is everyone ready?" Captain Ames didn't wait for an answer. He flicked the reins with a well-practiced shake of his wrists and moved the carriage at a quick pace from the bluffs down to the river. Short—but much too long—and silent, the trip took only minutes…long enough for the heat from Remy's thigh to warm hers.

Captain Ames brought the vehicle to a halt then swung down from his seat. He opened the door and held out his hand. Shaelyn slipped her hand in his and stepped out of the carriage, followed closely by the rest of the captains.

"Stay out of the way and stay out of trouble." With those parting words, Major Harte and his men left her to her own devices. Shaelyn didn't move from her spot for a few moments, caught up in the excitement, her heart pounding. Uniformed men swarmed around the *Brenna Rose*'s landing stage, and still more were coming from the warehouse, bringing crates and barrels of much-needed supplies.

The scene brought back memories of life before the war, when Natchez and Natchez-Under-the-Hill teemed with people embarking on leisurely trips down the Mississippi aboard fabulously appointed steamboats. Cargo, now as then, was scattered around the landing, waiting to be loaded. The sound of men shouting orders and grunting beneath their labors brought a lump to Shaelyn's throat. Tears misted her eyes and blurred her vision as the past flooded her. How many times had she stood here, beside her father, watching and learning? And how long ago it all seemed. Another lifetime.

She took a deep breath, wiped her eyes, and instead of memories of how it used to be, saw things as they stood at this moment. She left her spot beside the carriage and walked down the gravel road toward the *Brenna Rose*, neatly sidestepping a young man rolling a barrel down the graded path.

Oh, this is even worse than when the captains moved into Magnolia House.

She saw it all so clearly. There was no sense of order, no organization, no clear direction. The men—boys, really—were dropping crates and barrels and other supplies willy-nilly, most of them pushed against the far rail. Several of them pushed a Gatling gun on its giant wheels up the landing stage then just left it sitting there, in the way of those bringing other supplies. It was chaos and utter confusion.

Already, she could see the damage to her riverboat—torn carpeting, scratches on the new paint—small things, yes, but still…

And above it all, she heard the strident tones of Captain Vincent Davenport, ordering the men to "Hup to. Double time." He stood on one of the upper decks and leaned against the rail as if he were the king and the men scurrying below him his subjects. He pointed and shouted, as if he actually knew what he was doing, but in the few moments Shaelyn watched him, she knew. The man had never loaded cargo onto a steamboat before, had probably never loaded anything other than his pipe or his rifle. He may be quartermaster and in charge of the supplies, but she hated to think what the warehouse had looked like before the men emptied it. Probably as bad as her steamer.

Thinking only of the safety of the men the *Brenna Rose* would be transporting, Shaelyn climbed up on a barrel someone conveniently left in her path. What was in the barrel, she didn't know. Furthermore, she didn't care. What she wanted—no, what she needed—was to gain the attention of the men.

"Gentlemen! May I have a moment of your time?"

• • •

A frisson of uneasiness snaked up Remy's spine and the fine hair at his nape bristled as he felt it again—an unrelenting stare filled with malicious intent boring into his back. He remembered that same feeling, the same evilness, just before he and his men had been ambushed months ago.

Some feelings one never forgets.

He turned quickly, looking for the source of his discomfort, and stiffened, his hand gripping the head of his cane a little tighter. Captain Davenport stood a few feet away. Remy could have sworn he saw hatred—pure, unadulterated hatred—in Davenport's dark eyes, but that couldn't be. He blinked and looked again.

He was wrong. Hatred did not gleam in Vincent's eyes, only frustration. Furrows mussed his hair, as if his fingers had run through the light auburn strands many times, and redness tinged his face.

Irritation showed in his stiff-legged walk as he approached. "You really must do something about her, Remy." He had rolled the inventory lists into a tube and slapped his hand with it.

"Who?"

"Miss Cavanaugh." He spat her name as if it were a curse. "I don't care if she is your lover. She doesn't belong here. She's interfering with everything." He flung his arm wide, motioning to the men moving heavy artillery. "She is overriding my orders and rearranging all the equipment we've brought on board." He stared at Remy, his chest puffed out, face flushed with indignation and something Remy couldn't define.

Remy glanced over Vince's head and saw the object of his frustration. Shaelyn had, indeed, commandeered the men to move the heavy artillery. She stood on a barrel, her back to him, in the middle of a swarm of blue uniforms, shouting to be heard over the noise. "I'll take care of it." He started to walk away then turned. "Just for the record, Captain, Miss Cavanaugh is not my lover and I never want to hear you talk about her that way again."

"Yes, sir!" Davenport saluted, but in Remy's eyes, it wasn't a true salute, a sign of respect. Somehow, when Vincent raised his hand to his brow, there was something mocking in the action, almost scornful, and yet he just couldn't be sure. Davenport had been an underclassman at West Point before the war. Remy knew him as well as he knew any of the other men with him—knew their backgrounds, their military records, understood what drove them to accomplish what they had, but he'd managed to keep his distance. Except for Jock, he didn't have a personal relationship with any of his men.

After the ambush and losing the men he'd grown close to, he'd promised himself he wouldn't become that close to anyone again—at least until the war was over. It was too easy to lose a friend, a companion, or a superior to a sharpshooter's bullet or cannon fire, too easy to lose heart and hope when someone he cared for drew his last breath.

Remy mentally shook himself free of his own rambling thoughts, returned the salute, and strode away, the uneasiness making his back stiff as he limped over to Shaelyn. She had removed her hat, and her hair, tied up once more in the loose knot she preferred, gleamed with fiery brilliance in the morning sun. Wispy tendrils fluttered in the breeze.

The memory of pulling the pins from her hair and feeling the silken tresses between his fingers flared in his brain. He'd found every one of those pins—some gold, some silver, one with tiny seed pearls—this morning and returned them to her. She had taken them from the palm of his hand, blushed a deep red, thanked him quickly, and disappeared. Belatedly, the thought occurred to him that he should have kept them as a memento of their first kiss. He shook his head. He didn't need a reminder of the touch of her lips on his. He'd remember that always.

He watched her now, listened as she gave orders in a sweet, honey-toned voice, a natural-born leader. The men rushed to obey her commands, moving cannons and Gatling guns into position.

Remy cringed as he watched the movement on deck. They weren't men. They were boys. And so young. Some of them, their faces still shiny with youth, had never used a razor. Some had nothing but peach fuzz on their cheeks, and yet, here they were, fighting in a man's war, hungry for adventure, yet so naive of the hardship of battle. Not one of them considered that he might lose a limb—or worse, his life—or knew what it felt like to have bullets flying close to one's ears.

Remy shook his head and cleared his throat of the lump that had risen. He'd been that young once, that naive, so full of ideals and dreams. He cleared his throat again. "Shae."

She turned quickly, her lace-edged skirt swirling around her ankles. "Yes, sir?"

"Would you mind explaining what you're doing?"

She tilted her head as she looked down at him, her eyes wide and guileless. One shapely brow rose. "I'm having the men rearrange the cargo."

A smile threatened to curve his mouth and his heart beat a little faster in his chest. She looked utterly adorable. And capable. And for a moment, he forgot why he'd come over to her. With effort, he dragged his gaze away from her. "Why?"

"Captain Davenport tattled on me, didn't he?"

"He has every right, Shae. He is in charge."

She shrugged, as if she didn't care, then put her hands on her hips. "Then the boat will list, Major. All the heavy artillery had been pushed to one side of the *Brenna Rose*, creating an imbalance. Weight must be distributed evenly, otherwise you'll lose time and fuel and risk capsizing." She smiled then, her lips spreading into the teasing grin he saw even with his eyes closed, tempting him beyond reason.

He didn't care that the *Brenna Rose* swarmed with men and they weren't alone. He just wanted to kiss her, to taste and touch her as he'd done last night, feel her body next to his. She'd fit him so well, her curves melting into his hardness. Even now, he had some difficulty concentrating.

He almost reached out to touch her. Almost. Instead, realizing some of the men were staring at them, he focused on the task at hand and slowly nodded. He also realized she may be right. "Carry on."

Once again, Shaelyn flashed an impish grin at him and his heart thumped harder in his chest. He didn't know exactly why, but he trusted her, despite the pranks she'd played. She loved her steamers so much, she wouldn't let anything to happen to them.

Before long, all the equipment had been loaded onto the *Brenna Rose*, situated exactly as Shaelyn wanted it. After Remy, Shaelyn, and all his officers, except for Captains Falstead and Ames, left the boat, the landing stage lifted. Steam huffed from the pipe before a sharp whistle rent the air and the red-painted wheel began to turn, shushing the water. Captains Falstead and Ames leaned out the window of the pilothouse and gave another toot on the whistle.

The troops gathered at the *Brenna's Rose*'s railing and waved, although no one stood on the quay to wave back, wish them luck, or pray for their safe return except for himself, his other officers, and Shae, who stood beside him, her handkerchief a white flag.

Remy watched the water beneath the wheel churn faster, listened to the excited voices, and drew in his breath sharply. Dread, deep and dark, filled him, and a sense of foreboding he couldn't explain or deny added to the malice directed at his back.

Chapter 10

Shaelyn knew the moment she looked out the study window into the side yard, dust rag in hand, something wasn't right. Was it news about Ian? She didn't think so. Otherwise, Remy wouldn't be receiving the information.

He stood with his back to her, perfectly still, his entire body as rigid and unbending as steel while the young man facing him gestured wildly with his hands.

She pressed her nose against the window glass for a closer look and sighed. The young man couldn't be older than fourteen or fifteen. She noticed the difference in their dress. Remy in his spotless, pressed uniform, the boy's filthy and torn. Remy freshly shaved with his thick, dark hair brushed back from his forehead, the young man's dirty locks poking from beneath an equally dirty hat, and if she wasn't mistaken, his eyes glistened. Tears had made tracks through the dirt on his face.

Remy folded a piece of paper and stuffed it in his pocket, his movements slow and stiff, as if every motion pained him. He nodded several times then patted the young man's shoulder and directed him toward the back of the house and the kitchen, where Brenna would give him a good hot meal. The young man nodded, swiped at his dirty face, and followed the path.

Her heart in her throat, Shaelyn couldn't take her eyes from the major. He just stood there, unmoving, until finally his head dipped slightly as if he studied the ground...or prayed. She had an insane urge to go to him, offer solace for what had obviously been bad news and yet, she remained rooted to the spot, her nose touching the window, fighting her own sense of dread.

As if suddenly aware she watched him, Remy turned and faced the house. Shaelyn sucked in her breath. She felt his barely controlled rage through the panes of the glass. Perhaps it was just her imagination, but the heat of his gaze scorched her very soul.

As he made his way up along the flagstone path toward the veranda steps, he appeared to lean heavier on his cane. He seemed to have aged a lifetime in just the few moments she'd been watching him. He disappeared from view, going around the corner of the house. She heard his footsteps then and the heavy thump of the cane hitting the floorboards of the veranda surrounding the first floor. He came closer, ignoring the front door in favor of the study's French doors. So he wouldn't be seen? So he could gather his thoughts together in private?

Should she remain in the study? She could escape into the hallway before he reached the door. Undecided, she remained rooted to the spot, unable to move.

Too late.

Shaelyn stepped away from the window as he let himself into the study. "Major? Is everything all right?"

She must have startled him as well, for he jumped and barked, "Not now!"

His voice sounded hoarse and almost tormented as he closed the French doors behind him, limped across the room, and pulled the pocket doors open, but his tone gentled as he stood beside the open door and looked at her. "Please, leave me."

Shaelyn dipped her head, gathered her cleaning supplies, and made a hasty retreat, but not before she caught the glimmer of tears in his eyes. Her heart thumped painfully in her chest. Whatever the young boy had imparted to him must have been devastating. She took one last glance at him then hurried to the kitchen.

• • •

"How could this have happened?" Remy asked as he paced the study a short time later, his cane thumping on the thick carpet covering the floor. He'd had opportunity to share the news with his officers, each of whom had taken the information in the typical stoic manner he expected from West Point-trained leaders. It was he himself who struggled to bring his emotions under control. The only thing he felt as he turned to Vincent, who had remained behind after the other officers departed, was anger.

"How could they have known, Vince? How could we lose the *Brenna Rose* before she reached the rendezvous point? No one knew she was sailing for New Orleans except those of us around the table."

Anguish colored his voice. Stress made his shoulders stiff and the loss of innocent men made his heart hurt.

Captain Davenport sat up straighter in his chair and reached for the bottle of whiskey on the desk. "You're forgetting one thing, my friend."

Remy turned and faced the man. Frustrated, he ran his fingers through his hair. "What? What have I forgotten?"

Vince's brows rose in surprise. "You're so besotted with her, you can't see the obvious." He poured them both a healthy portion of liquor.

"Besotted? What the hell are you talking about?" He stepped closer and reached for the cut crystal glass Vince held out.

"Do you not know the meaning of the word?" Vince asked, his tone heavy with sarcasm.

"Of course I do," Remy snapped, and tried hard to ignore the cynicism and disdain he heard. Under normal circumstances, he would not tolerate Vincent's tone of voice, but these were hardly normal circumstances.

"Well then, you know what I'm talking about. You, my friend, have fallen under whatever spell Shaelyn Cavanaugh has cast over you," he scoffed. "Whether the *Brenna Rose* was ambushed, as Major Johnson suspects, or exploded and sunk, there is only one person who could accomplish that. And you know who it is." He drew in his breath, his eyes flickering away from Remy to stare at the amber brew in his glass. "I've seen the way you watch her. You're so blinded by your—shall we call it weakness?—you don't seem to recall Miss Cavanaugh being present while we discussed plans." He paused, looked up from his drink, and pinned Remy with a relentless glare. "She heard everything. She could have told anyone. She could have tampered with the engines, too."

The words Davenport uttered shocked him, rocked him to his soul, almost as much as what the captain didn't say, the label left hanging in the air between them without being spoken. Remy said nothing, despite the tone in which those sentiments were delivered and the feeling he'd just been kicked in the teeth.

He drew in his breath, his gut clenching. Could it be? Was Shaelyn a spy?

He took a deep swallow of the whiskey and replayed everything in his mind.

Yes, she had heard everything, but only the night before. She wouldn't have had time to tell another person what she knew. Unless she snuck out under cover of darkness. Between the time she'd learned of their plans and the moment he kissed her in the moonlight, she could have stolen away and met someone. Even after their kiss, she could have slipped away.

No. He would have heard her. He'd always been a light sleeper and that night, he hadn't slept at all, desire for her keeping him awake long after he should have surrendered to slumber.

The thoughts running through his mind made his head ache, made his heart ache as well, and yet he said nothing to Vincent. Didn't deny what the man said. It wouldn't have mattered anyway. Davenport had made up his mind, already thought he and Shaelyn were lovers. He'd stated as much before the *Brenna Rose* set sail.

Remy limped toward the desk and pulled out the chair, the sharp ache in his leg seeming to build with each passing moment. His gaze never left the captain's face. Something flickered in

Davenport's eyes. Was it disgust? Triumph? Something else? It didn't matter. "I would like to be alone now. There is much I need to do."

Pain burst in his heart as he took his seat behind the desk and pulled stationery and Captain Ames's file from the drawer. Though he knew the words on paper would never make up for the loss of Captains Ames and Falstaff, he'd write condolence letters anyway. He'd done it before, too many times since the fighting broke out in '61, and would most likely do it again.

And regardless of what Davenport thought, he'd have to tell Shaelyn the *Brenna Rose* was lost. He did not relish the task, but better to get it done now, as quickly as possible, though that wouldn't make the telling easier.

Vincent remained seated, swirling the remains of his drink in the bottom of his glass.

Can the man not take a hint?

Remy let out a long sigh. Davenport still hadn't moved from his seat, although he did reach for the bottle on the desk.

Apparently not.

He cleared his throat, drawing the other man's attention. Davenport caressed the bottle, but didn't pick it up and refresh his drink. His eyes slid over Remy and his lips pressed together. Was that annoyance? Irritation? Remy cleared his throat again. "If you should see Miss Cavanaugh, would you let her know I'd like to see her?"

Davenport finally took the hint, although not without protest. "But, Remy, she—"

"Dismissed, Captain."

"As you wish, sir." Davenport slid his glass onto the desktop, his movements slow, and rose from his seat. There could be no denying the man was unhappy—the sharpness of his tone could have drawn blood. Watching him, Remy couldn't be certain what irked the man more—that he'd been dismissed or that he hadn't agreed with Davenport's unspoken accusation.

The pocket doors slid closed silently as Davenport left the room. Remy shook his head to clear his mind, perused Cory's file, then dipped the pen in ink and began the letter to Cory's wife. The words were hard to find, even harder to write. He'd been fond of Cory Ames, regretted the fact he hadn't allowed himself to know him better. The words on the page blurred. Sympathy flared in his heart for the daughter Captain Ames had never seen and the wife he'd left behind.

Suddenly weary and overwhelmed, not only by the sheer loss of human life, but by the insinuation Shaelyn Cavanaugh could be a spy, Remy sat back in his chair and stared at the intricate design on the ceiling.

How had it come to this?

The answers he sought were not in the plaster hearts and flowers forming a border where the walls met the ceiling.

With a sigh, he took another swallow of whiskey and forced himself to continue writing the letter.

"You wished to see me, Major?"

Remy looked up to see Shaelyn standing in the doorway, frozen to the spot, as if afraid to come any farther into the room, her expression wary. She worried her bottom lip between her teeth and clasped her hands in front of her.

"Please. Come in."

She entered the room, but not full steam ahead like she normally did. She walked slowly, as if she already knew he had bad news to impart.

He gestured to the chair in front of the desk. She sank into it and adjusted her dove gray skirt, hiding a recently mended tear. Her eyes flitted toward the letter in front of him and widened, but she said nothing. Remy continued watching her, waiting for her to speak, but for once, she demanded nothing of him, remaining silent though her direct gaze seemed to settle on his heart and stay there. The thought of causing her pain hurt him all the way to his soul.

Remy cleared his throat and opened his mouth, but words would not come. He tried again and had the same result. He just didn't know how to tell this woman her beautiful steamboat was gone, perhaps sunk into the mud at the bottom of the Mississippi, after she'd been assured her riverboats would be safe, after she'd been asked to trust him. Remy tried one more time. "Shae—"

"Whatever it is, Major, just say it. I already know it isn't good news. I saw you talking to that boy. I saw your face." She held herself rigid, her hands gripping the arms of the chair, her knuckles white. Her voice lowered. "Just tell me."

Remy gave a slight nod then poured her a small draught of whiskey. He pushed the glass across the desk and waited until she picked it up and took a sip. "The *Brenna Rose* is lost. She never made it to the rendezvous point. There are reports she was ambushed and sank." He said it bluntly, as if saying the words that way could ease some of the pain.

Color drained from her face, leaving her cheeks pale. Sudden tears made her glorious eyes shine. Shock and sadness changed their color to a deep indigo, not the violet of anger he saw more often.

"I am sorry about your steamboat."

She gasped and every muscle in her body tensed. "Do you think me so callous and mercenary, Major, that I have only a care for my steamer?" Her eyes narrowed. "You are wrong."

He could see her struggle for composure.

"I was thinking of the mothers and fathers who have lost their sons." She took a deep breath and continued, "Of the wives and loved ones they're leaving behind. It doesn't matter what color uniforms they wore—they were just boys. Most of them weren't old enough to shave."

Her voice cracked with emotion, and though her eyes glowed with tears, she did not cry as one would expect. Or perhaps she just would not cry in front of him. "Captain Ames's daughter will never know what a wonderful, brave man her father was." She rose from her seat as stiff as an old woman and stumbled before she grasped the back of the chair as if it were an anchor, the only thing keeping her from collapsing to the floor.

"I won't deny I am devastated by the loss of the *Brenna Rose*, but…" She stopped speaking, as if unable to continue. The muscles of her throat moved as she swallowed—hard—several times and swiped at her eyes, which remained on him.

No, Captain Davenport couldn't have been more wrong. Despite his intimations, Shaelyn hadn't done this. Seeing the pain on her face, hearing it in her voice, Remy knew, without a doubt, she wasn't responsible.

She'd always been honest. Despite her pranks, which, he realized, were only aimed at him, she'd never done anything harmful. It simply wasn't in her to spy. Or to tamper with her steamboats.

He didn't know what to do. She needed solace, as did he, but would she swallow her pride and allow that from him? At this moment, would she allow that from anyone? Stubbornness alone, it seemed, kept her standing upright, although her hands still gripped the back of the chair for support.

"If that is all, Major?"

Whether she accepted his comfort and concern or not, he would offer it just the same. He needed to—not only to ease her sadness, but to ease some of his own. He rose from his seat and limped around the desk, for once forgetting the cane that was so much a part of him. "No, that is not all," he said as he swept her into his arms and wrapped them tight around her. There was nothing sexual in either his embrace or his intention. He simply needed to hold her.

Shaelyn didn't fight him, didn't struggle to escape his embrace. She sank against him, her arms snaking around his waist, head resting against his chest, accepting what he offered without so much as a whimper. She did not cry, not even then, but he could feel how stiffly she held herself, willing herself not to give into the tears she needed to shed.

How long they stood there in each other's arms, he didn't know, nor did he care. Whatever comfort he offered her, she returned.

"I am sorry about the *Brenna Rose.*"

She nodded against his uniform and sniffed. "She was just a steamer, Major, made of wood and paint, not flesh and blood like all those boys. I may have lost her, but I have not lost my memories." Her voice cracked with the emotion she couldn't quite hide as she pulled away from him. "I need to tell Mama."

Knowing how difficult the task had been for him, he sympathized with the anguish reflected on her face. Remy pulled a handkerchief from his pocket and gently blotted the wetness from the corners of her eyes, then handed her the square of pressed cotton. "Would you like me—"

"Thank you for the offer, Major, but no, I will tell her. It's not the first time I've had to share bad news with her, nor is it the first steamer I've lost." She let out a long sigh. "I am grateful the news wasn't about Ian. I don't think I could have borne that."

She left the room as silently as she had entered, walking slowly as if headed toward the gallows. She did not turn and look back at him, or change her mind and ask for his help in explaining to Brenna what had happened.

Shaelyn Cavanaugh was a remarkable woman. She truly was.

Chapter 11

Flour. Sugar. Molasses. Coffee. Stubborn. Strong. Spirited. Beautiful.

Remy blinked and tried to focus. He looked at the words he had written and grimaced, embarrassed by the turn his thoughts had taken. What had started as a list of needed provisions had turned into an accounting of Shaelyn's attributes. Actually, the list could pertain to Brenna as well. The good lady had taken the loss of the *Brenna Rose* as well as her daughter had. No hysterics, no accusations, no tears—just a calm acceptance and a prayer for the men and their families.

He shook his head, scratched out the words with a quick flourish of his pen, then thought better of it and scrunched the paper into a ball. He tossed the wad into the fireplace, where it quickly disappeared in a flash of flames, and started the list again. This time, with concentration and a dogged determination, he was able to complete it without writing down another one of Shaelyn's charms. With one task complete, he started on another that was much more pleasant…his weekly letter to his parents.

"Good morning, Major."

He looked up from the correspondence on the desk and smiled. General Ewell Sumner stood in the study's doorway, the medals on his uniform gleaming in the sunlight streaming through the window. Remy rose quickly to his feet and saluted, though the stiffness and throbbing pain in his leg reminded him he'd sat too long once again.

"I was at Rosalie and couldn't resist the opportunity to drop in on you as well, my boy." He returned the salute with a grin. A big man, not only in height but in breadth as well, General Sumner lumbered into the room as if he owned it and tossed his coat over a chair. He glanced around at the fine furnishings as he approached the desk and nodded with appreciation. He gestured for Remy to sit. "Nice home. How are you faring? How is your leg?"

"Fine, sir. Thank you for asking."

"I have a vested interest in that leg." The general took a seat in a comfortable leather chair pulled close to the desk, crossed his legs, and adjusted the sharp crease in his trousers. "You almost lost it on my account. Have I told you how grateful I am? I'd be standing before St. Peter's Pearly Gates, begging to be let in, if you hadn't thrown yourself in front of that bullet."

A blush spread over Remy's face. "It was my pleasure to serve you, sir."

He meant every word. General Sumner had been his instructor at West Point. Over the years, they had grown very fond of each other. When the opportunity arose for Remy to join the general's regiment, Remy considered the appointment an honor.

The general snorted. "Like hell, Remy. You could have lost your life with your actions. I'm just an old warhorse. My life isn't worth that much."

"I disagree with you, sir. And what's more, I would do it again. Without question." He grinned, catching the warm glow of pleasure in the older gentleman's light brown eyes. "And I'm certain your lovely wife would disagree with you as well."

"She misses me. I don't know why, but she does."

"She's a good woman, sir." And indeed, she was. Honor Sumner personified everything genteel and soft and sweet of her gender, but beneath all that, she had a backbone of steel. Ewell may have been a general and led men into battle, but it was Honor who led him. Remy remembered many an evening he'd spent with the general and his wife, lingering over coffee after dinner, discussing the politics of the day. Honor had her opinions and wasn't afraid to share them. Much like Shaelyn, although he rather doubted Honor would pour molasses in anyone's boots.

"That she is," General Sumner said as he rose from his seat, grabbed his coat from the back of the chair and patted the pockets. Remy thought he looked for his ever-present cigars, but something within the fabric thumped instead. A wide grin crossed the general's face as he pulled out a leather case and flipped it open. Within the box, on a bed of velvet, lay a Congressional Medal of Honor.

"She so wanted to be here when I gave you this, but wasn't able to join us." He blushed beneath the hair on his face. "Normally, this would have been presented to you in front of your men, with all the glorious ceremony receiving this entails, but knowing how much you hate a public display, I asked for the honor." Gratitude gleamed in the older man's eyes as his chest puffed out. He stood taller, back ramrod straight. "This gives me great pride, Remy, and I can think of no one who deserves it more. Congratulations, son." He extended the case with one hand and offered to shake with the other.

Shocked, his heart pounding a little too fast, Remy stood, grabbed the older man's hand, and shook. He looked at the medal in its bed of velvet. Though proud to receive it, he didn't think he deserved it. The general, apparently, thought he did. He took a breath. "Thank you, sir. I know this was all your doing."

The general shrugged and cleared his throat. "It was the least I could do. You did save my life." He took his seat once more, crossed his long legs, and let out a long sigh. "From horses to steamers." He laughed. "Do you miss being in the front lines, scouting ahead on Soldier Boy? Do you miss the bullets shrieking past your head? The thunder of the cannons?"

"Honestly, sir? No, I don't miss it. I do, however, miss being under your leadership. You are an excellent commander but you've taught me well, and I thank you for that." He slipped the leather case into a drawer then folded his hands atop the desk.

"I never would have helped you get this assignment if I didn't have complete faith in you."

High praise coming from General Sumner; however, after losing the *Brenna Rose*, Remy didn't think he deserved the general's praise, nor the medal in the drawer. "I suppose you've heard."

Sumner inclined his head. "About the *Brenna Rose*? Yes, I've heard. Damn shame losing all those men." He studied Remy, his eyes narrowing as he tilted his head to the side. "I hope you're not blaming yourself. I don't think it could have been prevented."

Remy said nothing. He could have argued the point. If he had been better prepared, perhaps those men could have been saved. If he had sent scouts ahead, the *Brenna Rose* might not be sitting at the bottom of the Mississippi, a watery coffin for her passengers.

"Do you know who is responsible?"

"I have my suspicions, General, but those suspicions won't help the men who lost their lives needlessly. Most of them were so young, they'd just begun to live." He ran his fingers through his hair in frustration. "In answer to your question, though—I believe it was the Gray Ghost and his band of rebels."

"Bastard," Sumner exclaimed as he smoothed his fingers along his mustache, an action Remy had seen many times before and one that signaled the general's concern. "I wish to hell I knew who he was. Where he came from. Where he hides when he's not sinking our boats, destroying our rails, or stealing our supplies."

"As do I, General." Remy sighed, forcing his own frustration with this unseen enemy to dissipate with his breath. "Perhaps he will make a mistake and show himself—" He didn't finish the thought, asking instead, "Would you like some coffee?"

The general shook his head. "You know my tastes run a little stronger than coffee."

"Ah, I have just the thing for you, sir." He turned in his seat, pulled open the door of the cabinet behind him, and withdrew a half-full bottle. The general's eyes lit up when he saw the silver and black label.

"Harte's Private Reserve Whiskey," he said, his voice filled with surprised pleasure. "I didn't know the admiral was still in business."

"Of course. It would take more than a war for my father to close down the distillery. The admiral," he said, referring to the man General Sumner knew well, "is already thinking about expanding when the war ends."

He poured the amber liquid into glasses and handed it to the general. "See if that won't soothe your parched throat." He put the bottle on the desk, within the general's reach. "I found four cases in the cellar. Apparently, the owner of this home enjoyed Harte's Private Reserve and kept plenty on hand."

"Oh, that's smooth," Sumner said after he took a sip and lingered over the taste in his mouth. After a moment, he cleared his throat. Uncrossing his legs, he leaned closer to the desk, his hand still clutching the cut crystal glass. "I had several reasons for seeing you, Remy, most importantly, I wanted to know how you were faring and personally give you your medal, but I also have an assignment for you, other than what you're already doing."

"Of course, sir. I am more than happy to do as you ask."

"I'm sure you've heard I've given up my command."

Remy nodded. The news had saddened him, but he understood the reasons. After the ambush and coming so close to losing his life, Sumner wanted nothing more to do with battlefields or bloodshed.

"I'm trying to work on an exchange of prisoners. Theirs for ours." He took a long drink of the whiskey and sighed. "You're aware of the deplorable conditions men are suffering in our prison camps. On both sides." Sadness tinged his voice. "I'd like to, if nothing else, ease a bit of that, perhaps enable these men to go home, especially those who are ill. I'd like your advice, Remy. And your help."

Remy said nothing, for he understood both the situation and the kind of man General Sumner was. He'd never been battle hungry. Instead, he promoted peace and understanding, even when it seemed impossible, and he remained, as always, humane. Remy often wondered why this compassionate and gentle man joined the military and how he became a widely respected, brilliant officer.

They spent the next hour going over details and how best to utilize the Cavanaugh steamboats to accomplish more than one goal. By the time the bottle of whiskey was gone, several plans were put in place and the general stood and stretched.

Remy stood as well, limped around the desk, and grabbed the general's coat from the back of the chair. He held it up, allowing Sumner to slip his arms into the sleeves.

"Major, it's been a pleasure, as always."

"Thank you, General, for everything. It's been wonderful to see you." He could have said more, but Ewell Sumner, as compassionate as he was, grew uncomfortable with shows of appreciation and sentiment.

The general pulled on his gloves as Remy ushered him into the hallway then he turned and whispered in a conspiratorial manner, "So tell me about this Shae Cavanaugh."

"Would you like to meet her? I'm sure she's around here somewhere. Or perhaps she's down on one of her steamers. Believe it or not, she has consented to maintain her boats for us, despite who we are."

"Is that wise, Remy?"

"Truthfully, sir, it was the wisest thing I could have done. Miss Cavanaugh—Shae—loves her boats. Of that, I have no doubt. She'd never do anything to hurt them in any way." Sunlight streamed in through the long, rectangular windows on either side of the front door, the glass sparkling, and if he wasn't mistaken, he could smell the distinct tang of vinegar in the air, which made him believe Shaelyn had just cleaned these windows. "I could find her if you'll give me a moment."

"Perhaps another time." The general waved away the offer. "I was just curious about her, that's all. The officers at Rosalie regaled me with some funny stories, but I must admit, I'm not sure if I believe them. It seems Miss Cavanaugh is quite the spirited lass. A handful, as it were."

"That she is, sir." Remy opened the front door and accompanied Sumner down the stairs, his cane tapping on the stone steps. The general's horse waited at the bottom of the staircase, reins tied to a post.

"Hmm, reminds me a bit of my Honor, being a handful and all." He chuckled, and for a moment his face took on a pinkish hue beneath the whiskers. "Did she really pour molasses in your boots?"

"Yes, sir, she did," Remy replied with a grin.

Sumner burst out in laughter. "Personally, I'd rather fight the enemy I know." He climbed into the saddle with the ease of many years practice. "Good luck to you, son."

"Thank you, General." Remy handed him the reins. "I think I need all the luck I can get." He grinned as he saluted.

"I'll be in touch." The general returned the salute then kneed his mount's sides.

Remy stood in the driveway and waited until the general disappeared from view before he went into the house, his mind not only on the exchange of prisoners they had discussed, but also on the loss of the *Brenna Rose*…and Shaelyn Cavanaugh. In truth, she was never far from his thoughts.

• • •

Shaelyn finished packing Captain Ames's belongings in the trunk she remembered him pushing across the marble tiles of her hallway. How long ago it all seemed. How quickly she'd become fond of the officers living in her home. She bit her lip in order to keep her emotions at bay and closed the lid. In tribute to the gentle man who was no longer with them, she said a silent prayer as she tugged his trunk into the hallway.

She'd already done the same for Captain Falstead's possessions.

She hadn't been asked to perform this particular task. She'd taken it on herself as a kindness, and though the chore was painful for her, she could only imagine how much worse it would have been for Remy. After he had held her and offered comfort when the *Brenna Rose* was lost, it was the least she could do for him.

Piano music floated up the stairway and a smile spread her lips. She recognized the tune echoing through the house. Beethoven's "Moonlight Sonata." Her mother's favorite piece.

Her heart lifted with joy. She hadn't heard her mother play in a very long time, the love of music almost dying within her when the man she loved passed away. How many evenings had they sat in the music room and listened to Brenna play? How many rousing reels had they danced?

Shaelyn wiped her hands on her apron and slowly made her way downstairs, the music becoming stronger and lovelier than she remembered…and somehow, subtly different.

"Mama! It's so good—" The words died on her lips and her heart slammed against her ribcage. Her mother did not sit at the piano. *Her* fingers did not splay over the keys and produce such beautiful notes.

Instead, Remy sat on the bench, dressed not in his uniform but in a white shirt, open at the collar to expose his strong neck. The cuffs of his sleeves were rolled to his elbows. She'd never seen him like this. Out of uniform. Relaxed. He'd given the officers a day to themselves to do as they chose and they'd taken advantage of the time. So, apparently, had he.

If she startled him, he gave no reaction, just kept playing without missing a note, though his gaze rose and rested on her. Goose bumps broke out on her flesh as his fingers gently caressed the keys, each touch vibrating through her body with exquisite sensation, even though he didn't touch her at all.

"I'm sorry," she whispered over the sudden dryness in her throat. "I didn't mean to interrupt."

"You're not interrupting. Please, come in." Remy smiled with his invitation, the little-boy grin melting her heart. "Join me."

"I really shouldn't." She hesitated in the doorway, torn between wanting to listen to him play and needing to stay away from him. He didn't help matters by looking so handsome, his smile so inviting. Nor did it help that she had dreamed of him again last night and had woken up with every nerve in her body feeling as if it had been stretched tight, like fabric pulled through an embroidery hoop. Why she dreamed of him kissing her, caressing her, she didn't know. She just wished it would stop. Longing filled her, a yearning for things she could not have, should not think about wanting, and yet, with each dream, the ache within her grew. The physical demands of her chores helped to take some of that away, but not all of it, and she struggled to maintain her composure. "I have chores to finish."

"Five minutes? Please?"

Against her better judgment, she gave in. "Five minutes."

Five minutes turned into fifteen as she sat beside him on the bench, shoulder to shoulder, while he finished playing the sonata and played another. And it was just a little bit of heaven. The scent of citrus and fresh air filled her, the warmth of his body next to hers making her so aware of him as a *man*—a virile, hard-muscled man. She glanced in his direction as his fingers splayed over the keys and caught the fine sprinkling of dark hair revealed by the open collar of his shirt. Oh, how she wanted to reach out and run her fingers through that silky hair, touch his strong, muscle-corded throat, kiss the spot where his neck met his ear.

"Where did you learn to play?" Shaelyn asked as she rose from the bench and put some distance between them…at least some physical distance. It didn't help. The impulse to touch him grew stronger.

"My mother taught me," he said, his deep rich voice as vibrant as the chords he played. "I know you play. Who taught you?"

His eyes twinkled, his crooked grin firmly in place, and it hit her suddenly. When had she grown to like this man, this intruder into her home? When had he stopped being the enemy and become… something more? Was it the afternoon they'd spent together? Was it when he told her about the *Brenna Rose* and she saw the pain and devastation on his face? When he offered—and she accepted—his comfort? Or when she read the letters he'd written to the families of Captains Ames and Falstead?

When?

Could she pinpoint the exact moment when she started to feel affection for him, affection that had nothing to do with the constant ache low in her belly?

"Mama. It was an enticement. Well, blackmail, really. If I wanted to be able to help Papa with the steamers, I had to practice piano for at least an hour. That was, of course, after I finished my chores and schoolwork. Mama placed high importance on education."

How could she keep a thought in her head and chatter about mundane things when all she wanted was to kiss him once more, follow through on the dreams that invaded her sleep night after night?

Did he feel it too? Did he want to hold her as much as she wanted to embrace him? Caress him? Kiss him?

The front door opened and closed and she heard the dulcet tones of her mother and the heavy Scottish brogue of Jock as they came home from their afternoon outing. Closer than ever, they didn't bother hiding their feelings for one another, and there was no need. Shaelyn heartily approved. Jock's footfalls as he strode down the hallway toward the kitchen covered her mother's lighter footsteps.

And still, she couldn't take her gaze from Remy, from the warmth showing on his face. Her eyes widened as he stopped playing, rose from the bench, and approached her, his expression somewhere between wonder and intention. For an insane moment, she thought he'd read her mind and would take her in his arms, but he simply took her hand, brought it to his lips, and kissed the slightly reddened skin of her knuckles. The soft glow of his eyes, however, told her he wanted to do more than just kiss her hand.

How easy would it be to fall into his arms and touch her lips to his?

"Oh, there you are," her mother's voice broke the spell.

Shaelyn jumped, startled, and snatched her hand away. She jammed both hands into her apron's pockets to hide their trembling; however, that did nothing to stop the blush from staining her face. She quickly took a step away from the major.

"I just bought the loveliest…" Brenna stopped speaking and looked at the both of them. Beneath the sharp perusal of crystal blue, Shaelyn felt as if her face were on fire. "What's going on in here?"

"Nothing, Mama. We were…that is, the major was… Nothing, Mama."

"I see." A perfectly formed brow rose over Brenna's eye and the hint of a smile played on her lips. "Well, come along." She motioned with one gloved hand. Shaelyn glanced at her feet then at Remy, and finally moved toward where her mother waited in the doorway. Brenna continued speaking as if she didn't notice

Shaelyn's hesitation. "I bought the nicest roast at Mr. Gaviland's. We'll have mashed potatoes and carrots and gravy. And of course, some of my biscuits and for dessert…" She held up a box tied with string. "Mrs. Blake's famous sweet potato pie."

• • •

Dinner seemed to go on and on, as did dessert. The men around the table, rejuvenated from an afternoon off, didn't run out of words as they told jokes and amusing anecdotes of what their lives were like before the war. At any other time, it would have been a lovely evening. But not tonight.

Shaelyn listened with half an ear as she pushed the remains of her pie around her plate. She sighed and tried, once more, to drag her gaze away from Remy's hands. They were all she could stare at, ever since she'd seen them splayed over the piano keys, making beautiful music. His long fingers ended in clean, short nails and all she could think about was those fingers pulling the pins from her hair, caressing the side of her face, or touching some other part of her that longed to be touched.

She glanced up from his hands and found his gaze riveted to her, his eyes warmly glowing, the crooked smile she adored lighting his face. Her breath froze in her lungs and a hot flush swept through her body, heating her from the inside out.

Abruptly, she rose from the table and started collecting the soiled dishes. Brenna laid her napkin beside her plate and began to rise, but Shaelyn stopped her. "I'll take care of it, Mama. You relax."

Brenna resumed her seat and poured a bit more coffee into her cup. "Thank you, dear."

Conversation around the table continued. Not one of them seemed to notice when Remy rose and grabbed his plate, but Shaelyn did. She sucked in her breath as her heart beat out a frantic tattoo. She had hoped to escape to the kitchen, where she didn't have to see Remy's smoldering eyes or charming smile, but her plan had just backfired…in the most alarming way. Instead of escaping him, she'd been thrown closer to him.

Just make the best of it. Don't look at him. Don't encourage him.

And yet, even as she reiterated the words in her head, on her last trip into the kitchen, she almost dropped the plates in her hand. The sight before her made her suck in her breath.

How could she ignore him?

Remy had removed his jacket and now stood at the sink, his broad back covered only in a pristine white shirt tucked neatly into his trousers, a shirt she had laundered many times. His muscles rippled as he rolled up his shirtsleeves then sunk his hands up to his elbows into the hot, soapy water filling the sink.

There was something to be said about a man who wasn't afraid to wash dishes.

Memories flooded her and for a moment, her vision blurred with tears. She could clearly see her mother and father, standing in front of the sink, side by side, talking quietly of the day's events as one washed and the other dried. Though there had been servants before war broke out, her parents had enjoyed doing this one task together. Her mother always said it reminded them of the days when they'd had nothing but each other, the *Brenna Rose,* and dreams.

"Are you all right?"

Startled, Shaelyn jumped. At what point had Remy turned from the sink and approached her? Her gaze rose to his face as he reached out and smoothed the wetness away from her cheek with his thumb. The breath she'd been holding released in a rush and her heartbeat—dear God!—her heart was going to pound right out of her chest. "Yes, of course," she managed over dry lips and even drier throat, then, in order to gain some semblance of control, she handed him the stack of dishes in her hands.

With a smirk, Remy took the soiled plates and laid them gently in the sink before he handed her a dishtowel then picked up a dishcloth and began to wash. They worked in companionable silence while Shaelyn listened to the conversation in the dining room. She grinned when she heard her mother's laughter, sweet and pure, as she took the clean plate Remy handed her, dried it, and put it away.

Her gaze drifted to him, and she almost smiled at the expression on his face, then forced herself to stop looking at him. She didn't want to be drawn to him and yet...she couldn't help herself. And this, standing side by side while his hands were in soapy water, just confused her more. What other officer, be he Union or Confederate, would wash dishes, especially in a home he'd overtaken?

In an effort to avoid looking at him, her eyes fell upon a ring on the counter. She'd seen it before, of course, on his finger, but never had the opportunity to inspect it. She did so now, under his watchful, curious eyes.

The stone was onyx, if she wasn't mistaken, with a small diamond chip in the middle. Around the stone were the words West Point. On one side, the initials USMA were engraved. Below the initials were two sabers crossed. On the other side, an eagle with an olive branch in its talons. Inside, almost faded, she read the inscription Honor Above All and his initials REH.

"That ring commemorates my graduation from West Point," he said as he leaned against the counter and watched her with that crooked grin plastered across his face.

"It's lovely."

"Thank you. I designed it myself. We all did. Cadets are given free rein to create our own rings, within reason, of course." He was too close and smelled too wonderful and the look in his eye conjured thoughts she shouldn't have...

Shaelyn put the ring back on the counter where she'd found it and concentrated on drying the plates that were stacking up. Eventually, Remy returned to washing, but the silence between them had grown uncomfortable.

"I thought your family distilled whiskey," she blurted out in the hopes of filling the disquieting silence.

Remy grinned as he looked at her. "We do."

"So how is it that you attended West Point? How is it that you don't work with your family in…"

"Kentucky," he supplied, then quirked an eyebrow and his grin widened. "I'm lucky my eyebrows grew back after than incident with the still." He wiggled his eyebrows for effect. Shaelyn couldn't help smiling at him, couldn't stop drowning in the pure pleasure of his voice.

"No, the whiskey business isn't for me. Never was."

"So why West Point?" she asked again. "Why the military?"

"I was twelve when I met Charles Foster, my mother's brother, but I'll never forget that day. It was the first time I'd ever seen a military man in full uniform. From the moment he stepped off the steamer onto our dock and I saw how his brass buttons and the stars on his collar shined in the sunlight, I was impressed. More than impressed. He regaled me—us really, but I thought he was talking just to me—with stories of West Point and his time there with the other cadets."

A sigh escaped him and his voice lowered, but he continued talking as he washed, handing her one plate at a time.

"From that moment on, I wanted to attend West Point, just like him. I wanted to be a general just like Uncle Charles. Father made me wait. He thought twelve was too young for life decisions, so I waited." He turned toward the table behind them, which now had all the dessert plates and coffee cups piled high on a tray atop it, and her eyes followed every move he made. She hadn't heard anyone come into the kitchen, hadn't heard anything except the sound of his voice and the beating of her own heart. Remy gently placed the dishes beneath the soapy water and continued washing. And talking.

"My mind was still made up when I turned sixteen, but to prove I was serious, I contacted a friend of my father's, a congressman, and had him nominate me. Between the congressman's recommendation and my uncle's influence, I was accepted at the Academy. I loved being there. Even though it was my first time away from home, I didn't become homesick. How could I? We were busy from sunup to sundown and I loved everything about it—the discipline, the camaraderie between the boys, the knowledge imparted by our instructors. I made some everlasting friendships during my time there, met some fascinating people. For me, it was the best decision I ever made."

His eyes glowed with warm memories. The smile on his face charmed her, crooked as it may have been. The tone of his voice seeped beneath her skin, settling in her bones and zinging straight to her heart. By the time the dishes were done, Shaelyn was a mass of bristling nerves.

It had nothing to do with their conversation and everything to do with his nearness and the smell of sunlight and citrus faintly clinging to him. Apparently, she couldn't be in the same room with him any longer without desire—yes, desire for him—coursing through her veins, heating her blood. Wanting him had become something she could no longer deny, no matter how hard she tried.

Once more, she wanted—no, needed—to wrap her arms around him, dishtowel and all, and draw him closer so she could taste his lips.

He leaned against the sink and studied her, those eyes of his staring deep into her soul...or so she thought. Was he thinking the same thing? Did he desire her as much as she desired him?

Coward. Just kiss him like you want to.

The voice in her head taunted her, daring her to do what she wanted…

Shaelyn swallowed hard. "I have some laundry still on the line." She ducked her head in an effort to tear her gaze away from him. "I should bring it in."

"Of course," he said, and tilted his head. "Good night, Shae."

She beat a hasty retreat outside, filling her lungs with crisp, cold air, hoping the shock of the chill beyond the warmth of the house would jolt her out of the heat simmering within her.

It didn't work. Her hands still trembled as she pulled the clean laundry off the line and folded each item before placing it in the wicker basket at her feet. At least the kitchen was empty when she came back into the house, set up the ironing board, and heated the irons.

Ironing done, clothes hung up in the mudroom until the morning, Shaelyn left a lamp in the middle of the kitchen table lit as she made her way to bed, too exhausted to think. Or so she thought. But as she changed out of her serviceable skirt and blouse, unhooked her corset, and shrugged out of her chemise and drawers, Remy filled her mind—his smile, his warmly glowing eyes, his hands…and everything else.

"Stop it!" she chided herself for the course her thoughts were taking. Exasperated, she tugged a thin nightgown over her head, slipped beneath the covers of her narrow bed, and closed her eyes.

And dreamed of him, touching her, caressing her, kissing her.

She awoke with a start, her heart thumping a wicked beat in her chest. She'd never be able to go back to sleep.

With a groan, she rose from her bed. The sound of the clock chiming midnight followed her down the hall to the study, where she hoped a boring book and perhaps a sip or two of whiskey would get her mind off the unreasonable yearning surging through her. But even that was a mistake. The study now smelled of citrus and sunlight, just like Remy.

She poured herself a small glass of whiskey then sank into the leather chair behind the desk, even more frustrated than before. She tucked her legs beneath her and inhaled. Couldn't she go anywhere in this house to escape the major from Kentucky?

Chapter 12

Remy couldn't concentrate. The smell of her perfume tickled his nose and conjured images in his head—as mundane as washing dishes together, or as erotic as seeing her head thrown back as he kissed her neck. Shaelyn dusted the books lining the shelves in the study and he watched her, becoming more and more enraptured with every passing moment.

He tried to focus on the correspondence on his desk, but every movement she made drew his attention. She hummed, too, while she worked, a little nonsense tune he didn't quite recognize. He glanced in her direction, intending to ask her to come back later… and wished he hadn't.

She climbed onto a stepstool, reaching into the highest corner of the room, where a cobweb fluttered in the breeze her feather duster made. Her trim ankles were displayed, as was the intricate embroidery on her stockings. The frothy lace edging her petticoats beckoned his perusal, and he caught a glimpse of her calf as she stretched even further toward the delicate cobweb. Her backside wiggled beneath the sensible gray bombazine skirt she wore.

It was too much for him, seeing her like this. He opened his mouth, intending to ask her to stop, but no words issued forth. Instead, Remy sucked in his breath. The way the sunlight hit her hair changed the color to molten fire, and as she reached toward the ceiling, her blouse pulled tighter against her body, emphasizing the lushness of her figure.

He was lost. Couldn't help staring. Or the unintended reaction of his body. He shook his head and tried once more to put her out of his mind, but the task remained impossible. How could he not be drawn to her?

She'd shown a kindness to him yesterday by packing up all the personal belongings of Captains Ames and Falstead, and he appreciated her efforts. Returning a soldier's possessions was not a common act, yet he tried. Every one of the men who'd died in the ambush that almost killed him had their things returned at his request, though not personally by him.

After the compassion and thoughtfulness she'd shown, she'd changed as soon as everyone else came home. Backed away from him. And blushed every time their eyes met, as if she'd done something she shouldn't have done.

He wanted to kiss her—then and now. He wanted to take her in his arms as he had done in the garden, feel her mouth beneath his, and experience once more her passionate response.

She teetered a bit, the step stool beneath her feet tottering on two legs for a moment as she reached toward the ceiling. Remy jumped from his seat and rushed to her. Shaelyn let out a stifled screech as he reached for her, placing his hands on her hips to steady her. "Good grief, woman, have you no common sense? Have Captain Beckett or Captain Williams help you."

He did not remove his hands from her person as he looked up at her. Shaelyn gasped at his touch, but didn't try to stop him as he let his hands slide down her skirt- and petticoat-covered thighs, feeling her muscles tense beneath his palms. He wanted her legs around him, squeezing him.

He should have let her go then. Instead, he took a step closer.

Her eyes widened, the irises turning the most luminous shade of dark amethyst as her pupils dilated. A vein throbbed along the column of her slim throat and he wanted to feel the rapid pulse beneath his lips and kiss that vein all the way down to where it disappeared beneath the collar of her blouse.

"Do you think this is the first time I've done this, Major?" she asked, a bit breathless, the words not at all in keeping with the low, sultry tone of her voice. "I've been helping to clean this house since I was old enough to hold a dust rag in my hand." She gestured to the wooden step stool beneath her feet. "And I have never, not once, fallen."

"Be that as it may, please come down from there. You're making me nervous." He reached up then, his hands spanning her slim waist, and pulled her from the top of the stool. She went into his arms quite willingly.

"Nervous, Major?"

He couldn't resist. What's more, he didn't want to. And why should he? He pulled her closer and once again, Shaelyn melted in his arms, molding her body to his. He felt her warmth seep through her clothing…and his. He dipped his head and captured her mouth with his, touching her lips tenderly, then with more hunger, like a parched man tasting water after a drought.

He pulled her closer still, wrapping his arms tighter around her as her hands smoothed along his back. A feather from the feather duster tickled his ear before it clattered to the floor.

"What is it you do to me?" he murmured as his lips found the smooth skin of her cheek, the soft flesh of her neck, the perfection of her ear. "Why is it I can think of nothing but you and the taste of your mouth? Are you a witch? Have you cast a spell on me?"

"No, I am no witch." Shaelyn sighed and tilted her head back, allowing him more access to her neck. She said not another word, but he felt her chest move as she drew in breath and the frantic beat of her heart as his fingers deftly unbuttoned the top button of her blouse, then the one below it and the one beneath that.

He moved with her, guiding her to the divan just a few steps away. Shaelyn followed his lead without hesitation, her mouth clinging to his, her fingers twisting into his hair. Remy would have gone further, would have laid her down on the divan and undressed her completely just so he could feel the softness of her skin beneath his fingertips, but the pocket door slid apart and a voice he didn't expect to hear, especially now, stopped everything. "Remy, I'd like…"

Remy stiffened as Shaelyn jumped and moved away from him, her face the picture of utter mortification. Color rose to stain her cheeks before she dropped her gaze and stared at the carpet beneath her feet.

"Oh, excuse me. I didn't know you were…ah…busy. Just wanted to let you know you're wanted at Rosalie." Amusement not only on his features, but in his words as well, Davenport bowed and beat a hasty exit, closing the same doors with a quiet snick.

Remy turned back to Shaelyn, but she was already buttoning up her blouse, her fingers shaking and clumsy. Her eyes seemed so much bigger in her still red face as she glanced at him, and her mouth opened several times, her lips swollen from his kisses, but no words came forth. She nodded once, her eyes shining with emotion he couldn't quite define, and left the study at a near run, leaving the feather duster on the floor and the step stool in place.

There was nothing he could do but watch her go.

"Damn."

• • •

Shaelyn dried the last dinner plate and put it away in the cabinet. She spread the towel on the counter to dry and sighed as she looked around.

Tonight, she had accomplished the chore by herself. Remy hadn't offered to help, which was a blessing because she didn't want—or need—a repeat of last night with him. Performing ordinary, mundane tasks, such as washing dishes, seemed so intimate when they worked side by side. Sitting across from him at dinner, knowing he watched her, his eyes smoldering with desire, had been difficult enough. She didn't need to tempt fate again…she'd already done so too many times, and if she admitted the truth, she didn't trust herself being alone with him at all. Their encounter this afternoon proved it.

Who knows how far she would have gone if they hadn't been interrupted? God knows, she hadn't tried to stop him. She'd been eager for his kisses, his touch. A small cry of frustration escaped her.

The house had grown silent. She was the only one awake as she made her way to her small room. She struck a match and lit the candle on the bedside table, changed into her flannel nightgown, and slipped beneath the thin blanket.

She lay there, eyes wide open and staring at the ceiling. Restless. Jittery. Every nerve in her body seemed to be pulled tight, like violin strings, and every time she thought of him, those delicate strings were stretched tighter. Exhaustion overwhelmed her, but she didn't want to sleep. If she closed her eyes, she might dream of him, as she'd done so many nights before, dream of them together, arms and legs tangled among the sheets. She'd feel what she'd felt with his lips on hers, his hands in her hair, caressing her.

What sensations he had awakened in her! Desire and longing didn't begin to define what she felt as she tossed and turned in the narrow bed, her body alive, her skin on fire. She *wanted* to be touched, to feel his fingertips caress her, his mouth on hers…

She gave up on the idea of sleeping. How could she with every nerve in her body taut?

With a sigh of resignation, she crawled out of bed and sat on the edge.

Perhaps a hot bath will take away this urgency.

The idea of dragging out the small hip bath and heating the water in the kitchen fireplace seemed like much too much work. Still, a bath might be just what she needed, and she knew exactly where she could go without too much bother.

Decision made, Shaelyn grabbed her robe, pushed her feet into slippers, picked up the candle, and left the room.

She wandered down the hall and into the study, where the scent of sunlight and citrus assailed her once more. She poured a large glass of her father's favorite whiskey; the healing powers of this particular drink had helped before—last night came to mind—and she took the glass upstairs with her.

A short time later, steam rose from the water filling the bathtub. She added a few precious drops of bath oil, letting the heat of the water release the provocative scent. She removed her clothing, leaving her robe and nightgown in a pile on the floor, and sank into the fragrant liquid with a sigh.

She took a big swallow of the whiskey then laid her head against the rim of the bathtub, using a folded washcloth as a pillow.

The hot water did, indeed, soothe the ache in her body, as did the warming powers of the whiskey. She closed her eyes, just for a moment, and let herself drift.

She awoke with a start and a splash, gooseflesh pebbling her skin. She stepped out of the bathtub, shivering, and wrapped herself in a towel. Groggy and disoriented, still half asleep, Shaelyn left the bathroom and, dropping the towel on the floor, crawled into her own bed. Warmth enveloped her immediately and the thick mattress cradled her as she settled back into the dream that invaded her sleep each night.

• • •

Fire and ice. Hot hands. Hotter lips.

Fire where a pair of lips touched her; ice when those lips left to ignite another flame somewhere on her body. All along the back of her neck, the incredibly sensitive spot just beneath her ear, her throat, she felt the heat of moist lips pressing against her skin. Her limbs grew languid beneath the onslaught of a hand caressing her flesh even as urgency and need filled her. She needed *him* where her desire burned at the juncture of her thighs. She squeezed her legs together and felt the swelling folds of her sex; dewy moisture scented the air.

Am I dreaming?

Flames consumed her. She wanted *him. Remy.* In her dreams, she could have him. Heat grew with every passing moment, building, burning. She moved restlessly as a hot hand gently cupped her breast. The nipple tightened into a hard bud when a thumb flicked the peak, sending another rush of anticipation through her.

Shaelyn drew her breath in sharply and held it. She had awoken from this particular dream many times, always with her body on fire, the center of the flame buried deep within, but the dream had never been this vivid, this real. Truthfully, she didn't want to wake, to end this sweet torment. She stilled, unwilling to move, waiting for the feelings to stop and her traitorous body to cease its unreasonable longing to leave her disappointed.

The fire raging through her didn't stop. The yearning grew as the warmth of a tongue laved the nape of her neck and the thumb flicking against her nipple quickened.

"Sweet Sassy," a voice whispered in her ear, sending chills down her spine, as his hand left her breast to caress her hip. *His* voice, as she knew it would be. *His* hand, as she had dreamed so many times. *His* lips pressing against the damp skin at the back of her neck.

Realization snuck into her dream with startling clarity. Her heart raced. Her eyes flew open only to close just as quickly. Fully awake and aware, but too far gone to stop, she pressed her back against his solid chest and stomach, her backside nestling against the hard muscles of his thighs. She felt something hot and rigid pressing against her soft flesh and moved closer. The reality was far better than her dreams.

His fingers grazed her hip, leaving a trail of fire along her skin, and her legs opened of their own volition. She grabbed his hand and pressed the open palm against the burning softness of her sex.

A groan sounded in her ear. "Do you want this?"

"Yes," she whimpered, her body drugged with need. She had wanted this for so long, from the moment she'd rushed into his arms.

"Tell me you need me," he murmured against her throat.

Under normal circumstances, never would she admit such a thing, but now, anticipation coursed through her, the heat of his body warmed her. Resistance to him and his charms seemed useless. And unnecessary. Caught in the power of her own need, Shaelyn whispered, "I need you." She felt the pressure of his hand as he began a slow, circular rhythm between her thighs. Her breath quickened as she rocked against his hand. Her instinct said this man would fulfill her, though her mind told her she shouldn't do this. She didn't care. She strained against his hand, losing herself and coherent thought in the tightening coil of desire.

He slipped a finger into her moist heat, then another, while he continued the rhythm, swirling, stroking, pressing down on the tiny bud that was the key to her release. Shaelyn gasped, not only from the intrusion into her innermost secret place, but by the way her body seemed to explode from the inside out.

Moonlight filled her room as Shaelyn's eyes flew open. The force of her response surprised her. She pulsed around the fingers he had slipped inside her, the liquid warmth of her release dripping from her body. Never before had she felt anything quite so exhilarating…and just a touch frightening. And yet, she wasn't afraid. Not of Remy. Indeed, she wanted more…of him and what he'd done to her. Wanted more of that feeling of floating to heaven and touching the stars.

Fully awake, no longer captured by the dream that had so enthralled her, she turned in his arms, offering herself fully.

"Finish what you started," she demanded as she wrapped her arms around his neck and pulled his mouth toward hers. "Take me."

"Are you sure?"

"Yes."

"With pleasure," he whispered as he gazed at her. Passion glazed his eyes. She knew he would have stopped, would have done the honorable thing, as he was an honorable man, if she had requested such. That thought was the last thing on her mind as his head lowered, his mouth slid over hers to take possession, and she responded, parting her lips. His tongue slipped inside, caressing the hot cavern of her mouth.

Her body felt weightless, her mind a dark void except for the sensations his hands and mouth and lips evoked. He caressed her, his hand smoothing over her skin as he explored every inch of her, his mouth taking hers then moving away to taste another part of her body, leaving nothing undiscovered.

She caressed him as he touched her, sliding her hands over his shoulders and back and lower. Beneath his skin, the muscles in his arms and back were taut, like steel bands that rippled and moved under her fingers.

When his mouth closed over her hard nipple and his tongue swirled around the crest, she gasped, the thrill intense. Her thighs pressed together as the exquisite sensation centered between them, once again building, like a spring coiled too tight, demanding to be sprung.

A soft chuckle met her ears. "Do you want me?"

"Yes. Now."

He rose above her, his thighs parting hers and eased into her slowly, so slowly she thought she would die from frustration. She caressed his firm, round buttocks then dug her nails into his skin, pulling him closer, deeper.

The sharp pinch of pain receded as quickly as it came when he seated himself completely within her, stretching her, filling her with such sweet sensations.

This is so right.

And then he began to move, again slowly, taking his time, sliding into her over and over.

Sweet torture! Sweet bliss! She caught his rhythm and met him thrust for thrust, her legs wrapping around his thighs. His pace quickened, as did hers, the sensations gripping her, growing stronger. She knew what she wanted now, knew what he could do to her. She rocked against him, straining for that sweet explosion. Blood rushed through her veins, her belly tightened…

"Oh, yes!" Her voice was a hoarse moan as she rode the peak of bliss and touched heaven once more.

He must have reached that little piece of paradise too, for the muscles in his arms became iron bands around her until he groaned, his entire body stiffening with his own climax.

"My sweet Sassy," he murmured as he peppered her face with light kisses then took possession of her mouth once more.

He rolled to the side and gathered her close in his arms, pulling the thin blanket over both of them, though with the liquid warmth rushing through her veins, she had no need of the coverlet. All she needed was *him*.

Not a word was spoken as she rested her head on his shoulder and smoothed her fingers through the soft hair on his chest. What could she say to describe the incredible feelings cascading through her? Her heart thundered in her chest. Her body felt sore, yet alive in a way she'd never known before. A smile curved her lips. Her dreams were nothing compared to the reality.

She stretched against Remy. The springy hair on his chest tickled her cheek as his arms tightened around her. "Don't go," he whispered, his voice heavy with sleep. "Stay. Please."

Shaelyn relaxed within his embrace, the warmth of his body lulling her, and closed her eyes once more. Only for a moment.

. . .

"Major Harte! Shaelyn!" Brenna exclaimed as the coffee cup and tray crashed to the bedroom floor.

Startled, Shaelyn jerked upright in the bed and clutched the blanket to her chest. She blinked to clear away the last remnants of sleep, the lingering languor of making love and experiencing the heights of passion. "Mama!"

Remy opened his eyes and groaned. He too sat upright in the bed, the blanket falling to his waist, exposing his hard, muscled chest and broad shoulders.

"Here." Brenna thrust Remy's robe at her. "Cover yourself! You too!"

Remy pulled the blanket higher to hide his nudity while Shaelyn slipped her arms into the too-big sleeves and tried to cover herself. Her face flamed with embarrassment, the heat rising up from her neck to stain her face. "Mama, I...I..."

"I thought you were down by the boats," Brenna said as she picked up the dropped tray and now empty coffee cup. "I didn't expect..." She gestured toward the bed, her eyes wide, her voice sharp and heavy with disappointment. "To find you here. Like this."

Jock ran into the room, his own robe wrapped tightly around his body. He stopped short in the doorway.

Captain Williams, the cowlick he usually persuaded to lay down standing straight up, nearly collided with the Scotsman. "I heard—oh, excuse me," he said as he took in the tableau before him. Face instantly red, perspiration popping out on his high forehead, he exclaimed, "Oh!" once more then took off down the hallway, his apologies trailing behind him.

"Would ye mind explainin' this, laddie?" Jock's heavy brogue seemed heavier and more pronounced. The redness in his face contrasted sharply with his ginger hair and mustache as he tied the sash to his robe with angry jerks. "Ye'll do right by her, Remy, by God, or ye'll be answering to me. Ye'll marry before the day is out."

"Oh, Shae, what—" Brenna never finished her question. She opened and closed her mouth several times, but no other words issued forth, as if everything she wanted to say was stuck in her throat. Tears shimmered in her eyes as she turned away.

Shaelyn's entire body flamed with embarrassment as everything became clear in an instant, despite the voices raised in anger and confusion. She knew how she ended up in Remy's bed. Or thought she did. She'd fallen asleep in the bathtub and dreamed of him, as she always did, her hands between her tightly clasped thighs. Caught in that dream, she had risen from the tub, simply walked into her room—his room—and crawled into bed, the wet towel she had used to wrap around herself crumpled on the floor. Had she done it on purpose?

Remy rustled the blankets beside her, but had yet to say a word. She couldn't look at him, wouldn't look at him, afraid of what she'd see in his eyes. Finally, after what seemed an eternity, he cleared his throat. "Of course I'll do the right thing. Miss Cavanaugh—"

Oh, the way he said *Miss Cavanaugh* made her shiver…with fear and dread and something else she didn't want to name.

"—and I will be man and wife as soon as the preacher can get here."

"No need for a preacher," Jock said as a huge grin stretched the ginger mustache on his upper lip. "I'm still an ordained minister. I'll perform the deed myself. Is twelve o'clock all right with everyone? In the study?"

The decision had been made though not one of them asked her if she wanted to marry *him*. Not one of them considered her feelings.

"But...but..." The words died in her throat as Shaelyn turned to face Remy. It was a mistake and she instantly averted her gaze. Suppressed anger showed in the firm set of his lips. And his eyes! Glowing like polished pewter, they seemed to see right through her, as if she wasn't there. He cleared his throat again and began moving the blankets away from him.

"Now, if you'll all excuse me. It seems I have a busy day ahead of me."

Chapter 13

Tears blurred her vision as Shaelyn stood before her mother and Jock. Remy's robe, still wrapped tightly around her body, smelled of him.

What have I done?

The servants' room that had become hers seemed crowded, not only because there were too many people inside, but because disappointment was a tangible thing, a fourth entity that grew bigger, stealing the air...and her pride.

Both Brenna and Jock glared at her. The displeasure on her mother's face sunk into Shaelyn's bones. The last thing in the world she wanted to do was hurt and disappoint her mother. The other last thing she wanted to do was marry Remington Harte.

"He'll do the right thing fer ye, lassie. He's a good man," Jock said as he rocked back and forth on his heels. "Ye'll be married. And we can all put this unfortunate incident behind us."

He patted the pocket of his robe, looking for his ever-present pipe. "After breakfast, I'll go down to the courthouse and get a marriage license. Bertram Tealing down there owes me a favor," he said, and with a nod to Brenna, left the room.

Shaelyn ignored the part about the unfortunate incident, but the marriage part, she just couldn't. Finally alone with her mother, she stated her case. "I don't want to get married...not to him! He...he—"

"You should have thought of that before...before you gave yourself to him," Brenna hissed and moved toward the armoire in the corner of the room. "All the plans I made for you, Shae, gone in a flash. This is not how your father and I pictured your wedding day. There will be no church, no grand party afterward." She shook her head as she pulled the ball gown out of the armoire and shook it free of wrinkles. "This will have to do in lieu of a wedding gown." She held the dress up then peered at her daughter, unmistakable reproach written clearly on her face. "I had such plans."

"I don't want to marry him, Mama."

Her mother rattled on, her words rapid-fire and as sharp as the major's saber. "Be that as it may, you'll just have to make the best of it, Shae. Your own actions brought you to this place. No sense being upset and angry with me, or Jock, or with the major." She laid the ball gown across the bed. "And don't you dare cry. Crying never solved anything."

"What about James?" Shaelyn sniffed as she glanced at the gown and swallowed against the lump in her throat. The last time she'd worn the dress her mother held, she had danced the night away with James. In the garden, with the moonlight shining down on his face, she'd promised to wait for him.

And what had she done? Since Remington Harte had walked into her life, she spared very little thought for James. Very little thought at all except for how the major made her feel. James seemed to be an inconvenient reminder of what her life had been like before everything changed.

"What about him?"

"He'll come home, Mama, and find that I broke my promise to him."

"That, my dear, is something you'll have to face when the time comes and another thing you should have thought about before you went to the major's bed." She tossed the gown on the bed then pulled out a plain, black skirt and blouse and handed them to Shaelyn. "Now, I suggest you get dressed and help me with breakfast. We're already behind schedule and the major, as you know, likes his schedule kept."

"I'm sorry, Mama." She sniffed again and swiped at the wetness clinging to her lashes. "I never meant for this to happen. I never meant to hurt you."

Brenna said nothing although her eyes glowed with unshed tears. She nodded once then left the room, her back stiff, her head held high.

Shaelyn watched the door close behind her and collapsed on the bed, willing to give in to the tears blurring her vision. Brenna's disapproval and disappointment, and her own actions, weighed heavily on her heart. How could one night of passion have ruined everything? How could Brenna force her into marriage knowing she'd always wanted to marry for love and love alone? The major didn't love her and probably already thought she'd done this on purpose, so he'd be trapped into marrying her. And what could she possibly do?

She hid. That's what she did. Despite the fact the major had requested she eat all her meals with him and his men in the dining room, Shaelyn made sure she didn't step foot outside the kitchen. And the thought of food? Well, that was enough to turn her already fragile stomach.

But she couldn't hide for long or stay busy enough to forget how her life would change in a few short hours. If twelve o'clock came and went and she didn't make an appearance, someone would look for her—either her mother or Jock or, heaven forbid, the major himself. She had no doubt Remy would drag her into the study, whether she wanted to be there or not, whether *he* wanted to be there or not.

To avoid such an event and further embarrassment, when the grandfather clock in the hallway chimed the hour, Shaelyn, dressed in the ball gown that now held a mix of memories, left her room and made her way down the hall.

They were all there, the officers who had invaded her home and turned her world upside-down. Hair brushed, faces scrubbed clean, silly grins firmly in place, they waited, eyes turned toward the door as the clock finished its dainty little tune.

Shaelyn took a deep breath and forced herself to walk through the doorway, although how was a mystery. Her heart beat so quickly, she saw spots before her eyes, and her legs…her legs felt as soft as butter on a warm day and didn't want to move any further into the room.

"Courage, little miss," Randall Beckett whispered as he approached from the side of the room, grabbed her hand, and tucked it into the crook of his arm.

She nodded once, unable to speak, as he escorted her to where Remy waited. Shaelyn sucked in her breath. Remington Harte held himself rigid, as if a steel pole replaced his spine, his expression dark and forbidding and yet, he was still the handsomest man she'd ever laid eyes on. She forced herself not to dwell on that fact as she took her place beside him.

Jock stood behind the desk, the Bible open in his hand, the buttons on his uniform and the high polish on his boots gleaming in the sunlight coming in through the window.

"Dearly beloved," he began softly, and every muscle in Shaelyn's body trembled as the man she called Uncle read the words that would make her Remington Harte's wife, his brogue almost musical.

One mistake. One moment of weakness and her whole life changed. The plans she'd made for her future flew away like birds on the wing as Remy repeated the words Jock intoned and slipped his ring from West Point, the one she had admired just a short time ago, over her finger. Too big for her, the heavy stone forced the circlet to twist, the diamond chip cutting into her flesh as she clenched her fist.

One mistake. And every one of the officers living in her home knew the circumstances of this impromptu wedding. She'd been found in the major's bed, and Major Harte had been forced into this marriage just as she had been. Embarrassment heated her face and made her tremble as Jock recited from the family Bible.

She glanced at Captain Bonaventure, who gave her a slight nod. No recrimination showed on his face. Instead, he beamed like an overindulgent uncle. Her eyes flitted toward Captains Williams and Beckett. Again she saw no reproach in their eyes, nor in the smiles stretching their mouths. She couldn't fathom the expression on Captain Davenport's face. Though his lips were curved in a smile, there was something about his eyes that gave her pause.

Her gaze slid to Brenna. Her mother returned her stare, unblinking. No sympathy whatsoever glowed in her eyes nor in her expression. No forgiveness either, which made Shaelyn's stomach clench. And yet, no one else would see what she saw. Brenna would remain charming and sweet and generous and pretend to the world that her daughter's marriage was nothing but planned.

Unsettled by the look on her mother's face, Shaelyn's focus drifted to Remy and her breath seized in her lungs. The charming grin he normally wore was nowhere to be seen; his lips pressed together so firmly, a white ring formed around his mouth and his eyes—no longer soft gray-blue—resembled polished pewter.

"I do," Remy's voice jerked her out of her thoughts. She hadn't heard Jock intone the vows, only Remy's promise to obey those vows.

Her heart slammed against her ribcage as those same vows were directed to her. "Do you, Shaelyn Rose Cavanaugh…"

The rest of his words disappeared in the dull buzz droning in her ears. It was only when he stopped speaking, when he stared at her and mouthed the simple response that she realized she must answer. "I do," she managed, although how she didn't know. Her throat constricted to the point where she could hardly draw breath. Perspiration, despite the icy chill taking up permanent residence within her, dampened her back, underarms, and trickled between her breasts.

"I now pronounce ye man and wife. Ye may kiss the bride," Jock said the words then placed the Bible on the desk and waited. Shaelyn almost backed up a step as Remy turned toward her. As it was, she had to force herself to breathe as her husband—husband!—leaned forward and lightly kissed her cheek.

He wasn't the only one to buss her cheek. Each one of the officers did the same as they offered their well wishes then shook Remy's hand, congratulating him.

"If you'll all come into the dining room—" Brenna clapped her hands to draw everyone's attention and moved toward the door, "I have prepared a lovely meal to celebrate this occasion." As her mother led the way out of the study, followed by Remy's officers, Shaelyn took a deep breath and glanced at the man still standing beside her.

"All I need are yer signatures," Jock said, once more jerking her out of her own thoughts.

One of Remy's dark brows rose as his eyes gave her a slow, thorough perusal. "It has been said, Mrs. Harte, that some battles are hard won," he commented, his voice a low, hoarse rasp. "But you got what you wanted." He took the pen Jock handed him, signed his name with a flourish on the marriage certificate, then handed her the pen.

Instead of signing her name with the implement, Shaelyn wanted to stab him with it. "You think this is what I wanted? To be married to—"

"Go ahead. Say it." When she said nothing, he supplied the answer. "A stubborn Yankee ass."

"You're wrong, Major. This was not what I had planned for my life. You...you—This is all your fault. If you hadn't taken over my room..."

"Don't you dare say I took advantage of you." Once again, he stiffened, holding himself rigid, and his eyes flashed a warning. "I only took what was offered. What else was I to think when you climbed into my bed?" An eyebrow rose, but the rest of his face seemed to be carved from granite. His voice was as hard as that cold stone.

How his words stung. He did think she'd done this on purpose, allowing them to be caught so he'd be forced to marry her. She didn't regret making love with him, or staying with him as he'd asked, but she regretted them both being forced into marrying.

"I hate you, Major!" It was mean and childish of her to say, but no more so than putting vinegar in his coffee or molasses in his boots. She really didn't mean it though. She didn't hate him and yet, she couldn't stop the words from falling from her mouth. "I'll hate you until I draw my last breath."

"As you wish, Mrs. Harte." Remy bowed from the waist and strode to the open door, his limp more pronounced, perhaps because he'd held himself so rigidly for so long. He stopped and stood still for a moment, his back moving as he drew air into his lungs, before he turned around and pinned her with his stormy blue eyes. "You may move your belongings back to your room. Your mother may move back upstairs as well." He nodded briefly then quickly left, closing the door behind him.

It took less than a minute from the moment the pocket door slid closed before Shaelyn gave in to the tears she'd held at bay.

"Now, now," Jock said as he came around the side of the desk. He opened his arms. Shaelyn immediately stepped into the comfort he provided. "Come now, Sassy lass, this is not the way to start yer married life."

Shaelyn sniffed and tried to stop crying. "But I never wanted this, Uncle Jock. I didn't want…this."

He stroked her back and his voice lowered. Shaelyn smelled tobacco on his clothes, the scent reminding her of how many times this gentle man had offered solace in exactly this way in the past. "He's a good man, lass. I've known Remy all his life, watched him grow from a boy to the honorable man he is, much as I watched you. Ye'll find none better." He pushed her away a little and stared into her eyes. "I suggest ye make the best of it."

"The best of it? With him? He hates the fact he was forced into this marriage as much as I was. Hates me."

"And didn't ye just yell the same words to him?"

Ah, the voice of reason. She could always count on Jock to make her see what she didn't want to see. This time, his words had little effect. She might be married, might not hate Remy as she said she did, but that didn't mean she would share his bed. Or even be nice to him. Never again.

They said making mistakes is how one learns. Well, she learned. Her chin raised a notch as she pulled out of his embrace and signed her name to the marriage certificate. She stuck the pen in its holder, took a deep breath, and swept from the room.

• • •

I'm married. The thought jolted Remy as he joined his men at the dining room table. He accepted their congratulations once more while he mused on the reality of his situation with some amount of incredulousness. No, it was not the way he had always envisioned his wedding day. In truth, he had hardly thought of it at all, instead planning to get as far ahead in the military as he could, and eventually return to his boyhood home in Kentucky when wearing a uniform no longer suited him…if he didn't teach at the Academy.

That had been the plan for his life. Marrying Shaelyn had not been part of that plan, but he hadn't had a choice. That option had been taken from both of them when he'd asked her to stay instead of letting her leave with the dawn. Remorse for his anger and for behaving like such an ass, as she'd already accused him of being, swept through him. He needed to take responsibility for his actions and not place all the blame squarely on her shoulders.

The object of his thoughts strolled into the dining room as if she hadn't a care in the world. The moment he saw her though, he knew it was an act. There were telltale signs of both her anger and nervousness. She pulled her bottom lip between her teeth and chewed just a bit before she realized what she was doing and stopped. She also held herself stiffly, as if bending would break her. Tears had made her lashes spiky, but there were no signs of them now.

Remy glanced around the table and let out his breath in a sigh of relief—the carving knife was nowhere to be seen, although the tines of a fork could do some damage if she decided to stab him, though he didn't think she would. Slowly, he rose from his seat as she drew closer. The room grew silent. Not a sound was heard… no utensils clattering against each other, no indrawn breaths, no comments at all as his officers—and Brenna—stopped passing the meal around and watched with wide, curious eyes.

He pulled out Shaelyn's chair. She slid into her seat with a nod to the gentlemen around the table then turned slightly as he pushed in her chair.

"Thank you." Her voice was prim, proper, and polite, but nothing else. Her response did not surprise him. He'd expected as much.

What he had not expected was her passion.

She had surprised him last night, first by being in his bed, then by how she responded to his every touch. She made love like she was born for it. He still bore the marks of her fingernails. And if he were telling the truth, he'd admit something had changed in him. Touching her, sinking into her warmth—making love to her—made him feel like he'd found where he belonged.

Perhaps being married to her wouldn't be the worst thing that could happen. Other marriages had started with less. He could and should make the best of it. Happiness was worth the effort, wasn't it? *She* was worth it, wasn't she?

He studied her now as she picked at her meal, pushing the green beans around her plate. She didn't look at him. She didn't look at anyone, but her cheeks were a pretty pink. Fine wisps of auburn hair teased her cheek and he resisted the urge to sweep them away from her face.

Yes, she was worth it.

His smile widened as he thought of ways to win her over. He'd been told he could be quite charming when he chose to be.

Let's see how long she'll hate me.

• • •

Shaelyn climbed the servants' stairs at the back of the house and wished her aching muscles on someone else.

So much for a wedding day. After the brief ceremony, which bound her to Major Remington Harte until death do them part, and the cozy luncheon her mother had prepared, she'd gone back to doing her chores. Nothing had changed except her name. She still washed uniforms and hung them in the sunshine to dry, dusted and polished and mopped. She'd also moved her mother's belongings back upstairs into the master bedroom.

Just before dinner, she had packed the major's belongings into his trunk and pushed the chest into the hallway. He could move his belongings wherever he wished—outside in the pigsty or Hades for all she cared. A tired smile spread her lips...*he* could sleep in the servants' quarters now.

Her arms laden with the last of her clothing, Shaelyn entered her bedroom and stopped short. Her breath seized in her lungs at the sight before her. And what a sight it was.

Remy sat up in bed, the glow of the lantern illuminating not only the book in his hand, but the dark hair covering his bare chest. Beneath the blanket pulled up to his waist, she could see that his legs were crossed at the ankles. He seemed relaxed and at ease, quite comfortable in her bed. She was also quite aware of how his muscles resembled corded steel and how they had felt beneath her fingers.

In truth, he looked more delectable than any man had a right to. Wanton desire surged through her quicker than she could snap her fingers, making her knees quiver. Her stomach clenched and blood rose to stain her cheeks. Was it only last night she had made love to him? Less than twenty-four hours ago?

With determination she didn't know she possessed, Shaelyn tamped down the wicked inclination to drop her clothes right where she stood and jump—yes, jump!—into bed with him, for despite their current circumstances, she wanted him again, wanted what she knew he could do to her.

Finding her voice, she asked instead, "What are you doing in here?"

"Reading," he replied and gave her that crooked grin, the one that had melted her heart on more than one occasion. But not tonight. She tore her gaze away from his broad, muscular chest and noticed the open doors of the armoire in the corner. His uniform trousers hung neatly next to her skirts, as if they'd done so for years. There were other changes as well. His brush and comb joined hers on the bureau, and his boots were lined up beside her shoes on the floor.

He'd emptied his trunk, she realized, after she'd gone through so much energy and time to pack it. He'd also taken her side of the bed, a most unforgiveable sin.

"I thought...you said..." she stammered, unable to get the words out and finish a coherent thought. She took a deep, weary breath. "You're in my room."

"Correction. *Our* room. We are man and wife now."

"That doesn't..." She stopped before she said something she'd regret. She'd already done that once today, when she'd said she hated him. "I'd rather sleep on the floor."

He did not move. He stayed utterly still for a moment, as if holding his breath. He released it slowly, his chest moving as the breath left his body. He gave a slight nod, closed his book and placed it on the bedside table, then pulled the covers back, inviting her to crawl into bed beside him.

"I would prefer that you sleep with me…if only for appearances' sake." Remy cocked an eyebrow, but his smile remained. "However, if it will ease your worries, I have no intention of touching you."

His words jolted her. "What?"

"Rest assured, Mrs. Harte, you are the last person I want to touch. Tonight…or any night." And with those words, he blew out the lamp, casting the room in darkness except for the moonlight streaming in through the window.

Shaelyn heard rustling as he settled himself for sleep, heard something that sounded suspiciously like a chuckle, then nothing more.

Dumbstruck, she stood and stared for the longest time, unable to decide what she wanted to do. "Damn Yankee," she muttered, just loud enough for him to hear.

This time, Shaelyn was certain she heard a small chuckle. "Are you going to stand there and call me names? We could, I'm sure, do that all night, but we have a lot to do in the morning. Come to bed, Shae."

And still, she stood there, her clothes still in her arms, undecided, unprepared…unhappy, glaring at him. "A gentleman would…"

"I never said I was a gentleman."

She jumped and a shiver rushed down her back. Did she imagine his voice was closer? Her heart thumped as she let out her breath. He wasn't closer. It was just her imagination…and her nerves. "All right, Major. You win."

"Hmmm. I wouldn't exactly call this winning."

With a sigh of exasperation, Shaelyn dumped the armload of clothes on the chair then stubbed her toe on the trunk he'd pushed back into the room.

He may have said he wouldn't touch her, but Shaelyn had her doubts. Too tired to argue with him, too sore deep in her muscles to want to sleep on the floor—or in the chair or back in the small, lumpy bed in the servants' quarters—she tugged open the bureau drawer and chose a nightgown, one that buttoned all the way up to her chin. The sleeves went to her wrists while the hemline dusted the floor. Nothing alluring in the least about this piece of flannel, she mused as she laid the nightgown over the privacy screen and slipped behind it.

Finished changing her clothes, Shaelyn sat at the vanity and began brushing her hair with scalp-scratching strokes before she plaited the thick, curling mass into one long braid that swung down her back. With a sigh, she finally crawled into bed, brought the blankets up to cover her shoulders...and scooted as close to the side of the mattress as she could, leaving an emptiness the span of the Sahara desert between them. She may have to share the same bed, but she didn't have to touch him!

"Sleep well, Mrs. Harte," he murmured.

This time, she was certain she heard him chuckle!

Chapter 14

Despite the rough beginning, Remy enjoyed married life…at least the first two weeks of it. And he loved sleeping next to Shaelyn. Without her realizing it, she brought a comfort to him as no other had been able to do, and the nightmares he generally suffered through were not as frequent. She crawled into bed now without argument, although she continued to hug the edge of the mattress, which simply amused him because no matter how hard she tried, at some point during the night, she would wander to his side of the bed in her sleep and they ended up holding each other, a fact that annoyed her beyond reason.

Feigning sleep in the mornings had become a favorite pastime for him as well, for as much as he loved sleeping beside her, he loved watching her when she was relaxed and not so guarded.

She rose early, whether she could hear Beelzebub's crowing or not, and slipped from bed after wrestling herself free of entangled blankets…and him.

This morning was no different…for either of them. He lay on his back, holding her close, while her head rested on his shoulder, her body pressed against his side. Her hand splayed across his chest, fingers hot against his skin, but not nearly as hot as her bare leg thrown over his, her nightgown bunched up between them. Remy lay still, and hoped she wouldn't move. Better yet, he hoped she would, but not to get out of bed.

With a heartfelt sigh, Shaelyn carefully disentangled herself and crawled from the bed. Remy instantly felt the chill without her beside him, even though she adjusted the blankets over him, which warmed his heart if not his body.

She lit a lantern against the darkness, but kept the wick low to provide only meager light, then gathered her clothing from the armoire. He watched every graceful move she made, mesmerized, until she left the room.

She returned shortly, fully dressed in a simple skirt and blouse, which she preferred, the flannel nightgown, which she also preferred, thrown over her arm. Through slightly closed eyes, he studied her as she untwisted the braid hanging down her back and brushed her long, shining tresses until they gleamed in the lamplight. A few quick moves and she twisted the light mahogany locks into a loose knot atop her head. He wished she'd leave her hair loose, like that night in the garden when he had pulled the pins from the heavy mass and weaved his fingers into the softness. His fingers flexed now, remembering how soft her hair had been.

The last thing she always did before she headed downstairs was dab a little perfume on the pulse spots behind her ears. Not a lot, as the bottle was nearly empty. The fragrance not only filled the room, but filled his mind with images, his heart with wonder, and his body with longing.

This morning, though, she surprised him. She added something new to her routine after she put the stopper back in the perfume bottle. Something unexpected. Remy kept his eyes half closed as Shaelyn turned from the mirror on the bureau and approached their bed. She hesitated as she stood beside him, as if undecided. He wished he could see her expression.

Instead, he concentrated on breathing normally and watched her face through the veil of his lashes, resisting the urge to grab her and bring her back to bed. She hesitated a moment more then quickly dropped a kiss on his lips before making a hasty exit.

Remy lay in bed after the door closed and grinned. Ah, was his prickly rose beginning to soften toward him? Simple kindness had brought them far from the days when he had first taken her home and her boats. What else could he do to complete the transformation and make her love him?

He sat up, thoroughly surprised by his own thoughts, but quite at home with them, too. Did he want his wife to love him? The answer came to him quickly.

Yes. Yes, I do.

His grin widened then he began to chuckle. It was the beginning of a good day. He was still smiling when she brought him his coffee.

••••

Shaelyn headed upstairs after washing the breakfast dishes, intending to strip the bed and put on fresh linen, but the bed had already been made. Had Remy done that? It wouldn't surprise her. He'd been especially kind and solicitous since saying "I do," but why would he make their bed if she needed to change the sheets? She pulled back a corner of the coverlet and realized the linens had already been changed.

What is going on?

She left her room through the French doors and strolled toward the back of the house. No one was in the yard, but from her vantage point, she could see the door to the little shed behind the carriage house stood wide open. Already, several sheets hung from the clothesline, pristine white, fluttering in the breeze.

Shaelyn traipsed down the back stairs and made her way across the yard, shivering a little, despite the warmth of the shawl wrapped around her shoulders.

A fire burned merrily beneath a huge cauldron in the shed when she slipped in through the open door. A tall, thin young man had his back toward her. He whistled a nonsense tune as he stirred the contents of the cauldron with a long wooden pole. The sleeves of his uniform were rolled to his elbows and he paused to wipe perspiration from his forehead several times before he lifted a sheet from the pot, using the pole, and dumped it in the galvanized washtub on the table next to him. He looked vaguely familiar, but then so many of the young boys in blue did.

"Who are you?"

The boy gave a guilty start and dropped the pole. A blush rose up his face as he turned to look at her. He couldn't have been more than fifteen years old. "Private Connors, ma'am," he responded, his voice cracking.

"Private Connors, what may I ask are you doing?"

"I'm to do the laundry, ma'am." He swallowed and his Adam's apple bobbed as he did so. The redness never left his face. "Major Harte said so. As'ed me if I liked goin' on the riverboats, which I don't—my stomach gets a bit queasy on them boats, ma'am—then as'ed me if I wouldn't mind doin' some chores at Magnolia House and here I am." He picked up the pole, but didn't make another move, as if he waited for an order.

"I see." She resisted the urge to smile at him. Poor thing seemed nervous in her presence. He stood ramrod straight although he studied the ground instead of her. "Have you seen Major Harte?"

The boy shook his head as his gaze rose from the ground to face her once more. He grinned, making dimples appear in his smooth cheeks. "No, ma'am. Not since earlier today."

"Thank you. You may carry on, Private Connors, and when you are done, you may come up to the house and have some pie."

"Thank you, ma'am, already had some o' Miz Cavanaugh's fine pie. Wouldn't mind havin' more though. Best pecan pie I ever had."

She left the boy to finish his chores and headed back toward the house. The kitchen was clean, but empty. Several bowls were on the table, each one covered with a dishtowel. A familiar sight and she knew what it meant. Her mother would make bread today. The bowls were filled with dough, beginning the rising process.

A thick, hearty soup simmered on the stove, scenting the air with the delicious aroma of chicken and vegetables. She wondered briefly if there would be dumplings, too.

Shaelyn stepped through the door into the hallway. "Mama?"

"In here, dear."

She swept into the sun parlor and found her mother sitting in a ray of sunlight coming in through the window. She worked on a quilt stretched between the wooden rods of a quilt stand in the natural light, a cup of steaming tea on the small table beside her. In the past, she would have been in the company of other ladies, fabric spread out between them as they sat in a circle, gossiping as they sewed quilts for those in need.

"Is there anything I can do for you, Mama?"

Brenna glanced up from her work in progress, the needle poised above a multicolored ringlet. "No, dear, but thank you. With all the captains gone right now, there isn't much to cook. I do have some dough rising and soup already simmering. Perhaps you can help me later?"

"Just let me know when," she said as she studied the design of the quilt. Her mother called it a double wedding ring. "I met Private Connors."

"Isn't he a sweet boy? He and I had a long discussion earlier today." She took a sip of her tea. "I thought it was rather sweet of Major Harte to have him help you."

"Speaking of the major, have you seen him?"

Her mother put the cup back on its saucer and moved her spectacles further down her nose. Questions lurked in her crystal blue eyes, questions that remained unasked except for one, "Is everything all right?"

"Everything is fine, Mama. I just wanted to ask him a question."

She gave a slight nod then went back to her needlework. "I believe he's gone to Rosalie. I heard him mention something about the Gray Ghost and cut telegraph wires."

Shaelyn nodded as she wandered around the room, then paused in front of the French doors and studied the small vegetable garden.

"Are you certain everything is all right, dear? There aren't any problems…" Brenna didn't finish the sentence.

Shaelyn added the rest of her mother's question silently…*with your marriage?*" and bit back the sharp response on the tip of her tongue. *Of course not, Mama. What could possibly be wrong with a forced marriage? Did you think it would be all peaches and cream once the ring was on my finger? The major hates me and I…I don't know how I feel.*

She said none of that as she moved away from the door. "No, Mama. Everything is fine. I promise."

Brenna smiled and pushed her spectacles back into position. "That's good, dear," she said as she bent her head over the fabric. "I knew you two would work it out."

Shaelyn said nothing as she left her mother to her needlework, something she'd never had an interest in, and wandered down the hall to the study. The house just seemed so quiet, and in the quiet, there was too much to think about.

Like the major.

And herself.

And the pretend marriage they shared in a real bed.

And the myriad of feelings rushing through her, all jumbled and confused and utterly frustrating.

So this is what being a lady of leisure feels like. How can they stand it? All the thoughts going through their minds, playing havoc with their emotions?

She'd never been a lady of leisure. There had always been something for her to do. Before the war, she'd had more steamboats and worked in the office, selling tickets to passengers, or in the warehouse, keeping inventory and such.

The truth? She was bored, didn't quite know what to do with herself. Or the thoughts screaming in her head. Private Connors had washed the bed linens. She had dusted just yesterday and scrubbed the floors the day before. Indeed, the house gleamed with cleanliness.

She couldn't even go down to her beloved steamboats…both were gone—the *Sweet Sassy* to Memphis with Captains Becket and Williams and the *Lady Shae* to St. Louis with Captains Bonaventure and MacPhee. There were no letters she needed to write, and reading one of the many books in the study didn't interest her at the moment. Shopping didn't interest her either. There was nothing she wanted. Or needed.

Except something to do.

They didn't need her help at the warehouse. Beside, she didn't want the risk of running into Captain Davenport. Ever since she had usurped his authority on the *Brenna Rose*, he regarded her with disdain or downright hostility, but never in Remy's presence. When the major was present, Davenport treated her with the utmost respect, which only served to deepen her distrust of the man.

So what am I going to with myself until Remy comes home? The thought made her stop and take notice. When had that become important? When had seeing his soft blue-gray eyes become the highlight of her day? And why bother asking herself questions she wouldn't answer?

She left the study and wandered around the nearly empty house.

A smile slowly came to her. Before Remy and his men intruded into her home and she'd struck the bargain with him, she had volunteered her time at Airlie, the plantation house turned Federal hospital. She hadn't been there in quite some time, but imagined a volunteer would never be turned away. Dr. Shaunessy might be happy to see her.

"Mama, I'm going over to Airlie."

"That's nice, dear," Brenna said, then went back to her quilting and her tea.

• • •

Later, after she'd returned from Airlie, where Dr. Shaughnessy, the man in charge, welcomed her back, Shaelyn rose from her chair in the study as Remy swept into the room, bringing with him a rush of fresh air, the smell of wood smoke, and the unmistakable thump-thump of his cane. "I'd like a word with you, Major."

"Well, good evening, Shae." Remy grinned as he doffed his coat and flung it over the back of the settee.

"I met Private Connors today."

Remy stopped in the process of tugging his gloves from his hands and studied her. "I see."

A fiery blush rose up her face, burning her cheeks, and she glanced away from his scrutiny, but not for long. No matter that her emotions were a jumbled mess, she couldn't lie...Remington Harte, husband or not, remained one of the most handsome men she'd ever known...and she *enjoyed* looking at him. Her gaze wandered over his clean-shaven face and came to rest on his eyes, then moved lower to his mouth, his perfectly kissable mouth. She realized she wasn't listening.

She was lost...in oh-so-many ways.

Mentally, she shook herself and paid attention.

"I hope you don't mind—" she finally heard. Her gaze dropped from his face to his hands as he finished removing his gloves, but even that was a mistake. She remembered the feel of his hands on her, touching her, caressing her, and it was all she could do to concentrate. "I thought having Private Connors perform all the heavy manual work would make your life a little easier. You've been spending more and more time on the boats and it's plain to everyone that you are exhausted."

"That's very sweet of you, Major, but why? Why would you do this for me?" Working hard wasn't the reason for her exhaustion. Fighting off her desire for him was what exhausted her. Even now.

It had been different when she'd slept downstairs, but night after night, sharing the same bed, trying not to touch him was proving to be a lot more difficult. And she failed more often than not. Indeed, she'd begun failing that very first night when she awoke to find herself in his arms, her head resting on his shoulder, his arm around her, holding her close.

"You're my wife now. You shouldn't be taking care of everyone," he said, his voice low and sensual, just a purr really. "Just me. I also asked your mother if she'd like to give up her chores as well...I was going to hire someone, but your mother said no, she enjoyed cooking for us."

For once, Shaelyn had nothing to say. He was killing her with his many kindnesses, not only to herself, but to her mother as well. And he made it more than impossible to retain her anger and keep her balance. In fact, it seemed most things he did, those little thoughtful acts, did more to undermine her sense of stability and poise than anything else he could have done. To her utter mortification, his plan of attack, if it was a plan, was working.

Hadn't she kissed him the other morning? Granted, he'd been sleeping, but she hadn't been able to stop herself from touching her lips to his and wishing...

"Oh, by the way, I brought you this." Once again, he caught her drifting attention as he lifted his coat from the settee and rifled through the pocket to produce a small bottle tied with a pale yellow ribbon. As he handed the bottle to her, their fingers touched, setting off a whirlwind of physical longing that seemed to reach into her soul and steal her breath from her lungs. Her skin tingled from the inside out, as if the butterflies that usually congregated in her stomach now fluttered against every inch of skin on her body.

Shaelyn forced herself to breath then glanced at the bottle in her hand. He'd bought her perfume. And not just any perfume, but her own signature fragrance. She would know the shape of the bottle and the delicate color of the ribbon as Madame Lamoureaux's anywhere.

"I saw that you were almost out."

She was touched, so touched tears misted her eyes and her vision blurred. "Thank you, but how could you possibly know?"

He shrugged with nonchalance, but she didn't miss the hint of a blush creeping up his face. "I have my ways, Mrs. Harte. I am nothing if not resourceful." He grinned then, showing a full complement of pearly white teeth. "Madame Lamoureaux asked me to pass along her regards."

It took every ounce of her strength not to rush into his arms and kiss him. Every ounce. She gave a slight nod instead and slipped the bottle into her pocket. "Thank you, Major. You've been most kind."

"My pleasure, Shae."

His deep voice rumbled through her, setting her already frazzled nerves on fire as she nodded one more time and nearly ran for the door. She stopped for a moment and turned to look at him, which gave her both a jolt a pleasure and a shiver of dread as she realized she was quickly losing the battle she fought with herself. "Dinner will be ready shortly," she informed him, then beat a hasty retreat.

• • •

Something tickled her. Shaelyn snaked her arm out from beneath the blanket and scratched her nose. Her fingers touched the slightly curling hair at the back of Remy's neck.

She'd done it again. No matter how far over on the bed she was when she crawled beneath the covers, she woke up spooning Remy, her legs bent and snug against his, her breasts pressed flat against his back, her nose scrunched against the back of his neck, where his scent lingered.

Or he cuddled her, his leg thrown over hers possessively, his arms wrapped tightly around her.

It was enough to make a girl scream…or sigh with comfort and go back to sleep.

This morning, she wanted to scream.

She moved slightly, intending to pull away from him, but he laid his hand firmly on her backside, keeping her tight against him.

"Stay," he begged.

"I…I can't." And truthfully, she couldn't. It had nothing to do with the chores that awaited her…or that used to await her. It had to do with the tightening of her belly, with the tingle of her skin, with the heat of his body so close to hers. Desire, hot and sweet, swept along her veins, leaving her a shaking, trembling mess. She wanted him. Wanted him more than anything she had ever wanted before.

"Please," he whispered, his voice a seductive beacon she no longer had the strength to fight. "Stay with me."

Why not? They were married. Why should she deny herself the pleasure she knew he could bring her?

A small smile tilted the corners of her mouth as she reached around him and splayed her fingers through the soft hair on his bare chest. At the same time, she moved slightly and kissed the back of his neck where his hair curled. His skin was warm beneath her lips, even warmer beneath her hand, and the small fluttering sensation deep in her belly grew.

"Shae." Her name fell from his lips in a husky moan, but he didn't move. He did draw in his breath as her fingertips slid over his nipple, which grew pebble-hard in an instant. Her hand moved lower, sliding over his taut stomach and lower still to smooth along his bare hip and thigh. For once, she was grateful he did not wear clothes to bed, preferring to sleep naked and unencumbered.

"Hmmmm?" she murmured as she moved closer to him, her breasts crushing against his hard back, her leg slipping over his, her nightgown bunching up between them as she peppered the back of his neck with more kisses.

"If you don't stop…" He didn't finish the statement, but his hand pressed against her backside, pulling her closer.

Her voice lowered to a whisper. "I don't want to stop, Remy. I want…I need…" She reached between his thighs, closing her hand around his fully engorged erection.

His muscles contracted and tensed as her grip around him tightened and she stroked slowly, up and down. His breath left him in a rush, his back and chest moving as he exhaled. "Then have your way with me." His words came out in a hoarse groan. "I am yours to command."

She felt bold and empowered by his complete surrender, as if she had a choice, something she hadn't felt in a long time. But now, now, she had a choice. She moved again, coming up on her knees to hover over him, all the while pressing kisses against his neck, his shoulders, and his face until he rolled onto his back with a groan.

Dawn had yet to break, but moonlight flooded the room. She could see the expression on his handsome features, saw the softness of his eyes before he whispered her name then cradled her face between his hands and kissed her, a deep, soul-searching kiss she felt down to the tips of her toes…and every place in between. A kiss so full of promise, it left her gasping for air, for sanity, freeing her of the last vestiges of modesty she might have had, as well as the resentment she had harbored.

He hardly let her catch her breath before he captured her mouth once more, his lips sliding over hers as his hands caressed her neck through the softness of her flannel nightdress.

"Touch me," she whispered against his lips, not realizing Remy had already unbuttoned her nightgown until he slipped his hand beneath the fabric and cupped her breast. His thumb flicked over her nipple as his mouth continued to play over hers. If she thought she'd been lost before, she'd been mistaken. His touch drove her to madness, his kiss pushing all thought from her head except that she needed him. Wanted him.

"This has to come off," he murmured, and slid the garment over her head, tossing it to the floor beside the bed. His lips replaced his hand, his tongue swirling around the nipple before drawing the pearl-hard peak into his mouth and suckling gently.

Shaelyn gave herself over to sensation completely. His fingertips lightly skimmed her flesh. Goose bumps pebbled her skin. The warmth of his breath on her face and neck, the pressure of his lips against hers, and the delightful heat of his tongue as it brushed hers held her spellbound.

She straddled him then, reveling in the raw power of his steely arousal between her thighs, rubbing against her moist core before she impaled herself on his thick shaft. Remy placed his hands on her hips and guided her, as his teeth grazed first one nipple then the other. Waves of pleasure shot through her. She found a rhythm and moved slowly, rocking back and forth, riding him as the coiled spring that was her release spiraled and tightened.

And Remy helped her reach that climax as he slipped a hand between them, finding that most sensitive spot within the moist folds of her flesh.

Shaelyn's eyes flew open as the coil sprung free. She was flying, soaring among the stars in the heaven, touching those glittering points of light as her body convulsed over and over. She bit her lip to keep from screaming, the sensations whisking through her intense and wonderful.

And she wanted more. Much more. She leaned down to capture his mouth with hers, tracing her tongue over his lips, and started moving on him once more, rising up on her knees then slowly sinking down, feeling him fill her.

Remy moved so quickly, she drew in her breath and let out a startled squeak. One moment she was atop him, her legs on either side of his hips, the next, she was beneath him, the steel-hard length of him still within the wet, swollen flesh of her body.

"Oh yes," Shaelyn hissed as she pressed against him and surrendered herself to the sweet seduction of his touch.

He moved in her slowly, drawing out almost entirely before settling against her again. Shaelyn couldn't help the moan that escaped her, nor could she help moving against him, her hips rising up to meet his every slow, torturous thrust.

Why had she denied herself this? She reached her peak, her body pulsing around him once more. She couldn't help groaning, "Oh, yes, Remy!"

He smothered her voice with his mouth, drawing the words as well as her breath into him. His pace quickened as he slid into her moist, giving flesh and whispered words of encouragement, demanding she come for him one more time. The muscles in his arms bulged as he held her close and his hips settled between hers, grinding against her in the most provocative way, his movements tight and controlled until he grunted and groaned with the force of his own release. A slight chuckle escaped him as he thrust into her, the heat, the pulsing of him pushing her over the edge.

Shaelyn followed his release with her own explosive climax. One last time, she touched stars. They exploded all around her, little shards of light showering down on her as she soared into bliss, more powerful than before. Her body rocked beneath his as her legs tightened against his thighs. She couldn't speak, couldn't hold a coherent thought as she pulsed around him, every inch of her skin alive and tingling. Tears flooded her eyes and rolled down either side of her face as she pulled in a deep breath.

"My God, are you all right?" His deep, rich voice reflected his concern as he slowly withdrew from her. "Did I hurt you?"

She shook her head, unable to say a word. Emotions, deep and mysterious, filled her until her heart seemed full to bursting. She couldn't explain even if she had the power to speak. She settled next to him, feeling the heat of his body seep into hers, and rested her head on his shoulder as she'd done before, but this time she knew what she was doing. She wasn't asleep. She laid her hand on his chest, too, and smoothed her fingers through the soft matting of hair there.

"Are you certain I didn't hurt you?"

"I'm certain," she whispered into his chest, finally finding her voice. He hadn't hurt her, not one bit. She'd just been overcome with emotion. "You didn't hurt me."

He grew quiet for a moment then wrapped his arm tighter around her. "I rather like it when you lie against me like this." He pressed a kiss against the top of her head and let out a long contented sigh.

"I admit, I like it too," she responded between yawns, just before her eyes closed and she slipped into an exhausted yet satisfied slumber for as long as Beelzebub would let her.

Chapter 15

"May I come in?"

Remy looked up from the letter in his hand and grinned as he rose to his feet and saluted. "I was just thinking about you, General."

General Sumner returned the salute as well as the grin, his woolly mustache stretching across his upper lip. "Good thoughts, I hope."

"Always, sir." Remy gestured to the comfortable chair in front of the fireplace next to him, folded the letter, placed it on the table, and then poured the man a generous draught of whiskey. The temperature had dropped outside, but the study remained warm and cozy—flames crackled and jumped along the logs behind the grate, while sunlight filtered in through the window and dust motes danced in the beams.

The general removed his gloves and hat, shrugged out of his coat, and tossed them over the back of the divan. He rubbed his hands together in front of the crackling fire as he took his seat.

"I understand congratulations are in order." He picked up his glass and swallowed the whiskey in one gulp, then licked his lips and gestured for more. "Honor was quite happy when I told her about your marriage. She said she always knew there was a woman out there for you. And who would have thought it started with vinegar in your coffee. We both hope you'll be happy."

Remy could have disabused him of the notion his marriage was anything but planned or based on love, but he didn't say a word. No sense in letting the entire Union army know he had been well and truly trapped.

Ah, but that wasn't fair. He hadn't been trapped. Not at all. He could have just as easily said no, as he very rarely ever did anything he truly didn't want to; however, in all fairness, and the circumstances being what they were, he was an honest and honorable man. He had married because it had been the right thing to do.

And since he was honest, he needed to admit there was more to it than simply being principled and proper. His relationship with his wife had changed. Shaelyn wasn't nearly as prickly as before. Perhaps that had something to do with his unspoken campaign to win her heart. Passion simmered between them, passion she had once denied, but now accepted. This morning was a perfect example. After holding herself back, she had seduced him. His body still thrummed with the force of his release, her cries of pleasure still echoed in his ears.

With a simple nod, he said, "Thank you for your kind wishes, sir."

"Not at all, my boy. I can't think of anyone who deserves to be happy as much as you." He chuckled. "However, if you want to know the secret to a long and happy marriage, you'll have to ask my wife." He chuckled again but with obvious adoration for the woman he had married. Honor Sumner was the perfect match for the general and had been from the moment they met thirty years ago. They shared a mutual respect and a deep abiding love for one another that hadn't diminished over the years. Instead, it had grown stronger.

Remy hoped his marriage would turn out to be the same. He was willing to work for it.

"Now, to the reason for my visit," the general said, interrupting Remy's thoughts. "EJ has been hurt."

"EJ? Hurt? What happened?"

The general explained the details while Remy listened, his heart hammering in his chest. He knew EJ—Ewell Junior—and admired the young man's determination to follow in his father's footsteps, but to do it on his own, without any special privileges.

"Right now, he's in a hospital in New Orleans. I left him a few days ago, but Honor is still there. She's staying with friends in the city." He sighed as he gently stroked his mustache, a motion he performed whenever upset. And there was no doubt the man was upset now. Seeing his son injured had to have been devastating.

"The next time you make a run for supplies, I'd like for him to be brought here, to Natchez. I don't trust the trains, and going over land in a carriage or wagon would not be what's best for EJ." He continued stroking the bushy hair on his upper lip, dragging his fingers down along the sides of his mouth to stop at his chin. "Doctor Watson at the hospital has been notified and is awaiting further instructions, so the sooner, the better."

"Of course, General. I'd be happy to make the arrangements."

Shaelyn swept into the room, balancing a silver tray in her hands. "I thought you might like some coffee." She stopped short, her eyes opening wide, the lovely blush staining her cheeks most becoming. "Oh, excuse me. I didn't know you had company."

"It's all right, Shae. Come in. Please."

Both men rose from their seats to watch her cross the room and place the tray on the table between them. Remy noticed there were two cups along with the coffee service. Had she intended to join him? The thought pleased him, especially after this morning. "General, I'd like to introduce you to my wife. Shae, this is General Ewell Sumner."

"General." Shaelyn gave a quick curtsey then extended her hand.

The older man bowed and took her hand in his. "A pleasure, my dear," he said as he kissed her knuckles. "And my warmest congratulations on your marriage. You've got yourself a fine man."

Shaelyn's blush deepened as she nodded and quickly left the room, closing the pocket doors behind her. Remy stared at the doors for a while then poured coffee for both of them.

General Sumner added whiskey to his and took a sip. His face dissolved in an expression of pure pleasure. "Good coffee," he said, then gestured to the door. "I see why you were so taken with her, my boy. She's a beauty."

"Yes, she is." And it occurred to him that he had the power to make her happy. More importantly, he wanted to, for suddenly her happiness seemed vital. "I wonder if I could impose upon you, sir."

"It's only fair, Remy. I'm imposing on you. Whatever it is, son, just ask. I'll do anything I can to help. Remember, I owe you my life."

"My wife hasn't heard from her brother since he joined his regiment." He passed the general a white linen napkin, which the older man placed across his lap. "She is, understandably, worried about him. I think it would ease her mind tremendously if she knew he was safe."

"And you'd like me to look into his whereabouts?" Sumner helped himself to several shortbread cookies, dipped one into his coffee-whiskey mixture, and took a bite. Again, a momentary expression of pleasure appeared on his face as he chewed and swallowed. "Of course. What's his name? When did he enlist?"

"Ian Alexander Cavanaugh. He joined a Union company out of Natchez two years ago. No one has heard from him since."

"Nothing?"

"No, sir. Nothing. He enlisted with a young man named James Brooks and they marched off together. She hasn't heard from either one, doesn't know if they're alive or if they've perished in battle."

"I see." He placed his plate and cup on the table then rose from his seat and dug through the pocket of his coat. He produced a small notebook and a stub of pencil, then asked for the name again and quickly wrote it down. "I'll see what I can find out."

"Thank you, General. I appreciate it. And if you wouldn't mind, please don't mention anything to Shae. I don't want to get her hopes up in case…" He didn't finish his statement, but the general understood. All too well.

"Of course, my boy. Anything for you." He tucked the notebook away and took his seat once more to indulge in the shortbread cookies. "By the way, I'm not sure if you've been told, but I've been permanently assigned to Rosalie. Honor will be joining me once you can bring EJ here."

"That's wonderful, sir."

"Natchez is a lovely city." He finished all the shortbread on the plate and wiped his mouth with the napkin. "We're renting a little house not too far from here. She'd love to see you once we're settled. You'll have to come to dinner. And bring your lovely wife. I'm certain Honor would love to meet her."

"Thank you, sir, we'd love to." He poured more coffee into their cups then passed the bottle of Harte's Private Reserve to the general, who liberally added the whiskey to his once again. "Speaking of dinner, would you like to stay this evening? Brenna Cavanaugh is a fabulous cook."

"Thank you for the invitation. I'd love to," he said as leaned back in his chair and crossed his legs, the picture of a man comfortable enough in his surroundings to relax. "Since I've come back from seeing EJ, I've been taking my meals at the King's Tavern or Rosalie. Neither place is up to Honor's fine standards. I could do with a meal that isn't burnt to a crisp or half raw."

• • •

Shaelyn did not serve dinner. Young Private Connors did the honors and did it very well. Even with an unexpected guest, as well as the sudden return of Captains Becket and Williams from another successful trip, the young man performed his duties graciously.

She sat at the table while the private waited on her, and enjoyed the general's company, actually enjoyed the company of all the men, most especially Remy. Every time he glanced in her direction with his smoldering eyes and knowing smile, the flames of desire curled in her belly and she couldn't wait until they were alone again.

He'd been most charming this evening, sharing stories of his time at the Academy, as did the others around the table. The only one who didn't share was Captain Davenport. Though he chuckled when amused, he never did so aloud, and his smile didn't quite reach his eyes. Several times, she caught him staring at both Remy and the general with something akin to disdain—and superiority?—in his expression. The same expression he sometimes gave her.

Curious, she watched him from the corner of her eye, but made sure his attitude didn't spoil her mood. The dampening of her good spirits came as coffee and dessert were served and the talk turned to the general's son and the special request he'd made.

"Can you be ready to leave again by Friday?" Remy addressed the captains sitting across from him. "That'll give you two days to rest and recuperate from your last trip." He turned to the general and asked, "Is Friday all right with you?"

"I prefer right now," General Sumner admitted, "but I understand you need a few days."

"Friday it is then," Captain Beckett replied for both himself and Captain Williams as he dug into his dessert. "I'll notify the other captains."

"Supplies, Vince?" Remy directed his attention to Davenport. "Since our ultimate destination is a hospital, perhaps we could bring extra medical supplies aside from what we normally do."

"Consider it done." Davenport removed a small leather-bound notebook from his pocket and jotted a quick note. "I'll have a list prepared from our inventory for your consideration shortly."

Shaelyn listened to the plans being made and the more she heard, the more her stomach tightened. She pushed her dessert away, unable to take a bite over the constriction in her throat and the fear building within. This would not be the first time the *Sweet Sassy* had delivered supplies, nor would it be the first time she transported passengers. The men who guided her, Captains Williams and Beckett, as well as the other captains who shared the duty, all experienced and competent, brought her back safely to Natchez after each trip, but this time something *felt* different. No matter how she tried to convince herself it would be all right, dread and doubt grew.

"Shae?"

She realized Remy had asked her a question and waited for her answer. Her gaze rose to meet his and she wanted to blurt out a warning, but couldn't get the words out. Not now, with everyone watching her. "She'll be ready. I'll see to it."

• • •

Later, when they were alone, after the general had taken his leave and the house had settled for the night, Remy watched Shaelyn as they readied for bed.

"I like him," she said as she unbuttoned her blouse and pulled it free from the waistband of her skirt before slipping behind the ornate screen in the corner. She still hadn't become so comfortable that she'd undress completely in front of him, but she'd made progress.

"That pleases me," he replied, and he meant it. General Sumner was an important person in his life and he meant to retain the friendship. "He was quite taken with you as well."

"How long have you known him?"

He could see the top of her head over the edge of the screen as he removed his trousers and folded them neatly on the chair, then doffed his undergarments and socks, pushing them into a small wicker basket beneath the same chair. "We met my first day at the Academy. He was my favorite instructor, not only teaching me mathematics, geography, and strategy, but French as well. You wouldn't know it to look at him, but he speaks the language fluently. His wife taught him."

He limped to his side of the bed, placed his cane in the space between the bed and the bedside table, then slipped beneath the blankets. He settled against the pillows behind him, waiting for Shaelyn to reappear and wondered, briefly, when they'd begun to act like an old married couple. "I think you'll like her as well. Honor Sumner is a gracious lady," he said, "and very much like you."

She stepped out from behind the screen a moment later, her nightgown buttoned up to her neck and down to her wrists, which lifted the corners of his mouth in a grin he tried to hide. What pleasure it would give him to undo all those buttons and expose her creamy skin to his view. The material billowed around her as she moved to the small vanity and sat in front of the mirror.

Watching her pull the pins from her hair had to be the most erotic sight he'd ever seen. Her light auburn curls slowly fell down around her shoulders to glisten in a multitude of shades in the lamplight, a sharp contrast to the virginal white of her nightgown. He thought of nothing more than inhaling the fragrance of her hair as he buried himself deep within her warm, welcoming body. Blood rushed through his veins and the grin he had tried to hide, as well as the words he was about to say, simply disappeared.

Shaelyn ran her fingers through the glossy tresses and then began to brush the long, shimmering locks. Remy watched every move she made and when she hesitated in the midst of sliding the brush through her thick, luxurious mane, he noticed immediately.

"Is something bothering you, Shae?"

She turned on the small stool and raised luminous eyes toward him. He saw the concern shining in their violet-blue depths. "It's just a feeling," she said as she put down the brush, leaving her hair loose instead of braiding it as she usually did. "I can't explain it, but I don't think the *Sweet Sassy* will come back."

Her voice held a certainty he couldn't deny, as well as pain and fear. He did the only thing he could do. He moved the blankets aside and then opened his arms wide in invitation. "Come here."

Shaelyn rose from her seat and crossed the floor in her bare feet, coming to a stop beside the bed. He reached out his hand. She placed hers in his and crawled into bed, snuggling within his embrace, laying her head on his bare chest. Her breath fluttered against his skin as he adjusted the quilt to cover both of them. When she spoke, her voice trembled. "I know it's silly, but I can't help it."

"It isn't silly, love. These are dangerous times and you've already lost so much." He stroked her back through the flannel of her nightgown and inhaled the fragrance of her hair, the scent uniquely hers, sending a rush of desire hurtling through him once more, but whatever thoughts he had about making love to her faded as he tried to comfort her. "What makes you think this trip will be different than all the others? Captain Williams and Captain Beckett regard the *Sweet Sassy* as their own, as do Captains Peterson and Simpson. They're knowledgeable and skilled and have made the run to New Orleans several times."

"It has nothing to do with how competent or experienced they are, Remy. Or how many times they've successfully made a run." She sighed against his chest and snuggled a little closer. "In my heart, I know something will happen. Don't let them go. Postpone the trip for a few days at the very least."

"I don't think the general would appreciate that." He continued to caress her back, feeling the tautness of her muscles beneath her flesh. "He's anxious to have his wife and son with him. I can't say I blame him."

"Would you try? Would you ask him? For me?"

"Yes, I'll speak with him. I don't promise to change his mind, but I'll try."

"Thank you." With his promise, she relaxed against him.

Remy held her until her even breathing told him she slept, but he remained awake for quite some time, thinking about what she'd said. Was there merit in her fears? Of course. These were dangerous times as he'd said, and anything, as he well knew, could happen. Anything at all.

● ● ●

A strange, strangled noise woke Shaelyn from a sound sleep before an arm was flung wide, nearly hitting her in the face. Remy's hand slammed into the headboard instead, the sound of his knuckles hitting wood sharp. Shaelyn quickly scrambled out of bed…and out of reach before Remy kicked out.

Deep in the throes of a nightmare, he kept pushing—at what, she didn't know—and emitting the most pitiful, desperate, and heart-wrenching sounds she'd ever heard. He spoke in his night terror as well, calling out names and orders to take cover.

She raced around to his side of the bed and reached out to shake him, but his arms were flailing about so much, she couldn't get close enough.

"Remy! Wake up!" she commanded. Her words did little good. He remained asleep, trapped in a battle she couldn't see or hear… and didn't want to either.

Shaelyn struck a match, lit the lamp on the bedside table and tried one more time to shake him awake, but again, she couldn't get close enough.

Sweat gleamed on his face and his expression showed fear and pain and made her heart ache.

Dear God, what is he dreaming about?

She spotted his cane and grabbed it, grasping it tightly in her hand. She tried speaking his name one more time and when that didn't work, she poked him with the cane. Hard.

He awoke with a stifled scream, his eyes wide and unfocused. And glistening with tears.

"Remy! Look at me!"

He faced her and his expression turned from one of confusion to one of horror. "My God, Shae! Did I hurt you?" He reached out and grabbed her, skimming his hands along her arms as if seeing for himself he hadn't.

"You didn't hurt me, Remy." She kept her voice even in tone though concern rushed through her.

Shaelyn placed the cane back where it belonged and climbed into bed beside him, enfolding him in her arms, offering comfort as he had done for her earlier. His entire body trembled. She laid her hand over his heart on his bare chest and felt the thundering beat beneath her fingers. "What were you dreaming about? You were shouting names, telling them to take cover, to get down."

He drew a deep, shuddering breath. "I haven't had one that bad in a long time."

"Tell me," she whispered as she blew out the lamp, casting the room into semidarkness once more, then held him tight, her fingers stroking through his soft, thick hair.

"We were ambushed, as you know." Slowly, hesitantly, he began to speak, his voice low and hoarse. "We were scouting ahead along a path surrounded by old growth trees and bushes. The path, if you could call it a path, was a ribbon of mud that sucked at our horses' hooves." He stopped and drew in his breath. Shaelyn squeezed him a bit tighter and kept stroking his hair until he continued. "Sunlight dappled the ground through the canopy of leaves over our heads, but cast shadows everywhere else. Mist rose from the earth from recent rains. Everything looked…otherworldly, if you know what I mean. Eerie. Strange."

"Is that when you were hurt?"

He nodded against her and shifted slightly so he could get closer, his arms wrapping around her as if she were an anchor, holding him steady. "There were six of us—myself, the general, Beau Ryland, Landry Hopkins, Richie Streuble, and Big Jim Piper. You would have liked Big Jim, Shae. He could make us laugh about anything." He sucked in his breath and let it out slowly.

"He wasn't making us laugh that day though. We were all on edge and cautious as the path seemed to sink lower. It was like being in a tunnel." His voice dropped to a whisper. "It was so odd…there were no sounds except for the steady thud of our own horses' hooves—no birds chirping from the branches of the trees around us. No animals moving through the dense underbrush."

He shivered, his entire body shaking as if he were cold despite the warmth of the blankets over him and her arms around him. "I didn't like being there. I remember thinking, if I were planning an ambush, this is where I'd do it and as soon as I had that thought, I heard the crack of a rifle being fired. The sound came from my left, I think, but I couldn't be sure because after that first shot, there were hundreds more. I didn't know if there were ten sharpshooters or fifty or a thousand. Bullets came flying from all around us, from all sides."

His voice tightened, as if saying the words had become too painful. "Big Jim got hit first. I saw him fall from the saddle into the mud. He didn't move, didn't make a sound. Then Beau got hit. I heard him scream as the bullet—I shouldn't be telling you this. It isn't for ears as lovely as yours."

"It's all right, Remy," she whispered, "Just tell me. You don't have to be afraid of hurting my delicate sensibilities. I think you've kept this locked up for far too long. It needs to come out, whether you tell me or someone else."

"My men, those I'd sworn to protect, were dying all around me. They hadn't had time to draw their weapons. And I...I hadn't been touched. Neither had the general, and I thought, for a moment, we would be captured by whomever shot at us."

He began to shake again, but he didn't stop talking, as if the trunk where he kept these memories had become unlocked and all the things he'd hidden within would no longer obey the command to stay concealed. "I'd just drawn my rifle when I heard this laughter I'll never forget. I swear, Shae, time seemed to stand still. I didn't see the bullet leave the rifle, but I sure as hell heard it, and then I *could* see it, heading straight for the general. I didn't think. I just reacted. I had to get Sumner out of there, at least protect *him* as I hadn't been able to protect the rest of my men. I'm still not sure how I did it, but I managed to take the bullet meant for him at the same time the bastards shot my horse."

Absently, he rubbed his thigh and she wondered if the scar pained him now. Perhaps it was what was beneath the scar, and he massaged the puckered skin to find some relief. Or perhaps just talking about these horrible memories made him ache. "I remember screaming for the general to go as I fell into the blood-soaked mud, the pain so intense I saw flashes of white, and Soldier Boy fell on top of my legs. I passed out at that point, I think, but I knew I had saved the general and that was what mattered. I could see him ride off between the trees."

Tears flooded Shaelyn's eyes and rolled down her cheeks. Her breath seized in her lungs. She couldn't even begin to imagine what he'd gone through, what he'd seen and suffered, and it hurt, more than she dared to admit. Yet she didn't have the heart to stop him. She had asked him to tell her before she realized how utterly devastating his story could be.

"General Sumner came back...with help, even though he had been hurt. A bullet had found its mark despite my efforts, but the wound wasn't life threatening. By that time, it was full dark. I don't know how long I lay beneath Soldier Boy. Trapped. Unable to move my legs. Pain so horrific, it made my stomach twist and brought tears to my eyes every time I tried."

He sucked in his breath and held her tighter, as if drawing strength from her. "Memories are a little hazy, but I remember trying to push against Soldier Boy's body despite the pain, I remember tasting mud and blood. And I remember bargaining with God. I thought I was going to die, Shae. I prayed for it. The next thing I knew, I woke in the hospital. A surgeon stood next to me, holding a saw, and he was telling me he was going to take my leg, the damage had been too great and I would never be able to walk again."

A shudder wracked his body and his voice deepened and grew ragged. "I begged. I bargained. And I was lucky, Shae. The surgeon listened and I kept my leg, but for a long time, none of us were certain it had been the right decision. I came close to dying so many times…sometimes I begged God for it."

Shaelyn was grateful for the darkness so he couldn't see the tears on her face. "And you relive all that in your dreams?"

He gave a sharp bark of laughter, but there was no humor in it. "That and more, but I don't need to be asleep to see it or hear it or remember it all. With my eyes wide open, I see the muddy path, I see my men, I hear the shots being fired…hell, I can smell the mist rising from the ground. The pain reminds me to be grateful I am alive, and I am grateful. The pain also reminds me of the promises I made and what the experience taught me."

She continued to run her fingers through his soft, thick hair as he grew quiet. They hadn't moved since she'd taken him in her arms, but she had no desire to let him go. The silence between them deepened, but it wasn't oppressive or awkward. Rather, after such heartbreak, such tragedy, the stillness was much needed, at least for Shaelyn. She needed the time to absorb everything he'd said. She supposed he needed it as well—not only the calm after his torrent of words, but the sharing of those memories.

"I bet you're sorry you asked." He broke the sense of tranquility that had expanded between them.

Shaelyn shook her head. "No, I'm not sorry I asked. I'm just sorry you had to go through that. This war is…" She couldn't finish the sentence as her throat constricted, not only because of Remy but for the thousands of other boys who hadn't been quite as lucky as he. She swallowed hard and asked, "Do you know who ambushed you? Was it Confederate soldiers?"

She felt his shoulders shrug against her. "It could have been anyone, Shae, anyone who didn't like the color of my uniform, not necessarily Confederate sharpshooters."

"But you want to know, don't you?"

"Oh, yes. One of the promises I made to myself as I lay in the mud beneath Soldier Boy was to find the men responsible for killing my boys. It's a promise I intend to keep."

The conviction in his voice told her he would keep that promise, no matter what it cost him. She wanted to caution him against vengeance and bitterness, neither of which had worked for her, because here she was comforting—and yes, loving—a man she swore would be her enemy forever, but she didn't detect either in his words. Just a simple promise. "Do you think you can sleep now?"

He nodded against her and admitted, "Only if you hold me."

"I won't let go," she whispered, and held him in her arms as he fell asleep. But she didn't sleep. Her brother's face floated before her. Had he met the same circumstances at Remy? Had someone saved him? Or was he in a shallow, unmarked grave?

Where was he? And why hadn't he let her and her mother know he was safe?

Hours later, her body stiff from holding Remy for so long, Shaelyn fell into an exhausted sleep, though none of her questions had been answered.

Chapter 16

Despite her fears and misgivings, Shaelyn helped load the *Sweet Sassy* for her journey to New Orleans. Boxes and crates filled with bandages and much-needed drugs for the hospital were crammed side by side with ammunition and food for troops so in need. There would be several stops along the way to New Orleans to distribute supplies. As a Southern woman, she wished one of those stops could be for Confederate troops who were just as hungry and in need, but she might as well wish for a cease-fire. It just wasn't going to happen.

Before she knew it, the loading was complete. A core group of young men—boys she had personally trained—who would feed the boiler to produce the steam were on board and already doing their jobs. Steam belched from the stack pipe. The paddle wheel began to turn, water sluicing between the slats, propelling the steamboat forward.

Shaelyn's heart thundered against her ribcage and her throat constricted as she waved to Captain Beckett in the wheelhouse. He returned the greeting then tooted on the whistle.

The feeling of dread had not left her since it first appeared, but Remy had only been able to postpone the trip by one day, though he'd given every argument he could to the general. In the end, she knew there was nothing he could do—and nothing she could do either. One could not stop the world because of a feeling, no matter how much one tried.

Tears blurred her vision as Captain Beckett tooted the whistle one more time and the *Sweet Sassy*, paddle wheel churning water faster and faster, sailed out of view.

She watched for a long time, standing at the river's edge, her gaze glued to the horizon, the lump in her throat massive, until another feeling, different than the dread that filled her, made her take notice.

A shiver wound its way up her spine as if icy cold fingers touched her back. She turned, quickly, and scanned her surroundings. Nothing seemed out of the ordinary. Several soldiers were making their way back to the warehouse, while a few others stood not far away, talking amongst themselves. None paid the least bit of attention to her.

The feeling persisted though—not only persisted, but grew stronger. As she made her way to the buggy parked down the lane, her eyes darted back and forth, searching for the cause of her discomfort.

She saw him then.

Captain Davenport.

He stood next to his horse, a beautiful black stallion he called Vindicator, the reins held loosely in his hand.

And he watched her, stared at her as if she were the most loathsome woman on earth. She saw anger in his gaze, distrust and hostility in his stance. Shaelyn didn't know what she'd done to deserve or provoke such emotions from the man. They barely spoke. When they did, their words were civil, though hardly much more. She shivered beneath his glare of contempt.

"Are you ready to go home?"

Shaelyn jumped and let out a small squeal of surprise as Remy came up behind her and lightly grasped her elbow. She whirled around to face him and found herself drawn by his charming grin. Whatever concern she had over Captain Davenport disappeared in the soft gray-blue of Remy's eyes. "Yes, I'm ready."

When she turned back toward the buggy, Davenport was gone, a trail of dust rising from the road the only evidence he'd been there at all. Curiosity burned in her as Remy tucked her hand into the crook of his arm and escorted her to the waiting conveyance.

She climbed into the buggy and settled herself on the seat. "How long have you known Captain Davenport?"

Remy limped around to his side of the buggy and climbed in beside her. He shrugged as he picked up and flicked the reins. "I met him at the Academy, but I was ahead of him by three years so we didn't have much opportunity to get to know each other." Jezebel started walking at a fast clip, tugging the buggy up Silver Street. "I didn't see him again until he walked into the general's lodgings at our last post, announcing he was the new quartermaster." He glanced at her. "Why do you ask?"

She shook her head. "No reason. He just doesn't seem to be very happy here."

Again, he shrugged. "He probably isn't. A lot of men aren't happy to be involved with the circumstances they currently find themselves in."

"Does that apply to you as well?"

The grin that suddenly appeared on his face made her heart thunder and heat curl in her belly. "What do you think?"

She didn't answer. The words died in her throat beneath the warmth in his glowing eyes. Perhaps when he'd first come to Magnolia House, he hadn't been happy, but now? Perhaps he was. Just a little bit.

• • •

"I've been looking for you."

Shaelyn turned away from the French doors—where she'd been staring at nothing—to see Remy standing in the doorway of the sun parlor, his hand clenched around a wad of paper, though he couldn't hide it all. She sucked in her breath, muscles tensing beneath her skin. The book in her hand, the one she hadn't been reading, slipped from her fingers and thudded to the floor as anxiety and fear knotted in her stomach.

She knew this moment would come, had been waiting for it for several days now. The *Sweet Sassy* was overdue—she should have returned to Natchez almost a week ago.

Remy didn't have to say another word. The expression on his face, the sadness clouding his eyes told her the *Sweet Sassy*, like the *Brenna Rose*, was gone, the men aboard her lost. She'd seen enough telegrams to know one, even crumpled in his hand as this one was. Her heart already breaking, tears burning her eyes, she begged, "Don't say it."

"I'm sorry." He held out his arms. Shaelyn was in his embrace within seconds, holding on to him as if she couldn't let go, taking comfort from his strong, hard body, feeling his heart beat.

His voice shook, "The general just left. The *Sweet Sassy* never made it to New Orleans. It's like she left Natchez and just disappeared off the face of the earth. No one has seen her."

She pulled out of his arms and studied his face. The pain and confusion she saw there reflected her own, but she couldn't give in to those emotions, not now, though she wanted to sink into the floor and release the tears that stung her eyes. Instead, she grabbed the telegram from his fingers and smoothed out the wrinkles.

There were three simple words written by the telegrapher. *Where are you?* It was signed simply *Honor*.

"Anything could have happened." He visibly shuddered with his words. "A boiler explosion. She could have hit a snag and sunk. She could…"

His voice hitched and he stopped speaking. Pain, not physical but emotional, radiated from his eyes and matched the ache breaking her own heart. Since the war began, she'd lost four steamboats. Made of wood and steel, they could be replaced someday. It was the loss of human life that devastated her and she wished, more than anything, this War Between the States would end before more lives were lost.

"Will you be all right?" Concern for her echoed not only in his voice but in his expression.

That caring became her undoing. Shaelyn cleared her throat, hoping to dislodge the lump there. Tears blurred her vision, and she blinked several times, forcing them away as she stepped into his open arms once more. She hoped she gave as much comfort as she received because he needed it just as much.

• • •

"What say you now, Remy? The evidence is irrefutable. She was there. She heard the plans for the *Sweet Sassy* just as she heard the plans for the *Brenna Rose*. For God's sake, man, she knew every piece of equipment we loaded aboard both steamers. Right down to the number of bandages!" Captain Davenport slammed his open hand on the desktop. "She made the boat ready. She could have easily tampered with the boiler so it would explode."

They were ensconced in the study with the door closed after the captain had insisted upon this private meeting. Remy had agreed, although a bit reluctantly. After seeing Honor Sumner's telegraph and acknowledging the *Sweet Sassy* may have sunk or exploded, he wasn't in the mood to listen to Captain Davenport, who lately had nothing good to say.

"You didn't do anything about it before but you cannot deny it now. Your *wife* is helping the Confederacy!"

Remy studied his second in command, noticing, not for the first time, how very little the man smiled and how angry he seemed to be all the time. Right now, Davenport's face held a tinge of redness, but something else too. Something Remy couldn't define.

He said nothing, just listened to the captain's accusations as he limped back and forth, stopping now and then to glance out the window and see the one Davenport denigrated. Shaelyn sat on the bench beneath the grouping of magnolias where they'd shared their first kiss. She didn't look at the house. Instead, she huddled within the confines of a heavy shawl and dabbed her eyes with a white handkerchief, the one he had handed her earlier to dry her tears.

"She's a traitor of the worst kind," Davenport insisted, then reached for the whiskey and poured himself another drink as Remy turned away from the window and the vision of Shaelyn.

"Enough!" Remy shouted, coming to Shaelyn's defense, before he pulled his temper back under control. "She is no traitor, Vince. How could she be? She has never, not once, championed the rights of either the Union or the Confederacy. She doesn't care about this damned war at all. All she cares about is the loss of human life and the young boys who will never go home. She doesn't give a damn about who is right or who is wrong."

He sank into the comfortable leather chair behind the desk and stared at Davenport. "We don't know what truly happened to the *Sweet Sassy*. She could come back to Natchez at any time. She could have simply been delayed."

The captain's face reddened even more and his eyelid took on a peculiar tic. "Ha! You just don't want to see what's right in front of your face. The evidence is there if you would only look for it."

"You're wrong, Vince."

"Am I? If so, then ask yourself why she didn't offer to pilot or navigate the *Sweet Sassy*. She's done so for every other trip her boats have made."

Seen from Davenport's view, the evidence, such as it was, seemed damning, and though Remy didn't want to believe it, he couldn't deny suspicion from creeping into his mind.

Why hadn't she asked to accompany the *Sweet Sassy*? Could Shaelyn Cavanaugh Harte cry over the loss of human lives and still be that devious? Would she sink her own boats to further a cause? She was a woman of the South and yet she'd made her feelings clear on more than one occasion, as he had just reminded

Vincent. It wasn't the color of the uniform, it wasn't North and South or Yankee and Rebel, it was the color of the blood that offended her the most. And damn it, she had told him of her fears, believed something would happen. Had she tampered with her own steamer? Would she go that far?

Remy shook his head and dismissed the thoughts. He'd never believe that. From what he knew of Shaelyn, she didn't have the heart to harm anyone. She had been devastated when he told her about the *Sweet Sassy*. He couldn't deny that.

And yet, once doubt took hold in his head, he couldn't help asking himself—had Shaelyn made love to him simply to deceive him? So he'd let down his guard? So he'd trust her? The thought left a sour taste in his mouth.

His muscles grew taut and the throb of pain in his leg seemed to increase with every beat of his heart. He remained grateful the steamer had been lost before General Sumner's wife and son were on board. However, the loss of men devastated him. Despite his own rules, he'd grown fond of Captain Beckett. Shaelyn had grown fond of him too. To lose both him and Captain Williams, as well as the other men, had destroyed them both.

Davenport put both hands on the desk and stared at him. "You don't have to believe me, Major, but you should ask yourself where she goes in the afternoon. Who does she see? What does she do?"

Remy snapped back to attention and heard the unbecoming whine in Davenport's voice, something he hadn't heard before.

"It's not just to maintain her steamboats. They're hardly ever here anymore." Davenport paused a beat or two then said, "You know I'll have to report my suspicion to General Sumner."

Remy sighed. "No need, Vince. I'll do it myself. She's my wife." How his heart hurt. Granted, she'd never said she loved him. For that matter, he'd never said those words to her either, but he did love her. From the moment she dared to pour vinegar in his coffee, he'd fallen for her, and despite the fact she said she hated him, he knew he'd love her forever. "I'll take care of it."

Davenport finished his drink in one swallow, slammed the heavy-bottomed tumbler on the desk, and rose from his seat. He strutted across the room and paused at the closed door. He turned with a look of triumph he tried to hide, though not quickly enough. "Make sure you do, Major. I will report my suspicions— not only to General Sumner, but to Ulysses S. Grant himself if I must."

Remy quirked an eyebrow but said nothing as he tamped down his rising ire. What could he say? There wasn't any point in arguing. Davenport would believe what he believed and there would be no changing his mind.

Davenport saluted, a half-hearted raising of his hand to his brow, then left the room. Suddenly, the air didn't seem quite so heavy as it had been a minute ago.

A few moments later, Remy heard the heavy pounding of Vindicator's hooves down the drive.

I should write him up for insubordination. At least report him for his conduct.

He rose from the desk, overwhelmed with exhaustion and pain, and grabbed his cane. He moved slowly toward the window. Shaelyn was still on the bench where he'd last seen her. She hadn't moved except to wrap the shawl tighter around her shoulders, but at least she no longer dabbed her eyes. He couldn't accuse her of wrongdoing without proof. All he had right now was Vince Davenport's suspicions. And his own doubts.

Ah, Shae, my love, are you, as Vince believes, a spy? A traitor? Are you helping the Confederacy?

He'd have to find out, no matter how much it hurt him, and do it before Vince made good on his threat.

He'd learn the truth. The whole truth.

And what then? What will you do if she is abetting the Confederacy? What will you do if she is a spy?

• • •

For two days, after Shaelyn hooked Jezebel up to the buggy and started down the long drive toward the road and her beloved steamboat, the *Lady Shae*, the only one left to her, Remy saddled his horse and took off after her, despite the strain and pain sitting in the saddle caused him.

He watched from behind a group of trees as she swept and mopped the decks, washed windows, and polished brass on the small riverboat. Sometimes she'd disappear for a while, stepping into a stateroom with her bucket full of soaps and oils and old rags, only to reappear hours later, the kerchief she tied around her head askew and damp with perspiration. He'd never seen brass so bright and shiny or saw a person work so hard.

He never saw anyone else approach the boat either.

He was beginning to feel like a fool, but he couldn't stop. He had to have proof Shaelyn was innocent so he could shove it in Vincent Davenport's face before he recommended the captain perform his duties elsewhere. He couldn't wait for that day and so, despite his own growing sense of shame, he continued spying on his wife.

On the third day, she surprised him and didn't take Silver Street down to Natchez-Under-the-Hill and the *Lady Shae*. Instead, she snapped the reins a little harder and headed north. Remy hung back, just until she disappeared from view, then kneed his mount.

He followed at a discreet distance until the buggy disappeared. He almost passed the shaded drive hidden behind a wealth of trees and low shrubs, which offered privacy as well, but pulled back on the reins just in time. As he turned and made his way toward the manse, he studied the structure. It was a beautiful home, surrounded by lush green lawn and stately trees.

He stopped a woman strolling down the drive toward him, her arms filled with a bundle of blankets. "Excuse me, can you tell me what this is?"

"It's a hospital."

He nodded in thanks then applied pressure to his mount's sides. The horse walked toward the steps at the front of the building. *A hospital? Is she ill?*

No, she couldn't be. Earlier today, she'd been trading quips with Jock and her mother, her face alight with pleasure, her wit as quick as always. If she'd been ill, she wouldn't have done so. At least he didn't think so. A sigh escaped him. Would he ever truly know the woman he'd married?

He gave a gentle tug on the reins and his horse stopped. Shaelyn's buggy was there and Jezebel munched contentedly on the oats filling her feedbag. Other buggies were there too, and several horses had their reins tied to a long railing.

Warm light spilled from the multitude of windows, and a few men lounged in rocking chairs and on benches on the front porch, taking in some fresh air, blankets slung around shoulders to protect them from the chill. Many had bandages wrapped around various parts of their bodies. Behind several chairs, he spotted the canes and crutches the men used to ambulate outside. Nurses, both male and female, helped other patients.

Remy dismounted, his leg almost collapsing beneath the weight of his body. Pain, sharp and nausea-inducing, shot up his thigh and he nearly lost the lunch he'd eaten. Sweat broke out on his forehead, and for a moment, everything seemed to darken as his head grew very light. He dragged several deep breaths into his lungs and managed to not only drive the nausea away, but the dizziness as well.

He climbed the front steps without falling on his face, despite the residual pain. Several of the men saluted, recognizing the stripes on his uniform, a few standing as they did so.

"At ease." Remy returned the salute. As he walked down the gallery and greeted the men, he took the opportunity to peek in the windows, searching for any sign of Shaelyn. At last, he found her and his heart ceased its frantic pace.

She wasn't ill. Not in the least. He watched as she shrugged out of her plaid jacket and spoke with a man and several other women gathered in what must have been a parlor at one time. A settee, several chairs, and a large desk remained, but that was all.

Shaelyn tied an apron over her dark skirt, rolled up the sleeves of her white blouse, slipped a basket over one arm, and strolled into another room, her skirts swishing around her ankles.

Remy moved to another window and continued watching her as she spoke to a young man reclining upon a familiar army-issue cot. The dizziness returned and the ache in his thigh sparked to life when he noticed the boy was missing his leg from far above the knee down, exactly the same place the surgeons wanted to cut his own leg. Remy sucked in his breath.

The loss of the boy's leg didn't seem to matter to Shaelyn though. She kept a smile on her face as she pulled a chair closer to the cot and sat beside the young man. She reached for the boy's hand and held it as they spoke.

After a few moments of conversation, Shaelyn released the boy's hand and pulled a writing tablet from the basket. She laid the tablet on her lap and for the next twenty minutes or so, the boy spoke and she wrote.

This was a Federal hospital, he learned from the men on the porch in various stages of recuperation. He knew there had been one in the area, he just hadn't known where. Union soldiers filled the beds inside and the chairs lining the gallery outside. Shaelyn hadn't lied to him. She truly didn't care what color a man's uniform was. What mattered was the comfort she could bring to someone.

And there was a great deal of comfort. He watched with fascination as she moved from one man to the next. Her smile never faltered, at least not that they could see, but he could tell how difficult keeping the smile on her face had become—he knew her that well at least.

The heat of embarrassment suffused his face, making him sweat despite the chill of the day. He'd been a fool, a damned fool. Not only for listening to Vince, but for believing him too. How could he have doubted her? His own wife?

"May I help you?"

Remy jumped, startled, and quickly turned to see the man Shaelyn had been talking to earlier, his starched white coat brilliant in the late-afternoon sun. Behind wire-rimmed spectacles, his eyes were bright with intelligence, warm with welcome, and gleaming with good humor.

"I'm Dr. Shaughnessy." He held out his hand. "Is there a soldier you wished to see? A relative?"

Remy didn't quite know what to say as he shook the doctor's hand. "Major Harte," he managed, and cleared his throat as his eyes darted back to Shaelyn.

The good doctor peered in through the window and a slow smile stretched his mouth into an understanding grin. "She's quite lovely, isn't she? The men adore her." His grin widened as he clasped his hands in front of him. "I must admit, I'm quite fond of her as well. She's been one of my best volunteers." His eyes snapped back to Remy. "Her name is Shaelyn Cavanaugh."

"Harte."

"Excuse me?"

"Shaelyn Cavanaugh Harte. My wife."

"Ah, I see." The doctor rocked back on his heels as understanding dawned on him. He studied Remy, but said nothing more.

Beneath the doctor's scrutiny, heat rose up to warm his cheeks and his stomach clenched. Now, not only was he embarrassed, but the wicked tongue of jealously licked at his gut as well—a most uncomfortable feeling.

"Why don't you come in and see what kind of hospital I run?" Dr. Shaughnessy squinted behind the lenses of his spectacles. "I can assure you, Mrs. Harte is treated with nothing but respect and kindness. As I said, the men adore her and look forward to her visits."

Remy shook his head. "Thank you, but no." He turned and started walking away, every muscle in his body taut, sweat dampening his back, his one thought to get away and get home before Shaelyn saw him and learned how big a fool he was.

"Major, you're limping. Are you hurt?"

Again, Remy shook his head. "No, sir." He stopped, turning around to face the man. He thought about asking the doctor to keep his visit here today a secret, but that would have made him look like more of fool...and would reflect badly on Shaelyn as well. After a moment, he simply nodded his thanks and continued on his way, his hand clamping the railing as he descended the stairs as quickly as he could. He climbed into the saddle and kicked his horse into a gallop.

He'd learned a valuable lesson today. Trust his wife.

Chapter 17

Three days later, Remy closed the study doors and limped toward the desk. His men, including his officers staying in the other homes in Natchez and the warehouse, watched his every move. He was aware of their scrutiny as well as their confusion and curiosity, but he had his reasons for asking for this meeting.

He gave a slight nod to Vince. His second in command sat to the right of the desk, long legs crossed, fingers tracing the label on the bottle of whiskey, though he hadn't poured himself a drink. A smug, knowing smile curved Vince's mouth but did not reach his eyes, and for a moment, Remy wondered if his smile *ever* reached his eyes.

It was because of Vince's accusations that he chose to say what he had to say away from the women of the house, especially one woman. His wife. And it was because of Vince's accusations that he had learned something wonderful about the woman he married… and something about himself too.

It still rankled him that he'd actually followed her, hurt him that even after learning she volunteered at the hospital, he followed her the next day, and the next, only to learn that she visited those unable to leave their homes, bringing with her news of the outside world as well as Brenna's cakes and muffins. He watched her bring foodstuffs, a fresh ham and a chicken already fried to golden perfection, taken from the pantry he had stocked, to a new widow and her children, and his heart pounded with pride and something else. Shame. And when Shaelyn came so willingly into his arms each night, that shame and unworthiness flared brightly.

No, if there was a spy, a traitor, within his group, and he was beginning to think there was, he'd find out. He glanced at the men gathered around him and mentally tried to figure out who it could be.

Jock, whom he'd known all his life and trusted with that same life? Never in a million years would Angus MacPhee betray his country. Daniel Bonaventure, with whom he'd felt an immediate bond when they'd met? Again, he didn't think so.

What of the others? Respected officers, one and all. Granted, he didn't know them well, at least not as well as those living in the same house with him, but he believed in his ability to judge men on their behavior, on their attitudes. None of them had given him reason to distrust them.

Except for one.

The man who had done the accusing.

"We're going to look for the *Sweet Sassy*," he announced as he leaned against the desk, his heart beating a steady conviction-filled cadence in his chest. "I find it impossible to believe a boat that size could simply disappear. If she sunk, if she exploded, then I must know." He pinned each one of them with an intent stare. "We leave tomorrow afternoon."

No one said a word, each man giving him his undivided attention, again, except for one. He glanced at Vincent once more, a little disappointed the man still studied the whiskey bottle instead of paying attention to him. "I trust the *Lady Shae* will be ready."

"Of course." The man finally took his gaze from the bottle and glanced at Remy.

He saw it then. Not only saw it—he felt it as well. Hostility. Shining brightly from the dark brown of Vincent Davenport's eyes. But only for a moment, a flicker actually, a tick of the clock so brief, he wasn't quite sure it truly was hostility. Perhaps it was something else. Jealousy?

Remy shook his head and got back to the business at hand. For the next hour, he and his men discussed plans for finding the *Sweet Sassy*.

"Thank you, gentlemen. Until tomorrow then. Dismissed." His men rose from their seats, talking among themselves as they headed for the door. He saw Jock start to approach the desk, but quickly turn around when Remy shook his head and directed his attention to Captain Davenport. "I'd like you to stay."

Remy took his seat behind the desk and leaned back in the soft leather chair, fingers steepled, as his men left the room and closed the door behind them. Vince eyed the door and uncrossed his legs, planting both feet flat on the carpeted floor. He looked ready to jump out of his skin.

Without preamble, without warning of any kind, Remy turned all his attention to Davenport and said, "I think it may be time for you to transfer to another unit."

This time, the hostility shining from his eyes left no doubt in Remy's mind, as Vincent sat up straight, his face taking on an unhealthy reddish hue. He did not raise his voice. In fact, his voice lowered to a menacing timbre. "Why? Because your wife is a spy? Because I had the audacity to tell the truth and say she tampered with her own boats to make them sink. Or explode. Perhaps you're not fit to command, Major." An eyebrow raised and a smirk settled on Davenport's lips. "Perhaps you're helping the Confederacy as well."

Such rancor dripped from his lips that Remy was taken aback. He stiffened beneath the onslaught of malice, his temper flaring at the belligerence and lack of respect.

"That's enough, Captain! One more word regarding Shae and I'll make sure it's the last word you utter in this house. She is my *wife* and you will keep a civil tongue in your head when you refer to her." He reined in his temper with an effort that left him shaking. When had he started disliking the man? Was it after his accusations? Or had it been there all along, going as far back as the Academy? As a lower classman, Davenport had tested his mettle on more than one occasion, but this...this he would not tolerate.

Remy took a deep breath and stared at the man sitting before him. Though his heart pounded and every muscle in his body tensed with the struggle not to punch the captain in the mouth, he folded his arms across his chest and continued in a much softer, yet firm, voice. "Actually, I owe you a debt of gratitude. If it weren't for you, I would never have known what an exceptional, loving, giving woman my wife truly is." At the expression on Davenport's red face, he smiled. His second in command seemed to be having a little difficulty keeping his temper as well.

"Oh, yes, much to my chagrin, I followed her, as you asked. Do you know what I found?" He rose from his seat, grabbed his cane, and started to pace…in front of the desk and in front of his guest. "No, I don't suppose you do. My *wife* volunteers at a Federal hospital, Captain. She visits the sick and infirm. That's right. Our boys in blue. She also gives of her time to the widows and orphans of this war. And I am ashamed for ever having doubted her. As for you—" He stopped pacing in front of Davenport, leaned forward, and lowered his voice even more. "You will leave this house immediately. Find other accommodations and send someone to pack up your possessions. I expect you to be on board the *Lady Shae* tomorrow, but after that, I don't want to see you again. Ever. Dismissed."

Davenport rose to his feet, his entire body stiff with anger. His eyes narrowed as he pinned Remy with a glare. "You will regret this, Major."

Remy straightened, his shoulders thrown back. "Is that a threat, Captain?"

Captain Davenport said nothing more as he turned and stomped across the room. He didn't pause at the study door, simply opened it, walked through, and slammed it closed. A moment later, the front door slammed as well, and Remy took a deep, calming breath.

• • •

Curiosity glistened in Shaelyn's eyes as she lay across the bed on her side, her head supported on her hand. Those eyes had watched him all through dinner and focused on him as he finished dessert, before he closeted himself in the study with Jock. They followed him now, still full of inquisitiveness, as he unbuttoned his shirt and tossed it over the back of the chair.

"Are you going to tell me?" Exasperation colored her voice.

Remy hid his grin as he sat in the chair and removed his boots and then his thick socks. "Tell you what?"

Clearly, she was frustrated with his lack of response, as evidenced by the look on her face and the way she nibbled at her bottom lip. A long sigh escaped her and Remy wanted to laugh. Despite the events of the day, she, and her curiosity, amused him.

"What happened today?"

He shrugged as he stood and started unbuttoning his trousers. "Nothing happened." He glanced in her direction and this time, he did grin. He couldn't help it. She didn't believe him. That much was obvious.

"You know you'll tell me eventually."

He slowly lowered his trousers to expose himself and his steel-hard erection.

"Why not just tell me now and save..." Shaelyn stopped speaking. Her gaze rose to his and her eyes widened, the pupils dilating. Her small tongue darted out to lick her lips and his erection jumped in response to that incredibly erotic motion. He wanted nothing more than to sink himself into her incredibly hot, slick sheath and for a little while at least, forget everything.

Instead, forcing himself to go slow, he moved to the bed and, lowering himself to his hands and knees, crawled along the bottom until he reached her feet. Slowly, he licked the arch of her foot, then sucked one of her toes into his mouth. Shaelyn inhaled deeply, her eyes widening even more, but never leaving his face.

"You're doing that in hopes I'll stop asking questions, aren't you?"

He said nothing as he moved up her leg, pushing her nightgown toward her hips, kissing every inch of her skin as he uncovered her. He loved her legs. They were long and shapely and tightly muscled, especially when she wrapped them around his hips and squeezed. He loved other parts of her too.

Her perfect breasts that fit into his hands just right, her luscious lips meant just for kissing...or smiling that charming smile. Her belly, which wasn't flat, but gently rounded and sensitive to the lightest of his caresses. Her hands. So delicate, yet strong and capable, able to fix steamer engines and bring him to his knees with a simple caress. Her eyes, flashing at him with anger, nearly violet, or dark with passion, seeming almost black, like now.

He had enjoyed getting to know her, exploring her. It thrilled him to know there was so much more to learn.

"Aren't you?" she asked again, but this time her voice was breathy and hoarse. A light push at her hips and Shaelyn rolled to her back, her nightgown now bunched around her waist, exposing her long legs and the fiery thatch of hair between them. Remy settled between her thighs, one hand reaching up to gently knead her breast beneath the soft fabric of her gown, teasing the nipple until it became hard, the other hooking around her leg to reveal even more to his gaze.

"Something like that." His breath fanned her inner thigh. She shivered in response. He smiled as he dipped his head and blew gently on the springy curls at the juncture of her legs. Parting her flesh, he was amazed how slick her soft folds were, how pink and flushed. Her delicate fragrance rose to him, mixed with the musk of her arousal. Again, he blew gently then pointed his tongue and tenderly touched the little pearl that was the key to her release.

"It's not going...ah!" She gasped, then gasped even louder when his mouth settled on that most intimate part of her, at the same time that he eased first one finger, then two, into her tight, welcoming flesh. "Remy!" she panted, her breath coming in short gasps as he worked her, his fingers moving in tandem with his tongue. Her hips bucked upward, rising off the bed as her thighs tightened against him.

Her fingers delved into his hair, her nails digging into his scalp as she tried to pull him closer, her hips moving faster, keeping up with the pace he'd set. Small cries filled the quiet of the bedroom. Remy could feel her body tightening and knew she was close, so close to release, but he wasn't quite ready to give that to her just yet. He slowed his pace, just a bit, just enough to make her beg.

And beg she did. "Please, Remy!" Her voice became a deep moan as her fingers pulled at his hair, bringing his head closer to where she wanted it, her heels digging into the soft mattress as her hips rose higher and moved faster.

Remy complied with her plea, his mouth, lips, tongue and fingers bringing her to the height of ecstasy. This time, he didn't hold back, didn't tease her, let her continue on the journey to find her bliss. "Oh, Remy!" Her deep groan of his name made him smile. She shuddered, her body quivering, the snugness of her sheath pulsing around his fingers, and his smile widened.

He kissed his way up her stomach, tasting the honey of her skin, dipping his tongue into her belly button before moving higher. And all the while, her soft cries of pleasure filled his ears. Indeed, filled his heart to nearly bursting.

He pressed light kisses on her neck, nuzzling that most sensitive spot beneath her ear as he made quick work of unbuttoning her nightgown, a task he'd become quite adept at, and one he enjoyed immensely. He tugged a little and the nightgown moved just enough so he could caress her warm skin with his tongue as well as his fingertips. She felt like silk beneath the rough pads of his fingers. He kissed his way to her breast then captured a pert nipple between his lips, satisfied by her small squeals of pleasure and the shiver that pebbled her flesh in goose bumps and made her gasp.

"Remy…" She said his name, but that was all.

There were no other words, no other questions as he positioned himself over her and then slid into her, seating himself up to the hilt in her hot, moist, still-pulsing flesh.

Home.

The word filled his brain as he moved in her slowly, letting her become accustomed to his width and breadth. Her eyes were open, watching him, the color so dark blue, her irises appeared almost black. Lamplight shimmered on her hair, turning the light mahogany locks into liquid fire.

He moved faster, sliding into her, and marveled at the most incredible feelings coming over him. For a man who needed control, he didn't mind losing the same within her.

Her eyes fluttered closed and she drew in her breath. Perspiration glowed on her face as her hands left his shoulders and smoothed down to his backside, her nails digging into his flesh. By the sounds coming from her throat, the way her eyes flew open wide, she was once again close to reaching bliss. Her sheath tightened around him as her hips moved, meeting him stroke for stroke.

"Come for me, my sweet. Just let go."

"Oh yes, Remy," she moaned as her body convulsed around him, her legs tightening around his hips, exactly where he wanted them. The heat of her drove him wild and he sank into her over and over again.

He could have given over to the feeling of her body pulsing around him, her sheath squeezing him. He could have let himself go and found his own release, but he didn't. Instead, he slowed his pace and rocked into her, his body pressing against hers in such a way, he felt every inch of her. And she rocked with him, her hips matching the rhythm he set as he tasted her mouth once more, swallowing the cries she made.

And suddenly, he couldn't hold back any longer. She was so incredibly warm, so wet, so *giving*, her body pulsing around him, her fingernails digging into his skin. Such pleasure could not be borne and he lost himself in her heat, thrusting into her one last time, filling her with his essence, his shaft vibrating with the force of his release. So amazing was this feeling, he couldn't help the chuckle that escaped him.

With a great deal of reluctance, Remy withdrew from Shaelyn, rolled onto his back, and pulled her close. They both breathed heavily. Remy's heart pounded in his chest and thundered in his ears.

Shaelyn drew lazy circles on his chest, her breath warm on his skin. "Are you ever going to tell me?"

He smiled. He couldn't stop himself. "So we're back to that, are we?"

"Did you think I would forget simply because we made love?"

"I was hoping."

Remy pulled her closer, her warm body stretched out beside his, one of her long legs over his, her thigh touching him most intimately. Her head rested on his shoulder. He smelled the fragrance of her hair and wondered exactly what to tell her. The truth, of course, but how much of it? Should he confess that he'd actually believed Davenport's poisonous lies and thought her a spy? Should he admit he followed her?

No, better to keep that to himself. "I asked Captain Davenport to leave."

"Is that why he stormed out of Magnolia House," she asked, "slamming doors so hard I thought he'd break the glass? Why? What did he do?"

"I have little tolerance for insubordination," he said as his fingers brushed the soft, sensitive skin of her arm. "Except from you. Captain Davenport stepped over the line."

"What else aren't you telling me?"

He kissed the top of her head and drew in his breath. "We're taking the *Lady Shae* to look for the *Sweet Sassy*. I don't believe she just disappeared into thin air. If she sunk or exploded, I need to know."

She inhaled deeply and rose up on her elbow. She gazed at him, her eyes wide and guileless in the lamplight, the lids heavy with expended passion. He felt himself falling into their fathomless depths. "I want to go."

"I...I don't think that's wise, Shae."

"Wise or not, the *Sweet Sassy* is my boat. I want to find her too."

"I know." He didn't want to argue with her or tell her point-blank she couldn't come with him. Truthfully, he was afraid of what he might find, if he found anything at all. He was even more afraid he might not be able to return to her.

In the end, he said nothing, just pulled her closer, his lips finding hers once more, wanting to take as much of her with him as he could.

Chapter 18

Shaelyn listened to Remy's even breathing and light snore as she mentally counted to one hundred again. It had taken a long time, but he finally slept. She rose up on her elbow and studied him. He looked so peaceful. The lines radiating from his eyes didn't appear as deep now as they usually did, and a slight smile curved his lips.

A twinge of guilt tweaked her as her thoughts touched on James, but only for a moment. James was part of her youth, a childish dream she'd once had. What she'd felt for him couldn't compare to what she now felt for Remy. Her Remy. For now and always.

She took a deep breath and resisted the urge to rouse him from sleep so they could make love again. The corner of her mouth lifted. He thought he could change her mind or make her forget everything simply because he made love to her, but he had a thing or two to learn. Her amnesia was temporary and lasted only as long as his kisses.

Does he really think he can stop me from searching for the Sweet Sassy?

She would try one more time, in the morning over breakfast, to change his mind. If she couldn't, well then, she'd just need to do things her own way. She'd been thinking about searching for the *Sweet Sassy* for several days now—actually, since he first told her the news of its loss.

Shaelyn slipped from bed, grabbed her robe from the floor where it had fallen, and left the room on her tiptoes. She didn't take a breath until she'd closed the door softly behind her, crept down the hall, and slipped outside.

A slight breeze full of the smell of wood smoke ruffled the edges of her robe and nightgown. Shaelyn shivered as she drew the robe closer against the chill in the air and ran down the wrought-iron stairs. Her bare feet hardly made a sound. A bright full moon lighted her way to the small shed beside the stable. She left the door open as she slipped inside. The smell of wet wool and soap assailed her as she grabbed a pair of trousers and a shirt hanging from the clothesline within the small room. Clutching the uniform in her hands, Shaelyn closed the door behind her, grateful Private Connors hadn't finished the laundry, and ran across the grass toward the kitchen.

She let herself into the house through the service room attached to the kitchen, satisfied no one had seen her mad dash across the yard. Despite the late hour, she still needed to be careful. Private Connors now slept in the servants' quarters she had previously occupied. She stepped into the kitchen.

"Shae! What are you up to?"

Shaelyn jumped, clutching the uniform closer to her chest, and squelched the scream of surprise as she came face to face with her mother. She hadn't expected anyone else to be awake, least of all Brenna.

Two glasses of milk resided on a tray beside two clean plates, the glass dome covering the cake platter resting beside it as Brenna sliced into the cake.

"Nothing, Mama."

A smile played at the corners of Brenna's mouth and her eyes focused on the uniform in her hands. "Nothing?" she asked, "Now, why don't I believe you?"

"They're planning to search for the *Sweet Sassy*," she whispered, her heart still thumping in her chest.

"I know." Such wisdom glowed from Brenna's face, Shaelyn sucked in her breath, but the question in her mother's eyes remained unasked.

"I'm going with him, Mama. I can't afford to lose my last steamer, but more importantly, I won't lose him."

"And does he know you're going with him?"

"Not exactly. He said it wouldn't be wise."

"But you don't agree with him."

"No, I don't. I…" She shrugged, unable to explain further.

Slowly, Brenna nodded as she transferred the sweet, rich cake from the platter to one of the small plates then licked the icing from her thumb. "You love him."

"Yes, I love him."

Brenna smiled, the corners of her eyes crinkling in the glow of lantern light. She gestured to the uniform with the knife she held in her hand and then proceeded to cut another slice of cake and transfer it to the plate. "So you plan on…what? Following him? Sneaking aboard the *Lady Shae*?"

"Yes."

The smile on her mother's face brightened even more, if that were possible. She said nothing as she put down her knife, walked into the pantry, and pulled her own uniform from hiding. "I'm going with you."

"Oh, Mama, you can't. It's too dangerous."

"Too dangerous for me, but not for you?" She shook her head and a steely determination darkened Brenna's eyes. Shaelyn hadn't seen that gleam of purpose and resolve in her mother in a very long time. "Why? Because I'm older? I'm fragile?" She returned the uniform back to the pantry.

"No, Mama, it isn't—"

"Why?" Brenna stood before her, her head held high, demanding an answer. She raised one eyebrow. "Just as you cannot let Remy go, I cannot lose my last chance either. Jock is captaining the *Lady Shae*," her voice cracked and lowered to a whisper, "and I want to be with him."

What could she say? What argument could she give her mother that couldn't be turned right back on herself? Shaelyn reached out and grabbed her mother's hand. "We are a pair, aren't we? Now all we need is a plan. You wouldn't happen to have one, would you?"

The grin on Brenna's face slowly turned downward. "I hadn't thought that far ahead, but you're a smart, resourceful girl. I was hoping you would have a plan." She grabbed Shaelyn's uniform and tucked it away in the pantry with her own, then picked up the tray loaded with her midnight snack and headed for the swinging door. "By the way, Jock doesn't know I plan to be on the *Lady Shae*, at least not until we are well under way. I would appreciate it if you didn't say anything to him." A conspiratorial grin tilted the corners of her mouth. "And I won't say anything to your husband." With that, she left the room, balancing the tray in her hands.

Shaelyn stared at the door, a bit unnerved, not only because of what she planned to do, but because her mother—her mother!—planned on doing the same.

She grinned as she made her way back up to her bedroom and crawled into bed beside her sleeping husband. She should have remembered Brenna Cavanaugh was made of sterner stuff than what she'd shown the world in the past two years.

• • •

"I'll see you when I get back."

Remy leaned down and kissed her, his mouth sliding over hers in such a way, she felt the tingle down to her toes. Desire flared, hot and tumultuous, making her senses come alive beneath the touch of his lips.

He broke the kiss and took a step back, studying her, then caressed the side of her face, the softness of his eyes reaching deep into her soul.

Does he know what I plan? Does he suspect?

She didn't think she gave anything away, but she'd been careful not to show any emotion other than sadness at his departure. Remy was not a stupid man, though.

"Be safe," she whispered.

He pulled her to him and dropped one last kiss on her lips, seemingly reluctant to leave. After a moment, he let her go.

Shaelyn stood on the top of the stairs at the front of the house as he, accompanied by Jock and Captain Bonaventure, made his way down the steps to where his horse, and the buggy the other men were taking, waited. She was relieved to see that Jezebel wasn't harnessed to the little buggy. That would have put a crimp in her plans for certain.

He tucked his cane into the slot beside his rifle on his saddle and then mounted. He stared at Shaelyn for the longest time, as if memorizing her face, saluted, then nudged his horse.

Shaelyn watched him ride away, her heart thundering in her chest. An overwhelming sadness filled her, battling with the excitement coursing through her veins. She watched until he turned south at the end of the drive, toward Silver Street, the buggy with Jock and Captain Bonaventure following closely behind him.

She took a deep breath to slow her racing heart and turned to her mother. She grasped Brenna's hand in her own. "Are you ready?"

Her mother grinned, a blush turning her cheeks rosy. She'd received her own kiss from Jock as he said goodbye. "Oh, yes." No fear colored her voice as they entered the house, only anticipation.

A short time later, Shaelyn left her room and strode down the hall to her mother's, her boots clumping on the marble floor. Dressed in a private's uniform, cap perched on her head, she knew she wouldn't bear close inspection…she had too many curves, which were somehow enhanced by the blue clothing, but it would have to do. Belatedly, she realized she should have wrapped her breasts to flatten them against her chest, but she was afraid time would fly too quickly and she'd miss her chance to be aboard the *Lady Shae* when she sailed. "Hurry, Mama! I don't want the *Lady Shae* to leave without us."

She knocked on her mother's door, but received no response.

"Mama?" She opened the door and peeked in. The room was empty, no sign at all of her mother, although the gown she'd been wearing earlier lay strewn across the bed.

Stifling a sigh, she ran down the servants' stairs and entered the kitchen, only to stop short and stare. She'd always thought her mother a beautiful woman, but now, clad in the uniform of a Union private, she looked stunning. And if she wasn't mistaken, she looked younger too, especially with her hair curling down her back. Perhaps once the dark chestnut locks were pinned up and a hat pulled low on her head, no one would notice how lovely she was. Shaelyn could only hope.

"I'm ready." Her mother held up two burlap sacks, the bottoms bulging. "I thought we might need food. Some bread, some cheese, and a few pieces of chicken left over from last night."

"Mama, you're a wonder. I hadn't thought about food." She noticed her mother's high color and the slight trembling of her hands. "Are you certain you want to do this? It's not too late to change your mind."

"I won't be changing my mind." A sigh escaped Brenna as she tied one of the burlap sacks with a piece of string. "I've been in the shadows too long, dear. Ever since your father died, I haven't been myself, but seeing Jock, falling in love with him, I feel like I'm finally living again."

Shaelyn swallowed the lump crowding her throat and gave a quick nod. "I'll saddle Jezebel then. We'll ride double."

Within minutes, they were heading north, the opposite direction Remy had taken, and turned down Silver Street, which made a sort of circle around the bluffs and Natchez-Under-the-Hill.

Behind her, Brenna held on tight, arms wrapped around her waist. The burlap sacks bumped against her thighs.

By the time they reached the warehouse, Shaelyn's heart thundered against her ribcage. Sweat, cold and clammy, made the uniform stick to her skin, and yet, she had no desire to turn back. She doubted her mother would either. She nudged Jezebel's sides and slowed the horse to a walk.

A young man tended Remy's horse outside the warehouse, but she didn't see her husband at all—and he would have been easily seen among the young men milling about outside the building. No one's hair gleamed as black in the sunlight as Remy's. No one else had his commanding presence. Was he inside? Already on the *Lady Shae*? All this would be for naught if he saw her before she could board the side-wheeler.

Holding her breath, Shaelyn guided Jezebel along the alleyway beside the warehouse then slipped behind the building and continued on the narrow path to Dixon's livery a few doors down. She slid from the saddle and then reached up to help her mother. Leading the horse by the reins, she stepped through the open door. "Mr. Dixon?"

"Just a minute. I'll be right there." Mr. Dixon's voice rang out from his office. He appeared a moment later, two pieces of bread wrapped around a thick slab of ham in his hand, his jaw and big teeth working the food in his mouth. "Can I help you?" He stopped in his tracks and stared, his mouth opening and closing several times, exposing half-chewed sandwich, before he stammered, "M-miss Shae?" He swallowed hard and his voice rose as his gaze slid past Shaelyn and settled on Brenna. "Mrs. Cavanaugh! What...why..."

"No time for questions, Mr. Dixon." Shaelyn dug a few coins out of her pocket. "I need you to keep Jezebel for a few days."

"But—"

Shaelyn handed him the coins as well as Jezebel's reins, grabbed her mother's hand, and made a quick exit before Mr. Dixon could get his wits about him. She almost chuckled at the stunned expression on the livery master's face as they headed back toward the warehouse.

As they stepped inside the cool, dark interior of the building through the back door, she warned, "Don't look at anyone and don't talk to anyone. Keep your head down."

Brenna simply smiled, from all appearances not nervous, not even a bit. Indeed, she seemed to be enjoying this adventure into sheer lunacy. They tucked the ends of their burlap sacks into their belts then fell into step with a group of men collecting crates of fruits and vegetables, and followed the line toward the *Lady Shae*.

Shaelyn still hadn't seen Remy. She didn't see Davenport either and with every step she took, she prayed she wouldn't see either of them, at least not until the *Lady Shae* was well under way.

She felt it then—the unmistakable sensation that someone watched her. She glanced up toward the side-wheeler's pilothouse, and almost stumbled over her own feet. Remy stood at the open window, posture rigid, eyes narrowed and intent…on her. In an instant, her heartbeat quickened and her stomach clenched with panic. She glanced at her mother, who seemed oblivious to Remy's presence.

Don't recognize me. The words popped into her head.

Ignoring her alarm, Shaelyn concentrated on putting one foot in front of the other, a litany of prayers repeating in her head. She snuck another glance toward the wheelhouse and nearly choked on her own breath. Remy hadn't left his station, for which she was grateful. However, his gaze remained fixed on her, as if he saw through her disguise. His hands were now clasped behind his back, a posture he assumed when heavily in thought, and she couldn't help feeling she'd be caught any moment, especially when he leaned forward and narrowed his eyes.

Her knees went weak beneath the intensity of that stare, and her heart, already pounding, thundered even harder. She stumbled and quickly caught herself, unable to glance to the side to see if anyone saw. To her surprise, her mother drew a little closer and said in an even tone that commanded obedience, "Don't lose your nerve now, Shae. He's not looking at you. He's not looking at anything."

"How do you know that, Mama?"

She shrugged as her grip on the crate of apples tightened, her knuckles gleaming white. "I just know. I've seen that exact same expression on your father's face. Jock's too. Remy may be looking right at you, but I doubt he's seeing you. Just keep walking. We're almost there."

Her mother was correct. The landing stage loomed ahead as they followed the line of men. There were others already on the boat, collecting the crates, stacking them one on top of the other in small columns so they could be distributed to the correct place.

Shaelyn followed the private in front of her and held her breath. No words were spoken as a young man relieved her of her crate. Indeed, she didn't dare look at him. Instead, she glanced at the floorboards beneath her, hunching her shoulders forward.

Beside her, Brenna did the same. And just like that, they were aboard the *Lady Shae*.

"Well, that was easy," her mother said as they strode away from the staging area at a fast clip. She tried to wipe fruit juice from her hands by rubbing them together, but ended up using her trousers to clean it off. "He didn't even look at me."

"We're not out of danger yet, Mama. We still need to make it to the Texas deck without being seen. Or stopped."

On previous trips, the *Lady Shae's* decks had swarmed with men in blue. She and Brenna would have perhaps not quite blended in, but been ignored. This trip was entirely different, as it wasn't to bring supplies or transport troops. There was one purpose for the *Lady Shae* to leave Natchez—to search for the *Sweet Sassy*. Her crew numbered only a few.

It turned out to be surprisingly easy to slip up to the Texas deck. No one paid any attention to them as they stepped into one of the cabins not far from the huge paddle.

Shaelyn crossed the deep-pile area rug covering the floor, Brenna trailing behind her, saluted the portrait of George Washington on the wall, and pressed her hand against the wood paneling above and to the right of the first President. She heard a click before the section of wall moved a fraction of an inch, just enough space for her to slide her fingers in and push the panel open all the way to reveal a small but comfortable room.

Two cots, like those issued by the army, were placed against the walls, blankets folded neatly at the bottom. The narrow space between the cots made maneuvering a little difficult, but it didn't matter. This little hidden room contained everything they'd need for a few days, including a commode hidden behind a curtain. "We'll be safe here," Shaelyn said, "as long as no one decides to take the other cabin for the duration of the trip."

Brenna sucked in her breath as they stepped inside and Shaelyn closed the panel behind them. "What is this? I've never seen this before."

Shaelyn shook her head. "Oh, Mama, you're so funny. You know what this room is. It's where Papa hid the goods he smuggled."

"Your father was a smuggler?" Disbelief colored her tone and her eyes widened. "You mean—oh, I don't believe that for a minute, Shaelyn. You're making that up."

Shaelyn turned in the small space between the cots and stared at her mother. "You didn't know?"

Brenna said nothing, but she didn't have to. The expression on her face spoke for her.

"I'm sorry, Mama. I thought you knew." She took her mother's hands in her own and offered comfort against what had to have been a shock. "I found out quite by accident on a trip to Memphis. When I confronted Papa, he confessed everything. Our other steamers have rooms like this, too. Not only did Papa smuggle goods, he helped people get north before the war. This is where they hid."

"People? What people?"

She winced, realizing that Brenna truly hadn't known any of Sean Cavanaugh's ventures. Too late to take back her careless words, Shaelyn said, "Slaves, Mama. Papa helped slaves longing for their freedom."

Again, Brenna sucked in her breath. "Sean was part of the Underground Railroad?"

Shaelyn nodded, but didn't say another word. Weak sunlight filtered into the space from a small, round window covered with a heavy curtain. It illuminated the expression on her mother's face.

Brenna sat heavily on one of the cots and removed the cap from her head. "Well, that explains so much." A slow smile curved her mouth. "I didn't know, but I should have. Your father had some very definite ideas."

Chapter 19

Boredom was her enemy. Shaelyn wasn't used to inactivity, and she hated being cooped up in the small room aboard the *Lady Shae*. She wanted to be out in the fresh air or standing at the wheel in the wheelhouse, caressing the worn wooden spokes, the wide Mississippi spreading out before her. She wanted to be in the boiler room, helping to shove cords of wood into the boiler to keep the steam coming.

Instead, she blew out a breath, dealt another hand of cards to her mother, and tried to remain calm. She should take lessons from Brenna, who had not once complained. She did, however, make a humorous comment regarding the uniform she wore and how much different the long trousers felt against her legs…and how freeing it was not to be covered by yards and yards of fabric.

As Shaelyn discarded the ace of spades, the same sense of dread she had experienced before settled in her stomach. Icy cold fingers of fear wrapped around her heart, squeezing hard. They skipped up her spine, one vertebrae at a time. She shivered beneath the onslaught.

And then she heard it—the ringing of the bell in the wheelhouse just before the *Lady Shae* changed course. The steady rumble of the engine thumped as the blades of the big paddle wheels shifted into reverse, slowing the steamer down, the shush of water pushed by the blades dying in the silence of the night when the engine shut down completely.

They shouldn't be stopping, as they'd picked up fuel earlier in the day. Judging by the landmarks they had passed, New Orleans wasn't far. A few more hours at the most. Unless…

Had they hit a snag? She hadn't heard the telltale thump and scrape of a log hitting the hull. The *Lady Shae* didn't list to either side as if she took on water.

Had she struck a sandbar? No. Shaelyn had been traveling this river long enough to know the sound and sudden jerk of becoming stranded on a hidden sandbar.

No, the *Lady Shae* went off course for a reason, the engine shutting down with purpose and not due to something else.

Had someone spotted something along the shoreline?

"Dim the lantern, Mama," she requested as she climbed up on a crate for what seemed like the hundredth time, moved the heavy curtain covering the porthole window, and glanced outside. She couldn't see much in the darkness, but she heard the landing stage drop and men running on the deck, their boot heels heavy on the wooden planks. A frisson of fear raced up her spine to settle at the base of her neck.

"What's happening?" Brenna asked, her voice tinged with the same anxiety Shaelyn felt.

"We've stopped, but I don't know why." She climbed down from the crate and squeezed past her mother in the confined space. She tapped the wall panel in the proper place, waited while the false partition slid open, and stepped into the cabin proper. "Stay here. Don't make a sound."

Brenna nodded. The last things Shaelyn saw as the panel slid closed were her mother's wide, fear-filled eyes.

Shaelyn let herself out of the cabin and stood on the deck, her back touching the wall. She took a deep breath, stepped away from the wall, and clutched the brass railing surrounding the Texas deck. Lantern light bobbed in the darkness and her eyes followed the bouncing lights until she saw the reason the *Lady Shae* had stopped. Her heart thudded in her chest as she sucked in her breath. The *Sweet Sassy* loomed south of her, close enough to almost touch, close enough that someone could swing from one of the landing stage ropes and land on her deck! She hadn't sunk after all, hadn't exploded!

Tears stung her eyes even as a storm of questions skittered through her mind. If the *Sweet Sassy* was here, where was her crew? What happened to them? Had they walked into the heavy wooded area along the riverbank in hopes of finding help? A plantation at the end of the dirt path she spied between the trees, perhaps? Why had the steamer been abandoned in the first place? Had she been damaged? Run into a snag?

No answers presented themselves. Her questions only brought more questions, but she had no time to dwell on them. Conversation from above floated to her ears—Jock's heavy brogue and Remy's smooth-as-molasses accent as they stepped out of the pilothouse and started down the wooden stairs, the warm glow of a lantern spilling golden light.

And just her luck, they chose to exit the wheelhouse on the port side. *Right above her.*

Each heavy footfall sounded like a death knell in her ears. If she didn't move, and move now, they'd see her. She glanced around. There wasn't enough time for her to head down to the cabin deck below or run to the end of the Texas deck and hide in the lifeboat suspended over the wooden planks by heavy ropes.

No matter what she did, even if she tried to go back the way she came and slip inside the cabin, she might be seen. Her heart beating a crazy tattoo in her chest, she did what anyone else would do—she plastered herself against the wall beneath the stairs.

And prayed the shadows would protect her.

Fear reached deep within her and left panic in its wake. She didn't move. Didn't dare even breathe, not until Remy and Jock stepped onto the Texas deck and continued on to the next flight of stairs to the cabin deck below. They didn't even glance in her direction. At least she didn't think so. They would have stopped, wouldn't they?

Relieved she hadn't been caught, Shaelyn exhaled and crept out from her hiding place in time to see both men step across the landing stage, which had been lowered, and leave the *Lady Shae.*

Without a thought to the consequences, Shaelyn ran around to the starboard side of the steamer and slipped down those stairs to the deck below. She made it all the way to the cargo deck, but could go no further. There were too many soldiers milling about, waiting for direction. She couldn't cross the landing stage without being seen.

The only thing she could do was conceal herself.

And wait.

Knowing the *Lady Shae* as well as she did, Shaelyn found a convenient hiding place, one that enabled her to still see and hear what went on around her without drawing undue attention to herself. She hunkered down to consider her options, which weren't many to her way of thinking.

Could she be bold and slip unseen into the water? She could swim, but the Mississippi's currents might pull her away or worse, pull her under, if the icy cold water didn't sap her strength first.

As she debated her choices, the decision was taken out of her hands. She watched Remy and Jock cross the landing stage and step aboard the dark and abandoned *Sweet Sassy*.

Something just wasn't right. She felt it in her bones. She wanted to scream at them to get off the *Sweet Sassy* right now, but the words died in her throat.

The knot in Shaelyn's stomach tightened and fear made her draw in her breath as Vincent Davenport stepped out of the shadows of the *Sweet Sassy*'s cargo deck. He carried a pistol in his hand, the bore pointing toward the deck until he raised his arm and aimed at Remy's heart.

Neither Remy nor Jock could do anything, surprise rendering both helpless as another man joined Davenport on deck and came up behind Jock, his revolver pointing at the captain's head. Davenport took a few steps closer and carefully slid Remy's army-issue Colt from its holster. He slipped it into the belt around the waist of his Confederate uniform. "So nice of you to join us, Major," he said, his clipped Boston accent replaced by one dripping in Southern charm. "Don't even think of doing anything foolish. The first man I kill won't be you. It'll be your good friend Jock." He nodded toward the older gentleman, a wicked grin stretching his mouth.

"You bastard," Jock hissed, and received a sharp rap to the back of his head. He staggered beneath the blow and dropped to the hard planking of the deck.

Davenport grabbed the lantern from Remy's hand and raised it high over his head. A mighty roar came from the darkness beyond the river as men poured from the shelter of the trees, their gray uniforms almost white in the moonlight. They clambered over the landing stage of the *Lady Shae*, their rifles pointed at the soldiers waiting on the cargo deck. There was no time for the soldiers to draw weapons, even if the men had been so equipped, or for her to leave her hiding place and rush back to her mother.

Shaelyn shrank further into the shadows and sucked in her breath as the implications became a little clearer. The *Sweet Sassy* had been left where she was to entice the *Lady Shae* to stop. Davenport, who had stormed from the house just a few days before, had orchestrated the whole thing, of that she was certain. But why? Had he known Remy would search for the missing steamer?

Rage radiated from Remy. She could see it in his rigid posture and the set of his jaw, both visible in the glow of the lantern. His hands curled into fists at his sides. Given the opportunity, Remy would strike the man, but he could do nothing now, not with a pistol pointed at his chest and innocent lives in the balance. Neither could Jock, who faced his own mortality as he sprawled on the deck, the revolver pointed at his head shaking just a bit. The Scotsman's features glowed a deep, dark red in the light of the lantern. Shaelyn could only imagine his anger.

"Traitorous bastard!" Remy hissed, his voice low enough to make Shaelyn strain to hear. "It was you the whole time. You who gave up our plans. You're the spy. It was never Shae."

He thought I was a spy?

If the circumstances weren't so dire, she'd have found that fact amusing. Or perhaps not. She had no time to absorb the information or to become upset over it. As it was, she missed part of the conversation. She didn't miss Davenport's cruel laughter though.

"You both played into my hands so effortlessly." Vincent's tone mocked him. "She was perfect. So angry with you, so spiteful, but even I couldn't have predicted you'd marry her or fall in love with her." His teeth gleamed in the beams of moonlight as he began to pace along the deck of the abandoned steamer. "It was easy to make you think she spied for the Confederacy. So easy until I made the mistake of suggesting you follow her. How could I have known she'd become a saint in your eyes?"

Followed? Remy followed me?

"Why?" Remy asked, his voice filled with confusion and sorrow. "Why did you do this? I thought we—"

"Ah, you thought we were friends. At the very least, good acquaintances. There are no friends in war, Major. There are simply people to be used. And you were so easy to use."

Again, Vincent grinned, but he said nothing more. He shifted his weight from one leg to the other, then moved with the speed of a copperhead, bringing the butt of the pistol against Remy's head. Blood spurted from the wound as Remy sank to the wooden planks beside Jock, his cane clattering to the floor. Davenport took the opportunity to kick him—in the thigh—not once but three times in quick succession. Remy grunted with the impact each time and tried to protect himself.

A cry of anguish built in Shaelyn's chest, threatening to spill from her lips. She tamped it down, although her inclination was to attack Davenport as viciously as he attacked Remy. It took every ounce of willpower she possessed to stay exactly where she was.

There was nothing she could do to help him.

Not now.

She couldn't leave her hiding place while the Confederate soldiers led the boys in blue off the *Lady Shae* under threat of death and marched them along the sliver of dark brown path between the trees. Jock could do nothing, either, as Davenport's accomplice helped him to his feet, the bore of the pistol still pressed against his head.

"Get up!" Davenport demanded, his voice a little higher pitched, as if he enjoyed inflicting pain.

Remy crawled first to his hands and knees, grabbing his cane in the process, then slowly gained his footing. He winced, but said not a word. In the moonlight, in the glow of lantern light, she saw the pain etched clearly on his face and the rage he didn't bother to conceal. He whispered something, words she couldn't hear. A threat toward the captain, perhaps? A promise?

"Walk," Davenport commanded as he swiped the cane from Remy's hand then pushed him forward. Remy stumbled and turned quickly, his hands fisted. Davenport took a step back, gestured toward Jock, and warned, "Remember, his life is in your hands."

A white ring formed around Remy's mouth as he clenched his jaw and limped off the *Sweet Sassy*, leaning heavily on Jock for support.

Shaelyn, tears running freely down her cheeks now, watched until they disappeared into the trees before she crawled out of her hiding place and took to her heels, carefully making her way back to her mother. Twice, she had to hide, almost caught by the men in gray as they searched for more soldiers on the *Lady Shae*. By the time she entered the cabin on the Texas deck, a cold sweat dampened her entire body. She wiped the tears from her face on her uniform sleeve.

"Mama," she whispered as she knocked twice on the door, then twice more, pressed on the panel to the right of Washington's portrait and let herself into the room. The dim glow of the lantern offered very little light, but it was enough to see the worry on her mother's face. "We have to go."

"What happened? Why did we stop?"

"Captain Davenport has taken Remy and Jock and the rest of the men." She could have said more, could have told her mother how the captain had held Remy and Jock at gunpoint, but she took one look at Brenna's round eyes and pale complexion and decided not to say a word.

"Davenport?" Brenna whispered, her expression mirroring the horror in her voice. "But why? He seemed like such a nice young man."

"I don't know." Tears blurred her vision as she blew out the lantern, leaving only the glow of the moon's beams coming in through the rounded window to light the room, then took her mother's hand and led her into the cabin proper. "He isn't at all who he proclaims to be. He—"

The thumping of boots on the deck outside the cabin made Shaelyn jump. They stopped just outside the door, moved away a little, then came back.

"Get down!" Shaelyn whispered, and pulled Brenna behind the huge bed that took up so much space in the room, moments before the door swung open.

Shaelyn flattened herself on the floor and peered at the doorway from the space under the bed. All she could see were boots, polished to a high gleam, but nothing more. The boots didn't move, nor did the person who wore them. Shaelyn held her breath, hoping—praying—he didn't come further into the cabin, for then they'd be caught just as the soldiers had been.

How long that person stood in the doorway, she had no clue, but her lungs began to burn with the need to breathe. She could hear her mother beside her and squeezed her hand, offering silent comfort, hoping to gain some from her as well.

A moment later, the boots moved and the door closed. The breath flowed from her lungs in a huff. "Are you all right?"

"Yes. No. I'm—" Brenna's voice trembled.

"Afraid. So am I, Mama, but we can't stay here."

"What are we going to do?"

Shaelyn rose to her feet and drew in her breath. "Follow them."

"Oh, Shae, we can't."

"We have no choice, Mama. They have Remy and Jock and all the other men. We have to save them."

Something happened to Brenna in that moment. Instead of wilting like a hothouse flower, the courage she'd displayed earlier made itself known once more. She smoothed her hair back beneath the cap on her head, sucked in her breath, and stood. "Of course, dear. We must do what we must do."

Leaving the *Lady Shae* proved a bit easier than boarding her. Still, they kept to the shadows beside the thin ribbon of path the men had taken, darting behind graceful magnolia trees, their branches adorned with lacy Spanish moss. It didn't take long for them to catch up to the Union soldiers being driven toward an unknown destination, although Shaelyn worried about her mother. Brenna had not spoken since they'd left the steamer, and her breath came in gasps.

"Do you need to rest?"

"No, keep going," she panted, her voice barely above a whisper.

A sprawling, single-story plantation home came into view, one that bore all the ravages of war. Or neglect. Or both.

In daylight, perhaps she'd be able to recognize where they were, but with only the moon and a few lanterns to cast any light, she couldn't tell. Moonlight played along the edge of the roof, showing the gaping holes, missing tiles, and sagging woodwork of what was once a beautiful place.

Dim light spilled through a window, which remained, by some miracle, unbroken. Other than the one tiny beacon, the house was dark, forbidding, filled with the ghosts of better times. A shiver rushed up Shaelyn's spine. She ignored the feeling as best she could and continued on, dragging Brenna behind tree after tree.

The column of men disappeared behind the huge home. Two separated from the group and went toward the house, one limping badly while the other shoved a revolver in his back, prodding him along. Her heart thundered in her chest as they stepped onto a dilapidated porch and disappeared into the house.

There was no mistaking that limp.

Torn between following Remy or following the other men, Shaelyn kept a tight grip on her mother's hand. It didn't take long to make her decision. "Come on."

A stable, in poorer condition than the house, came into view, light shining from between the huge gaps in the slats that made up the structure's walls. There was something familiar about the stable, but she didn't have time to pay attention to the nagging at the edges of her brain. Shaelyn sucked in her breath as the doors slid open and the soldiers they'd been following were pushed inside, none too gently.

Chapter 20

Shaelyn crouched behind a Gatling gun—possibly one that had once been loaded aboard the *Brenna Rose*—and pulled Brenna down beside her.

Through the open door of the stable, illuminated by moonlight beaming through the holes in the roof, she saw them—not only the soldiers they'd been following, but others too. She recognized many from the *Sweet Sassy* and the *Brenna Rose*. Those exuberant young men were now so weak, they could barely raise their heads. Some sported bruises on their faces. Others showed blood, not only on their flesh but dried to dark stains on their clothes as well.

They crammed into the confines of the old structure, sitting on bales of hay or on the cold, hard ground. Some leaned against the walls, but none stood. A few men glanced toward the door—and freedom—but none appeared ready to escape. They had to be disillusioned and hungry after so much time in captivity. Many didn't move at all, not even when one guard kicked at a young man or when another swung his rifle toward an older soldier's unprotected head and laughed—cruel, heartless laughter that echoed in her ears.

Shaelyn sucked in her breath. This wasn't a prison camp, at least not a sanctioned one, but it certainly had the look and feel of the nightmarish ones she'd heard about. Though tears blurred her vision, her gaze swept the confines of the interior, as much as she could see through the open door, and her breath escaped in a rush when she spotted Captains Ames and Falstead.

Cory Ames, tearstains cutting through the dirt on his face, sat on a bale of hay and held a rag against the bloody wound on Captain Falstead's head. The other man didn't notice. He didn't stir at all, never even opened his eyes. The more she watched them, the more her heart broke. Captain Falstead was obviously dead.

Beside them, offering what comfort he could, sat Captain Beckett, his normally smiling face devoid of all emotion except sadness.

She couldn't hear his words, but she could certainly read his gestures and the haunted expression on his face. A moment later, Beckett stiffened as one of the guards approached and leered at them. The guard spoke. Beckett's face reddened, his eyes squinting as he glared at the guard. The guard kicked both Captain Ames and the man he held in his arms. She sucked in her breath. Beside her, Brenna let out a strangled cry.

The reaction of Captain Beckett to such cruelty was swift. He rose to his feet and grabbed the guard by the collar of his uniform, intention to cause bodily harm clear on his face. He never had a chance to retaliate. The second guard came up behind him and hit him across the back with his rifle. Beckett staggered then fell against a bale of hay.

Captain Bonaventure, sporting an ugly purple bruise on one side of his face, was quick to help Beckett to his feet. The first guard raised his rifle, threatening both men, said one more thing with a sneer of contempt, then kicked Captain Ames one more time before he left the building. He slid the door closed, but not all the way, and not before Shaelyn caught sight of Jock's bloody face as he crouched to the ground and tried to comfort a visibly grieving Captain Ames. For his efforts, he received a blow to the face from the second guard, though with a fist and thankfully not the rifle, before the man joined his partner outside.

The guards, both young but hardened, lines of cruelty stark on their moonlit faces, stood in front of the door, laughing as they threaded a heavy chain through the door handles and locked it, leaving a gap. One guard—Shaelyn designated him "the copperhead" because his hair gleamed copper in the moonlight—pulled a silver flask from his pocket, took a long swig, then offered it to his partner. With a big grin, the other guard tipped the container to his lips and then wiped his mouth on his sleeve before handing the flask back to the first man. They separated then and wandered toward opposite ends of the stable, where they turned the corner to disappear into the darkness.

"We've got to get these men out of here," Shaelyn whispered as she turned around to face her mother, but Brenna wasn't beside her.

Panic struck, making her entire body tremble. A strangled cry built in her chest. Where had her mother gone?

"Mama!" Her harsh whisper sounded loud in the dark, even above the sound of the moaning men. She saw the slim figure of her mother then, her uniform seeming black in the moonlight as she moved quickly toward the space where the stable doors remained open a bit. She didn't hesitate at all before she hunkered down and squeezed herself between the gap and slipped inside. The top of her cap set the chain and lock swinging, but thankfully, no noise issued forth to alert anyone.

Shaelyn had no choice. She stood, keeping to the shadows behind the Gatling gun, and glanced toward both sides of the stable where the guards had disappeared. She saw neither man, but that didn't mean they weren't watching. Taking a deep breath and gathering her courage, she sprinted across the yard and slipped through the doorway the same as her mother had.

The smell hit her immediately. Unwashed bodies, sweat, and blood. Rotted food. Damp wool. Despair. Death.

She nearly gagged, then forced herself to breathe through her mouth. She threaded her way between the soldiers to where her mother sat beside her Scotsman, doing her best to clean his wounds with a lace-edged handkerchief, as Captain Bonaventure did his best to comfort Captain Ames, whose arms were now empty of his friend and fellow officer. Captain Beckett was nowhere to be seen, and she wondered where he'd gone before she dropped to her knees in front of the small group of men.

Jock shook his head at her, his mouth twisting into a frown of disapproval, and yet she could tell by the gleam in his eyes he was glad to see her. "Ach, lassie, what are ye doin' here?"

Shaelyn shrugged. "I had to come."

"And why am I not surprised?" he asked. "I am surprised by this one." He nodded toward Brenna. "Thought I'd died and gone to heaven when I saw her face under that cap. Even a private's uniform can't hide her beauty." He grunted as Brenna pressed the now bloody handkerchief against his wound. "Ye, I expect to find trouble. It's yer nature, but Brenna? I thought she'd have more sense."

"Hush now, Jock," Brenna murmured as she continued dabbing at the blood that wouldn't stop flowing from the cut on his head. "I think you need stitches."

As if he didn't hear her, he said to Shaelyn, "That bastard Davenport took Remy to the house."

"I know."

"Damned son of a bitch." Anger made his brogue heavier and in the moonlight, his features were hard as if carved from granite. "Never liked that man. He always seemed so arrogant, like he was too good for everyone." He pounded his thigh with his fist and then drew in a deep breath. "We'll have to get him out of there. I've no doubt Davenport plans to kill him."

Shaelyn nodded as she struggled to keep her emotions under control. It wouldn't do to become angry or hysterical. Thankfully, she'd never been one of those women who suffered from the vapors. She had to keep a level head on her shoulders and think. She already knew she'd have to help Remy and these men escape, but how?

Though only two guards patrolled the outside of the stable, she knew there were more. A lot more. The little derringer hidden in her boot wouldn't be much good against the rifles the guards carried. It was designed for one shot and would only succeed in drawing attention to her if she should shoot it.

"I can help with whatever you're planning. I'm not injured," Captain Beckett said as he joined them. "And I haven't been here as long as some of the others."

His meaning was clear. The other men, deprived of good food and exercise for so long, were in no shape to help. Even if the desire was there.

"I need to show you something." He helped her to her feet then moved toward the back of the building, directing her to several bales of hay that had been piled atop one another, forming a wall. Perhaps the guards thought the bales were pushed against the side of the stable, like she did at first, but they weren't. It wasn't until she followed Beckett to a space about two feet wide behind the straw barrier that she saw why they were there.

Beckett grinned at her. "I've been planning an escape," he whispered, "but the opportunity had not presented itself. Until now." Shaelyn followed his eyes as he glanced over the bales of hay at the men crowding the structure. A concerned expression came over his face when he focused on Cory Ames, who now seemed lost and so alone without Captain Falstead in his arms. "Truthfully, I couldn't leave without them, and Cory refused to leave without Aaron, so I put my plans on hold." Beckett returned his attention to her, his voice still low, his eyes shining with moisture. "I don't think I could have lived with myself if I survived, but they didn't. I've already lost too much." He took a deep breath, blinked several times in quick succession, then seemed to get control of himself.

"I've been working on this whenever possible." He carefully shifted one wooden plank away from the rest, only by an inch or so. The piece of wood moved easily—the nails had been removed and littered the dirt floor beneath his feet. "So far, I've removed the nails from four planks, large enough for even the biggest among us to slip through."

Shaelyn glanced at his fingers and realized, with no tools at his disposal, he'd used his bare hands to pry the wooden board away from its mates. She could see the raw and shredded skin of his fingertips, the blood under what remained of his previously clean, nicely pared nails. "What is your plan?"

He shrugged and looked at her, his eyes sharp with so many emotions she didn't want to define. "Walk out of this stable and head straight into the woods. Find help." He grinned suddenly. "Under cover of darkness, of course, but now that you're here…"

She could have hugged him. In fact, she did. When she pulled out of his embrace, she said, "Gather the men. The *Lady Shae* is docked and undamaged. We can use her as our escape."

He gave a slight nod and followed her orders.

Stepping out from behind the bales of hay, Shaelyn glanced around the dim confines of the edifice while Captain Beckett started gathering the men together. Those who were badly injured were helped by those who were not, and her heart lifted. She only hoped their escape would be successful and these men would taste freedom, which they so deserved.

As she watched the soldiers congregate around Jock, Captain Ames, and Daniel Bonaventure, she realized one of the officers was missing.

Where is Captain Williams? He should be here.

She didn't have time to ponder, nor did she ask, as Captain Beckett motioned for her and she stepped inside the circle of men. Her mother reached for her hand and squeezed, "I'll keep watch at the door."

Shaelyn watched her mother walk away then cleared her throat. "Captain Beckett has a plan for your freedom." The soldiers before her visibly perked up, hopeful smiles appearing. Several of them inhaled deeply and puffed out their chests.

Captain Beckett quickly explained the simplicity of his plan and finished with, "But we need to do something with the guards before we do anything else." His hand moved to his belt, where his army-issue Colt revolver should have been. He frowned, his dark brows drawing together with frustration.

"How many are there?" Daniel rose to his feet, but remained beside Cory, his hand resting on the other man's shoulder.

"I don't know. There are eight that come in here often," Beckett said, then admitted, "but God knows how many are patrolling other parts of the grounds. I have no idea how big this plantation is. Or who's in charge."

"I say we kill them," Cory said quietly as he wiped his hands on his trousers, trying to remove the bloodstains from his skin. "Kill them all."

"And how do we do that? Ain't none of us as has a gun," a young man, no older than eighteen by the looks of him, shuddered, his face gleaming white in the glow of moonlight streaming through the holes in the roof.

Cory stopped wiping his hands and held them out, palms up. "With these."

"There's been enough death," Jock whispered, his accent deep, his voice harsh. "It'll be enough to incapacitate them and lock them in this stable."

"I saw rope outside by the Gatling gun. We could use that to tie them up." Shaelyn glanced toward the door.

"And gag them," Beckett added. "We don't need them alerting anyone else."

"Once the guards are in here, it'll be up to you officers to lead everyone to safety," Shaelyn said. "The *Lady Shae* is waiting at the river, as is the *Sweet Sassy*. I'm not sure of the *Sassy*'s condition. She floats, but she still may be damaged. The *Lady Shae* is in fine condition though. At least she was when we left her." She glanced at Captain Ames. She didn't like the expression on his face and couldn't help asking, "Cory, can you help?"

He looked at her, his eyes brimming with tears, and swallowed before he whispered, "Yes, ma'am."

"I'll stay with the guards," Captain Beckett offered, "until the rest of you are safe."

"I'll stay as well," Jock said.

"What about the injured?" Someone, a young man she recognized from the *Brenna Rose*, spoke up. He stood beside a boy whose arm had been clearly broken and had begun to heal, though crookedly. A strip of someone's uniform had been used as a sling, but it was his eyes that drew her attention. They glowed with illness, and his skin, instead of being pink and healthy, seemed to have a yellowish cast to it. She resisted the urge to lay her hand across his forehead to see if he felt as feverish and hot as he looked.

"No need to worry, son. No one will be left behind, no matter how ill." Captain Beckett touched the young man's arm gently. The boy visibly relaxed and grinned at his companion. "If I remember correctly, I saw a wagon the night they marched us in here. We could utilize that to get the injured and wounded to safety." He paused, drew in his breath and asked, "Are we ready? Does everyone know what they're to do?"

Each officer nodded, understanding the role he was to play in their bid for freedom, the one and only chance they all might have.

Shaelyn glanced at the officers and pride made her heart swell.

"And what am I to do while you're off seeing to the guards?" Brenna asked as she slipped up to the group of soldiers.

"You're going back to the boats," Jock announced softly as he pulled Brenna closer to him, his gaze caressing her face.

"The hell I will." Brenna Cavanaugh never cussed, but she did now. "You want me to sit there and wait for you, not knowing what's happening. I think not, Angus MacPhee. I can help."

Though she feared for her mother, Shaelyn couldn't have been prouder. If she'd had time, she'd tell Brenna so. She didn't have a chance though. Brenna didn't wait for a response from Jock— or anyone else. Instead, she moved away from the circle and positioned herself at the front of the stable, where she continued keeping watch through the crack between the doors.

"And what will you be doing?" Beckett asked, interrupting Shaelyn's thoughts.

"I'm going to get Remy out of that house." She looked at all of them, pinning each one with an unflinching stare. "And don't try to talk me out of it."

Beckett grinned. "I wouldn't dream of it. I only ask that you wait until the guards are all in here."

"And wait for one of us to help you," Jock suggested.

"I'll consider it."

• • •

Pain.

Unrelenting. Excruciating pain. Not only from his leg, thanks to Davenport, but from his heart and mind as well. The sure knowledge he'd been betrayed by a man he'd trusted left a sour taste in his mouth and a hole in his heart. He couldn't understand why. Had countering Davenport's lies about Shae, forcing him to leave Magnolia House, precipitated this treachery?

No. Judging by how well everything had been set up, there had to be other underlying reasons for Davenport to be this disloyal. Remy doubted he would ever learn the truth.

There was one saving grace to the situation he found himself in. Shaelyn wasn't here with him. She was home. Safe. Unaware of the danger that had been residing at Magnolia House right under both their noses and the circumstances he found himself in now.

He was thankful she hadn't argued with him when she begged to come along and he'd denied her request.

He closed his eyes, and saw her as he would always see her… violet-blue eyes grown darker with passion and twinkling with just a hint of mischief, her hair spreading out on the pillow as she lay back in the bed they shared, beckoning to him, offering comfort and relief. To sink into the solace she promised, to…

Remy shook his head, erasing the image. He sucked in his breath and concentrated on not passing out, refusing to surrender to the blessed darkness overshadowing his mind. He had to remain awake and alert and figure a way out of this. But what? One of his eyes had swollen nearly shut, and the vision in the other kept blurring. His hands were tied behind his back. Tight. Numbness crept up his arms and already his shoulders ached from the unnatural position. Even if he wasn't bound, he doubted he had the strength to crawl to freedom, let alone stand.

He watched Davenport flit around the room, building the fire, laying out bread, cheese, and fruit. He even produced a bottle of Harte's Private Reserve. Someone was expected. Someone important, judging by the way Davenport kept peering out the window.

The captain—no, traitor—turned away from the window and glanced at Remy. Coldness radiated from his eyes, the black eyes of a snake, as he sauntered closer.

Why had he never noticed before?

Remy prepared himself for another kick, another punch, but neither came. Instead, Davenport hunkered down and grinned. Remy wished he hadn't. There was nothing friendly in Davenport's smile. "Do you know how lucky you are?"

"Lucky?" Remy swallowed hard and tasted blood. "I'm not feeling so lucky right now."

Davenport chuckled. "No, I don't suppose you would, but I swear, Remy, you have the nine lives of a cat. Do you know how many times you should have died?"

"At least once."

"Oh, the ambush? That, actually, was a mistake." He grinned a bit sheepishly, as if he should be forgiven a mistake that cost men their lives. "You weren't supposed to get shot that day, but things got a little out of hand. My companions saw blue and that was enough for them to start firing." He shrugged, the gray of his uniform stretching across his broad shoulders and wide chest.

Remy's stomach twisted as the betrayal deepened. "You tried to kill me." He grit his teeth, clenching his jaw so tight he saw flashes of white behind his eyes.

Davenport shrugged. "I wasn't aiming for you. I was actually trying to kill General Sumner, but you had to go and make yourself a hero." He chuckled and shook his head. "Both of you were getting too close to our headquarters. You had to be stopped." He rose, standing tall. "It was that simple."

Remy strained his neck to look up into Davenport's smug face. "Why? Why are you doing this?"

"It's nothing personal, Remy. Not in the least. I have nothing against you." His shrugged again as his attention was drawn to the window.

"Not personal?" Remy gestured to his thigh with a nod of his head. "This feels pretty personal to me."

"I've been given orders, Remy, and I have every intention of following through on those orders. You, above all others, should understand that." He began to pace, going back and forth between the window and where Remy rested on the floor, his hands clasped behind his back in a perfect imitation of General Sumner. "There were days when looking at you, having to take orders from you, made me physically ill." He turned and grinned. "But it was all worth it, as there were days when I could rejoice in your suffering. I will be greatly rewarded for my service."

"Rewarded?" Remy couldn't keep the contempt from his voice.

If Davenport noticed the derision, he didn't act upon it, for which Remy was grateful. He kept pacing and speaking. "When this war is over and the South rises again, there'll be new opportunities for me. I will have power and authority. Control. No more will I take orders from someone who is not my equal."

"And that day is coming sooner than you realize, Davenport," a man said as he stepped into the room. He wore a Confederate general's uniform, complete with gold epaulets and a gold-handled saber hanging from the scarlet sash around his waist. As he stood at the threshold, he removed his leather gloves and waited, expectantly, for Davenport to salute him. The captain didn't disappoint.

"Sir!" Davenport straightened, puffed out his chest, and brought his hand up to his brow, showing respect for the general. "My apologies, sir. I did not hear your horse. I would have…"

Remy watched the exchange. He didn't recognize the general, but he acknowledged the carriage and bearing of one who was used to giving orders and not taking them.

"At ease, Davenport," the general commanded as he strode across the room to the blazing fire. He tossed his gloves on the table and then held his hands out to the roaring flames. "No harm done," he said over his shoulder, then turned and faced Remy.

"Ah, good evening, Major Harte. It's a pleasure to finally make your acquaintance. I've heard a great deal about you." He removed his saber, placing it on the table next to his gloves as he spoke. "My name is James Brooks, *General* James Brooks, though some call me the Gray Ghost." He held out his hands to encompass the room. "Welcome to my humble abode."

Remy studied the man who had once been the fiancé of his wife, his heart thundering in his chest with the knowledge he'd never see Shae again. Having made the acquaintance of the Gray Ghost, he doubted he would be permitted to live.

Chapter 21

Shaelyn stood at the back of the stable, just inside the space where the planks had been, and watched Jock return with another guard. She recognized the young man as the one who had so cruelly kicked at Captain Ames. A small smile of satisfaction twitched at the corner of her mouth as Jock dragged the younger man across the dirt by his shirt collar.

The boy certainly didn't notice. He was unconscious. By the time he awoke, he'd be no threat to anyone.

There had been so many more guards than Beckett had realized. Aside from the eight who frequently came into the stable, there were ten more. All were now under the watchful eye of Captain Beckett, who proved to be most restrained and actually quite polite in his treatment of the men who had abused all of them.

After they had captured and bound the guards, Daniel and Cory, armed with the rifles and revolvers confiscated from those men, led the soldiers out of the back of the building and into the woods. Shaelyn could no longer see them.

She prayed they'd make it to the steamers before anyone realized what was happening. The wounded, the ill, and those too weak to make the journey to the river, waited until it was their turn.

She turned around and watched her mother comforting those boys, her soft words bringing solace and hope. Shaelyn's gaze drifted to Jock, tying the hands of the guard he'd just dragged into the stable, then to Randall Beckett, who sidled up to the space where the doors didn't quite meet.

She couldn't wait any longer. Neither man paid attention to her. Seeing her opportunity, she took it. With a deep breath and a prayer, Shaelyn slipped through the opening and disappeared into the moonlit night.

She darted behind a tree. They may have rounded up eighteen guards, but that didn't mean there weren't more patrolling the grounds. Reasonably assured she was alone, she ran toward the house, her footsteps light despite the heavy boots on her feet.

Something tripped her. One moment she was running, pulling air into her lungs, the next, she landed on her hands and knees, hard. Remarkably, there was no pain. Something soft had cushioned her fall. It only took a moment before she realized she'd hadn't fallen on a pile of compost, but on a person. Her nose nearly touched his as she stared into his face.

Captain Williams. He'd been shot. Moonlight filtering through the trees illuminated the perfectly round hole in his forehead. His eyes were wide open and stared, unseeing, at the canopy of limbs above him.

She squelched the scream rising from the depths of her being as she scrambled to her feet. Bile rose in her throat, threatening to choke her. She took a deep breath, but her mouth watered and filled with the taste of metal.

She wouldn't vomit. She wouldn't.

She concentrated on just breathing, said a silent prayer, for there was nothing more she could do for Captain Williams, and forced herself to move on.

Several lights now glowed from the windows of the plantation house as Shaelyn crawled onto the porch. The scent of wood smoke filled the air. She held her breath, afraid to make a sound, as an armed guard came into view. To her relief, he paid her no mind. All his attention was directed toward the cigar he tried to light. She ducked under a small table between two chairs on the veranda until he succeeded. Smoke billowed around his head before he moved on, blending into the shadows at the opposite end of the house.

Shaelyn let her breath escape and then closed her eyes for a moment and tried to still the frantic beat of her heart.

What am I doing? This is insane!

The thoughts screamed through her mind as she crawled along the porch on her hands and knees, yet it was too late to turn back, too late to consider another plan. She came closer to a window, which was open just a bit. She clearly heard the voices drifting into the night. Two of them. One was Davenport. She'd recognize his superior tone anywhere, though the clipped New England accent had been replaced by the silky drawl of the South.

The other man in the room replied to Davenport's comment. Her stomach clenched.

That voice! She knew it as well as she knew her own.

James.

She peeked in through the window, through the dirty lace curtain covering the glass, which made everything hazy, and saw him. He sat in a chair beside the fireplace, his long gray-clad legs stretched out before him. Her eyes drifted upward to his face. A nicely trimmed dark beard now covered his chin and rose up on the sides of his face to meet his sideburns. Her gaze rose and she inhaled. There was no mistaking the distinctive green of his eyes, but why had she never noticed the cruelty in them before? Or his stern countenance? Her heart banged against her ribcage and her palms grew damp as the truth hit her with all the subtlety of an explosion.

Shaelyn flattened herself against the wall and tried to draw air into lungs that seemed unable to expand.

James Brooks, the man she'd promised to wait for, was the Gray Ghost. The scourge of the Union Army.

What happened? How had he become the man behind the taking of her steamers, the destruction of train rails and telegraph wires? She didn't remember him as being particularly sympathetic to the Southern cause. Actually, he'd enlisted in the Union Army as a lark. He said the blue of the uniform emphasized his good looks. She thought he'd been teasing her. At the time, he'd said with his money and education, he'd be an officer for certain.

At least that part was true. He was an officer. The insignia on his uniform declared him so. Yet, she couldn't believe he had the blessings of the Confederate Army. Then again, perhaps he did. She'd heard of other men, guerilla fighters, they were called, who ambushed Union patrols and supply convoys and delighted in creating havoc and fear wherever they went. The Confederates were not the only ones to employ such methods. The Union army had guerilla fighters too.

If James was here, then where was her brother, Ian? Had he traded in his blue uniform for gray as well? Was this why she hadn't heard from either of them in so long?

And Remy? Where was Remy?

She peeked in through the window one more time, gathering her courage, though fear made her tremble. This time, her gaze moved beyond the man so comfortably ensconced in a chair. Davenport, the traitor, looking much too smug for his own good, refilled James's glass from a bottle of whiskey on the little side table. Amazingly enough, the whiskey was Harte's Private Reserve. She recognized the silver and black label from Remy's family.

James grabbed the glass and drank deeply, finishing all of the liquor in one swallow. "At least he makes a damn fine whiskey." He put down the glass and rose to his feet, directing his comment to Davenport as he turned and faced the man huddled against the wall.

Tears instantly filled her eyes as she followed Davenport's progress across the room.

Remy!

Her heart sank at the same time anger coursed through her veins. He looked horrid, his face swollen, his arms behind his back at an unnatural angle, his legs twisted, but she didn't think broken.

"Take him in the other room. I'm tired of looking at his face." James strolled to the door as if he hadn't a care in the world, then stopped with his hand on the knob. "When you're done with him, take care of my horse." He stood still for a moment, his gaze traveling over Remy before he smiled, a slick smile filled with contempt that made Shaelyn's fear intensify. "Tomorrow, as an example to the other men, he'll be hanged."

"Yes, sir!" Davenport snapped to attention, then quickly obeyed orders as James left the room. "On your feet, soldier!"

"Go to hell!" Remy snapped, his voice strong despite his obvious pain. He received a kick to his injured leg for his efforts.

Shaelyn squelched the cry of anger that rose in her throat. Beneath the rainbow of bruises on his face, he blanched, and even from her position at the window, she could see sweat bead on his forehead, but he uttered not a sound. He seemed to draw strength from the pain.

"Get up!" Davenport grabbed him by the arm and pulled upward. Remy didn't buckle, but she saw his agony, felt it as if it were her own as the captain half-dragged him into the other room.

"Kill me now." The words were barely audible, but she heard them.

Oh, Remy. Don't provoke him. She wanted to scream the words at him.

"Don't tempt me, Harte," Davenport said, then smiled, the same nasty smile she'd grown to hate. "The general wants you to hang in the morning so that's what'll happen."

Shaelyn sank to her hands and knees and crawled, once more, along the porch, pressing herself against the side of the house, and followed their progress. She came upon another window. This one wasn't merely open. The glass had been shattered, the lacy draperies partially hung outside and billowed with the breeze. She didn't dare take a peek though. She heard Remy's grunt as he was thrown to the floor and Davenport's laughter, the sound making her shudder with revulsion and fear.

"Don't even think about trying to leave. The guards are armed and won't hesitate to shoot you. I, personally, prefer to see you hang in the morning, so don't disappoint me." He chuckled before he took his leave, slamming the door behind him. She heard the twisting of the key in the lock then nothing but receding footsteps and blessed silence. Why did he bother to lock the door when the window had no glass? Did Davenport want Remy to try to escape? And get killed by one of the guards? Or did he think, even given the chance, Remy couldn't escape due to the fact he'd been hurt?

She shook her head. Davenport's reasons didn't matter in the least. The glassless window was to her advantage and she wasn't about to question her luck. All she had to do was get Remy out of there.

Rising to her feet, Shaelyn peered in through the window and studied the layout of what was once a formal dining room. Candles flickered in the wall sconces on either side of a fireplace. An empty china hutch hugged the wall on the opposite side of the room and matched the table in the middle. Other than those items, the room was empty...except for Remy, who had slowly gained his footing, but he only stood for a moment before he collapsed to the floor with a surprised grunt.

Shaelyn glanced down to the end of the porch, looking for the guard she had seen before. Satisfied he wasn't around, she made sure no one else was in the room with Remy, then climbed over the windowsill into the plantation house.

"Remy," she whispered, drawing his attention.

He looked up through swollen eyes and her heart thumped painfully in her chest.

"Shae?" He slurred her name. His lip had been split and was now distended to twice its normal size.

"Yes." She tiptoed closer.

"Good God! I thought you were home, safe at Magnolia House. What in the name of all that's holy are you doing here?" He licked his lips and winced. "Don't you realize the danger you're in? You have to go. You have to go now!"

His left eye was completely closed, the skin puffy and bearing the colors of red and purple. His right eye wasn't much better. Could he see at all?

"I can't go. What's more, I won't. I'm going to save your miserable hide whether you like it or not." She dropped to her knees beside him. "Turn a little so I can untie you."

"Why, Shae? Why would you do that? I thought you hated me."

"Shh. Keep your voice low. We don't need Davenport coming back in here, nor do we want to draw the attention of the guards." She tried to work the knot, but her fingers were clumsy and the twisted rope tight, unlike any knot she'd ever seen. She wished she had taken one of the knives they had confiscated from the guards, but wishes were useless right now. She did have the little derringer, but that wouldn't do much good for his bonds. "For the record, I don't hate you. How could you think such a thing?"

How could he still think she hated him? They shared a bed... and passion. Hadn't her actions spoken louder than words?

Despite the obvious pain it caused him, he turned his head. The corner of his mouth lifted. "You told me so, Sassy. You stood right in front of me on the day we wed and told me you'd hate me until you drew your last breath."

Shaelyn shrugged as she picked at the twisted loops of the rope. "I lied. I was angry. You were angry. I knew you didn't want to marry me and only did so because you were forced."

"Yes, I was angry at the time, but Shae, don't you realize that I never do anything I don't want to do? If I hadn't wanted to marry you, I wouldn't have."

His statement confused her. "What are you saying? You would have married me anyway?" She stared at him, trying to see truth in his eyes, but they were too swollen, and they really didn't have time for this discussion right now. Davenport could come back at any moment. So could James. Or a guard they hadn't found. "Wait. Don't answer that. We've got to get out of here."

Beneath the blood and bruises on his face, his pallor bordered on a sickly greenish-white and he huddled within himself. The pain in his thigh must have been intense. She glanced at his trouser leg when he winced and noticed the blood staining the fabric. "Can you walk if I help you?"

He shrugged. "I don't know. Davenport kept kicking me on our short journey here." The sadness of the ultimate betrayal reflected in his voice. "It was him, Shae. The whole time. Right under my nose. It was Davenport who almost cost me my life, who staged the ambush that killed so many men." His voice grew hoarse as he swallowed several times. "He nearly convinced me you were a spy when all the time, he was supplying the Gray Ghost with information. I should have known. I should have stopped him. How could I let him fool me so completely?"

The heartbreak in his voice was nearly her undoing, and yet she couldn't give in to the devastation staking claim to her. She had to get him out of here.

"Don't think about that now, Remy." A frustrated sigh escaped her. "I can't get this blasted knot untied!" Her voice trembled just as much as her fingers, and exasperation made it worse. "I'm just making it tighter."

"Take a deep breath, Shae," he suggested, and did so himself, drawing air deep into his lungs. "I didn't have a hope in hell of escaping before I saw you, but everything is different now. Try to stay calm. We'll do this together."

Shaelyn, taking his advice, took a deep breath and then another. Despite the circumstances, his voice soothed her and his belief in her compounded the feeling.

"About the Gray Ghost—"

"He's James," she finished for him. "I know. I saw him. I just don't understand why he's doing this. He's not the same man I knew."

"War changes people," Remy said. "It can bring out the best in some people, like bravery and courage. For others, it brings out the worst. Davenport is a great example." Remy grunted as she pulled on the ropes around his wrists, the action tugging on his shoulders.

"I'm sorry," she whispered, and concentrated on breathing and working the knot. Finally, she could feel it loosening just a bit.

"Well, isn't this sweet?"

The voice came from just inside the doorway.

James.

Shaelyn stiffened and then jumped to her feet to confront the man she'd once thought she loved. They had shared some wonderful times, but now her heart hurt to look at him and her palm itched to connect with the side of his face. She said nothing though. The words in her brain tumbled too quickly, and truthfully, she didn't know where to begin or how to tell him what she thought of him.

"So lovely to see you, Shae. Or should I call you Mrs. Harte?" He came further into the room, his smile as wide and charming as it had always been, but beneath the calm veneer, she sensed triumph and arrogance, anger and hatred.

He tilted his head as he gazed at her and fondled the key in his hand. She could see the lights dancing in his eyes. The sight filled her with panic. Her hands clenched at her sides.

"You seem surprised. Did you think I wouldn't find out you married the major here?" He shook his head, his smile never leaving his face. "Tsk, tsk. You should have waited for me, Shae. We could have done so much together."

James grinned at her as if neither of them had a care in the world, and the desire to hit him grew, overwhelming her. She'd like nothing better than to bring him to his knees somehow and make him feel the pain Remy felt—she felt—but she couldn't seem to move or make her arms and legs obey the silent commands of her mind, not even to retrieve the derringer from her boot.

He held out his hand and came closer still. "Come, my dear. We have many things to discuss."

"Leave her alone, Brooks!" Remy struggled against the bonds that held him, his voice rising with fear and rage. "She has nothing to do with this."

"On the contrary, Major, she is here. She broke into my home—"

Surprised, Shaelyn couldn't stop herself from gasping. They were here? At Brookshire, the plantation where James grew up? What had happened to the lovely home she'd visited?

"—with the intention of freeing my prisoner. She deserves to be, at the very least, reprimanded." He grinned again. Shaelyn's stomach clenched and bile rose to her throat, threatening to choke her with its acidic bite.

"It's me you want, Brooks. Not her."

"Oh, you are so very wrong about that, Major." James's voice lowered to almost a whisper. "I do want her. I've always wanted her." One dark eyebrow rose, giving him a sinister appearance as he focused on her. "If you want him to live, you'll come with me."

"No, Shae! Don't go with him."

Shaelyn had no other option. James would keep his promise to have Remy hanged in the morning if she didn't go with him, but perhaps, if she did as he asked, Remy could be saved. She'd take that chance, however slim.

She slipped her hand into his and allowed him to escort her from the room. The last thing she heard was Remy struggling against the ropes around his wrists and the anguished cry escaping from his swollen lips.

"Don't touch me!" Shaelyn snatched her hand from his as soon as they entered what had once been the formal parlor at Brookshire. The urge to slap the smug expression from his face still made her palm itch, but she couldn't follow through on the impulse. She had to remain calm and think of the consequences of her actions *before* she acted. To do less would be more than foolish. Remy's life—and her own—hung in the balance. Fortunately, he didn't seem to take offense. He stepped away from her without a word; his smile, once so charming, now made her ill.

"What happened to you, James? Why have you done this? And where is Ian?"

James shrugged as he took his seat next to the fireplace. His eyes followed her as she paced the room. Despite the flames dancing behind the grate, the room felt cold, but perhaps the chill had nothing to do with the temperature and everything to do with the man sitting so regally in his wingback chair. "Do sit, Shae. You're making me dizzy watching you pace back and forth."

He poured himself a drink, then poured one for her and held it out for her. Shaelyn refused to take the glass. Instead, she asked again, "Where is Ian?"

"I don't know." He placed her glass on the table beside him, without anger, in complete control of himself, then took a sip from his own. "Honestly, my dear, we may have marched off together, but we were separated shortly after. The last I saw of Ian, he was joining a troop heading toward Washington. Beyond that, I know nothing."

Relief surged through her, but it was short-lived. Did she dare believe him? Or was Ian dead like Captain Williams? She tried to keep her anger and her fear at bay—the task seemed next to impossible. She wanted to know why Remy had been singled out, sentenced to be hanged, but was afraid to know the answer. Was it because of her? Was James taking revenge on Remy because she'd married a Union officer? She didn't dare ask those questions either.

"What of you? How did you come to be the Gray Ghost?" Tears sprang to her eyes. She couldn't help it…this was the young man she had once thought she loved.

"Because I could," he said simply.

Shaelyn drew in her breath and glared at him, her entire body shaking. "Because you could," she repeated slowly, as if she hadn't a brain in her head and needed him to explain it to her one more time, or two more times, or however many times it took before she understood.

"Look around you, my dear." He swept his hands to encompass the room and laughed, the bitterness undeniable. "What do you see?"

She did as he asked, and her heart hurt. She remembered what a magnificent place Brookshire had been once upon a time, and the long, slow summers filled with barbecues and grand balls where friends and neighbors came from as far away as St. Louis or New Orleans to attend. To see what it had become devastated her, as it must devastate him—every time he looked around.

"I marched south with my Union brothers, taking my orders, burning crops and plantation homes—until I came to my own home…" Sadness tinged his voice now, the bitterness gone, and he shook himself free of his recollections. "And saw what had been done to it. The only reason Brookshire wasn't burned to the ground is because the Yankees thought they could make use of it, which they did."

He stopped speaking for a moment and swallowed, his Adam's apple bobbing as he did so. When he resumed, his voice had turned hard, the bitterness back. "They burned the furniture, I would imagine to keep warm. Why they broke the windows, I haven't a clue. That just defeated the purpose of burning the furniture. They set my horses, cows, and chickens free or took them, I'm not sure which."

His gaze rose to hers and Shaelyn sucked in her breath. His eyes held a faraway quality then, as quickly as she saw emotion, the wistful expression vanished, replaced with an iron-hard determination. "I was so young and foolish, Shae, and stupid, thinking…never mind what I thought. I am a Southern man, born and bred, and yet I joined the Union Army. Why? Why would I do that? So I could wear the uniform of an infantryman? So I could burn the homes of my friends and see the betrayal in their eyes?" He shook his head. Sadness reflected on his face and for a moment, he seemed so weary and disillusioned, so *hurt* by all of it.

"It didn't take me long, actually took me no time at all, to realize I could no longer blindly follow the orders of men who knew nothing of the Southern way of life—my life. Do you realize there are men in positions of power who delighted in the destruction of the hard work of others? Men, like my commander, who took utter joy in causing pain." A grim smile curved his lips. "He'll never know joy again. I saw to that." He glanced around the room. "I found others who thought as I did, gathered them all together. I became the Gray Ghost and this…this is my legacy. A house falling down upon itself and land that no one will work."

"Where are your parents?" Shaelyn asked as she moved slowly toward the door they'd come through, her back against the smooth wood, her hand reaching for the knob.

"Gone." He shrugged. "Away from the fighting and the memories. Colorado, I heard. I can't say I blame them. I have nothing left, not even you." Something in his voice changed, grew deeper, harder. His attitude changed as well, and he became more arrogant and self-important. "But, as the Gray Ghost, I have power, I have authority. The Union Army fears me. Civilians fear me too." He swirled the remains of the whiskey in his glass before he stood suddenly and tossed the glass into the fireplace. The crystal shattered with a brilliant flare of light, the alcohol feeding the flames along the logs. "I can even have you, my dear, if I so choose."

His grin became frightening…and merciless. "I think I will." In three strides, he was at her side, the fingers of one hand cruelly digging into the soft skin of her cheek as he brought his mouth to hers in a brutal kiss meant to hurt and humiliate. He curled the fingers of his other hand around her throat as he pushed his body against hers, slamming her back into the hard wooden planes of the door.

The scream lodged in Shaelyn's throat died before she could utter a sound. She turned her head, tearing her mouth away from his. A moment later, James's fist clipped her chin. Her last thought before darkness descended was that she'd never told Remy she loved him.

Chapter 22

Shae!

Anger surged within Remy's veins as he violently sawed his hands against the ropes binding him. Despite the chill of the room, sweat rolled down his face, stinging his already swollen eyes. The rough cord cut into his flesh. Pain flashed in his shoulders and through his numb hands, but paled in comparison to the pain in his heart.

A muffled thump drew his attention and he stilled. What was that? A moment ago, he'd heard the murmuring hum of conversation and the shattering of glass. Now? Nothing. Not even footsteps. Only frightening silence and the sound of his own heart pounding.

Fear for Shaelyn's safety gripped him with iron talons and refused to let go, but he persevered, using that fear to his advantage. He resumed his struggle to free himself and felt the ropes, slick with his own blood, loosen a bit. He struggled harder, biting his lip to keep from groaning aloud as the blood flowed back into his numb hands. He gave one final tug. The pain that surged through his shoulders as the rope slipped to the floor stole his breath.

Freedom!

Shae. He had to find her and get her away from the Gray Ghost.

Remy climbed to his hands and knees and slowly gained his footing, but immediately collapsed to the bare wood panels beneath him, unable to put any weight on his leg. After sitting hunched on the floor for so long, his body had stiffened, his muscles cramped and aching.

The abuse he had suffered at Davenport's hands hadn't helped. He was almost sure he'd heard the cracking of bone at one point, courtesy of Davenport's boots.

He gathered what little strength he had and tried again, crawling to his hands and knees then rising upward, using the wall to steady himself. He tasted metal before he fell to the floor.

Dragging in a ragged breath, fighting the helpless feelings of hopelessness careening through him, Remy forced every other thought from his mind except Shaelyn. Despite the physical and emotional agony, he began to crawl, pulling himself forward on his arms by sheer force of will until he reached the table in the middle of the room.

He pulled himself up, pain exploding in his thigh, forcing him to suck in his breath. His stomach churned, but he took a tentative step, then another, using the table to help him. Determination kept him on his feet. Fear kept him moving, slowly, toward the door. He needed to get out of this room and find Shae.

How am I going to save Shae when I can't even save myself?

The thought weaved through his weary mind, shaking his conviction. He fought his uncertainty and took another cautious step, still resting his palm on the tabletop.

A slight noise drew his attention toward the window Shaelyn had crawled through earlier. He stopped as a wave of panic rushed through him.

Was it Brooks outside? Davenport? Another guard? Would he be shot dead before he found Shaelyn?

He didn't have very many choices. He couldn't run, that was most certain. He could throw himself to the floor and attempt to hide beneath the table, but if he did so, would he be able to stand again? Getting this far had taken almost more strength than he had. He could defend himself, but doubted he could overtake whoever came into the room. The knowledge wouldn't stop him from trying…he'd fight to the death if need be.

Remy tried to focus, but with the sweat dripping into his eyes, everything blurred. He blinked several times but it didn't help.

More noises from outside. Remy stood up straight and puffed out his chest. If this was death, then he'd face it head-on.

"It's me, laddie."

Relief surged through him, a reprieve from the terror that had rocked him. "Jock," he whispered, surprised but infinitely grateful as the Scotsman climbed in through the window.

"I'm here too." Captain Beckett followed the older man inside. They both approached the table where Remy waited, unwilling to let go of something stable beneath his hand.

"Ach, laddie, look at ye!" Jock exclaimed as he studied Remy's face. "Davenport worked ye over pretty good."

"If my hands hadn't been tied, I could have fought back."

"I know that, laddie." Understanding and sympathy glowed from the man's eyes as he reached out and gently touched Remy's shoulder. "No need to worry about that. Or him anymore, either. Davenport'll get what's comin' to him. We caught the bastard leadin' a horse into the stable. He's trussed up and waitin'." He chuckled then and smiled, his mustache stretching across his upper lip. "Brenna's holding a gun on him. She's a bit shaky with that pistol so I doubt he'll be making any moves."

"Brenna is here?" Remy couldn't hide the surprise in his voice, nor the sinking feeling in his gut.

"Seems she's got a bit of stubbornness in her too. I'm guessing almost as much as her daughter." He rocked back on his heels, his pride showing. "I suppose ye seen Shae."

"She loosened my ropes so I was able to get free before she left with Brooks." Remy swallowed hard. "James Brooks is the Gray Ghost and he's got her, but I don't know where."

"I knew that boy was no good, first time Ian brought him home from school!" The Scotsman cussed in his native tongue then shook his head. "An' her! Damn fool woman. Runnin' off on her own. She was supposed to wait for us, but as soon as our backs were turned, she lit out, lookin' for ye." He cleared his throat, as if dislodging the emotion growing there, then pulled a revolver from where it had been tucked in the sash of his uniform and handed it to Remy.

And not just any revolver, either, but his own army-issue Colt, the one Davenport had taken from him. The grip felt comfortable and familiar in his hand. Truthfully, Remy couldn't wait to see if the weapon still shot as cleanly as it had before. Though he'd kept the revolver clean, he hadn't used it since the day of the ambush.

Self-doubts rushed through his mind, eroding his confidence. The revolver might fire true, but could he see clearly enough to aim?

He shook his head, trying to dismiss the demon of skepticism nipping at the edges of his brain. It wouldn't do anyone any good if he doubted himself.

The Scotsman took a step back, his eyes bright as they drifted from Remy's feet to his hand, resting on the table, to the top of his head then back, stopping briefly at this thigh. "Can ye walk, laddie?"

"Of course." Remy let go of the table and took a step. Pain, sharp and hot, flared in his thigh, nearly bringing him to his knees with its intensity. Nausea curled in his stomach once more and a cold, clammy sweat chilled him to the bone. He took a deep breath, then another, and remained on his feet. Given his condition though, he didn't know if he'd be a help or a hindrance. The last thing he wanted was for his weakness to be the cause of more heartache.

"Maybe this will help. It's not your cane, but it'll do." Beckett handed him a stout, crooked stick. Thicker than his cane, it was just as sturdy and the perfect height.

Remy hefted the piece of wood, felt its heaviness. Not only could he use it to take some of the pressure off his leg, but it would come in handy for cracking a skull or two. "This will do nicely. Thank you."

"So what's the plan, laddie?"

"We'll have to take care of the guards before we can do anything."

"No need. It's all been done," the Scotsman said. "The guards are waiting for us on the *Lady Shae*, bound and gagged and under the watchful eyes of Daniel and Cory."

"Our soldiers are on the steamers as well," Beckett chimed in. "And the wounded are being looked after."

For a moment, Remy was overwhelmed by what had been accomplished without his leadership, but the feeling passed. Being a good leader meant those under one's authority could do the right thing even when one wasn't there to help. "Then there's nothing left for us to do except get Shae, capture the Gray Ghost, and get the hell away from this place."

"Which way?" Beckett asked as his gaze swept the room.

Remy pointed toward the door Shae disappeared through earlier. "There's a parlor that way. What lies beyond the parlor, I don't know." He turned to Beckett and gestured to a door at the opposite side of the room. "Why don't you take that direction?"

"Of course." Beckett drew his revolver and stepped quickly but quietly across the room and through the door.

"Can you make it, laddie?" Jock asked when they were alone.

Remy didn't answer. He stood up straight, chest out, shoulders back. Renewed confidence swirled through him. Even his vision was beginning to clear. "Let's go."

They left the dining room, Jock in the lead, his pistol drawn. The formal parlor, where Remy had first met the Gray Ghost, was empty, though a fire burned behind the grate. A glass of whiskey and a half-empty bottle were on the table beside the fire. There was another glass on the table as well, but that was empty. Had Brooks offered Shaelyn a drink? Had he tried to be social before…

He didn't finish the thought, forcing himself, instead, to move on. Pocket doors, which he hadn't noticed when he'd been in this room before, stood wide open.

He hadn't had time to analyze the floor plan as he was being pushed and shoved toward this house, but he did remember clearly the home had only been one story. Remy crossed the room, every step a new experience in pain, and entered a long, dark hallway. He smelled mildew and despair and shivered.

A faint light glowed from beneath the door across from him. He stopped and listened, but heard nothing. He turned and motioned to Jock, then took a hesitant step forward, his heart beating double time in his chest.

His hand closed over the doorknob. He took a deep breath then twisted. Unlocked, the knob turned easily. He opened the door and stepped into the room.

Candles flickered in the wall sconces, illuminating the scene before his eyes, and it was all he could do not to scream Shaelyn's name as soon as he saw her sprawled on a bed. His heart, which had been beating so quickly before, nearly stopped. She breathed, her chest moving with each inhalation, but her eyes were closed. She didn't make a sound.

Brooks sat on the side of the bed, hovering over her, his back to the door. He had already unbuttoned her uniform shirt as well as his own, and now his hands were on her, sweeping through her long hair, caressing her face. He whispered, words Remy couldn't hear, but he didn't have to.

The urge to kill surged through him like an out-of-control fire. *He's touching my wife!*

He cocked the revolver and aimed.

"If you value your life, Brooks, you will move away from my wife," he warned, his voice deadly calm. "Now."

Brooks stiffened, but didn't do as he was told. Instead, he stayed exactly where he was, his hand resting firmly on Shaelyn's chemise-covered ribcage, but he turned slightly. His gaze swept Remy from head to toe and back, as a slow, contemptuous smile spread his lips. "You won't shoot me." Even his voice held contempt. "You won't risk hitting her."

"Don't kill him, laddie," Jock said as he entered the room and came up behind him. "Let 'im hang."

The urge to shoot the man wouldn't be appeased, but Jock was right. Killing him now was too good for him. Remy uncocked the pistol and slowly lowered it.

Triumph flared in Brooks's eyes, but it was short-lived.

Remy sucked in his breath as Shaelyn's eyes sprang open. She moved quickly, rolling off the bed and out of James's reach, pulling the edges of her shirt together. "Shoot him!"

Despite his pain, Remy moved quickly toward the bed, swinging the heavy makeshift cane toward Brooks's head. The wood made a satisfying crack as it connected with its intended target. Brooks slumped to the mattress. His eyelids fluttered once, twice, then closed.

"Are you all right?" Remy asked as he rushed to Shaelyn. She met him halfway, falling into his arms as Jock pulled the cords from the draperies and tied Brooks's hands behind his back. The Gray Ghost didn't make a sound, nor did he move.

Her eyes bright with unshed tears, she nodded.

"He didn't hurt you, did he?" He gently touched the bruise forming on her chin.

"No."

Remy enfolded her in his arms and squeezed gently. "You have no idea what I thought when I stepped through that door and saw you." Relief made him weak, more so than the beating he had received. That feeling didn't last very long, though, as anger replaced it. "What the hell were you doing? I know you weren't unconscious when I came in this room."

"I was waiting for my moment." She brought her knee up to her stomach and pulled the small derringer from her boot. "I was going to shoot him."

"You...I...damn!" Remy stammered, then closed his mouth and shook his head. The woman would be the death of him. She was decidedly too daring for her own good. And too...

There were so many things he wanted to say to her. They were on the tip of his tongue, but he didn't utter a single one. There would be time for that later, once they were home. In the meantime, he was just happy she was safe and, aside from the bruise on her chin, unharmed, though he was certain he'd have nightmares of this day for years to come.

"The next time I tell ye to wait for me, I expect ye to listen, lassie," Jock admonished her as he finished tying Brooks's hands behind his back.

"Yes, sir."

"Is everyone all right?" Beckett rushed into the room, his revolver drawn and aimed. He stopped short, uncocked his pistol, and shoved it back into the sash around his waist as three pairs of eyes turned toward him. "Shae." He grinned and gave a slight nod of his head, then glanced at the man on the bed. "So this is the Gray Ghost. He doesn't look like much, does he?"

The man on the bed moaned and moved his head slightly.

"He's coming around." Jock nudged him, trying to speed his recovery. "What do ye say we get out of this place?"

"Yes, let's go home," Remy agreed, and let out his breath in a long sigh. Shaelyn was safe. They'd captured both the Gray Ghost and Davenport and freed the men who'd been held prisoner.

Beckett and Jock hauled Brooks to his feet and walked him out of the plantation house toward the stable and the wagon waiting in the yard. Defeated, hands bound behind his back, the man didn't even try to wrestle himself free, didn't look at anything except the ground.

Remy and Shaelyn followed. He leaned heavily on his makeshift cane, but managed to hold her close, determined never to let her go. "You and I are not done with this adventure of yours," he whispered in her ear.

She shivered against him and then turned that impudent grin toward him, reassuring him once again she had not been the least bit hurt from the events of the night. "Yes, sir."

"Brenna?" Jock called as they got closer to the stable. "You can come out, my love. It's all over. We've captured the Gray Ghost."

Brenna slipped out of the stable, the pistol gripped tightly in her hand. She stopped short and looked at the man standing between Jock and Captain Beckett. Her eyes opened wide as she sucked in her breath.

"James? You're the Gray Ghost?" Her voice was soft and hoarse with repressed tears before she slapped him across the face, her expression a mix of anger and disappointment. "I am ashamed of you!" she declared, her warm blue eyes frosty at the moment. "You were welcome in my house, sat at my table, and ate the food I cooked for you and this…this is what you've become." She raised her hand, intending to slap him again. "Where is my son?"

"He's not here, Mama. He went to Washington." Shaelyn rushed forward just as Jock grabbed Brenna and pulled her away before she made good on her threat.

"That's enough now, my love," the Scotsman said as he led her toward the wagon. He helped her up and then went back to assist Beckett with the prisoners. Hands bound behind their backs, both Davenport and Brooks were loaded into the back of the cart, much more gently than they deserved. Both were tied to the cart's railings before Jock climbed in and joined Brenna behind the seat.

Remy watched the proceedings and then helped Shaelyn into the wagon seat. He studied the height of the seat and wondered briefly if he had the strength to follow suit.

"Need a hand?" Beckett asked from the other side of the wagon.

"No, thank you. I got it." He took a deep breath, then another, forcing the pain away, and climbed into the seat.

Beckett swung up next to Shaelyn and grabbed the reins. With a well-practiced flick of his wrist, the wagon started moving.

Sunrise was still hours away as they rambled down the path toward the river, Brooks's horse clopping along behind the wagon. All were weary, not only physically but mentally as well, and no one spoke. Not even Brooks or Davenport, although Remy felt the heated glare of Davenport's unrelenting stare in the middle of his back. He resisted the urge to shudder, as well as the impulse to turn in his seat and use his makeshift cane on the man's head.

Shaelyn rested her head against his shoulder and entwined her fingers with his. He rubbed his chin against the softness of her hair, so thankful she hadn't been hurt…or worse.

The *Sweet Sassy* and the *Lady Shae* came into view, moonlight illuminating the smokestacks and pilothouses, while lantern light glowed intermittently along the railing. Men crowded against the balustrade and along the landing stage, ready to lend a helping hand.

Beckett tugged on the reins. The wagon rolled to a stop at the river's edge.

"Take him to one of the cabins and lock him in." Remy gave his orders as he climbed down from the wagon seat and then reached up to help Shaelyn. "We'll hand him over to the military authorities when we reach New Orleans."

Jock and Beckett did as they were told, leading the Gray Ghost to the upper deck, each man taking an arm. Remy followed, leading a complacent Davenport toward the same steps, while Shaelyn and Brenna trailed behind. He planned to hand his prisoner over to someone else, realizing his ever-present, worsening pain would prevent him from climbing the stairs. He signaled to Daniel and Cory.

"What will happen now?" Shaelyn asked, her nose wrinkling as she glanced from Captain Davenport to the other two men who would take over from here.

"He'll be handed over to the authorities as well. He's a traitor and will be judged as such." Remy looked upon the man who'd been his second in command. He shook his head and realized he'd never understand what had driven Davenport to do what he did. Perhaps he'd simply been hypnotized by promises of power. There was no sign of remorse, even now. Given the chance, Remy thought the captain would do the same again.

The man didn't beg for forgiveness. Davenport stood on the cargo deck of the *Lady Shae*, his hands tied behind his back, arrogant and defiant. "You may think you've won, but you haven't," he said, his voice cold and calm. "You might have the Gray Ghost, but there will be more to take his place."

"That may be true, but he will stand trial for his crimes. As will you, Vincent."

"I think not, Remy," he said, then with a nod and a grin, Vincent Davenport threw himself over the railing into the swirling waters of the mighty Mississippi. "The South will rise again," he yelled, then quickly sank out of sight.

"Get him!" Remy yelled, and someone grabbed a grappling hook, intending to save the man, but it was too late. He was gone. "Aw, hell!"

He felt a hand touch his sleeve and glanced at Shaelyn beside him. "It wasn't your fault." She squeezed his hand. "He couldn't face the future, knowing he'd hang for his crimes. Let the Mississippi have him and let's go home."

Slowly, he nodded. "Yes, my love, let's go home."

They started walking along the *Lady Shae*'s railing before she stopped and turned to stare at him, her brows drawn in question. "Did you just call me 'my love'?"

"I did." He grinned at her, despite the pain it caused his swollen lip. "Do you not wish for me to call you that?"

"I'm just surprised, that's all." Her eyes twinkled with doubt... and hope. "Why? Why would you call me your love?"

"Because you *are* my love, Shae. Didn't you know? Haven't I shown you?"

Her voice lowered to a whisper. "But you've never told me."

She was right. For all the passion they shared, he had never uttered those three simple words, had never told her what had been in his heart for so long. "I love you, Shae. I think I've loved you from the moment you flew into my arms and nearly knocked me over. I haven't been the same since."

Tears made her eyes luminous as the doubt shining in them disappeared in a flash. Once more, she fell into his arms and pressed her face against the buttons on his chest, like she had the first time they'd met. "And I love you, Remy."

Epilogue

"Are you all right?" Remy asked with a smile as Jock paced the confines of the parlor. Sweat beaded on the Scotsman's forehead and his normally ruddy skin seemed a bit pasty and white, making his ginger mustache stand out in stark relief. He looked like he'd have an apoplexy if his bride-to-be and the man who would marry them didn't show up soon.

"Ye don't think she's had second thoughts, do ye?" Jock paused in his pacing and slumped into one of the chairs, which had been set up to create an aisle down the center of the room. "Perhaps she doesn't want to marry me after all."

"Nonsense! Brenna Cavanaugh's love for you is as wide as the Mississippi." A knock sounded on the front door, interrupting the words of encouragement he'd been about to say. "Ah, that must be the preacher."

Jock jumped to his feet, a bundle of nerves. His hands shook as he pulled the high collar of his uniform jacket away from his Adam's apple, which bobbed as he swallowed. "Well, answer the door, man."

"Of course." Remy gave a slight bow then motioned to his parents, who had arrived just last night to witness the marriage of their dear friend and the woman he'd loved for as long as they'd known him. "See if you can't calm him down," he whispered as his mother and father drew closer.

Melissande Harte moved past him. "Come now, Jock, I've never seen you so nervous. Everything will be fine. The preacher will arrive in time and your lovely bride-to-be will walk down this very aisle soon." She soothed the man with her gentle tone and almost singsong cadence.

"It's not every day a man gets married, ye know," Jock admitted, then let out a long sigh.

"I know," she commiserated, "and you've waited a long time for this day."

Remy smiled as he limped from the parlor where the wedding would take place. He smiled quite often these days, despite the pain in his leg. His life, such as he'd known it, had changed for the better. Three weeks had come and gone from the moment Shaelyn had attempted to rescue him from certain death at the hands of Davenport and the Gray Ghost. He was now secure in the knowledge that his wife loved him. She had proven it by coming to his aid and kept proving it every day.

Dr. Shaughnessy at the hospital where Shaelyn had once again taken up her volunteer duties seemed to think he could ease some of Remy's pain with one final operation. It was an option Remy would seriously consider.

EJ, General Sumner's son, was now safely in Natchez, recuperating from his injuries, and the prisoner exchange the general had been working on was about to commence.

Remy had many reasons to be happy as he opened the door to find Ewell Sumner standing on the steps, the medals on his uniform shining in the midday sun. "General!"

"Are we late?" Sumner stepped aside and allowed his wife to enter Magnolia House before him. "We would have been here sooner, but Honor couldn't quite decide what to wear."

"Oh hush, you old goat." Honor Sumner waved away her husband's comment and kissed Remy on the cheek as she swept into the foyer with a swirl of violet and gold skirt and a hint of lemon verbena perfume. "Don't believe a word he says. I wasn't the reason we were late." She stepped aside so their son could come into the house as well, his crutches tapping on the marble tile.

"EJ!" Remy exclaimed and heartily pumped the young man's hand. "I didn't expect you to be up and about so soon."

"I'm feeling so much better. Dr. Shaughnessy thinks I'm healing very well." EJ blushed as he shook Remy's hand. "I'm not the reason we're late, either." He grinned. "He is."

A young man, one Remy had never seen before, but who reminded him very much of his wife, came into the foyer and held out his hand. "I understand you are my brother-in-law."

• • •

"Mama?" Shaelyn knocked on her mother's bedroom door. She could hear the guests in the formal parlor making themselves comfortable, the buzz of conversation rising up to the second floor. Remy's parents had arrived just last night and welcomed her into the Harte family with warmth and not a few tears of happiness. Remy's officers were here as well, all to witness the wedding of Brenna and Jock.

"Come in, dear."

Shaelyn opened the door. Brenna sat at her dressing table in her chemise, corset, and pantalets, her hair a gleaming mass of pure mahogany flowing down her back. "Mama, you're not dressed. Is everything all right?" She noticed the picture of Sean Cavanaugh in her mother's hands.

"I was thinking about your father and the wonderful life we had together and how much I've missed him these past two years." She looked up with a sad smile on her face. Tears shimmered in her eyes, making them more luminous. "Do you think he would approve of Jock and me?"

"Of course he would. Papa loved Uncle Jock like a brother." Shae knelt down beside her mother, removed the picture, then took Brenna's cold hands into her own. "He would want you to be happy, as you deserve to be. He'd want you to find love again." She kissed her mother's long, slender fingers. "I'm sure Papa is up in heaven looking down at you right now and I know he is smiling."

"Thank you, dear. You always know the right thing to say." Brenna took a deep breath, grabbed a handkerchief from the top of the dressing table, and swiped at the moisture in her eyes. "Will you walk down aisle with me and give me away?"

Tears immediately sprang to Shaelyn's eyes as well. "Of course, Mama. It would be my honor." She rose to her feet. "I'll help you dress," she said as she kissed her mother on the cheek. "Jock is waiting. I think he's waited long enough, don't you?"

Brenna nodded and then rose from her seat and grabbed the ivory satin and lace gown from the bed. She slipped into it, adjusted the puffy sleeves, then glanced in the mirror. Her eyes met Shaelyn's in the reflection.

"Oh, Mama, you look beautiful."

"Button me up?" Brenna asked as she turned and presented the long line of buttons along the back of the gown.

"All done. Are you ready?"

"I need a moment."

"Of course." Shaelyn let herself out of her mother's room. She strode toward the staircase and stopped at the top of the stairs. Movement below caught her eye and she looked down to see Remy standing in the hallway. He spoke with someone in deep conversation, someone she couldn't see. Her heart swelled with love as she watched him. He glanced up and noticed her, his mouth—that kissable mouth—spreading into a grin before he gave her a slight nod and then winked, put his finger over his lips, and disappeared into the study.

Curious, Shaelyn leaned over the banister and tried to follow him with her eyes even though it was impossible. He returned in a moment, his grin wider, his eyes twinkling with mischief and again, he placed his finger over his lips, urging her to silence. A second later, a young man appeared in the hall and looked up the stairs.

Shaelyn sucked in her breath as her heart thundered in her chest. Tears instantly flooded her eyes as she gazed into the handsome, grinning, much thinner face of her brother, Ian.

He, too, put his finger against his lips, swearing her to silence and secrecy before slipping back into the study.

Remy winked and grinned, then answered the knock on the door, allowing the preacher to come into the house. "We're ready, if you are," he called up the staircase before leading the man into the parlor.

Shaelyn rushed to her mother's room and knocked. "Mama, the preacher's here."

The door swung open and the vision that was Brenna Cavanaugh, soon to be Brenna MacPhee, stepped into the hallway.

Shaelyn enfolded her in her arms and hugged her. "Just in case I don't have a chance to tell you later, Mama. I love you."

Brenna returned the embrace and whispered, "I love you too." She pulled away, then took a deep breath and smiled. "I'm ready." She tucked her hand into the crook of her daughter's elbow. Together, they traversed the hall and walked down the curving staircase.

"Do you have everything?" Shaelyn whispered as they made it to the bottom of the stairs. "Something old? Something new?"

Remy limped out of the parlor and strode to where they stood. He reached out, brought Brenna's hand to his lips, and kissed her gloved knuckles. "You look lovely," he said, then let go of her hand with a nod toward Shaelyn.

"Wait here. I forgot something," Shaelyn said, and then quickly relinquished her hold on her mother's arm and moved to the study doorway. She motioned to Ian, who joined her in the hall. She kissed him on the cheek, welcoming him home, then stood aside as he grasped his mother's hand.

"What did you forget, dear?" Brenna asked while craning her neck to view the inside the parlor.

When she didn't answer, Brenna finally looked at the hand holding hers and turned slightly. "Oh, Ian! I'm so…"

Her eyes filled with tears and her mouth opened, but no words issued forth as she hugged her son.

"I know, Mama," he said as he held her tight. "I'm happy to be home too. And it looks like I'm just in time." He broke the embrace and grinned at her. "I'm so sorry I never wrote. I couldn't tell anyone where I was or what I was doing. It would have been too dangerous, but I've been re-assigned to Rosalie, so we have plenty of time to see each other. Right now, though, Jock is waiting, and he's waited a long time." He pulled a handkerchief from his pocket and dabbed at her eyes. "Are you ready?"

Brenna took a deep breath as mother and son entered the parlor and strode up the aisle where the preacher and a very nervous Jock waited. The guests rose amid oohs and aahs and comments of how beautiful the bride looked and wasn't it wonderful that her son, whom she hadn't seen in over two years, could be here for this occasion.

Shaelyn reached for Remy's hand and entwined her fingers with his. She studied him for a moment, realizing how much she truly loved this man. Over the lump in her throat, she asked, "You arranged this, didn't you?"

"No, I…" Remy blushed to the tips of his ears and gave her the crooked grin that melted her heart. "Truly, I had no idea he would show up today. Now. I had simply asked General Sumner to see if he could locate your brother. I thought it would make you happy to know he was safe."

He drew her into his warm embrace and when he spoke, it was a whisper in her ear. "I could think of no better way to show you how much I love you."

Emotions overwhelmed her, but Shaelyn took a deep breath and whispered in return, "I love you too, Remy. Always."

About the Author

Marie Patrick has always had a love affair with words and books, but it wasn't until a trip to Arizona, where she now makes her home with her husband and her furry, four-legged "girls," that she became inspired to write about the sometimes desolate, yet beautiful landscape. Her inspiration doesn't just come from the Wild West, though. It comes from history itself. She is fascinated with pirates and men in uniform and lawmen with shiny badges. When not writing or researching her favorite topics, she can usually be found curled up with a good book. Marie loves to hear from her readers. Drop her a note at *Akamariep@aol.com* or visit her website at *www.mariepatrick.com*.

More from This Author
(From *A Treasure Worth Keeping* by Marie Patrick)

Charleston—1850

Music, raucous laughter, and light spilled onto the street as soon as Tristan Youngblood, captain of the *Adventurer*, opened the door of the Salty Dog. He stood still for a moment and let the atmosphere of his favorite tavern in Charleston wash over him.

The *Adventurer's* crew filled the room with the exception of Coop, who stood watch aboard ship, and Jemmy, Tristan's son, who was too young to join in the celebration. A more trustworthy, patient, experienced group of men he'd never find. He loved and respected them all, found comfort in their company, and trusted them with his life—and his secret. To the world, he was Captain Trey, treasure hunter. To those who shared his confidence, he was Tristan Youngblood, Lord Ravensley.

They had reason to celebrate this night, even if he did not. After months and months of searching, they'd found the legendary lost treasure of the *Sierra Magdalena*, a Spanish galleon savagely torn apart in a hurricane almost two hundred years ago off the coast of Hispaniola. Each and every one of them thought they had found heaven—or at least a little part of it.

Pockets bulging with pieces of gold, they turned, almost as one, and raised their tankards toward him. "Captain!"

"Tippy." He signaled the tavern owner. "Drinks are on me."

Loud cheers met his pronouncement as Tippy lined up clean tankards on the bar and proceeded to fill them one by one with thick, foamy ale.

Tristan accepted his crew's slaps on the back and handshakes as he made his way through the crowded room to drop a small pouch of gold coins on the bar.

Graham Alcott, the *Adventurer's* navigator as well as Tristan's second in command and oldest friend, sat at a table in the corner, his arms around the two winsome barmaids perched on his knees. A cigar smoldered in the brass tray surrounded by the remains of a hearty meal.

Tristan grinned as he strode toward his friend. It never failed. No matter where in the world the *Adventurer* put into port, Graham found the loveliest, most willing ladies.

He cleared his throat. Graham took his eyes off the tantalizing bosoms presented to him and glanced up. His smile could have charmed the birds from the trees—or the drawers from even the most discerning young woman.

"Tristan," Graham acknowledged as he nodded to the chair opposite him. "Sarah, my love, get the captain a glass of your finest rum." He gave each girl a sound kiss on the cheek and a promise to meet them later, then he patted both behinds to usher them off his knees. With squeals and giggles, the women rushed to do his bidding.

Tristan dropped into the chair and stretched out his long, leather-booted legs, crossing them at the ankle. He grabbed a serrated knife and cut a piece of bread still warm from the oven, then slathered it with sweet, creamy butter and took a bite.

"Well?" Graham prodded as Sarah delivered two heavy-bottomed glasses and placed them on the table. Tristan grinned as Graham's merry brown eyes followed the gentle sway of her hips.

"Well what?" Tristan replied after he swallowed.

"Don't play games, Tristan." Graham rested his elbows on the table. "I've known you too long. I was there when Tippy gave you the letter. I know the family seal when I see it. Was it your father? Is he here?"

Tristan stared at the light amber brew in his glass as he chewed the last of his bread. "No, my father isn't here. He sent his henchman, the honorable Theodore Gilchrist, Esquire. If we'd made port in Jamaica, I would have met Paul Farnsworth, another in my father's employ. Apparently, Father has all my regular haunts covered. The earl was bound and determined to give me the news." The information Mr. Gilchrist imparted made his stomach churn, made the bile rise in his throat, made him want to disregard convention and lose himself on the high seas.

Brown eyes twinkling with curiosity, Graham sat up straighter. "What news?"

Tristan pulled a half-smoked cigar from his vest pocket and used the candle on the table to light it. As he exhaled, blue-grey smoke swirled to the ceiling. "I have a little less than four months to put my affairs in order, go back to England and then—"

"Then what?" Graham lifted his glass and took a long drink.

"I am to be married."

"Married!" The navigator choked on his rum as he spit out the word. He coughed into his hand, his face red. For a long time, he stared and said nothing. "I would offer congratulations, but I gather you don't regard this as good news."

Tristan twisted the signet ring on his finger while he looked around the room—at the hunk of bread on a plate in the middle of the table, at the cigar smoke drifting around him—anywhere but at his shipmate. "No, I do not." He stopped twisting the ring long enough to rake his fingers through his hair; then he picked up his drink.

"You can't be surprised." Graham leaned back and folded his arms across his chest. His black-booted foot rested on the empty chair next to him. "Your father has been trying to marry you off for the past five years. Every time you go home, he introduces you to another eligible young woman. Perhaps he sees this arrangement as the way to get the deed accomplished."

Tristan tossed back the rum as if it were water and ignored the burning sting the liquor left in his throat before he gave voice to his concerns. "God help me, I don't want a marriage like my parents'. They barely tolerated each other before my mother passed."

He twisted the ring on his finger and caught the glitter of the lion's amber eye. "There was never any love between them. I doubt there was even fondness." He lowered his voice. "My father has had the same mistress since before I was born and my mother . . . my mother went through lovers like . . . well, like you and I go through bottles of rum."

Sarah sashayed to the table and refilled both glasses. Tristan nodded his thanks but didn't offer her a smile, as was his wont. The news of his impending marriage settled like a rock in his stomach.

"Was your parents' marriage arranged?" Graham swept his tongue over his lips in anticipation then reached for his refilled glass.

"Of course. It's the way it's done." Tristan let his breath whistle between his teeth and crushed his cigar in the tray, frustrated by his father's announcement. "I don't want to marry a woman I don't know, have never met. I believe—"

"But you don't have to, Tristan. You're an adult. Almost thirty. Tell your father no."

Tristan snorted. "If it were that easy, I would. You don't understand. Your parents met, fell in love, and married, the way I would like to, but . . . marriage is expected." He lowered his voice to a whisper though he doubted his words could be overheard in a room full of laughing men and women. "For a man of my position. As the next Earl of Winterbourne, I have an obligation to make the most advantageous match, which means marry for money to fill the family coffers and produce future earls. And as my father's solicitor informed me, though my younger brother and his wife have been married for nine years, there are no children from the union." He rubbed his fingers over his freshly shaved face and found he missed the beard he'd grown during his last voyage. "Father wants heirs."

"You jest."

"I wish I did."

Graham leaned back in his chair and studied the liquor in his glass. A smile crossed his face after a moment. "What about Jemmy?"

Tristan shrugged. "Father doesn't know the adoption papers have become final, but I don't think he would accept Rielle's son as his heir. She was my friend and I loved her as such, but Jemmy isn't of Youngblood . . . blood."

The navigator nodded, and Tristan knew he understood more than his spoken words. Graham shook his head. "No more treasure hunting. No more sailing around the world at a moment's whim. No more getting stinking drunk and spending our time with willing women." He grinned to reveal a compliment of pearl white teeth beneath his shaggy beard. "I pity you, my friend."

"Four months," Tristan repeated, his tone and mood somber until an idea grabbed hold and wouldn't let go.

Izzy's Fortune. If he could find the infamous treasure of Queen Isabella, he could fill the Youngblood coffers with more than enough gold to last several lifetimes. He wouldn't have to marry a woman he didn't know, wouldn't have to spend the rest of his life with a woman he didn't want. He could have the time he needed to find what he wanted most.

Love.

Passion.

A woman who could share his dreams.

Who am I trying to fool? There is no such woman.

But Izzy's Fortune. That, at least, had a chance of being real.

And if he found the treasure before Wynton Entwhistle of the *Explorer*, so much the better. An open rivalry existed between the two men and had from the moment they met some years ago when they'd both gone after the same fortune. Since then, Tristan had managed to stay one step ahead of the scheming seaman, much to Entwhistle's regret and frustration.

Tristan glanced at Graham, smiled, then started to chuckle. "Four months is long enough to try one last time to find Izzy's Fortune." His gaze darted around the room to the crew in the midst of their merriment. "Do you think they'd mind?"

"Hell, no!" Graham slammed his glass on the table. "When do we leave?"

"Three days. No, four. We'll need that long to gather supplies. Once we leave Charleston, I don't plan on coming back—at least for a long time. Remember, I'm expected in England to—" Tristan choked on the word "—marry."

"Again, you have my pity." Graham laughed. "Who is this woman? Is she at least pleasant to look at?" He waved his hands in front of his face as his grin grew wider. "She isn't some ugly beast with rotten teeth and pitted skin, is she?"

"I have no idea. I didn't even ask her name." Tristan wasn't surprised he had not asked a most important question. He supposed the announcement that his marriage had been arranged without his knowledge or consent had shocked him into not thinking at all. "I should find out, shouldn't I?" He tossed back his drink in one swallow. "I'll pay another visit to Gilchrist in the morning, but in the meantime, I'm going back to the ship." He stood and flipped a gold coin on the table. "I'll relieve Coop so he can celebrate with his mates."

"Are you certain?" Graham rose as well, although he never released the glass of rum in his hand, nor did he take his gaze from Sarah MacNamara and Rosie Flint. "I could just as easily take the watch."

Tristan shook his head. "No, you stay." He glanced at Sarah wending her way through the tavern's rowdy customers. Her hips rocked back and forth as she sidestepped with innate agility the various hands aiming for her backside. She met his stare and grinned. "Sarah and Rosie would be disappointed if you didn't keep your promises."

Tristan made his way through the men, and again accepted their congratulations and well wishes before he handed another small leather bag filled with gold to the barkeep. He saluted his crew. "Drink up, me hearties! You've earned it." He resisted the urge to tell them to keep their eyes, as well as their hands, on their gold.

"Aye, Cap'n!"

His men would be in sad shape tomorrow, sporting colossal headaches, perhaps still drunk from this night's revelry, so he gave them a reprieve. "I expect you all to be onboard the *Adventurer* in two days."

Again, their rousing chorus of "Aye, Cap'n" met his ears.

He grinned as he pushed through the door and left the deafening din of the Salty Dog. A senseless whistle escaped him as he strode over the cobblestones toward the three-masted clipper at berth.

His shoulders relaxed as his stride grew longer. He inhaled and caught the scent of a hearty beef stew as it simmered in someone's pot. Warm light spilled through the windows of the homes he passed and he heard the telltale sounds of people settling in for the evening.

He loved harbor towns—the charming, quaint villages of England, the rowdy, yet oddly cosmopolitan ports like Charleston, the rough and tumble atmosphere of Port Royal. The sight of the ships from all around the world lined up side by side, their colorful flags waving in the breeze, comforted him as nothing else ever could. He would miss these ports when he obeyed his father's command and married the woman the earl had chosen—a woman whose name he didn't even know.

Beneath the glow of a street lamp, he stopped and shook his head.

An arranged marriage. God, he hated the thought.

Shoulders tight once again, he kicked at a rock on the cobblestones and scowled. The earl had given him no choice.

If the truth were known, Tristan didn't object to the idea of marriage—he just hated the idea of being coerced into it, forced to give up the life he loved.

Part of it was his own fault. All the years he'd searched for treasure, he could have and should have searched for a wife. He could have remained in England and attended the debutante balls where most of the eligible bachelors of his class chose their future wives from the best families.

But marriage and the responsibilities of the earldom wasn't the life he wanted.

The sea called to him, lured him, begged him to feel its power and glory. From the moment he'd first stepped foot on a ship, he'd known he wanted to sail for the rest of his life. The warmth of a woman's hand on his cheek could not compare to the cool touch of spindrift on his face. The tedium of running the Winterbourne estates could never measure up to the exhilaration of riding out a storm on the high seas while the sky raged around him. In those moments, Tristan knew he truly lived.

He glanced up as he drew closer to the *Adventurer*. A shadow passed before the windows of his cabin, back and forth, as if someone waited for him with great impatience. It couldn't have been Jemmy. The boy had been fast asleep when Tristan had left to see his father's solicitor.

It wasn't Coop Milliron, either. His faithful crewman paced the length of the deck from bow to stern, his footsteps heavy on the wooden planks. They grew louder in the still night when he climbed the stairs to the quarterdeck. Moonbeams lit his path. He had no need of a lantern to guide his way.

Tristan studied the shadow and grinned. The silhouette belonged to a woman—he couldn't deny the full thrust of her breasts or the long skirt that twitched with her step. His grin widened, but only for a moment.

Who was she? What was she doing aboard his ship?

There could be two reasons a woman would be on his ship at this time of night. Either she was a strumpet . . . or a thief.

If she was looking for the spoils from the *Sierra Magdalena*, she'd wasted her time. Though it was common knowledge in Charleston that he and his crew had found the treasure, only a fool would have kept it on board. Tristan had never been a fool.

The other alternative pleased him much more. If she was looking for a night of pleasure, well then, she'd come to the right man.

Tristan quickened his step and bounded up the gangplank. Cooper jumped, startled, and pulled his cutlass from the sash around his waist in one easy, practiced move. The sharp blade glinted in the moonlight.

"Coop!" Tristan raised his hands and sidestepped the weapon.

"Cap'n, ye scairt the hell outta me!" The crewman lowered the cutlass and shoved it back into his sash then patted the handle for good measure. He stood as tall as his short stature would allow which made the white cotton of his shirt strain against the roundness of his belly. "Doncha be knowin' not to sneak up on a man? Coulda got yerself killed!"

"Who is the woman in my cabin?"

"She dinna give me her name, Cap'n. She been waitin' on ye fer pert near a hour." His grin spread from ear to ear then faded as his bushy eyebrows disappeared beneath the red kerchief tied around his forehead. Tufts of dark brown hair, peppered with grey, spiked around the square of cloth on his head. In the moon's glow, his cheeks were ruddier than normal and his bulbous nose, a result of years of heavy drinking, shined like a beacon in the middle of his face. "Were ye not expectin' her?"

"No, I was not."

The crewman mumbled beneath his breath words Tristan couldn't quite make out before he apologized. "I'm sorry, Cap'n. It ain't unusual fer ye to have a woman in yer cabin, though it ain't happened in a while."

"It's all right, Coop," Tristan said. "Why don't you join your mates at the Salty Dog? You shouldn't miss the celebration."

The seaman's sharp brown eyes disappeared in the wrinkles of his face as he grinned. "Aye, Cap'n!" He needed no further urging as he scurried down the gangplank.

Tristan watched him for a moment then strode across the deck, the hard soles of his boots loud in the silent night.

At the end of the hallway, his door stood wide open. Candles lit against the darkness created a warm glow on the mahogany paneled walls. He glanced around the room. All the built-in cabinets were ajar. Maps littered the floor, some flat, some curled into long tubes, which rolled back and forth as the ship moved. Perturbed, but not angry, his jaw clenched but only for a moment as he took in the sight before him.

The woman stood at his desk, her hands flat on the surface as she studied a map. Covered in yards of pale blue silk, her backside wiggled as she shoved the current map out of her way to study the one beneath it.

The glow from the candles brought out the golden glints in her hair, which curled down her back in wild abandon. With a well-practiced flick of her hand, she pushed long, light brown hair away from her face then reached for the snifter of cognac on the desktop, finishing the amber brew in one swallow.

Tristan leaned against the doorjamb and twisted the ring on his finger as he admired the tantalizing view before him, no longer bothered by her uninvited presence. A new feeling took hold, one that filled his veins with desire. It had been a long time since he'd had a woman. "Are you finding my maps of interest?"

"Oh!" She gave a guilty start and whirled around. A pretty shade of pink colored her face and contrasted with the pale blue of her gown. Her eyes, the color of the deep blue sea, were wide and twinkled in the candlelight. "I'm . . . I'm . . ." She paused to breathe. "You must be Captain Trey."

"I must be." He took two steps into the room. She backed into the desk, unable to retreat further. "And you are?"

The muscles in her throat moved as she swallowed hard.

"I . . ."

"If you're looking for the *Sierra Magdalena's* treasure, you won't find it here. Nor will those maps help you."

She drew herself up as his words hit her. "I beg your pardon. I am not a thief."

Tristan smiled as wicked thoughts careened through his mind and took another two steps into the room. He stood only a breath away from her, close enough to see the faint scar on her forehead, close enough to notice her eyes weren't merely sea-blue, but had flecks of green in their depths as well. Long dark lashes fluttered as she stared into his face and licked her lips.

He knew an invitation when he saw one. Without hesitation, he wrapped his arms around her, lowered his head, and tasted those tempting, moist lips.

The woman stilled in his embrace, then melted against him. She tasted of brandy, warm and intoxicating, while her perfume filled his senses and surrounded him with the clean scent of a forest after a rain. The combination of her taste and smell tantalized him; the heat of her response excited him and made him realize one kiss was not enough.

His mouth slid over hers, gently at first, then with more force. Her lips opened beneath his, and beyond the initial taste of brandy, he detected the cool freshness of mint.

"Captain," she breathed as she turned away and his lips touched the softness of her cheek. Small, dainty hands pushed against his chest. "I am not a common . . . strumpet here for your pleasure."

Tristan grinned. Oh, she was a beauty with the color of roses in her cheeks and the sparkle of indignation in her sea-blue eyes. Contrary to her words, she had responded to him. Her body still trembled within his embrace.

"My apologies." He released her and she staggered. "When a man comes aboard his ship and sees a beautiful woman who claims she is not a thief, he can only think one other thing."

Those beguiling eyes flashed, and for a moment, Tristan battled with himself to keep from falling into their fathomless depths. He pulled a chair away from the table before slumping into it and crossing his legs. "If you're not a thief and you're not a harlot come to fulfill all my carnal desires, then who are you?"

"My name is Caralyn McCreigh," she said and waited, as if she expected him to recognize the name.

He wasn't listening. He couldn't tear his gaze away from the beauty of her face, the wild curls of light brown hair held back from her small features by a ribbon the same pale blue as her gown, or her full figure emphasized by the cut of her dress.

"I . . . ah . . . I have a proposition for you," she blurted and raised wide eyes to him.

In that moment, Tristan was lost. Still intoxicated by her taste and smell, he now had to contend with desire sweeping through him with incredible speed and urgency.

"I want to hire you to help me find Queen Isabella's treasure."

Tristan said nothing, although his fingers drummed the tabletop. Was it possible? Had she overheard him talking with Graham? How did she know about the treasure?

Of course, everyone knew about the treasure, but how did she know he had searched for it and planned to search for it again? Was it coincidence?

Before he could voice his concern, she said, "You know my father, Daniel McCreigh of the *Lady Elizabeth*." She smiled with obvious love for her father. "He told me he'd met you in Kingston. He thought you were an honorable man."

Recognition dawned for Tristan. He did, indeed, know Daniel McCreigh, the fine, upstanding man who captained the *Lady Elizabeth*. They had both been in Finnegan's Crooked Shillelagh, commiserating that neither could find Izzy's Fortune, though each had searched for quite a few years. He remembered sharing an enjoyable evening with the man, hoisting tankards of ale and regaling each other with tall tales of life at sea. At one point, they'd even compared notes on where the treasure was not.

Tristan studied her, looked beyond her beauty, and saw the resemblance. "Many have searched for the treasure, Miss McCreigh, and yet, no one has found it. Queen Isabella's treasure may not even be real."

"Yes, that is true, but I believe it is." Her voice lowered to a whisper. "I know, in my heart, the treasure is real."

As did he, but he couldn't tell her that. They'd just met. "What makes you think you will succeed where others have failed? Your own father couldn't find the treasure."

"I know, but I have these." She reached for the soft-sided valise on the floor beside the desk, which Tristan hadn't seen when he'd come into his cabin. She pulled an oilcloth wrapped package from the depths of the case and laid it on the table in front of him. Her fingers trembled as she tugged the string and moved the protective covering aside to reveal a journal before she pulled out the chair beside him and sat.

The leather binding was cracked and brittle. As she lifted the cover with her gloved fingers exposing pages fragile and delicate with age, Caralyn said, "My father was never serious about finding the treasure. For him, it was a lark, an adventure he and I could share, but I was raised on stories of Izzy's Fortune and I . . .I always believed. Even when I found this journal, Papa refused to come out of retirement to find it."

Tristan looked from the book to her face. Her eyes were animated and sparkled in the glow of candlelight. Pink stained her cheeks. Enthusiasm colored her voice. He said nothing as he watched her, but his thoughts ran riot.

"This is the journal of Alexander Pembrook," she said. "He sailed with Henry Morgan."

She lifted one page after another with a touch so light, so dainty, Tristan's body responded as if she caressed him. The fine hair on his arms rose as he imagined her fingers on his skin. Excitement rippled through him, and his heart beat a little faster in his chest.

She stopped about a third of the way through the journal. "Here." She pointed to the page and pushed the book toward him. "Start here."

He moved the candle closer and started to read. The journal entry, dated June 1670, described separating the *Santa Maria* from her two flagships and overtaking her in a battle, which left the ship with gaping holes in her bow and her crew in bloody heaps. The passage further related how Morgan's men transferred the treasure to their own ship, set the *Santa Maria* on fire, and watched her sink into the ocean.

"This is all very exciting," Tristan commented as he slid the journal back to her, "but is it true?"

"I believe so." She stared at him, and in the depths of her fathomless eyes, he knew she did. With great care, she searched further through the journal and stopped at another page. "Morgan didn't trust very many people, and he moved the treasure several times. The last time he did, Alexander was one of the men he selected to help move the treasure and swore to secrecy."

Tristan rose from his seat. He grabbed her brandy snifter from the desk, found another one for himself in the cabinet over his head, and poured them both a draft of fine cognac. He swallowed his without even tasting it then refilled his glass.

"According to his journal, Alexander moved the treasure once more—stealing it from beneath Morgan's nose the year Morgan was arrested and sent to England for breaking a peace treaty between England and Spain."

She tapped the journal with her forefinger. "The final resting place of Queen Isabella's treasure is the Island of the Sleeping Man. He describes the island quite well, but I have never been able to locate it on any map. I can tell you where it is not because I've accompanied my father on several of his adventures." She took a sip of her brandy. "After he hid the treasure, Alexander . . . *reinvented* himself, I suppose would be the correct term. He changed his appearance, changed his name, changed everything about himself and settled in Jamaica, but he never stopped writing in his journal." She turned more pages and pointed to various paragraphs, but she never read from the writings themselves, so he knew she had committed certain things to memory.

"He married Mary Collins, a plantation owner's daughter and lived happily at Sweet Briar in Saint James Parish before Henry Morgan returned to Jamaica as the lieutenant governor." Her fingers smoothed over the written words.

"Alexander became very ill after Morgan returned. He didn't leave the plantation, wouldn't see visitors. I have the impression he spent a lot of time in a little chapel on the plantation, praying. I don't know if part of his illness was due to his constant consumption of rum, but I know he believed he'd been cursed for stealing the treasure. He believed Morgan would come for him at any moment." She paused and took a deep breath before continuing in a rush.

"His writing reflected his illness and his fear. Many of his words are gibberish, out of context, and make little sense, even though I've read this over and over. His last entry is August 10, 1680. I imagine he died a short time later."

Fascinated, Tristan watched her take another sip of brandy then lick her lips once again.

"To my knowledge, Izzy's Fortune is still hidden on the Island of the Sleeping Man."

Anticipation surged through Tristan's veins, and yet he couldn't allow himself to show it. Why should he trust her? She was simply a woman he'd found on his ship, going through his maps. Perhaps she'd made it all up, wrote the journal herself, but to what purpose? Was she bored with her life? Did she long for adventure?

He studied the book, noticed again the brittle pages, the ink so faded in places he had trouble reading it, and knew with certainty, the journal wasn't forged.

He felt her intense stare and looked at her.

"You don't believe me," she blurted, as if she'd read his thoughts. "I have this." She reached for her valise again and laid a wooden box beside the book, slipped the lock, and lifted the lid. Nestled in a bed of black velvet lay a golden goblet encrusted with precious gems. Rubies and emeralds sparkled in the soft glow of the candles and created rainbows on the dark mahogany walls. "It was with Alexander's journal. I found them both hidden in the false bottom of an old grandfather clock my father had purchased many years ago. I don't think they were ever meant to be found. If an earthquake hadn't toppled that clock to the floor, I never would have known."

Stunned, Tristan swallowed hard. He'd never seen anything so beautiful in his life, aside from the woman next to him. He said nothing as he lifted the goblet from its bed of velvet and inspected the gems, the perfection of the craftsmanship, the tiny inscription at the base.

"I will finance the expedition on the condition I am allowed to join in the hunt and we split the treasure—half for you and your crew, half for me." She held her breath and waited for his answer.

He came to a quick decision. There were those, he knew, who would think him insane, unstable. A superstitious group, his crew would regard him as quite mad and would object to a woman on board the *Adventurer*, but he had to take the chance—on her. On the journal. On the golden chalice in his hand and the possibility of finding Izzy's Fortune.

"I accept your proposition. We leave in four days."

In the mood for more Crimson Romance?
Check out *Blinded by Grace* by Becky Lower
at *CrimsonRomance.com*.

Printed in the United States
By Bookmasters